The Taos Massacres

John Durand

D1572234

Puzzlebox Press

Cover design by John Durand. Cover © 2004 by John Durand. Cover images are adapted with grateful acknowledgement from photographs of unidentified individuals in various collections in the American Memory Collection, U.S. Library of Congress. Photo of older white man is from Fred Hulstrand History in Pictures Collection, North Dakota State University Institute for Regional Studies, North Dakota State University, Fargo, ND.

1st Edition

First printing 2004

ISBN 0-9743783-0-5

Library of Congress Control Number: 2003096200

For further information contact

Puzzlebox Press

PO Box 765

Elkhorn,WI 53121

www.puzzleboxpress.com

For my children: John (1964-2002) and Peter

Much water goeth by the mill

That the miller knoweth not of

John Heywood, *Proverbs*

Author's Note

This narrative follows several months of New Mexico's turbulent past, when the American occupation of 1846 provoked a rebellion against American authority.

To construct *The Taos Massacres* I drew heavily on historical records and scholarly works. When the historical record is clear and credible I remain faithful to the history. In cases where the historical record is silent or ambiguous I keep within the boundaries of the plausible.

Although the major characters in this work are historical and their participation in these events was along the lines depicted, *The Taos Massacres* does not pretend to represent the actual people. Rather, I used historical figures and their experiences to help bring to life this complex and important episode in America's history.

Contents
Prelude
The Messenger   The Santa Fe Trail   Bent's Fort
Rebellion
Picuris Mountain   Charley's Ranch   Turley's Mill   The Loft
The Distillery   John Albert   Mormon Town   Haun's Mill
Simeon Turley   The Pueblo
Suppression
Santa Fe   The Volunteers   La Cañada   Embudo   Taos
Casa Martinez   The Pueblo   Taos Mountain
Retribution
The Plaza   The Poinel   The Trials   Turley's Mill   Fort Mann

----

Illustrations
The Santa Fe Trail
Simeon Turley's Mill and Distillery
John Albert's Flight to Safety
March Route and Battle Scenes
Diagram of the Battle of La Cañada
Diagram of the Battle of Embudo
Diagram of the Battle for the Taos Pueblo
Locations of the Murders in Taos

Chronology of Events
Teresina Bent's Eyewitness Account of Her Father's Murder
Further Reading

Prelude

The Messenger

Major George Howard woke from a deep afternoon nap to the sound of voices. The tent-light was dim, his neck sweat-soaked, and he grunted with relief when he realized the Mexican firing squad had once again vanished with his waking. Outside he heard the lieutenant speaking and several unfamiliar voices. Vaguely irritated but curious, Major Howard sat up, swung his legs off the camp cot, and bent over to pull on his boots. His mouth felt dry and scummy as he emerged from the tent groggy and adjusting his suspenders.

"Ah, Major Howard," the lieutenant said, presenting him with a sweep of one hand to a half dozen horsemen in various stages of removing saddles and gear. Most travelers on the Santa Fe Trail camped at this place called The Crossing, where wagon trains loaded with trade goods bound for Santa Fe crossed the nearby Arkansas River and entered Mexico territory.

Eyes bloodshot, his breath sour and liquor-laden, the major began shaking hands all around. When he heard the name of Charles Bent he expressed surprise. "Ah, Mister Bent!" He offered the man a bleary smile and a wink as they shook hands. Interrupting the rest of the greetings, Major Howard ducked into his tent with a gesture of just-a-minute. Gray-haired, bronzed by sun, Charles Bent stared after the disheveled officer. The major reappeared a moment later with a half-gone bottle of whiskey and paused in his approach to pull the cork with his teeth. "Mister Bent," he said. "I've looked forward to the honor of meeting you." He held the bottle aloft. "To victory," he said to the circle of men, then took a pull, the bottle trembling at his mouth. He presented the whiskey to Bent, who hesitantly raised the bottle towards his own lips, his expression quizzical. "Well...if it's come to war...."

The major and the lieutenant exchanged looks. With a touch of pride the lieutenant said, "It's war, Sir. Almost a month now."

Bent threw an uneasy look at one of his companions, a burly, black-bearded man attired in a worn buckskin jacket and an incongruous white, frilly-front shirt. Then with a hint of embarrassment Bent raised the bottle in salute to the others. "Well," he said again, his tone oddly strained, "to victory then." He drank a quick draught and passed the bottle to the bearded

1

man, who sniffed the liquor with a look of mild distaste and exchanged a long look with Bent before taking a quick swig.

Later, Bent was rummaging in his saddlebags when the major approached. "Mister Bent," the soldier said, his voice conspiratorial. "I have a message for you."

Bent straightened with a look of annoyance. Not only had he taken an instant dislike to the boozy man who stood before him, he was dismayed by the news of war with Mexico. He lived in Taos, a small city in northern New Mexico, and his Mexican relatives and friends numbered in the dozens. "For me?" he asked.

"Yes, from the President." The officer extended a letter.

"The President? You don't mean President Polk?"

The major nodded. Seeing Bent's dubious expression, he continued, "This letter will explain. It contains my instructions."

Addressed to the major, the letter was a month old, dated May 13, 1846. Bent read: "The President has this day declared by his proclamation, issued in obedience to an Act of Congress, that war exists between the United States and Mexico...." The letter went on to charge the major with warning any American wagon trains on their way to Santa Fe of the state of war, to secretly get word of the war to Americans living in New Mexico, and to find Charles Bent.

Major Howard put a finger to his lips to indicate secrecy. He leaned close and placed a hand on Bent's shoulder to steady himself. His breath reeked. "The President wants you in Washington, Mister Bent. Right away."

The Santa Fe Trail

Two months later a youth with a wan, boyish face was writing at an ornate table on the mezzanine floor of the opulent Planters' Hotel, the grandest building in St. Louis. His quill moved easily across a thick sheet of embossed hotel stationery. Fair-haired and slight, Lewis Garrard wore a pale yellow shirt with white collar and cuffs. Dun-colored trousers complimented a wrinkled linen coat draped over his chair-back.

Outside the morning was already muggy, heavy with the familiar odors of horse manure, wood smoke, tar, decaying fish, and the hundred other smells of a busy river city. But on the mezzanine the ambience remained almost pleasant. The slow, silent blades of a spring-wound ceiling fan stirred memories of cigar smoke and women's perfume. The most intrusive sounds were subdued voices from the lobby, the methodical tick-tock of a massive floor clock, and the slow, rhythmic stroke of a porter brushing the heavy brocade of an over-size sofa.

When the youth sneezed, the brushing stopped. The porter straightened from his work - ebony face, white shirt, purple trousers - his look inquiring if the dust he raised had caused the young gentleman's discomfort, if the young gentleman had taken offense. But when the young man didn't look up, the porter bent again to his slow, rhythmic task.

Indeed, so intent was Lewis on rereading his words he didn't stop as he fumbled in his pocket to take a habitual swipe at his nose with a well-used handkerchief. He smiled to himself as he read: "I trust you will not be angry with me for going off like another Ulysses." He'd wanted to say "like another Fremont," but thought an allusion to the popular explorer of the American West too obscure for a female. She would know of Ulysses, however, and the story of how the Greek's clever wife had fended off suitors while Ulysses pursued his adventures. "Oh, Lewis!" the youth imagined his cousin saying as she pressed his letter to her bosom. Yes!

He passed a slow hand through his hair as he fantasized his homecoming months hence, his cousin's kiss of welcome, her lips soft and sweet. She had surprised him at their farewell in the garden by suddenly rising to her toes to kiss him full on the mouth, a kiss that thrilled him. His first kiss! He could still feel the soft, warm, moistness of her lips on his.

3

A smile curled his lips as he bent to finish his letter. "I have sent my trunk to the wharf and will reboard the riverboat *Saluda* this afternoon to continue my journey up the Missouri River to Independence, so it now remains only for me to tell you that I have been invited to join a wagon train of Bent, St. Vrain, & Co, one of the premier houses of the Santa Fe trade. I know you will feel reassured that *Mssr.* St. Vrain himself has taken me under his wing. *Messieur* is a bear of a man who puts me in mind of a gruff Blackbeard. He is no-nonsense and looks to be more than a match for any Indian after my hair, so you need not be concerned for my safety on that account.

"We hope to set out from Westport in early September and reach Bent's Fort in about six weeks. Although my desire is to be bold like Ulysses, dear cousin, prudence dictates that I not go into Mexico until it is safely in our hands. So I send my adieu for now. I promise to be careful, to 'watch my hair' (as they say out here in Indian Territory), and to write again when there is news as,

Your most admiring cousin,

Lewis"

He leaned back in the chair, wondering if he'd been reassuring enough about the war. All St. Louis was war! war! war! Talk of 'Manifest Destiny' was everywhere! After all, everyone knew the Pacific Ocean was America's rightful western boundary. Of course! And President Polk had every right to secure that boundary, even if it meant taking the land by force. Godspeed Colonel Kearny as he marched forth to wrest control of the West from Mexico.

But while all St. Louis cried "War! war! war!" Lewis wasn't especially concerned about America's western boundaries or the first battles with Mexico being fought in Texas. And what did the march of Colonel Kearny's Army of the West have to do with him? No, here on the threshold of the vast American frontier his thoughts were a mish-mash of youthful fantasies - of broad-shouldered, buckskinned companions and buffalo chases and the untasted fruit of connubial embrace, of his cousin's soft, gold curls and bluebonnet eyes and rose-petal lips and delicate hands, of a dusky Indian princess with long black hair scented with exotic wild herbs beckoning from a bed of boughs, her eyes dark and bold in piney, sun-dappled shadows. Oh, young Lewis yearned for love with an awful ache! Adventure and love, love and adventure. What greater joys for a youth in bloom than adventure and love? Ho! for the Rockies! he wanted to cry for the world to hear! Ho! for the Santa Fe Trail!

Several weeks later young Lewis was merry with claret on the Santa Fe Trail. One of St. Vrain's freight wagons tipped over while crossing a steep-banked creek, breaking open a case of the merchant's favorite wine. The men around the campfire took full advantage of the accident. They sat in the center of a circle formed by St. Vrain's huge wagon transports, each loaded with some 2½ tons of boltcloth, kitchenware, farm implements, soap, coffee, sugar, and whatever else might turn a good profit in furs or specie from the Mexico trade. At other fires French-Canadian teamsters joked and laughed and sang. Somewhere in the distance one of the Mexican herders practiced a deliberate little melody on his guitar. When darkness gathered the herders would drive the oxen and horses into the wagon fortress for the night.

All day St. Vrain's wagons had traversed horizon-wide, undulant hills of brownish-green grass under a bright, cloudless sky. Mile after mile of monotony, the wheel ruts of the Santa Fe Trail wove an endless random pattern, crossing and recrossing until they disappeared in shimmering heat-waves. The heavy sun, the plodding pace of the patient oxen, the creaking axles and the hum of insects were mind-numbing, and young Lewis had dozed several times, weaving dangerously atop the high-pommel Mexican saddle he'd borrowed for his western adventure. Once he awakened to see the friendly dark green of a few ragged trees along a creek and felt relief that not everything familiar in his life had disappeared. Still, his Cincinnati home seemed as remote as the fabled Pacific shore.

Although Lewis did not know it, *Messr.* St. Vrain had indeed taken the youth under his wing, but with an idea in mind. With well-born young white men in distant New Mexico as rare as white buffalo, why not throw a rope around the neck of a prospective son-in-law and lead him back to his daughter in Taos, a raven-haired beauty? That was the sensible thing to do, and Ceran St. Vrain was a straightforward man. A second generation American of minor French nobility, he had journeyed to New Mexico with trade goods as a young man, trapped beaver, married into a New Mexico family, then decided to assume Mexican citizenship about the time he and Charles Bent formed Bent, St. Vrain, & Co, fur traders. Since then he'd become an unabashed expansionist and a tireless promoter of the Far West. His favorite dictum was: Where Americans go, prosperity follows! Now in his forties, one of the richest men in New Mexico, comfortable in several languages and Indian signing, St. Vrain indulged himself with good food and drink, fancy-front shirts, storytelling, and the pontifications of a man of stature. With his badly pocked face partially hidden by a glossy, black beard, burly St. Vrain was a princely merchant, a patriarch of the prairies.

Around the campfire that evening St. Vrain digressed from talk of the war with Mexico to tell a story about a fur trapper, Peg-leg Smith, who tried to amputate his own shattered leg. "'Wul, gol' dang it!" St. Vrain imitated."Git to it a'fore I pass out, ya gol' dang fools!'"

The listeners laughed. "*Vraiment!*" St. Vrain assured them. "We just stood around. We didn't know what to do - bones sticking out of his leg and all. So ol' Peg-leg took his Green River and started cutting off his own leg! I saw it with these two eyes! *Vraiment!*" St. Vrain pulled down his lower lids with two fingers.

Young Lewis had already concluded that "*Vraiment!*" was one of St. Vrain's favorite expressions, especially during stories of his fur trapping days, stories that Lewis suspected grew more incredible with each telling. Two or three men around the fire were holding their sides with laughter. "Yup! Ol' Peg-leg!" St. Vrain said, his tone droll. He repeated the punchline. "'Wul, gol' dang it! Git to it a'fore I pass out, ya gol' dang fools!'"

One of the laughing men tumbled off the upended bucket he sat on, which made everyone laugh all the harder.

"Yup, I can still hear him," St. Vrain said."'Wul, gol' dang it!' Oh, he was an ornery cuss, ol' Peg-leg. Danged if after that he didn't carve his own peg leg from a lodgepole."

After the laughter subsided, St. Vrain puffed his cigar for a few moments, then noticed young Lewis wore a dubious look. "What'sa matter, young fella," he said. "Don't believe it?"

"No, sir," Lewis said, then quickly added I mean, it's an amazing story."

"Amazing, eh?"

"Well, sure." Then, sensing he'd said the wrong thing, he amended, "I mean, for someone like me. I mean, it's so different out here, everything's so different."

"Yeah, it's different all right," St. Vrain said, "but in buffalo

6

country you'll really see different."

The experienced men around the fire nodded. Many prairie travelers held that the pinnacle of good living was to gorge themselves on fresh-killed buffalo, especially the hump meat and tongue.

"Are we almost there?" Lewis asked.

"Oh, yes," St. Vrain said, "Pawnee country now." The Pawnee were one of several Indian tribes that derived food, clothing, and shelter from astonishing herds of buffalo that ranged the prairie in great migrations. "But mind you don't go chasing off like some greenhorn. Pawnee'll take your hair as soon as any."

"No, sir," the youth said, using a finger to loosen his neck-piece, a new, black silk handkerchief that he now regretted. In truth, almost every day on the Santa Fe Trail he learned an elemental lesson. Like the morning he couldn't catch his horse. Not thinking, he'd freed its picket rope and turned to fetch his saddle. As his back was turned his horse rather casually moved off. Lewis started after it, lugging his bridle, blanket, and saddle, but the horse kept a dozen yards distance. Growing impatient, Lewis made a dash. The horse frisked away. So Lewis waited until the horse began to graze again, then approached at a walk. But the horse moved off. Time and again when Lewis got within a certain distance, the horse would snatch a last mouthful and move away. Not wanting to appear more stupid than he felt, but sensing that every eye in camp watched his little drama, Lewis continued to pursue the horse at a walk, entreating the animal in a friendly voice, his saddle growing heavier, his frustration and anger rising. Finally, after trekking nearly out of sight of camp he noticed the wagons beginning to move. "Goddamn you to Hell!" he shouted at the horse. If he'd thought to bring his musket he would have shot the beast! If he'd been able to lay his hands on anything more sizeable than pebbles on the prairie he would have driven the stupid animal off to be eaten by wolves. He gave up the chase so he could catch the wagons.

A quarter hour later, panting and sweaty, too embarrassed to say a word, he was able to hang his saddle and gear on a wagon-hook behind the plodding oxen. He walked all morning, aware that his horse followed the wagon train at a safe distance. At the mid-day break ("nooning" in trail talk) one of the Mexican herders rode out to lasso the wily animal, and in gratitude Lewis gave him two dollars, almost a week's wages for the man. That night even Lewis managed to laugh about his morning misadventure.

Now St. Vrain addressed a youth at the campfire who was returning from college to his home in New Mexico. "And how about you, Narcisse, happy to be going home?"

Fifteen or sixteen, a smallish lad with liquid, brown eyes, Narcisse seldom spoke. Although his English was actually quite good, he was self-conscious among Americans, his accent having been mocked by Missouri schoolmates whose English was often burdened by French and German accents more obvious than his Spanish.

"Yes, very happy, sir," Narcisse blushed. He nervously stroked the sparse growth above his lip with a forefinger and thumb.

"Miss the mountains, do you?" someone asked.

"Oh, yes, very much! And my favorite horse!"

"Your horse?" one of the men exclaimed with a wink. "Not the *señoritas*?"

"Oh, no, sir!" Narcisse protested, blushing more deeply, squirming on his saddle-seat. "I do not miss the *señoritas* now! I am too young!"

Lewis joined the laughter that followed, and hoped no one would question his own romantic yearnings.

St. Vrain drained his claret. "Well, we're gonna need young fellas like you and Lewis in New Mexico," he said. He drew reflectively on a large cigar. "God gave us a gift not having to fight a war out there. It's a great opportunity."

So talk around the campfire returned to the war in New Mexico, or rather the lack thereof, because earlier that day they'd met Army messengers returning from Santa Fe with word that the Army of the West now occupied the dusty little capitol of New Mexico. The size of Colonel Kearny's force had apparently intimidated the Mexican governor. The Mexicans fled without firing a shot, and the Americans had marched into Santa Fe unopposed. All was calm.

"Hurrah!" cried the Americans in the wagon train, waving their hats in celebration. Grinning broadly, they'd shaken hands with the messengers and with each other. Several men fired their weapons into the air, a ragged volley of popping muskets. St. Vrain seemed to deflate with relief. "Well, by God!" he said half to himself, a wide smile spreading his lips. "Well, by God!"

He had been stiff with worry. For Americans with Mexican wives like him and Charles Bent - and there were many - going to war with Mexico was like going to war with family. No good could come of it. But with Santa Fe now under American control and with the secret that St. Vrain knew about his friend Charles Bent, prospects looked very bright indeed for Bent, St. Vrain, & Co.

"Well, Narcisse is going to be a rich man someday," St. Vrain said to young Lewis. They were riding ahead of the wagon train on the lookout for buffalo.

"Oh?" The idea of a rich Mexican was something of an oddity to Lewis. Weren't Mexicans backward and poor?

Narcisse was something of a puzzle to Lewis, and so far the two young men had found little in common. Indeed, when the other men in the wagon train raced horses or shot at targets, Lewis joined them with a puppy-like enthusiasm for competition and camaraderie. But Narcisse stayed apart, and Lewis wondered why a boy born and raised in a rough-and-tumble place like New Mexico was not a natural outdoorsman. Why wasn't he more manly? After all, he was a child of the frontier. Lewis found the doughy softness of Narcisse unsettling.

"Yup, got a kingdom on the Rio Grande, him and Elliott's brother."

"Elliott Lee? He's got a brother in New Mexico?"

Elliott Lee was another traveler in St. Vrain's wagon train, an older man who rode a huge gray because his weight would have punished a smaller horse. Sharing St. Vrain's mess with Lewis, Narcisse, and a couple of other men, Elliott ate with no apology for his appetite.

"A man of girth is a man of worth," he liked to say. Like Narcisse, he stuck close to the wagons and traveled in style...a servant, his own tent, a folding cot, a folding camp chair. For protection he carried a double-barreled shotgun loaded with small balls. "Wal,' if I gotta shoot I ain't gonna miss," he explained, "because I sure ain't gonna outrun 'em!"

Like Lewis, Elliott affected the crude speech of the Santa Fe

Trail, a good-humored bow to the leveling of life on the prairie. St. Vrain sometimes called him "General," but Lewis never knew why.

"Yup," St. Vrain said, "Elliott's brother lives in Taos. That's why he's coming out west. Gonna take a look at his brother's land. His brother needs help and the land needs men. Smart young men like you, Lewis. There's plenty of room. I expect there's more people in St Louis than in the whole of New Mexico. *Vraiment!* You just gotta see the land to believe it."

"How'd Narcisse get all that land? His parents rich?"

St. Vrain laughed. "Rich? Not unless they can sell rocks and sky! Oh, they're land rich, sure, but that's not rich, not in New Mexico, unless you got water and can make something of it. No, I trapped beaver with his pa when he couldn't rub *dos pesos* together because he didn't have 'em. None of us did. Then his pa married a Taos woman, and when the Mexican government started giving out land in big chunks he got some of the best. Got some for young Narcisse too. Smart fellas, those Lees!"

"But the land must be worth something, right? Worth the getting?"

"Oh, sure, it's worth the getting, but you gotta sweat the worth out, and to sweat the worth out you gotta have people. That's the problem with New Mexico, Lewis: Not enough people. And that's why an American New Mexico is good; it's gonna bring people to sweat the worth out."

Lewis said nothing. He pictured Elliott and Narcisse a-horseback, Mr. Big and Señor Little, surveying a vast rocky landscape, at a loss for how to "sweat the worth out." He smiled and imagined himself as a New Mexico. After he spent the day over-seeing fieldwork, his cousin would greet him under tall, leafy trees near the house. She would be wearing her long, high-waisted, white dress with small bows of blue ribbon. Her soft, gold curls would catch the late sun. As he handed off his mount to a servant, she'd smile and proffer a cool glass of something, perhaps lemonade...yes, lemonade. She'd take his arm and they'd stroll beneath the trees, the fullness of her long dress brushing his leg. He'd say something clever and she'd look up at him with her bluebonnet eyes, laugh delightedly, and squeeze his arm as she rose on her toes to kiss him on the cheek. Yes!

"Yup, the country needs young men like you, Lewis. I'd think it over."

Later, after Lewis learned more about St. Vrain's life in New Mexico, he wondered why the black-bearded merchant had said nothing of his own vast holdings.

Rising like a gigantic whale from the flat calm of the tree-less plain, Pawnee Rock was notorious for lurking Indians. Travelers approached with caution, but few passed on the Santa Fe Trail without stopping to add their names to the hundreds scratched on the rosy sandstone. While St. Vrain's wagon train nooned nearby, Lewis looked for names he might recognize - John Fremont, Kit Carson, Tom Fitzpatrick, Josiah Gregg, Jedediah Smith - famous men of the West who had surely visited the rocky outlook. He discovered a fresh name that intrigued him...Susan Magoffin, the only woman's name he saw. He wondered who she was, whether she was young and pretty, and if he might meet her in Santa Fe. Feeling devilish, he gouged his own initials just above hers and enclosed the two names in a crude heart. Then he climbed to the summit and was surprised to discover Narcisse.

The young Mexican sat on a jut of sandstone near a grave, scratching on the ground between his feet with a twig. When Narcisse saw Lewis he quickly wiped his eyes with the heels of his hands. "Sun is very bright," Narcisse said, his smile apologetic. He removed his huge Mexican hat and wiped his brow. Reseating his hat, he went back to scratching with the twig, a mosaic of nesting triangles. His hands were small, his fingers long and slender, almost feminine.

Lewis inspected the grave. Fairly fresh, its marker was a few stacked chunks of sandstone. He looked around. Except for a leafy fringe of trees along the Arkansas River in the distance, the midday sun shimmered on monotonous, pale brown emptiness as far as the eye could see, the colors of life gone with the late season. "Awful place to die," he said. "Know who he is?"

"No," Narcisse answered. He looked up briefly with sad, reddened eyes. "This grave was not here last year when I passed by. Now I was thinking how sad it must be to lie here alone."

Lewis nodded. "Mind if I sit?"

"Please, Señor Lewis, I would be honored."

11

Lewis leaned his musket and sat on the sandstone next to the youth. Narcisse shot him a glance and another shy smile. Lewis smiled back. He watched Narcisse go back to making triangles. Lewis felt awkward, at a loss for what to say. He wanted to ask the young Mexican what it felt like to own so much land. Lewis bent to pull some dry grass, nibbled, spewed it out, and tossed the rest away. He wondered why he'd bothered to sit with the shy youth. At last, embarrassed by the long silence, he said, "Well, I suppose we're the same now, huh? Americans."

"Ohhh!" Narcisse said softly. Then he quickly added, "Do you think so, Señor Lewis?" He did not look at Lewis as he added, "Yes...yes, I suppose that is true, the same now."

"I'm glad there wasn't any fighting, aren't you?"

"Yes, I am very glad also." A pause. "It was God's will. God's will that there was no fighting."

"Yeah, I s'pose." After days of chasing buffalo and eating great quantities of fresh meat, Lewis felt less like a greenhorn, and more and more he too affected the slurred, almost gruff speech of the prairie. He saw Narcisse wipe his eyes with the heels of his hands again. The sun wasn't that bright! He ventured to put a hand on the youth's back; the boy's white cotton shirt felt warm from the sun. "Something wrong?" he asked. "You feelin' all right?"

Narcisse shook his head. He snapped his twig, flung the pieces, and obliterated his doodles with a few angry scrapes of a boot. A long silence followed, during which Lewis felt so intrusive that he made ready to stand.

"Perhaps you will understand, Señor Lewis," Narcisse said at last, his voice strained. "I do not know, but I hope you will understand." He paused for a long moment. "I am feeling sad because we are almost to my country. Do you understand, Señor Lewis? We are almost to my country, but it is not my country anymore. I have no country. I go back to my home, but it is not the same home. Everything will be different. You Americans will change everything I grew up with." His words were a soft-spoken accusation. He looked away. "And you do not really think we are the same, do you? I will always be a Mexican to you, and you will always think you are better than me."

The blunt accusations of the youth took young Lewis aback.

He opened his mouth to protest, but realized the truth of what Narcisse said. Lewis remained speechless and the two said not another word, even to acknowledge one another when Lewis stood after a long, awkward silence and left the rock.

Bent's Fort

It was nearly dark when Lewis unsaddled, surrendered his horse to a Mexican, and slogged after his companions through the corral-side gate of Bent's Fort. Mud-spattered and soaked to the skin, he felt thoroughly discouraged. Adventure was fine, but jogging a-horseback all day in cold drizzle was misery. He was sick of the Santa Fe Trail, of cold nights of sleeping on the ground, boring food and the tedious landscape - and tedious companions. Ulysses and adventure be damned! He wanted a hot bath and sit-down meal. He dumped his borrowed saddle near a tangle of other saddles and gear on the muddy portico walkway and followed Elliott Lee into the fort's dining room.

St. Vrain welcomed them. "Why, hello there, Elliott! And you too, young fella! Enjoy the ride?" St. Vrain had gone ahead of the rest of the wagon train from eighty miles out, and in one long day covered the last leg of a journey that took Lewis, Elliott, and a couple of others two days. Freshly barbered and smelling of cologne, St. Vrain wore his usual white, frilly front shirt. In one hand he held a stemmed glass of claret, in the other a large cigar, which he stuck in the side of his mouth to shake hands. His eyes twinkled.

Aware of his own disheveled appearance and owly demeanor, Lewis returned the handshake and gave him a sheepish smile. "Why, yes, I enjoyed it," he answered, feeling better for the man's teasing, "and I'm ready for more!"

St. Vrain laughed and clapped him on his rain-soaked shoulder. "Elliott," he said to the other man, "how about a little something to warm you up?" Elliott brightened too, the heavy-footed, sodden man even more grateful than Lewis for the comforts of the fort.

The dining room was a roomy low-ceilinged chamber with huge, exposed beams of peeled logs. A dozen men or more crowded around a long table. Others sat at smaller tables or stood near a large fireplace at the far end. It was an assembly Lewis could not have imagined - grizzled men in greasy buckskins, harried-looking Army officers, civilians got up in jackets and shirts and starched collars, a couple of Indians who'd festooned their long hair with hammered coins and feathers and ribbons. He saw swarthy Mexican men and a female servant at the far end of the room attending a severe-looking Mexican woman in black, her wealth and station obvious. Others in the room looked like Lewis and Elliott - shaggy, unwashed, bedraggled, unfit for close company.

In what seemed like only a minute or two Lewis had a welcoming glass of brandy in hand and downed a couple of good swallows, relishing the warm slide of liquor down his gullet.

"William! Come on over!" St. Vrain called. "I want you to meet Elliott Lee and young Lewis."

As a grim-faced man approached Lewis drank again, already feeling warmer.

"This here is William Bent, boys - the man who built this fort, my partner's brother. William's the boss here."

The grim-faced man was dark-haired, clean-shaven, and solidly built, with piercing black eyes. Like St. Vrain, William Bent's face was badly pocked. He smiled a perfunctory, close-lipped smile.

"Elliott is Stephen Lee's brother, Lewis is from Cincinnati. His father was the newspaper man."

Lewis squirmed at the introduction. His father had been dead for ten years. How long would the world reckon Lewis's worth by his dead father's reputation?

"Lewis here might have the makings of a trader, William. The young fella took to the trail like an old hand."

William Bent's hand was horny-hard, his grip like iron. Feeling the strength of the brandy, Lewis tried to return the pressure of Bent's handshake. William gave the youth's hand a final quick squeeze that might have cracked a bone or two, then abruptly turned to St. Vrain. "Ceran," he said, "we gotta talk."

Lewis flushed at the snub, wondering if he'd somehow failed a test.

"All right, all right," St. Vrain said. "We'll talk in the morning, I promise." He put a friendly hand on William Bent's shoulder. The man nodded and crossed the room without another word. Elliott Lee and Lewis looked at each other with puzzlement.

"He's not rude," St. Vrain explained, reading their expressions, "but he doesn't like all the fuss around here." He winked, his eyes twinkling even brighter. "Oh, guess you didn't hear, eh? Well, fellas, his brother Charles is the new governor of New Mexico."

"Really?" Lewis asked.

"Yup, Charles Bent! I couldn't say anything before," St. Vrain continued, "but now word's come up from Santa Fe. I expect Charles is already on his way back from Washington."

"Well, that is good news!" Elliott said, offering his hand again to St. Vrain. "Congratulations!"

"Yup, but the news has William a little put off. With all this war business, nothing's like it used to be around here. All these soldiers and strangers are upsetting the Indians, and our fur trade's gone to hell."

Lewis nodded and drained his glass, glad of the explanation but still smarting from William Bent's rudeness. After all, St. Vrain's recommendation should have meant something.

When someone called St. Vrain's name the merchant clapped Lewis once more on the shoulder and also turned away. Lewis stood awkwardly by himself, looked around for the possibilities of another brandy, and spied Elliott Lee making for a seat beside two military men who were ready to attack huge platefuls of food. Glancing back at him, Elliott winked. Lewis grinned and half-raised his empty glass in salute. Then an arm in greasy, scarred buckskin reached up with an opaque bottle and gurgled liquor into the youth's glass. He heard a high-pitched, nasal voice say, "Hyar's the doin's what'll warm yer meatbag, son, drink 'er down!"

Next morning Lewis awakened in a strange room, still clad in his ripe trail clothes. Through a pounding headache, he surveyed his surroundings from the cocoon of his blanket. He lay on the floor on a buffalo hide inside a room devoid of furniture. Other buffalo hides and gear were piled around the badly scuffed, whitewashed walls. Supported by small, peeled logs, the ceiling was a herringbone pattern of close-laid peeled saplings darkened by smoke and soot. From outside he heard the ringing clang of a blacksmith's hammer, then became aware of voices and laughter and the braying of a mule. The nearby blare of a bugle caused him to duck his head under his blanket. Good God! What punishment! Through a small latticed window he noticed strips of bright sky.

Someone had put him to bed. He was not sure when, and couldn't remember who. He vaguely remembered being con-

16

veyed up a stairway by supporting hands. As he lay trying to reconstruct the evening, his head throbbing to the insistent beat of the blacksmith's hammer, he half remembered blurred faces, men dancing with men, himself dancing with a voluble black woman, loud talk of buffalo and Mexico and war and Charles Bent.

A strong whiff of frying bacon suddenly made his stomach churn, and he got to his feet in a hurry and staggered to the door.

Lifting the crude iron latch and opening the door, he recoiled from a blinding day. Under a breathtaking vault of intense blue, the morning sun sparkled on a thousand rain-wet surfaces. The air was crisp, pungent with the odors of wood smoke and barnyard and cooking bacon. Lewis crouched in the doorway, hands on knees, uncertain what his stomach would do. After a few moments of deep breathing, however, his queasiness settled and he began to feel better. He straightened and looked around at a strange new world - shining adobe, jutting pole-beams, porticos, men in serapes and buckskins and Army uniforms. Good God! Bent's Fort! He was really out west. The Far West!

Bent's Fort had sheltered a prosperous fur trading operation for more than a dozen years, first in beaver pelts brought down from the nearby mountains, now increasingly in buffalo and other furs acquired from the Indians of the plains. Passers-by stopped at the fort for storegoods, to repair their wagons and guns, replace worn-out or stolen animals, and enjoy the luxuries all travelers craved. On any given night the fort's high adobe walls might shelter a hundred or more people, the public rooms accommodating mountain men, European tourists, men in the Mexico trade, adventurers, an Indian guest or two, and a rare government official.

Home to men in the employ of Bent, St. Vrain & Co., the fort was a microcosm of the American West. Here lived traders and teamsters, herders, laborers, and artisans, many with Indian or Mexican wives. Few of the inhabitants could read or even write their names. Like most in the West, they spoke a colorful patois of English, French, Spanish, and expansive gestures. Life was simple. For most the pay was fifty cents or a dollar a day, sufficient to buy food, the comforts of shelter and tobacco, and the promise of better to come, God willing.

17

But the engine of war had transformed Bent's Fort from a busy frontier trading post into a bustling military hospital and quartermaster depot. Soldiers felled by scurvy and dysentery on the Santa Fe Trail convalesced in several of the public rooms. Army officers superintended the stockpiling of provisions and ordinance hauled from the "States" by road-weary oxen. Crates and barrels and bags marked "U. S. Army" crammed the storerooms and stood in heaps and stacks on the porticos and the central yard. Long trains of empty wagons came up from New Mexico to load the stuff of war from the new depot and haul it back to the south, for the Army's ever-lengthening supply line now stretched beyond Santa Fe and would soon reach hundreds of miles to the battlefields in Chihuahua and beyond. Troops in transition lounged about the fort, gawking and getting in the way and sometimes causing trouble. No wonder William Bent was upset.

Despite his hangover, Lewis mounted one of the fort's bastions to see what he could see. My God, he thought, the Rockies! To the southwest rose the famous twin breasts of the Spanish Peaks, snow-capped beauties a hundred miles into New Mexico. To the northwest he made out the faint up-thrust of Pike's Peak, also a hundred miles distant. He stood gazing at the mountain-rumpled horizon, longing to share his joy, to confirm with another human the wonder of his discovery. Oh, how he wanted his cousin at his side, his arm around her waist. Oh, Clio! Almost giddy, he descended to explore the rest of the fort, and found himself greeted with knowing grins and mock salutes by a succession of men he scarcely remembered. Lewis suspected he'd made a fool of himself the night before. Greenhorn!

In the middle of the yard he discovered big, wooden device used to compress furs for transport to St. Louis. Nearby he touched a small, burst cannon with his booted foot. He dimly remembered somebody saying the cannon had blown up during a salute to Colonel Kearny's arrival with the Army of the West. He explored storerooms, the wash house, and the blacksmith and carpenter shops. He revisited the billiard room with vague recollections of several games with the nasal-voiced trapper and losing a dollar or two but not caring. Peeking through an open door to the kitchen, he saw a female form bent to tend something in the fireplace, and when she straightened he recognized the voluble black woman he'd swung in dance with alcoholic exuberance. He tested his memory. "Charlotte?"

She turned, the shroud of irritation disappearing from her

round, ebony face even as she turned, just as quickly replaced with a toothy grin that lit the shadowy room. "Why, honey-chil'," she said. Lewis begged a cup of coffee, which she let him take away.

He passed through the dining room, smaller and more low ceilinged than he remembered, then peeked into a room being used by the Army. A hodge-podge of papers was piled on tables and the floor around the perimeter of the room. He wandered through an open door to the trade-room and gawked at the bounty.

Behind the rough plank counter an assortment of shelves held dozens of bright blankets for the Indian trade, bolts of showy red and blue broadcloth and flannel, a few of calico, muslin, and nankeen. He saw tinware, coffee mills, cans of gunpowder, percussion caps, gunflints, lead for balls, cans of shot, gun tools, writing supplies, needles and cotton thread, beads and bangles and tiny mirrors, combs and brushes. Other shelves held Green River knives, a wind-up clock, plugged and loose tobacco, soap, a smattering of apothecary items, steel ar-rowheads, tins of crackers and hardtack, jars of preserves, a ceramic figurine of an elephant and another of a dancing dog with a hat. Here were shirts and trousers and handkerchiefs, suspenders and stockings, rubberized rainwear, leather aprons and mittens. At one end stood a dozen upright muskets, some new. Near them on a shelf lay several used horse pistols and a couple of the new six-shot, cap-and-ball Colts. From smoke-darkened beams of peeled pine hung a balance beam for weighing skins. He saw dusty pots and pans, beaver traps, small tools and implements, more tin-ware, razor strops, can-dlewick, rawhide, bacon, and chilies. Beneath the shelves and under and atop the counter, an assortment of barrels and boxes and baskets and sacks held raw coffee-beans, cones of sugar, rice, eggs, wheat flour, a variety of beans, dried apricots, cob-corn, salt, jerky, tar. In odd places were half-forgotten lengths of Missouri ash and hickory for fashioning tool handles, shaped iron for plowshares, various kinds of axe heads and ironwork, horse gear, packframes, farrier tools, a small anvil. It was a frontier cornucopia.

He knew almost every item, every ounce, was pulled step by laborious step by plodding oxen over hundreds of miles of empty prairie, to sit on display as proof of St. Vrain's dictum: "Where Americans go, prosperity follows!" Lewis felt a surge of pride as he realized that more than once on the long journey from the States he'd lent his strength to get the huge wheels of a balky freight-wagon moving to bring these goods west. God, the excitement of it all!

The brief November day was fading quickly, the sun sliding steadily lower, the activities of the fort's main yard winding down. Lewis leaned against a post and puffed on his pipe, an instrument of manhood he'd taken up in St. Louis. After several days at the fort he felt quite at home. Among the sounds of the fort he recognized the rhythmic scraping of corn being ground into meal with antique stone implements and smelled supper smoke and cooking smells from several apartment fireplaces. His eye followed a beautiful young half-blood girl of eight or nine, clay jug atop her head, bearing water from the fort's cistern to her apartment with practiced grace. He watched a Mexican worker strolling to his quarters for supper, his hair plastered flat from a clean-up dunk in a water-trough, a child on each hand, a third behind proudly wearing his father's sombrero and trying to match is his long steps.

Something in Lewis's memory tugged. He felt his throat tighten with a sudden remembrance. When his own father had arrived home for supper he would doff his hat and give it to little Lewis to hang on the coat tree near the front door. Lewis caught the Mexican's eye and gave a wave. The man smiled politely and nodded back.

From the billiard room over the blacksmith shop came a burst of laughter, then Elliott Lee's stentorian voice of protest, which brought another round of laughter. Through the door to the kitchen Lewis heard Charlotte scold her kitchen help, an Apache waif bought from Indian slavery by William Bent.

"Yassuh?"

Lewis turned and saw a black man wearing raggedy "States" clothes - trousers held up by a length of rope, his faded hickory shirt draped with a gray velveteen vest, once stylish. He spoke through a wide, gap-toothed grin. "Missus sent this out fo' you."

"Why, thank you, Dick," Lewis said, taking the proffered mug of coffee. He'd noticed the black man around and knew both he and Charlotte belonged to Charles Bent. Until now Lewis hadn't dealt with the slave.

"Yassuh," Dick said, and affected a slight inclination of his upper body as he turned to go. Lewis sipped the rich brew.

20

"Ummm. Your woman sure makes good coffee, Dick."

The Negro stopped in mid-step. "Yassuh." After a few puffs on his pipe, his tone off-hand, Lewis asked, "Been west long, Dick?"

Dick took a half step back and scratched his head - wooly and graying - his gesture a parody of Negro servitude. "Well, suh, I's not sure," Dick answered, his eyes on the ground. "Lemme see now." He pondered as he scratched here and there and muttered to himself, "Um-huh, um-huh."

Lewis shifted, preparing to say something sharp. He knew he was being mocked.

"Well, suh," Dick said at just the right moment, "neahs I 'member it be bout fo'ty-one...yassuh, eighteen an' fo'ty-one, I b'lieve. Neah's I collec' now, masah, unnahstan? Neah's I collec' now. Las' see, dat mout be fi' year now. Tha's rah! Fi' year, ma-sah. That be afo' you's all growed up lak now, I 'spec." And with that Dick turned on his heel and walked away, whistling a familiar hymn. Lewis stared after him, his coffee and pipe forgotten.

After giving their animals a few days' rest, St. Vrain and his wagon train continued into New Mexico by the mountain route. Lewis had an invitation from St. Vrain to visit the family home in Taos, but for the time being he decided to stay at the fort and get a closer look at Indian life. Narcisse also extended an invitation to Lewis when the two shook hands in farewell.

"It will be a great honor for me and my family if you will visit us in Taos, Señor Lewis," Narcisse said.

"You bet, Narcisse, I'll see you in Taos," Lewis promised. Both affected more camaraderie in their farewells than they felt.

Soon after St. Vrain's departure, Lewis tagged along to a Cheyenne Indian village with a fur trader named John Smith, the greasy-sleeved, nasal voiced man who'd gurgled liquor into Lewis's glass and won a dollar or two from him at billiards. Like Charles Bent's brother William, John Smith had a Cheyenne wife. Unlike the taciturn William Bent, John Smith never stopped chattering. Ten years earlier he'd skipped out on his apprenticeship to a St Louis tailor to seek fur-trapping adventure in the west, and had never looked back. "Blackfoot" the

21

Cheyenne called him, because he was said to have taken seven scalps among that tribe. Now he was one of Bent, St. Vrain, & Company's most valued traders. He knew Indian ways, was proficient in Cheyenne, French, Spanish, and Indian sign language, and would share his knowledge with young Lewis in return for a little cultured company. Under Smith's tutelage the youth would live among the southern Cheyenne for almost three months.

The Indians called him *Veheo-kis*, Little White Man, and he was a novelty, for the Plains Indians seldom encountered young white males. And Lewis, genuinely awe-struck by his exotic surroundings, approached his experience among the Cheyenne with the enthusiasm of a scholar who stumbled upon a long lost manuscript. *Ten-o-wast?* he would ask a dozen times a day, pointing to an object, asking its name, then writing the words in his journal. Although he was determined to master the rudiments of the language, his efforts to speak regaled his listeners, especially mischievous older women who purposely fed him dirty words and expressions and combinations of sounds deliberately difficult to pronounce.

Among the young women he became a great favorite. In turn, their exotic faces and revealing skin dresses and form-fitting leggings and their love of decoration and bold play drew him like a bee to pollen. Smiling Moon and Morning Mist and O-ne-o (whose liquid hazel eyes made Lewis ache with longing) and a half dozen others repeatedly hauled him off to dances and games and youthful sport. They fussed over him with paints and brushes while he sat like a foolish, grinning puppy. Reveling in their attention, he let them dress him up and paint him like an Indian and parade him around the encampment for the amusement of all. He was passed on from family to family as a guest of honor. In short, he had a wonderful time among the Cheyenne.

He experienced a virginal adventure one night that he would remember forever. While living as a guest with the family of On-e-o, he slipped away one night from yet another round of dancing to go early to bed. Sometime later On-e-o returned home and invited herself under his blanket, hiding from her companions in a childish game. At first Lewis lay frozen with astonishment, his thoughts awhirl. What was going on? What was he supposed to do? Did On-e-o want him to "talk" with her? He was mindful of the girl's mother and younger sisters sleeping on the women's side of the teepee, their snoring forms obscure in the uncertain light of dying embers. What if her father discovered them together? The youth wondered if, like Po-cahon-tas, she would have to appeal for his life if they were discovered.

But before long the soft warmth of the girl's pliant form be-gan to melt his fears and his reserve. He extended a tentative, trembling hand over her middle and drew her close, their bod-ies spooning. He had never been so intimate with a nubile female. So soft. He smelled the sweat and wood-smoke in her hair and felt the moist warmth of her skin beneath her red flannel dance dress and the firm fullness of her backside against his thighs. When she didn't resist the closeness, Lewis gathered the blanket even more closely. He felt proud and pro-prietary. On several nights he had promenaded around the big dance fire with On-e-o under this same blanket, a favorite form of entertainment among the young people. But this! He won-dered what to do next, aware of a powerful erection that strained the leg of his trousers. He wondered if he could figure out how to do it without getting caught. Would it count with an Indian girl the first time? And could he tell anyone? And what about his cousin? Would she somehow be able to divine his car-nal knowledge of the Indian temptress?

Poor Lewis! His dilemma too quickly disappeared when sev-eral of the girl's friends burst into the teepee, waking everyone in a noisy search for their companion. For a minute or two Lewis thought he'd be able to keep On-e-o's soft, warm form for himself. He affected ignorance of her whereabouts while his erection strained even harder at the exquisite deception taking place beneath his blanket. The other young women seemed baf-fled at their friend's disappearance and were ready to give up the search when the little vixen reached back her hand under the cover of his blanket and gave his throbbing member a hard squeeze. And laughed!

Thankfully, Lewis's erection was almost gone by the time the young women pulled the two of them to their feet to return to the dance.

Next day Lewis sought a private place away from the camp and spent most of the morning composing a long letter to his cousin. He described John Smith and his family, what it was like to live in a teepee, his progress with the language, and sev-eral memorable personalities among the Cheyenne. "I will soon look like a mountain man," he wrote rather proudly, for he'd commissioned one of the Indian women to make him an outfit of elkhide "skins" to replace his increasingly threadbare

23

"States" clothing. After writing four sheets on both sides he closed his letter with a gush of feeling, realizing as he did so that he'd omitted any but the most general and innocent mention of On-e-o and his other young Cheyenne friends. He pondered this matter as he folded the pages, then began reliving the blanket-scene of the evening before and got an instant erection. "Jesus!" he said aloud and stood to duck under an over-hanging willow tree to masturbate. "I'm doing it for you," he said to himself as he imagined his cousin's moist, warm kiss, "for you...for you!"

Done, feeling an enormous pressure relieved, he tucked the pages of his letter into his journal, and soon found himself back at On-e-o's teepee.

During the time he lived among the Cheyenne, Lewis traveled back and forth between their scattered villages along the Arkansas River with John Smith and his family, making good progress with the language, writing and sketching at every opportunity. He spent hours playing with Smith's engaging two-year-old, a boy named Jack. Although Lewis liked the voluble Smith and enjoyed their time together, he felt challenged by William Bent's continued cool indifference, for William had left the fort to live with his Cheyenne wife and her relatives in the same village where Lewis was staying. But for some reason he kept Lewis at arm's length.

Although Lewis hung around William's teepee, volunteered to run errands, and tagged after William on his rounds (when permitted), nothing changed in William's demeanor. The taciturn fur-trader seemed to dislike the "little white man" from Cincinnati.

But perhaps it was Lewis's grinning efforts to please that kept William at a distance. In any event, the closest Lewis came to a real exchange with the man was the day when William acknowledged that he too had been called "Little White Man" when he first lived among the Cheyenne "They call you that if you're not quite a man," he explained.

"You mean you were as green as me?" Lewis asked, hopeful William would at last acknowledge a common bond.

"No," William Bent replied, his pocked face expressionless as he turned away from the youth. "I was never that green. I mean I was young."

Rebellion

Picuris Mountain

Charley Autobees later said he just couldn't understand how things had gotten so bad. Hell, in Taos everybody knew everybody, and Charley could name a dozen Americans like him who'd lived in the valley for years, taken up with Mexican women, married them, and become Mexican citizens. The Taos valley was their home. So why would he be alarmed in the cold mountain shadows of that fateful morning of Tuesday, January 19, 1847? As he urged his big, white mule up the last long pull to cross Picuris Mountain on his way back to Turley's mill Charley heard the dog barking and rounded a huge fallen slab to spot a Mexican hurrying toward him on a good-looking black horse.

Soon Charley realized the Mexican hat and serape had fooled him. "Why, hell, that's Town!" he said, surprised. Charley brought his mule and burros to a halt and turned in his saddle. "That's Town," he repeated to his brother.

Charley's voice was a rasp. His brother Tom nodded and stopped too, as did the three Mexicans farther back in the train of burros. Their packtrain of empty whiskey kegs stretched a hundred yards down the tortured, rock-strewn track, a portion of the old Spanish "royal road" running from Santa Fe up to Taos. Dust-covered snow littered the lifeless ground and lay deeper on the shadow-side of sparse juniper and tumbled rock.

When Town discovered Charley's packtrain he stopped, immediately wreathed in the vapor of his panting horse's breath and sweat. Horse and rider looked like an apparition. Then Town came clattering down the trail again, yelling and waving his big hat when he recognized Charley's red blanket coat and his white mule with the odd 'tch on the hip. Charley smiled. Town was always good for laugh. Sandy-haired, freckled, happy-go-lucky, Town had finally married and settled down with a Taos girl less than half his age.

At last Charley was able make out what Town was yelling. "Go back?" he repeated aloud. Tom heard too, but said nothing and leaned to spit tobacco juice.

"Go back, they're killing everybody! Go back!"

"What the hell's he talking about?" Charlie asked no one in particular.

27

Town reined in his heaving, lathered horse so violently he spooked Charley's mule and some of the burros, and there was confusion on the trail until the men got their animals under control. Town's face was flushed, his blue eyes wild, his nose running. His panicky words made little clouds in the morning cold. "Go back, Charley, go back, they're killing everybody! Get the hell out of here!"

"Who?"

"All of us! They're all over town, Charley, going crazy. They killed Bent. We gotta get out of here!"

"Killed Bent?"

"Charles Bent, damn it. The governor! They killed Charles Bent." Town was close to tears. "Everybody, Charley, they're killing everybody. Oh, Christ!"

"Jesus!" Charley said, his mind like molasses, "Bent! Who killed 'im?"

"Hell, Mexicans, Pueblos! I don't know! I was sleeping. My wife's pa came pounding on the door and told me to run. He said a mob had gone crazy and was killing Americans. I could hear the screaming, Charley. I got the hell out."

"Jesus, you believe it?"

"Christ, I heard the screams, Charley. I knew this was coming. Damned Mexicans! We gotta get to Santa Fe. We gotta get the Army. I mean it!"

Charley could hardly take in the news. He looked back to the rocky summits stretching south as if they would help his understanding. The mountains stood snow-capped and remote, brushed gold by the morning sun. The beauty of the morning made Town's news seem all the more strange. Town kept glancing back up the trail towards Taos.

"What about Turley?" Tom asked, and leaned to spit tobacco juice again.

Charley and Town looked baffled.

"Does he know about the mob?" Tom asked. At the awkward silence, he added, "We better let 'im know, Charley."

Charley regarded him. "Think so?" he asked.

Tom nodded.

Charley turned to Town. "You think they'll go up to Turley's too?"

"Jesus, I don't know, Charley. I s'pose! He said they were killing everybody."

Charley nodded, a corner of his mind aware that Tom had been the quicker again. He still wasn't used to his younger brother being the smarter one.

"Well, what you think?" Charley asked Tom. "Guess I should sneak around Taos and let Turley know, eh?"

Simeon Turley had fallen asleep in his chair after a big noon meal, so he didn't hear Charley shouting when he was still a hundred yards up the steep cart track that reached the bottom of the arroyo. Only after Charley's dog ran ahead through the gate, barking happily at old friends, did Turley awake with a jerk, hear Charley shouting, and hurry to the door. He saw Charley rein in so hard his mule almost went over backwards. Lord, now what? Turley thought as he left the house and limped across the frozen wheel ruts, mindful of his bad knee. Middle-aged, thick, with a cherubic face and ever-present gold-rimmed glasses, he wondered if Charley had run into Indian trouble.

Charley stayed in his saddle and kept up his raspy call of alarm as men hurried from the mill and the outbuildings to form an excited knot around the winded mule. A youth broke away to meet Turley.

"He says they're killing Americans, Mister Turley!" Except for bad teeth the boy was good-looking, a corn-haired laborer of an age with young Lewis.

"What's going on, Charley?" Turley asked as his men made way for him.

"Trouble. They killed Bent!" Charley doffed his slouch hat to wipe his brow with a sleeve of his blanket coat. Both he and the panting mule perspired heavily. "Town told us."

"Bent?" Turley said, squinting up at Charley against the bright blue sky. "The governor? Down in Santa Fe?"

"Hell, no! Right in Taos! Bent was in Taos. Listen, Simeon, they're coming, maybe two, three hundred. I seen 'em when I was circling the town. They're maybe four or five miles away."

"Who?" Turley asked.

"Hell, how should I know? Mexicans, Pueblos! A mob, Town said." Charley then told of Town in disguise riding hell-bent for Santa Fe to fetch the Army. "Well, damn it all!" Charley said, exasperated by Turley's muddled, disbelieving look. "See for yourself!" He pointed to the south skyline of the arroyo. "You can see from up there!"

"Maybe that's why the boys didn't show up today, Simeon." The speaker was John Albert, a smallish, wiry man with a squinty right eye. Like Charley, he was in his early forties and had given up mountain man life for a Mexican wife and regular employment with Turley. John Albert looked after Turley's men and machinery.

Turley nodded absently. He tended to trust John Albert, whose squinty eye and nasal drawl and worm-slow speech were jokes among the men. But though he was slow to speak his mind, John Albert usually spoke good sense, which was one of the reasons he was Turley's straw boss. And it was true that a half dozen Mexican and Indian laborers had failed to come to work that morning. Still, the idea of a mob in Taos killing Charles Bent seemed far-fetched. "Well, maybe," Turley said. "But I don't know what they'd want here. We didn't do anything." He pondered the ground, then looked at Charley as he rubbed the back of his neck in a habit that indicated he was thinking. "Well, I don't know, Charley," he said finally. "You know how Town is...." And the conclusion of his thought remained unspoken.

Charley stared in disbelief at Turley's reluctance to take alarm, then fished in his shirt. He jingled a little leather pouch and tossed it to Turley, proceeds from the sale of Turley's whiskey he and Tom had packed down to Santa Fe to satisfy the U.S. Army's thirst. That was Charley's job - packing Turley's whiskey and flour and furs. He was Turley's routeman. "That's everything but what you owe me. There's some Army script in there too. Tom's taking the burros back down to Santa Fe - figures the Army'll want 'em." Turley nodded absently, still rubbing the back of his neck.

Charley was turning to leave when John Albert put a hand on his mule's neck. "What about the Frenchmen and our families? Town didn't say anything about them, did he?" Two of Turley's men were French-Canadian trappers who had also settled in the valley. Like John Albert, they had wives and families on little farms close by.

30

Charley shook his head. "I don't know, John. I'd guess it's just us they're after, us Americans."

"But I got my British passport! They won't hurt me, right?" The speaker was a narrow-faced Englishman who did the milling and tended the grindstones, a man named Marshall.

Charley looked disgusted. "Well, get up there and wave the damned thing then!" he rasped at the Englishman. "Listen," he said to Turley, "if it's all right with you I'm going up to the ranch to see to our women. Then I'm getting out. If I was you I'd get the hell out too. At least you'll have a chance a-horseback. Let the Army handle it!" Without waiting for Turley's response he wheeled his mule and made for the gateway, where he halted and looked back. Turley and the others stared after him, slack-jawed. "Well, Goddamn it," Charley yelled, almost plaintive. "Do something! At least shut the place up." He kicked his mule into motion again and disappeared around the corner.

But the men didn't move. They stood gawking at Charley's sudden disappearance around the gate, then turned to Simeon Turley as if he should know what to do. Turley continued rubbing the back of his neck as he eyed the heavy portal that would secure his yard. What had he ever done that a mob should threaten his establishment? He'd always tried to be fair, to buy and sell for fair money. Why would they want to bother him, a man who always tried to get along?

Charley's Ranch

The shortest route to Charley's ranch crossed the narrow part of the arroyo where Turley had his mill, then continued north through the woodsy foothills of the Sangre de Cristos, a southern spur of the Rocky Mountains. As Charley pressed his weary mule up the steep slope, he spotted John Albert riding a horse bareback up the arroyo's other side — no doubt to verify Charley's story. Later, when Charley paused to let his mule catch its breath, he looked again.

Beyond the arroyo a wavery mass of men breasted a treeless swell perhaps three miles distant. Below, he had a view of Turley's adobe compound where the men still stood in a cluster. Charley shook his head sadly and urged his mule forward. "Let's get home, mule, there's nothing we can do now." The big yellow dog loped ahead.

With a fresh mount Charley figured he could reach American territory across the Arkansas River, a long, hard ride of almost 150 miles. But maybe he wouldn't have to. Maybe Turley would calm things. After all, the miller was a good talker. Or maybe when the mob realized the Army was coming up from Santa Fe they would quit their nonsense and go home.

Farther along the trail, after he had gotten into snow, Charley slowed, then stopped, the thought nagging that he should have offered to help get Turley's wife and little ones out of harm's way. He thought for some time before shaking his head again. They'd be all right, he decided. If it came to fighting the Mexicans would never let their own get hurt, especially women and children. They'd keep the Pueblos in hand if they could.

Charley had already tried to convince himself that his family and Tom's would be all right if he had to skedaddle north, especially with Jose around, his wife's brother. Still, a corner of his mind remained uneasy. It wasn't natural for a man to run off and leave his family in a time of trouble. Well, he thought, he'd see what he found at home, then make a decision.

Charley's home wasn't much of a home, nor did his ranch amount to much, because he'd only taken possession of it the previous spring. Thanks to a landgrant by the now-fled Mexican governor, he and Tom had acquired almost twenty-five square miles of ranchland in the foothills. If the Autobees brothers showed progress in developing their ranch for several years and helped forestall the depredations of roaming Indians they would get to keep the land. They'd been required to include a couple of Mexican partners in the deal, of course, but that was just a formality to satisfy the letter of the law. So far as Charley and Tom were concerned, the land was really theirs alone.

Although hilly and forested, their grant included promising land on Llamas creek, some ten miles north of Turley's mill. A half mile or so off the trail leading to the little community of Rio Colorado, the brothers had labored to build a one-room house of adobes at the edge of a mountain meadow, complete with a crude corral and small stable. Then they'd moved their families in. Shortly after they took up residence in their new home, Colonel Kearny and his Army of the West invaded New Mexico.

Like most Americans in the West, Charley had few opinions about politics in general and little interest in the war with Mexico. The thing so many people made a fuss about - "Manifest Destiny" - was beyond him. Oh, he'd heard of America's claims to all the land east of the Rio Grande, which included most of settled New Mexico and Charley's ranch, claims that dated back to the last war with Mexico a dozen years earlier. But to Charley the Taos valley was just a good place to live, no matter who was in charge. That was why he'd had given up a fur trapper's life to go to work for Simeon Turley, packing whiskey and flour to the vast country's scattered trading posts, bringing back whatever furs or cash or goods or promises he took in trade. He knew the land and the people; he did his job well.

As a younger man he'd dallied with a couple of Indian wives and had a daughter by one and a son by another, but after a few years of teepee life he decided to put down roots. He was married by the priest in Taos to his Mexican wife Serefina, and they settled on a little farm in Arroyo Hondo. That was about the time that his brother Tom came out from Missouri to join him. Now, with Tom married to a Mexican woman also, the brothers saw their huge ranch as the culmination of their ambitions. Not bad for two men who signed their names with ill-formed marks.

But after the invasion by Kearny's Army of the West plenty of Mexicans were embittered by their government's cowardly lack of resistance. The fat Mexican governor who fled without a

fight and abandoned their homeland to the American invaders had betrayed them. And New Mexico's landed gentry became all the more embittered when Kearny (by now promoted to General Kearny) annexed not just America's claims to everything east of the Rio Grande, but the whole of New Mexico - vast stretches beyond the Rio Grande never before claimed or even in dispute. These Mexicans saw America's venture in New Mexico as a greedy land grab, pure and simple.

After the invasion, wishful rumors circulated from time to time of great armies coming up from Mexico to right the wrongs of American annexation. But as the days and weeks passed and no military threat became evident, Mexican notables who'd fled to the south at Kearny's approach began drifting back. To safeguard their interests, most went through a formal ceremony to swear allegiance to the United States. Within weeks any hope of serious Mexican opposition seemed futile. The cause of keeping New Mexico a Mexican state was lost.

Heavy-hearted, local patriots could barely bring themselves to look an American in the eye. Others put on false faces and made the best of the situation. Men doffed their hats, women smiled. Fandangos and church celebrations lent an air of normalcy in their occupied homeland. To the Americans, all seemed fine.

Confident of his conquest, General Kearny swore Charles Bent and several other civilians into office to carry on the work of the new American government, then marched off with most of his little army to invade faraway California. The security of America's latest possession he left to the remnants of his invasion force, most notably a regiment of Missouri volunteers, the 2nd.

The new government had a little scare just before Christmas, some six months after the invasion, when a plot was betrayed to the American authorities. Through confessions and captured documents they learned of a grandiose conspiracy. A small cabal of New Mexicans planned an uprising that would take place on Christmas Eve when they would kill or drive out every American in New Mexico, whether invader or long-time resident. But it was a desperate, rather foolish plan, and few took the plot seriously. It mostly involved disgruntled Mexicans Kearny had deposed from office or diminished in standing. A few floggings and public threats aborted the Christmas Eve uprising, and life returned to normal.

Like most Americans, Charley paid scant attention to the

Christmas flap, not even interrupting his regular trips to Santa Fe with Turley's whiskey and flour for the new military market.

By the time Charley turned off the main trail toward his house, he'd been traveling through snow for an hour or so and the afternoon sun was fading. Gone from home for a week, frazzled by the events of the day, he was tired and glad to be home. Then his big yellow dog froze and growled at something ahead. His heart pounding, shaken by visions of violence, Charley dismounted, quieted the dog, and proceeded afoot with his musket at the ready. Through the trees he glimpsed strange horses near his house. He heard the baby crying and smelled coffee.

The coffee was a good sign, but just to be sure Charley circled through the woods until he could approach along the creek. As stealthily as a stalking fox he crept up the gully to peer cautiously over the embankment.

Wearing a red bandanna headdress and large copper earrings, a familiar Indian sat cross-legged in the failing sunlight by Charley's door. The Indian's musket leaned against the house. He wore an unbuttoned cloth vest, which left his torso and muscular arms bare where his blanket was fallen around his waist. Charley saw the Indian's eyes survey his surroundings as he took a sip of coffee from Charley's own blue, porcelain cup.

Beside the Indian, a woman and a child of six or seven were eating bread. Several ponies and packhorses stood patiently near the Indian's favorite, a beautiful sorrel that would have made one of General Kearny's Dragoons proud. By a corner of the house Charley's two older children sucked their fingers and stared at the Indians, their own crusts of bread forgotten. The corral was empty. Charley silently retreated to fetch his mule.

When he approached again, openly this time, his children ran to him and draped themselves around his legs. "Otabee! Otabee!" they cried. With Charley and Tom gone so much of time, their children heard little English, and that was the closest they could come to his name, Autobees. Charley smiled at them and ruffled their hair and stopped to sign a greeting to the Indian, then rasped, "Hello, Big Nigger, come to trade that horse?"

The Indian stood. Much younger than Charley, he was not quite as tall, but more powerfully built. "Hello, Hoarse Voice,"

he said, calling Charley by his Indian name. They shook hands. "Maybe I'd trade for that blown mule of yours and five good horses." Charley could tell by the man's expression that he'd been aware of Charley's earlier, cautious approach up the creek gully.

Charley Autobees had known the Indian for some time, a young Delaware who left his people's settlements on the Kansas River to roam the mountain surrounds of the upper Arkansas River. Charley first noticed the Indian at the mountain trading post near the Greenhorn River when he realized the man spoke good English. Many Delawares spoke English, but this man could also read and write, having gone to Indian schools and lived his early years near American settlements. Something inside had made him reject the reservation life, however. Two years earlier he'd come west on an extended buffalo hunt with a large band of Delaware hunters and stayed in the area to make a living taking furs. Now, with some of his band killed by enemy tribes, some gone west with John Fremont on his explorations, and others returned to their families, the young hunter was among the last of the Delawares remaining in the Rockies.

"Señor," Charley's wife met him at the door. Short, plain, and going to fat, Serefina carried their new baby in her arms, a boy not yet a year old. Charley gave her a brief embrace and a reassuring smile, then exchanged his musket for the baby.

"Muchachoo?" he asked, wondering about his oldest son, a half-blood by Picking Bones Woman, one of his Indian wives. He should have said "*el muchacho*," but even after living for years in the Taos valley, Charley butchered the Spanish language. He'd long ago given up trying to understand anything more than simple words and phrases, and after several years together Charley and his wife still communicated mostly by gestures and facial expressions.

Serafina made a face with downturned lips and pointed with her mouth towards the lower pasture. "Con Jose," Serefina said. "La caballara."

Jose was her brother. Apparently Jose and Charley's boy had taken the horses to a sheltered pasture. Were they hiding them? Did Jose already know of the trouble in Taos? In any case, Serefina was not happy at being alone on the ranch when the Indians showed up.

Tom's wife appeared in the doorway. She was swollen with

child and her face questioned why Tom wasn't with Charley. Charley gave her a significant look. "Back in Santa Fe," he said.

"Santa Fe?"

"Si."

Her face fell.

"Puhdee cumer?" Charley said to his wife. The women understood he wanted them to cook. They disappeared into the house, muttering between them.

"Been up to San Luis?" Charley asked the Indian. The San Luis was a broad grassy valley some fifty miles north where game sheltered in winter. It was a popular hunting ground when snow made mountain hunting difficult.

"Since fall."

"Good hunting?"

The Indian pointed with his mouth to the pack animals. Charley walked over to examine the pelts.

"Turley buying?" the Indian asked, approaching Charley near the animals.

Charley's heart jumped, but he made a point of shrugging. "Last I heard." He wondered what he could say about the trouble in Taos. He knew the Delaware was wintering in the Taos pueblo and the woman with him was probably his pueblo wife. He motioned for one of his children to take the baby from his arms and returned to unsaddle his mule. "That your new wife?"

The Indian grinned broadly. He motioned for his wife and the boy to approach. Charley smiled and shook hands with the woman, then the boy. The woman was taller than average, with a broad, attractive face. Beneath her blanket she wore a deerskin dress with long fringes and knee-high pueblo boots trimmed with bits of red ribbon. She would not meet Charley's eyes. The boy was also shy, and after shaking hands inched behind his mother. Charley signed to them that he was hungry and that they all would eat soon.

Charley's house was modest, but typical for New Mexico. Moreover, the brothers still had considerable work to do. For one thing, their adobe bricks stood exposed to the weather. If left unprotected by several coats of mud plaster the rain would

37

gradually dissolve the bricks into mud and grass straw again, and the house would simply disappear into the ground.

Their home consisted of a single, low-ceilinged, pole-beamed room with a front door and single, small, unglazed windows on each of the four sides, situated high on the walls. The windows were as much for defense as for light and ventilation. Dirt-floored, the room was bare of furniture except for grass-filled mattresses the inhabitants slept on and then rolled up in day-time and placed along the walls as bolsters. Belongings stood in stacks on the floor or hung from the beams. A small, corner fireplace provided warmth and a place for cold-weather cooking.

After Charley joined the Indian in drinking coffee by the door for a while, the women spread a cloth on the floor near the fireplace and placed a pot of peppery stew and a basket of tortillas and several wooden bowls in the center.

Seated opposite the Indian, the other eaters at the periphery, Charley decided after several minutes of silent eating that he had to tell the Indian about the trouble in Taos. If the Indian found Turley besieged he would know Charley had not been straight. He wondered if the Delaware would take sides.

"Hamigo," he began at last as he wiped his mouth with a sleeve, "if you go to see Turley you might find trouble."

Turley's Mill

W al, they're coming all right," John Albert drawled, sliding off the horse he'd ridden to the top of the arroyo. With a spank he sent it in the direction of the stables. "A couple hundred, maybe more."

"Why, hell, we can handle that many," said Billy, the cornhaired youth. He'd hurried to the bunkhouse to don a fringed overshirt and arm himself. He now stood before them with powderhorn and bullet pouch and a long sheath knife in his belt, his eyes bright with excitement over a big grin. His shaggy hair caught the sun, his face was a vision of youthful energy and confidence. Billy's proudest (and almost his sole) possession was his long-barreled Kentucky rifle, a weapon that had belonged to his father. His "cosset gun," one of the men teased - Billy's pet.

Turley rubbed the back of his neck and studied the ground. "Well, let's not get all excited. This might not come to anything at all." He addressed John Albert. "Pueblos too?"

John shrugged. "I s'pose," he said, his mind on his family. That morning he'd quarreled with his wife and smacked his young boy on top of the head for shirking his chores. He wished now he'd made amends instead of stalking off to Turley's like a growly bear. If worse came to worse that might be the last thing they'd remember of him.

Turley sighed. "Well, I don't know what they'd want here," he said again. "We didn't do anything." His tone was confused and hurt.

"Well, maybe not," John said, stirring from his regretful thoughts, "but if they're gonna come chasing after us there's no sense in leaving our shirttails hanging out."

Billy laughed, a short, maniacal cackle.

Turley glanced at the youth, then shook his head. "You mean shut the place up," he asked John Albert. "Like Charley says?"

John shrugged again.

Turley thought a long moment. "Well, I don't know, we didn't do anything."

"Maybe, but maybe that don't matter."

"But how can...?" Turley appealed with his hands. "We don't want to fight. I've got my family here. We've all got families. I didn't hire you men to fight."

"No matter, *monsieur*, damn Indian want horse, you fight. Want hair, you fight." The more talkative of the two French-Canadians, William LeBlanc looked to his compatriot for support and the man nodded his agreement.

"Well, I don't know," Turley said, rubbing the back of his neck again, "I don't see us fighting." He looked up. "Listen, maybe we can talk it out, but if anybody wants out...I mean, if you want to make a run for it, well, go ahead. I won't take it bad." He sighed. "I'll see to your families till you get back."

When no one made a move, Turley saw from their expressions that they were uncomfortable with his presence and he needed to let them talk among themselves. "Oh," he said with a touch of embarrassment. "Well, take a few minutes to see what you decide then."

After Turley limped out of earshot towards his house, Billy giggled, "Bet he's gonna hide his money." A couple of the men laughed nervously. With Turley's house having the only floors made of wood north of Santa Fe, stories had him hiding gold and silver beneath the precious planks.

"Well, boys," John Albert said, consulting the sun, "I'll tell you what - we got maybe twenty minutes. We better talk quick." He scratched his stubble, now gray, a mark of age that prompted Billy to call him "Grampa." Almost from the first day of their acquaintance the former mountain man and the youth had developed a special relationship.

A long moment dragged by while no one spoke. Finally John said, "Well, I don't know, we could head north, like Charley. They might not come after us. But if they do they'll chase us all the way to the Arkansas, and then what? We'd be out in the open."

A couple of the men nodded.

"But the thing is, all we know now is what Town told Charley. Hell, the way it stands right now we don't even know what they want. Turley's right about that."

"But what about me?" the Englishman lamented.

There was an awkward silence. No one much liked the narrow-faced Englishman. "Well, I'll tell you, Marshall," John said, "My thinking is, if they want our hair, they'll want yours too, what's left of it anyway."

The men laughed. The Englishman looked pinched and his voice had a catch when he said, "But that's not fair!"

"Well, scoot then, damn it! Goddamned Brit!"

"All right, Billy," John said. "That don't help."

"Well, I say fight!"

"Yeah, Billy, but what if they're not after us?" The speaker was Turley's distiller, a rosy-cheeked young man in his mid-twenties. "I mean, what if they just want Turley? You know, what if they're just after the bigwigs like Bent and Turley...the rich guys. What if Turley's all they want?" The idea seemed to strike the rest of the men for the first time. They looked at one another.

"Yeah, well," John said finally, "we don't know that."

"Listen!" Billy said, "I ain't gonna let 'em hurt Mister Turley even so! He's a white man, like us, an American! I say we fight them damn niggers till the Army gets here! Hell, we got a damn fort! We can shut this place up and pick 'em off like pigeons! I say fight!"

After another short silence John asked, "Well, anybody else want a say?" The men glanced at one another. Some looked down and scuffed their feet. They were used to taking orders. "All right, then," John said. "We'll stay. Now let's get moving." He addressed the Englishman. "Listen, Marshall, you're in or you're out. If you're gonna run, you better run now."

The Englishman wouldn't meet his eyes.

"All right then," John said. "You're in." He turned to the French-Canadians, men he liked. "All right, boys, we'll hole up in the mill. You fellas get in there and chock it up good. You know what to do. Billy, go pinch down the millrace, but make sure we get a little water. The rest of you boys grab everything we got to shoot and anything else you can think of. I'll get the gate."

The two-story millhouse that would be their fort was as solid as a blockhouse, but that was all that favored its defense. Situated in a gully, Turley's establishment snaked along a nar-

41

row shelf pinched between steep walls. By climbing only a few yards on either side one could look into the heart of his operation - the big millhouse and distillery at the narrow end and Turley's house opposite. Except for the churches in the Taos valley, Turley's millhouse was the largest building around, a marriage of adobe and pine. It featured a flat roof and a rare, many-paned window at one end of the second floor for light and ventilation, for that was where the milling was done. At the opposite end of the loft from the window was an oversize opening with shutter-like doors through which sacks of grain were hoisted up with block and tackle to the milling machinery. The entire second floor was an expansive area they called the loft. Between the adjacent distillery and Turley's house, smaller buildings were used for blacksmithing and coopering and bunking the workers and for accommodating the frequent visitors who traveled north and south on the so-called "royal road." A long shed by the mill comprised the stables and storage for Turley's gig and wagon and several utilitarian two-wheel carts. Adjacent pens confined hogs and sheep and Turley's milk cow and her calf. In Mexican style, the outer walls of Turley's buildings formed part of the perimeter wall of the entire compound. Skirting one side of the compound, a swift stream powered Turley's milling machinery by way of a long millrace. Downstream the millrace rejoined the stream, which twisted through a narrow passage for a couple of miles to the tiny settlement of Dolores. Upstream, just past a prominent knob of black rock a short distance from Turley's wagon gate, the arroyo widened into a narrow, flat-bottomed valley where Turley grew wheat and corn and where his newly arrived black cattle wintered. That was also where John Albert and the French-Canadians had their own little farms. Turley was still in his house when John Albert, now armed with his musket, rapped on the door. Inside the children were crying. When the miller came out and pulled the door shut John saw Turley's eyes were red and tearful. "We'll stick it out, all of us," John announced. Turley looked at him, breathed a big sigh, nodded, then extended his hand. "Thanks, John, you're a good man," he said as they shook hands. Rubbing the back of his neck, he said, "But listen, I was thinking, maybe it's just me they want! I mean, if they were after Bent...." He looked up at John Albert for his reaction, but the former mountain man only shrugged and looked away. "Well," Turley said, "I'll try and talk with them anyway. We have to see what they want."

John waved a hand to dismiss further discussion. "Listen," he said, "Let's get up on the roof so we can see what's going on."

Turley regarded him with a momentary blank expression, then said "Oh! Good idea," and moved woodenly to the ever-present ladder at the side of the house. He climbed, wincing at the pain of his bad knee. On the roof the men scanned the sky-line of the arroyo, then took seats on the low parapet to watch where the trail from Taos entered the arroyo. Fragrant smoke from the mud chimney carried the muffled sounds of whimpering, the broken voice of Turley's wife Rosita trying to shush her children. Turley looked pained as he listened to the sounds from below.

The Englishman was crossing the yard with his musket and accoutrements when he noticed Turley and John Albert suddenly stir themselves atop Turley's roof. "Bastards!" he cried at them, thinking that they were sneaking out over the outer side of the house. "Bastards!" Almost in tears, he started in their direction, then became aware of sounds that might have been high-flying geese and then heard the thud of hoofbeats and looked up to see a dozen horsemen and a mob on foot come pouring over the rim of the arroyo and down the cart track, yipping and yowling and hooting, sunlight catching bright colors and shiny, metallic surfaces. The Englishman felt his bowels loosen. "Mother of God!" he breathed. He might still find safety. He could still head north after Charley into the mountains. But where would he go, and what if the mob came after him? He'd be all alone! He groaned in anguish and ran for the mill.

Soon riders raced from behind the black rock knob where the mob had assembled to shake their weapons and retreat. Others climbed atop the rock to prance and strut and taunt. After several minutes of this display a half dozen men emerged on foot with a Mexican flag tied to a military-style lance.

"Know any?" John Albert asked Turley as the deputation advanced toward the compound. The former mountain man stood with one foot on the parapet, the barrel of his musket propped on his knee and pointing toward the parley party.

Turley had worn spectacles for near-sightedness since early manhood, and with age his vision was getting worse. Things at a distance were fuzzy. He needed new spectacles. Now he pushed his glasses up enough to massage his eyes with thumb and forefinger. The parley group was within a hundred feet of the gate before John Albert offered, "Well, there's Tomasito from the pueblo, and Pablo Montoya all dressed up like a peacock. And Pablo Chavez!"

43

"Pablo Chavez!" Turley echoed. He'd traded with the kindly Chavez for years, exchanging goods from the States for the influential Mexican's wheat and hides.

"Señor Turley," a voice called in Spanish, "Why have you closed your gate today?" The speaker was Pablo Montoya, wearing a gaudied-up, green militia coat. Despite his elaborately cocked hat he shielded his eyes with his hand from the westering sun.

Although neither Turley nor John Albert was fluent in Spanish, both could make do.

"You killed Governor Bent, Señor," Turley said in Spanish.

"Who told you that?" Montoya exclaimed. Turley didn't respond. Montoya said, "Señor Bent was not our governor!" Again Turley did not respond. "He was an American governor!" At the continued silence of the Americans, Montoya conferred with the others for a few moments, then said, "But you are a citizen of Mexico, señor. You will come to no harm."

"But Señor Bent was a citizen of Mexico, and a man of the Faith, too."

"Perhaps he was a man of the Faith, señor, but a true citizen of Mexico cannot be a citizen of the American government at the same time."

"Señor," Pablo Chavez interjected, "Why does Señor Albert threaten us with his gun? You know me well. You're a good man, a man of the Faith, a citizen of Mexico. We have no quarrel with you. But you must give us your guns."

"And what about me?" John Albert called out. "I've lived here for years. I'm a man of the Faith. I married one of your women. I've got children. What about me?" In his mind's eye he saw his wife's face wasted by lung disease and his son's teary, hurt expression that morning. Yes, he thought, and what about them?

Montoya ignored John Albert. "Señor Turley, you can see we have many men. It's growing late and we want to go home. We ask you to open your gate and give us your guns in the name of the government."

"What government?"

"The only government, señor, the government of Mexico, as you can see." He gestured to the flag. He ran his hand down the

44

front of his militia coat as if smoothing it. "You know our laws say that foreigners cannot have guns, señor, and some of your men are foreigners." John Albert snorted at the preposterous notion of men in the West giving up their arms. The law concerning firearms was one of the former Mexican governor's transparent efforts to extract still more bribe money from well-armed American traders.

"What about my men?" Turley said.

"They will come to no harm if they give us their guns."

"And what is my guarantee?"

Voices rose in disagreement during a long huddle around Montoya. John Albert spied figures beginning to filter among the scrubby piñon on the walls of the arroyo. The mob was spreading out to surround Turley's compound. When Montoya finally addressed the Americans again his words were a command: "Señor, open your gate and give us your guns. It is growing late and we will not bandy words."

"But why?" Turley cried. "What have we done? Señor Chavez, I have always been a friend! Why?"

"You must give us your guns for your own protection, señor. If you do not, then we must take them. That is the law."

"But the Army's coming up from Santa Fe! You can't fight the army, Señor Chavez!"

"Give up your guns, señor," Montoya said. "We are growing impatient."

"Damn!" John exclaimed under his breath. "This don't look good, Simeon. We give them our guns and we're cooked, all of us, understand? You understand? They'll take us prisoner and maybe shoot us all. It's an old trick."

Turley nodded but looked disoriented. His eyes roamed wildly. Finally he said, "But maybe I can still talk with them, John. At least I've got to try. Once we start shooting there's no turning back."

John Albert regarded the cherubic face. He knew Turley was right - that talk, even trading insults - was better than shooting and bloodshed. He raised his shoulders and let them drop. "Go ahead then," he said. "I'll cover you."

Turley turned to the delegation. "Señors, I wish to talk with

Señor Chavez...just the two of us...without guns. Señor Chavez, we will talk without guns, yes?"

"That is very good, Señor Turley," Chavez said. "Yes, we will talk without guns." Chavez handed over his musket and unbuckled his hanger.

"I am going to open the little door in the gate, Señor Chavez." Turley climbed awkwardly down the ladder and limped over to a portal in one of the big double-doors of the wagon gate. As he made ready to unbar the door he looked up at John. When the former mountain man nodded that all was clear Turley slid the bar. Chavez stepped into the compound. The two looked into each other's eyes as they shook hands with nervous smiles, then Simeon Turley turned to bar the little door again.

"He said that he was a man of honor and that he doesn't want bloodshed," Turley said after he had climbed up to rejoin John Albert. "He said that killing Bent was a mistake."

"Talk! Them buzzards want our hair too! Listen, Simeon, we can't trust 'em! They do this all the time. They did it to the Santa Fe Pioneers. They get you to give up your guns and then you're cooked! We gotta to buy time. The longer we stall the quicker it'll get dark and then some of 'em might get tired and go home."

Turley nodded absently, still picturing the face of Chavez. He'd always liked Chavez, a man with a kindly, earnest face. When Chavez had entreated Turley to comply with Montoya's demands the miller had felt a strong tug of desire to be done with this mad confrontation, to open his gate and to lay down his arms and say, "There, you have your wish. Now can we get on with our lives again?"

"Listen!" John Albert continued, alarmed at Turley's distant expression. "You don't believe him, do you? You don't believe they'll let us go, do you? Remember the Santa Fe Pioneers, how they gave up their arms and ended up in prison down in Mexico? It's an old trick! We can't give up our guns!"

But Turley wanted to say he believed Chavez. After all, what had he ever done to offend Chavez, or any of them? He'd avoided their politics and tried to be a good neighbor. He'd always tried to be fair in his dealings. He couldn't accept their religion, of course, but if he couldn't bring himself to be a man of the Faith he'd always been generous to the Church. Wasn't that enough? What more did they want? Turley raised his eyes as if to protest John Albert's words, but when he saw the hard look on the man's face he felt his strength suddenly leave him. No, of course it was foolish. They would be fools to let an armed mob into the compound. Not if they'd already killed Bent and who knows how many others in Taos.

Turley's entire being seemed to shrink. He sighed heavily. "I asked about our families. I said, 'If we don't give up our guns, what about our families?'" Turley forced a small smile. "Chavez said they would not be harmed. My family will have safe conduct."

"Good!" John said. "That I'll believe! Listen, tell him you need to talk to the men. Tell him we need time to talk."

Turley seemed flustered when he turned to address the delegation waiting on the cart track. "Señor Chavez, I must talk with my men."

Chavez conferred with Pablo Montoya, then made a show of taking out a pocket watch. "All right, Señor Turley, we will give you fifteen minutes. But no more." Turley consulted his own timepiece, slim and gold, looped across his paunch with a gold chain. A little after three o'clock. Two hours until dusk.

When they reached the ground Turley seemed more collected. "Go ahead, John, I need to get my family out." As he turned at the door he was surprised to find John Albert still rooted by the ladder and staring at him. After a moment of confusion a cloud of hurt crossed Turley's face. "Oh, no! No! Listen, John, I wouldn't let them in. I just want a few minutes with Rosita - you know, to tell her that everything will be all right. Listen, I'll send them up to your place. That way they can all be together. That'll be best, don't you think?"

John Albert dropped his eyes as he felt a wave of anger rise in his chest at Turley's simplistic notions. Who'd be all right? Every one of the men in the mill might be dead before morning! He wanted to grab Turley and shake him by the shoulders until the cherubic miller saw the truth of their situation - that this was life and death!

Instead, he suddenly wheeled and headed for the millhouse. "Do what you want," he barked over his shoulder. "I got work to do."

In the millhouse, John Albert found the men nervous and

fluttery. A couple of them were white-faced with fright. Billy paced back and forth giggling and joking and posturing with his rifle. Upstairs the French-Canadians were dragging and rolling things around, punctuating their efforts with *Merde!* and *Sacre!* and *Goddamn!* Several muskets and shotguns leaned on the stairs that led to the loft. John Albert saw a cooking pot and buckets for water and the rolled-up cloth that held Billy's gun-repair tools. The Englishman hunkered beneath the stairway fondling the dogs.

"What do they want?" someone asked.

"Our hair!"

"God damn it to Hell!" the narrow-faced Englishman cried, his voice shrill with fright.

"All of us?"

"I guess." John Albert stood near the door to keep an eye the house. If Turley tried to open the gate he'd shoot the son of a bitch! "They gave us fifteen minutes," he said.

"Owww!" Billy yelped, and began to mimic an Indian dance. "Whoo! whoo! whoo! whoo!"

"Cut that out, Billy!" John Albert snapped.

"What about Turley?" someone asked.

John Albert turned to see Turley's wife Rosita and their half dozen children and the servant-girl emerging from the house. Turley followed holding a carpetbag with one hand and a couple of weapons by their barrels with the other. Under an arm he also pinched his little medicine chest. Rosita and the children looked numb with fright. Their faces were frozen masks. They crowded around Rosita like baby chicks. As Turley turned after locking the door to his house one of the children began to wail. Immediately the others and Rosita began wailing too, and Turley dropped his burdens, fell to his knees, and gathered them close. Shoulders heaving with sobs, he buried his face in their midst.

John Albert raced across the yard and pulled Turley to his feet and dragged him roughly by an arm towards the gate, Turley's wife and children pulling awkwardly against him on the miller's other arm. "No, no, señor!" Rosita screamed in Spanish. "Don't take him! In God's name don't take him from us! Pray God, no!" John Albert felt such sudden rage at them all that his vision blurred.

After John Albert wrestled Rosita and the others safely out the little door in the gate he had to half drag Turley to the millhouse as Billy and the others watched open-mouthed from the doorway. Upstairs the Frenchmen were still dragging sacks of grain across the floor and tossing them with shuddering thumps. For a long moment Turley seemed oblivious. He stood with his hands covering his face, his shoulders shaking with silent sobs.

"Simeon!" John Albert cried angrily. "Simeon! Get ahold of yourself!"

At last Turley raised his face, his eyes red and swollen, but only to push up his glasses to massage his eyes with forefinger and thumb as if he had all the time in the world. "Simeon!" John Albert cried again. "God damn it!"

Turley looked up then, his reddened eyes mournful. His shoulders rose and fell with a huge sigh. "Well, ah, men," he began at last, "John, here, thinks...well, listen, it looks like we have to fight. John, I'd...I'd be grateful if you'd be our captain - our war captain - that is, if...."

John Albert surveyed the circle of workmen for objections, knowing there would be none. Better him than Turley! They watched his face expectantly. Billy wore a broad grin. A couple of the men nodded. John Albert suddenly dropped his eyes. Why should he take responsibility for them all? What did he owe the damned Englishman or the miller? What did he owe any of them? He didn't even like the carping Brit or the mouthy distiller. Maybe he should find a way to sneak out after dark, maybe just him and the French-Canadians and Billy. He stood pondering the possibilities for so long that Billy said, "Well?"

John Albert straightened, his insight suddenly clear. Of course they had to stick together, all of them, the strong and the weak, the oak and the willow. They had no choice. They were all in it together and had to hold the enemy at bay until the Army from Santa Fe came to their rescue.

He began making his case to buck up the men. They had plenty of powder and lead, he said, and a good place to defend against the Indians' arrows and the Mexicans' few muskets and rusty, old *escopetas*. The Pueblos might not have the stomach for a long fight anyway, because if Indians can't win quickly they think their medicine isn't right and will quit fighting. But

49

the men all had to stick together and make every shot count. To start off only the best marksmen would shoot - Billy, the Frenchmen, himself. The rest would load and keep an eye out and shoot if the going got hot. Billy rose on the balls of his feet and winked at the others, his chest swollen with excitement.

"Thanks, John," Turley said then, relief in his voice, "I'll, ah, be a loader too." He lifted the butt of his shotgun an inch from the floor. "I'm not much of a shot, even with this old *escopeta*." There were nervous chuckles at the honesty of the wealthy proprietor's admission.

"Señor Turley!" The name echoed in the sudden stillness. The Frenchmen in the loft arrested their work.

Except for the small gurgle of water through the millrace and the twittering of swallows among the portico beams the scene was quiet as death. They stood expectant, scarcely breathing.

"Señor Turley, your time is up!"

"One moment, señor," Turley shouted from the door.

"Well, boys, this is it," John Albert said. He started for the ladder-like stairs.

"Wait, John!" Turley stood in the doorway, hesitant. "I want to try one more time." One foot already on the bottom step, John paused and shrugged.

Turley stepped out and cupped his hands around his mouth. "Señor Chavez, this is Simeon Turley." A quick double echo sent his voice back from the arroyo walls - "urley, urley!"

"I've put my family under your protection. They have done you no harm. Neither have we. We want to live in peace."

"Eace, eace," the echo said. Except for the echoes, there was silence. "Señor Chavez, I cannot open my gate when you threaten us. You men are not the government. We ask you to leave us in peace."

Again the echoes, "eace, eace." Again the silence. Turley cupped his hands again. "Señor Chavez, we do not want to fight you."

Echoes. A silence that seemed to go on forever as Turley stood with a cupped ear.

50

"Open your gate and give us your guns, Señor Turley!" The distant voice was Montoya's.

Turley's shoulders slumped. He dragged back to the door with leaden steps. Inside he shook his head to confirm what the men already knew. He slowly shut the heavy door as he had done a thousand times before. It closed with a hollow, tomb-like sound he'd never noticed. He sighed again as he swung a heavy bar in place and stood with his head bowed low.

"Well, boys," John Albert said, seeking to draw attention from the mournful, defeated miller, "let's get going!" and he turned to lead his men to their positions in the loft.

After a minute or two John Albert called down, "I guess that's it, Simeon. Looks like they're done talking."

"Are they going home?" Turley asked. He climbed to the loft with quickened steps. John Albert knelt beside one of the small windows that flanked the big hoisting door. Turley knelt beside him in time to see Chavez and the others disappear behind the black knob.

"They're all over now," John said. "Every side."

Turley said nothing. He could make out blurry figures moving on the knob. Suddenly there was a loud *crack!* then *crack! crack!* Something struck the mica panes of the big window at the other end of the loft. John scurried over to see, knowing the missiles came from a jut of rock behind Turley's compound. Just as he reached a loophole, one of the panes was shattered by an arrow. He cowered from the flying shards while a hideous clamor built all around the compound. He hurried back to Turley.

"Damn!" he said. "They're on that outcrop back there. They'll shoot right down through the window." He pushed his musket out his own window. At the top of the black knob a gaudily attired Indian pranced and taunted. John cocked deliberately and sighted for several seconds. A belch of smoke left his muzzle, and a half second later his ball ricocheted off rock to smash into the leg of the Indian, who grabbed his knee and fell backwards to the ground and rolled with pain. John looked at Turley and made a face. Then another belch of smoke from Billy's long Kentucky rifle caught another figure on the black knob in the shoulder and spun him around in an awkward stagger.

All hell broke loose. Musketfire shattered the panes of the

big window and pattered like large hail against the hoisting door. A ball came through John Albert's window and struck a millstone. SPANG! it sang as it took new flight. Surprised at the onslaught, the men in the mill cringed, and John Albert suddenly realized the mob was much better armed than he thought, that their attackers must have looted every musket in Taos.

Turley looked at his war captain. The one-time mountain man huddled next to the window with his back to the wall. He wore an odd, puzzled expression, like a farmer who'd just been kicked by his favorite milk cow.

The Loft

There were nine men in the loft, and one was shot during that first afternoon of battle. Hatfield was wounded in the groin when his friend Slim accidently knocked over a loaded musket leaning against a roofpost. Time seemed to drag as Slim turned with mouth agape to witness the consequences of his wayward step. The weapon slowly pirouetted on its heel in the murky light, the dull gleam of the barrel described a lazy arc, then bounced off the housing of the millstones and discharged a sudden blast of light and smoke. Hatfield staggered back as if pushed by an invisible bully and fell sprawling onto a disordered pile of scrap lumber, then let out a horrible scream. As the others turned to peer through the gloom, now heavy with gunsmoke, Hatfield clutched his groin and screamed again and again. The ball had torn through his scrotum and lodged deep in the flesh of his right buttock.

Perhaps it surprised no one except Hatfield that Slim's clumsiness caused the first hurt. Lanky and slow-footed, Slim's intelligence sputtered like a starved candle. Having come west as drovers with Kearny's Army of the West, both he and Hatfield later drifted up from Santa Fe. Although they possessed few skills and less ambition, Turley had hired the two of them for grunt work a month earlier. The two Missouri men had quickly decided grunt work and New Mexico were not for them. They'd planned to head home to Missouri with the first wagon trains of spring.

Their decision to be quit of Turley's mill was all right with John Albert, who found coping with their laziness a challenge equal to coping with their speech - mindless utterances of half-swallowed, ill-formed, backwoods dialect that barely escaped monstrous cuds of chewing tobacco. John Albert shook his head slowly from side to side in half-amused wonder when he referred to the two Missouri men as "a matched team."

"Argh!" Hatfield cried. "Argh!" Hands at his bloody crotch, he writhed on the floor. Slim stood frozen in place beside the roofpost, his mouth agape.

Until that fateful moment the men in the mill had fared well. Enemy musketballs pecked harmlessly at the thick adobe walls without harm. Some had ripped jagged splinters from the wooden shutters and lattices, but the men behind them remained unharmed. Arrows also struck the walls, but none that flitted through the gaps in the big window in the rear of the loft had buried themselves in flesh. The men in the mill had meanwhile kept up a measured response and seen several wounded foes borne up the side of the arroyo by comrades.

But as daylight faded Turley and his men knew reinforcements for the enemy were coming from Taos and the nearby pueblos and ranchos to join the fray. They were gathering like vultures. Furtive figures scampering among the rocks and scrubby trees seemed to number in the hundreds. The incessant, yipping, nerve-wracking war cries of the Indians echoed in the winter air like frenzied dogs on the hunt.

The fateful, unspoken question that hung like the haze of gunsmoke in the loft was, of course, how long could they hold out? There was plenty to eat in the cellars. They had water in the millrace. But most already realized that an infinite enemy could not be defeated with finite powder and ball, no matter how much food or how good the fortress. While their supply of powder and percussion caps seemed plentiful at present, at some point one of them would fire the last shot. Inevitably the horde outside Turley's walls would overrun the mill.

It was growing dark by the time they finished bandaging Hatfield. Blood seeped steadily through his dressings as four of them each took an arm or leg and carried him down the stairs to the adjoining distillery. Turley led the way with a coal oil lantern. In the distillery they laid the wounded man in a storage bin of shucked corn. "It's the softest bed we got," Turley said as he knelt at Hatfield's side and smoothed the wounded man's shaggy hair. On the other side Slim knelt in the corn to put a cup of whiskey that trembled in his hand to Hatfield's lips, whose own hands never left his groin. After the others drifted away, their voices low, the two Missouri men talked of Slim's sorrow and Hatfield's pain and of those they'd left behind in their Clay County homes.

Into his second cup of whiskey, Hatfield began to ramble, his words indistinct except to Slim. "Know them Mormons, Slim, them Mormons that was just here? Too bad they ain't here now, eh? They'd be fightin' with us against these damned Mexicans. Think 'a that, Slim, them Mormons 'n us, fightin' on the same side!"

In late afternoon the wind had shifted to the south and the sky thickened with low, hazy clouds that promised snow. Now as night fell, darkness brought the suspense of the unseen, and the men in the mill saw fires flare up just out of musket range and the reflections of closer fires hidden by rocks and declivities. From time to time they fired at suspicious sounds or at the suggestion of movement or at the occasional flash of a musket, but their shooting was a waste of ammunition. They knew daylight would find the enemy in Turley's compound where they'd to assault the mill house from the cover of the other buildings.

With darkness John Albert put the men to work blocking the gaping window at the rear of the loft. Using whatever came to hand - empty whiskey kegs, scrap lumber, and sacks of grain - they built a precarious barricade. In the distillery Turley sat on a wobbly milking stool beside an open firepit and cut gun patches while waiting for lead to melt for making musketballs. On the other side of the fire pit the narrow-faced Englishman fried dozens of plump sausages in a massive iron frying pan and then stirred a thick gravy of sausage drippings and unbolted flour. One by one the men slipped down from the loft to consume the food. No one had much to say except Billy. The corn-haired youth left his shooting post reluctantly and arrived to announce that so far he'd hit seven, maybe eight men. He re-enacted the contortions of each victim from the impact of his shots.

The other men ate silently, their faces introspective as they chewed and swallowed and drank water spiked with whiskey. They watched Turley pour lead into the molds by the yellow light of the fire and then knock the shiny new balls free. They half-listened to Hatfield groaning and swearing and lamenting his wound, his speech now slurred by whiskey, his voice loud and complaining. "Gonna die, Slim, gonna die in Turley's mill! Ain't that a mystery, Slim, dyin' in Turley's mill?"

Deep into the night, when all fighting had ceased and even Hatfield fell asleep, Turley's cats emerged from their hiding places to explore old haunts. Billy heard them licking the blood where Hatfield had gone sprawling in the lumber pile. Outside the only sounds came from the plaintive mooing of the unmilked cow and her hungry calf, the constant, impatient rush of the mountain-fed Hondo Creek, and the occasional nervous growling of the dogs. With his lantern closed to a slit, as if afraid the enemy without might discover him moving about, Turley crept through the labyrinthine cellars of the distillery to put his ear to the walls and listen for sounds of the enemy. Would they burrow through the frosty ground to surprise the men in the mill?

The narrow-faced Englishman could not shake a dream that awakened him in the darkness of the loft after just an hour of fitful sleep. In his dream he'd searched for a hidden room in the distillery cellars, convinced Turley would keep knowledge of the secret room from the rest of them. In his dream the Englishman knew it was the room where Turley hid his money, a room he could picture as vividly as the kitchen of his family's cottage in Devon. He even saw Turley sitting at a small table in the room counting stacks of gold coins like some fairytale king. The Englishman knew the cellar room would be Turley's secret refuge when the enemy overran the mill.

He awakened from his dream just as he discovered the hidden floor-ring of a trapdoor in the dirt floor of the cellar, a trapdoor he knew led to Turley's secret room. Lying befuddled by his dream images for several moments, the Englishman got to his feet in a hurry when he felt his bowels cramping, then had to steady himself against a roofpost as a wave of dizziness rocked him in the darkness. His bowels fluttered as he carefully made his way down from the loft to light a stub of candle from the coals of the firepit and relieve himself of a foul discharge in the shitpot that sat in a corner. Feeling somewhat better, he gave a quick glance around, then crept through an open trapdoor and down a short, steep ladder into the distillery cellars. There several dank, stoop-low cubicles held whiskey and a few bins of cold-room vegetables. By the uncertain light of the candle he quietly explored the dirt floors of the cubicles with his foot. He tipped a few suspicious objects aside to peer beneath in search of the floor-ring to the hidden room. In his dream the rooms in the cellar had been large, their contents extensive, and he'd searched for a long time before finding the hidden trapdoor. Now after just a minute or two of fruitless effort he realized he was foolish in thinking Turley could have a hiding place in such small confines. He wiped a glaze of cold sweat from his forehead and was climbing the ladder again when he saw the light of an approaching lantern. It was Turley.

"I thought I heard something down there," the Englishman said quickly, as if he had to explain himself.

"Me too, but I guess it was just you." Their eyes met as each watied for the other to speak. Turley's eyes were obscured by the gleam of lanternlight on his glasses. "Hear anything?" Turley asked at last. "Anything like digging?"

The Englishman shrugged. "No, nothing."

"I thought maybe I heard something earlier, but now I guess

not. Just nerves, I guess." The Englishman nodded as he blew out his candle and emerged from the cellar to begin making coffee in a big metal pot.

Perhaps it was the smell of the Englishman's cooking that stirred the men in the loft long before a new day slowly revealed the dark outlines of Turley's buildings. A fine, rain-like snow sifted down from ominous skies. In the uncertain light the men scanned their fields of fire for signs of the enemy. The gate to Turley's compound gaped wide. Hearing sounds of movement in the loft, the Englishman brought up the steaming coffee pot and a couple of mugs, then returned with a half dozen small loaves of Turley's bread and the frying pan heaped with thick slabs of fried ham. Slim came up to report that Hatfield was sleeping, then hunkered down to help himself to a generous breakfast.

The warm, savory food seemed to cheer the men up, and they began speculating when the Army might arrive. After considerable discussion they concluded that if Town had reached Santa Fe late the day before, the Army might already be on the way. Hell, they might even get to Taos by the next day. In any event, as soon as the rebels got word the Army was coming they'd either quit and go home or break off the fight. If they broke off the fight then the men in the mill could all make it to the safety of the Arkansas.

Billy was looking out the window, not joining the talk, when a single shot silenced the cow in the middle of yet another plaintive moo. A following shot silenced the calf. The men in the loft looked at each other, their faces indistinct in the somber winter light.

"Those shots came from the house," Billy announced.

"Well, they're probably all over the place then," John Albert said.

Turley shook his head. "Poor Rosie! Why did they do that? It's not her fault." He'd brought the little brown-eyed Jersey cow all the way from Missouri to provide his children with the breed's rich, creamy milk.

"Yeah, we should have put the calf in with her," John Albert said.

"I should have thought of that," Turley said. "I should have sent the horses out too, and the pigs and sheep. It's my fault."

"Well, we didn't know it would come to this," John Albert said, strangely moved by Turley's obvious regret. Sometimes the miller's soft side surprised him, like the time Turley had plowed on foot to John Albert's house through a foot of fresh fallen snow on his bum knee to bring a basket of fresh-baked bread, butter, and apricot jam after he heard John's little boy had fallen ill.

"You're not to blame, Simeon. Besides, in all this mess, what difference does a couple more dead animals make?"

"Well, they didn't do anything," Turley responded, and said again that it was his fault.

By eight o'clock desultory firing was joined through the sifting snow. As the snow slackened and skies brightened the shooting picked up. John Albert had just loosed a shot at a musket poking through a window in Turley's house when Billy spotted Charley Autobees' mule in a procession of several animals disappearing behind the knob of black rock. "Hey, ain't that Charley's mule, with the patch on its hip? Some Indian's got him!"

John Albert waved gunsmoke away to peer out his window. Turley crouched beside him in time to see the last of the blurry figures slip out of sight behind the knob. "Them damned Indians," John Albert said. "They got Charley!"

Shocked voices repeated the news, "They got Charley! They got Charley!"

"There was three of 'em!" Billy said. "One was holding on behind like he was hurt!"

"Charley must have put up a fight!"

"Damn right he did! Them bastards!"

"They'll come out from behind that knob," Billy cried. "I can get 'em!"

"Yeah, get 'em!"

"Yeah, can you get 'em, Billy, can you get 'em from here?"

"Get 'em! Hell, I can take their peckers off if they stop to piss!" Billy knelt to rest his weapon on the sill as John Albert reached for a fresh musket. In a couple of minutes Charley's mule appeared from behind the knob. The rider wore a red headdress. The pony behind carried two figures.

"I'll get the one on Charley's mule," John Albert said.

"You got 'im," Billy said. Both barrels moved to track the riders for a moment, then Billy fired and a fraction of a second later John Albert. They saw Billy's target throw up his arms and tumble off, taking the rider behind down too. The figure on Charley's mule turned to see what happened, then leapt to the ground and ran to kneel over the fallen riders.

"Damn!" John Albert said, peering through the smoke. "I needed my own gun!"

Billy hurried to reload his long-barreled rifle while he kept one eye on the Indian with the red headdress. The Indian dragged the fallen riders towards the cover of the knob. By the time Billy was ready to fire again his opportunity had disappeared. He swore quietly, then took a careful bead on Charley's mule. It stood with its head drooping. When Billy's ball crashed into its skull the mule collapsed as if a giant hand had swept its legs from under it. "Well, at least we got one of them damned Charley-killers," he announced. "And they ain't going to be riding Charley's mule!" John Albert looked at Billy with a strange expression.

One of the French-Canadians took a ball in the temple about noon. Louis Tolque was probably dead before he slumped to the floor from where he knelt by a loophole. The lethal wound was a half-inch hole in his right temple and a gaping mess of brains and blood and shattered bone above his left ear. He'd turned for a moment to watch Turley stamping out a fire with his good leg and the ball chanced to find its way to his head.

By then the men in the loft had smothered two or three fires, for the enemy was shooting fire-arrows that at first buried themselves in the grain sacks of the barricade built up before the window. Then, as fire consumed the rough sacking, the grain ran out and the barricade began to sag and arrows arced through the gaps to start fires that had to be beaten out. Acrid smoke built into a thick black cloud among the roof-beams. Other fire-arrows targeted the big loading door at the other end of the loft and the doors on the ground level, even the wood of the waterworks. Although the fires posed little immediate threat, the smoke made for difficult breathing, and the men's eyes began to water.

59

William LeBlanc dragged his compatriot to a corner and cradled the dead man's shattered head in his lap. Unashamed of his tears, Turley knelt at Louis Tolque's feet and put out a hand to grasp the moccasined foot of his murdered workman, a man who'd done his smithy work for almost five years. Like many men of the west the former fur trapper had long preferred Indian footgear to shoes. "It's my fault," Turley said. "It's all my fault. I'm sorry, boys, I'm sorry."

But there was scant time for grief or remorse. Outside the sounds of tumult grew. After a few minutes LeBlanc rested his friend's head on a grain sack and joined the dead man's hands on his breast. He crossed himself and mouthed a brief prayer for his friend of more than twenty years. Coming west as young men to seek adventure and fortune in the fur business, he and Tolque had found adventure aplenty. But while fortune eluded them, they were now married and settled down and raising families, and their lives revolved around children and crops and baptisms and birthdays and the Holy Days of the Church. And for the first time since their own childhoods they were genuinely happy men.

LeBlanc returned to a loophole to pick up his musket. "*Sauvages!*" he said and knelt to find a target. Silently he vowed to avenge his friend's death tenfold.

"Go get Slim," John Albert said. "We need to get these fires out. Brushie, you start shooting too."

Brushie was the rosy-cheeked distiller, a St. Louis town-boy who'd come west in response to Turley's newspaper advertisement for "a sober young man." It was Billy who first remarked that the distiller's unkempt brown hair looked like a brushpile. Although the newcomer's name was Turbush, Billy began calling him Brushie and the name stuck.

The distiller had been making himself useful by cutting patches, refilling powderhorns, reloading muskets, and helping to put out fires, but he wasn't much interested in shooting. The shooting and horseracing and wrestling and other manly amusements so common in the West he thought rather silly. Now, a musket in his hands and fading hopes for rescue, he poked his heavy weapon through a loophole and fired in the general direction of the enemy. "Goddamn Turley!" he muttered. "Goddamn Turley!"

"Hey!" Billy cried. "Between the stables and the wagon shed! There's one shooting around that corner."

"Why's he shooting from over there? That's a dead corner!"

"Hell, I don't know! They must be all over now. Bastard!" Billy sighted his rifle on the corner by the stables. "Come on out, you damned devil!" he coaxed. "Stick your ugly head out again! Come on...come on." He waited for a full minute, then another, then his rifle popped. "Yowie! Got him! See that, Grampa, I got him!" The Indian sprawled on the ground with a ball in the shoulder he'd exposed to fire his weapon. As the enemy lay bleeding, invisible hands pulled him to safety. "Damn, there's more! I'll pop another one, I know I will, just watch."

John Albert watched the corner. Sure enough, when another of the enemy exposed his head and shoulder to shoot, he went sprawling too.

"They'll want outta there, Billy. They can't stay in that damned corner. Keep an eye out! Hey, LeBlanc, come over here! We're gonna have us a turkey shoot."

In the next few minutes Billy and John Albert and LeBlanc shot five more Indians caught in a trap of their own making. The first to sprint for the safety of the gate fell to Billy's marksmanship. When another dashed out to drag him back, he too fell, LeBlanc's victim. The third was John Albert's target, shot in the leg. Then a fourth and a fifth, gunned down by Billy and LeBlanc. Five Indians writhed in the snow.

The men in the mill went wild with glee. Billy whooped like an Indian.

"Seven down in seven minutes!" Turley cried, his face joyful. Bring 'em on!

The Distillery

And on they came. Enraged by the fate of their comrades, the enemy unleashed a furious, shrill onslaught. Sheer numbers overwhelmed the response of Turley's men as scampering figures poured through the open gate, climbed the perimeter walls, and ducked and dodged to find cover in stables and pens and outbuildings. The enemy set fire to every combustible at hand - the thatch of the stable roof, the small stableyard haystack, LeBlanc's carpentry shop, even the wood of the livestock pens. Smoke roiled from a dozen fires. They heard the hideous squealing of Turley's hogs and the frantic bleating of sheep. The men in the mill had wreaked a maelstrom of revenge.

"Shoot! Shoot!" John Albert cried as the confusion mounted. Those who'd loaded and fetched now grabbed any weapon at hand. They had to keep their enemies at a distance.

But their targets were ghosts. They emerged from the thickening pall of smoke to hurl a firebrand or to loose an arrow, then vanished before the men in the loft could bring a gun to bear. Turley's men fired too late at shadows in the smoke. They wasted shots.

As the pall grew heavier the enemy sneaked under the portico of the mill to smash through a shuttered window and throw burning brands inside. Hurrying down to investigate, Turley loosed a blast from his shotgun through the gaping window, but when he stepped aside to reload his weapon his foes threw in straw from the stables to feed the flames. Frantic, Turley stamped at the fires, but spears thrust through the window drove him back and he stumbled in retreat to the stairs, where acrid clouds of heavy black smoke billowed to the loft from the fires on the ground floor.

Then, miraculously, the battle slackened. Perhaps the enemy stood in awe, for the outbuildings burned unchecked and Turley's mill house stood mortally wounded. The main floor burned vigorously. Black smoke poured from windows and loopholes, from the roof, from the millworks, from every crack and crevasse. If the men inside did not suffocate they would be roasted alive. Once thought impregnable, the mill had to be abandoned.

The seven remaining fighters used the lull to retreat to the distillery. Gasping, coughing, their eyes streaming, they manhandled Tolque's body down the stairs and carried him to their next stronghold. There they barricaded themselves behind the big double doors that separated the mill and distillery. Now the cellars remained their only retreat.

Their faces and clothes begrimed, they recovered their breathing in the semi-dark granary where Hatfield lay. The wounded man was weak and feverish. He mumbled nonsense, his hands twitching at John Albert's coat, which one of men had thrown over him for warmth. Slim knelt beside him in the corn, his expression dejected, his bloody, throbbing, rag-wrapped thumb a trophy from the frantic last half-hour of fighting. An enemy ball had ripped off the tip.

The Englishman sat collapsed in a corner making himself as small as possible. His watery eyes were vacant. He absently scratched behind the ears of the dogs, which had flopped down with their heads on his outstretched legs. The rest of the men stood in a rough circle looking at one another, waiting for someone to speak.

No one needed to say that keeping the enemy at bay was a foolish fantasy. The men in the mill were losing the battle. In addition to Slim's wound, an enemy ball had gouged Brushie's upper arm and an arrow creased Billy's cheek. Their supply of powder and balls and percussion caps had shrunk dramatically. When the last of the caps was shot off they would have three fewer guns, all old flintlocks, plus two shotguns and two antique pistols. Like a relentless wolfpack the incessant nipping of the enemy was wearing them down. Even Billy saw that under the continued onslaught the bloodied defenders would ultimately fall. Rescue by the Army seemed impossible now. Escape was the only hope. But how? And to where? And what about Hatfield? They couldn't just leave the wounded man to be scalped and butchered.

"God, I'm gonna bleed to death," Brushie complained. He'd cut off his shirtsleeve at the shoulder to fashion a blood-stained bandage around his arm. Every few seconds he raised an edge of the bandage to peer at the fresh oozing. He looked at Turley as if expecting him to sympathize, perhaps apologize, but Turley only blinked away the tears streaming from his myopic eyes.

John Albert finally spoke. "Listen, it's gonna get dark. We got a chance if we can sneak out. With all this smoke and no moon we might be able to sneak out. Don't you think, Le-Blanc?" LeBlanc nodded.

63

"Not me," Turley said. "Not with my knee. And what about Hatfield? Maybe I should just give up. Maybe if I give myself up and let them take me they'll let the rest of you go."

"Yeah," Brushie said. "What about that? What about just him?"

John Albert snapped at Turley as if he were a naughty child. "Can't you get it through your head, Simeon? They want to kill us all!"

"Listen, Simeon" John Albert said more gently. "It's no good, this talk about giving up. There's been too much blood spilled. We've hit fifteen or twenty, maybe even more. We probably killed some."

"Hell, forty or fifty!" Billy cried.

John Albert glanced at him, then continuted, "They want our hair for sure now, and if anybody gives himself up he'll just make it easier for 'em to kill the rest of us. Running's the only chance we got. We run or we die. At least if we run we got a chance. Stay here and we're cooked."

Billy snorted and made a show of wiping his sweaty brow at John Albert's choice of words. The heat was building in the distillery from the burning mill.

"But run where?" Brushie asked.

"Hell, anywhere! Make for the Arkansas. Or hide in the hills and wait for...."

Slim screamed. The men whirled to see Slim slapping frantically at Hatfield, who'd grabbed Slim's wounded thumb and was struggling to sit upright. Slim bellowed as he tried to pry loose Hatfield's fingers, finally resorting to a fisted blow to Hatfield's head that caused him to release his grip. Slim rocked to and fro on his knees as he cradled his wounded hand between his knees, "Oooo! Jesus God! Oooo!"

Hatfield tried to raise himself again. "Listen," he implored. "You gotta know! You all gotta know!"

"It's all right, Bill, it's all right," Turley told him, crawling onto the corn to put a hand on Hatfield's shoulder. He pressed the wounded man back. "It's all right, Bill."

"No!" Hatfield cried. He struggled against Turley. "You gotta know. It's my fault. You won't get out and it's my fault. Me and Slim!"

"It's not your fault, Bill!"

"Yes, me and Slim's, Mister Turley. It's our fault!"

"No, Bill, it's not your fault!"

"Oh, Simeon, he's out of his head," John Albert barked. "We got no time for this."

"We can't hide from the Lord and we're gonna pay for our sins, me and Slim, all of us," Hatfield insisted.

"No, Bill, that's not so," Turley said. "We all got sins, me too. I'm the most to blame."

Hatfield shook his head as if trying to shake off Turley's words. He'd been speaking with his eyes closed, seeing with his mind's eye. Now they opened wide at Turley bending close. Hatfield's next words were so earnest and distinct that everyone heard. "It's our sins, Mister Turley, me and Slim's, for what we did at Haun's mill."

For a long moment Turley failed to respond. Then, disbelief in his voice, he said, "Did you say Haun's mill? Haun's mill, Bill? You were there? You and Slim?" Turley was aghast.

"No!" Slim cried. He scrambled from the corn bin and crouched with his wounded hand half raised as if to ward off a blow, his other hand a fist ready to strike. "Ain't so! Ain't so, Mister Turley, ain't so!" But Hatfield kept nodding, his eyes fixed somewhere on Turley's face.

"Haun's mill, Bill?" Turley said again, shock and disbelief in his voice. "You and Slim?" The miller's eyes blinked rapidly.

Hatfield closed his eyes slowly in acknowledgement and sighed deeply, as if relieved of a mental torment.

"Oh, no," Turley cried. His voice contained all the sorrow and disappointment in the world.

"Goddamnit! what's he talking about," Billy cried. John Albert stood stiff-necked and silent, scarcely containing his anger and impatience.

Turley sat back on his haunches, shaking his head, not wanting to believe. "You and Slim? Those terrible killings at Haun's mill?"

And Hatfield, his eyes tearful, croaked, "Me and Slim. And that's why we're gonna die, Mister Turley, why we're all gonna die in this mill."

"Listen, Goddamn it!" John Albert cried, his impatience bursting. "We got no time for this." The sounds of crackling and snapping of the flames in the mill were growing louder, the smoke in the murky granary growing denser.

"Well, all right then," Billy almost shouted, addressing John. "Tell us how we sneak out."

His question had swung the men's attention back to John Albert when a blood-curdling cry and the rapid tattoo of axe-blows on the double doors sent the men recoiling in fright. The enemy was inside the mill!

"Ready?"

John Albert's question was a whisper in the inky darkness by the slops door, a small portal at the back of the distillery. Outside they heard voices and the occasional sound of enemy movement in the frozen garden, a tangle of winter-killed weeds and garden foliage, canted bean-poles and broken-down trellises. At an earlier time the slops door was used to get rid of mash from the distillery, when the stone-fenced garden was a hog-pen. But after Turley converted the heavily manured hog-pen into a garden the little door was abandoned. It now stood almost invisible behind overgrown, winter-dead weeds and leafless creepers that climbed the rough adobe.

John Albert felt Billy's hand touch his shoulder and saw the vague form of Billy's face swim near. Billy whispered, "John."

"What?"

"You think we'll make it?"

For a long moment John didn't answer. How could he tell a boy of seventeen that he might be dead in a few minutes? "I don't know," he whispered. "But we gotta try." He sensed Billy's nod. Close by he heard Brushie make a sound. The young distiller was breathing hard, swallowing loudly. He was trying not to cry.

They were crouched near the floor where the air was a little better, waiting for rope signals that would tell them when Turley and LeBlanc and the Englishman were ready. Turley

66

and the others were in the cellars at the opposite end of the distillery quietly prying out foundation stones from the outer wall.

"John?" Billy said.

"What?"

"Slim and Hatfield - you think they'll make it?"

Again John did not answer immediately. After the enemy had attacked the big double doors of the distillery, flames must have driven them out, and with the reprieve the trapped men huddled near Hatfield and hastily considered and rejected plans. Retreat to the cellars? But then what? They'd be trapped there too. Work back through the burning mill and escape through the millworks? No, they'd be picked off one by one. Storm out with guns blazing?

The Englishman had roused himself from where he crouched with the dogs. "What about the dogs?" he cried. "We can't just leave these dogs." The men stared. Had the Englishman lost his senses? Then Slim announced that he could not leave Hatfield, that it was his fault Hatfield got shot and he'd been thinking that they could bury themselves in the corn and after the enemy was gone Slim would carry Hatfield to safety.

In the acrid gloom John and LeBlanc looked at each other as if Slim had gone mad. But they nodded their agreement with the foolish plan. At least it was a plan and answered for Hatfield, who seemed resigned to his fate as he lay quietly mumbling prayers.

The men finally decided on a coordinated breakout. From opposite ends of the distillery two escape parties would break for freedom at the same time. With the smoke and the darkness they might not be spotted at all, or might just slip through as shadowy figures unrecognizable in the uncertain light of the burning buildings.

They gave the two pistols to Hatfield and Slim and covered them with corn. They laid sacking over their faces like burial shrouds. The rest of the men double-charged their weapons with shot. It was every man for himself.

"John."

"What?"

"Where's your coat?"

John Albert felt his face drain of blood. He suddenly remembered it was his coat that covered Hatfield. "Hatfield," he said wearily. He wondered briefly if he could survive the winter cold without a coat, then decided the matter was hardly worth worrying about. Success seemed impossible. They'd hoped that the garden would be deserted, but with the enemy present he and Billy and Brushie would have to fight their way to safety.

John Albert took a big breath, let it out slowly, and pushed his hat down on his head as he tried to visualize his path. Outside the door he would cut to the right alongside the building, then get over the low stone wall that surrounded the garden. Then he'd sneak along the wall to where a thicket of willows grew alongside the creek. After hiding there he would try to work his way around the big rock outcrop and head north for Rio Colorado. Billy would charge straight ahead for the far wall and then run like hell down the trail to Dolores and hide in the belfrey of the church there. Brushie would bolt to the left, get across the creek, and make his way up the wall of the arroyo and hide in the church in Hondo. Three different routes, three different chances. They'd drawn straws for their routes.

"You want my coat? I got this heavy shirt."

"No, keep it. You'll need it."

"You can have it later," Billy whispered.

John Albert felt the rope almost jerk from his hand, slap the floor, then jerk again. "They're through the foundation," he announced. Two tugs on the rope that snaked between the escape parties meant Turley and LeBlanc and the Englishman had tunneled through the foundation stones to the outside. With a few more minutes to enlarge the opening, they would be ready to crawl out. John Albert wondered if LeBlanc would prevail in their plan to kill the dogs.

"I'm going with those other guys," Brushie suddenly announced.

"No!" John Albert croaked.

"You can't stop me. I'm going with them! They got a better chance!"

"We all got the same chance."

"No, they got a better place."

"Well, Goddamn it, go then!" Billy rasped. "Damned yellow-belly."

"I ain't no yellow-belly. They got a better place over there. Besides, maybe they just want Turley. He can go first."

They heard Brushie crawl back through the distillery to the cellar trapdoor. "Damned yellow-belly!" Billy rasped again.

The rope jerked and slapped the floor, then again, then a third time. "This is it!" John Albert said as he carefully began to lift the bolt-handle. The mechanism gave a small screech and refused to slide. The bolt was rusted fast. "Damn!" he said. He began to work the handle slowly up and down as he pulled with a steady pressure, worried someone in the garden would hear the squeaky, grating progress of rusted iron against rusted iron. The grating seemed to resonate on the door. Then a thought struck John Albert. With this delay Turley and the others might be a diversion that would better the odds for him and Billy. Maybe he and Billy should wait until they heard a commotion on the other side. He paused in his effort to free the bolt.

"Coming?" Billy asked.

"Yeah," John said, the darkness hiding his flush of shame. He resumed working the bolt and after a few more movements he felt the door release a little as the bolt finally cleared its capture. "Okay," he said, taking a big breath. "Got it! So...this is it." His heart pounded.

"John?"

"What?"

"Know what?"

"What?"

"I wish I'd learned how to read."

John felt a sudden lump in his throat. He tried to make his whisper reassuring, "Well, there'll be time for that...I'll teach you." Again he sensed Billy's nod. He felt Billy's fingers clasp his shoulder and release. "Listen, Billy," he said. He wanted to make things right with Billy. At least that much. But words refused to come, and after an awkward silence it was Billy who whispered, "It's okay, Grampa. Let's go!"

69

John nodded and unsheathed his long skinning knife and held it alongside the barrel of his musket. They cocked their weapons.

John burst open the door with his shoulder and broke to the right. A dozen steps away, six or seven men who stood watching the burning roof of the mill were startled by the sudden commotion. They began to raise their weapons. John Albert shot into their midst and from the corner of his eye saw a flash of light. He heard the blast from Billy's gun and saw two or three of the figures tumble backwards. A rattle of gunfire and he felt his hat fly from his head and something tug at his waist. Billy laughed as he charged straight into the knot of enemy. John heard Billy's rifle butt strike flesh and bone and sensed something and turned to see two shapes come flying over the low stone fence straight at him. He barely had time to raise his musket, knife protruding like a bayonet, before the first with a hideous, painted face was on him. They sprawled together in the garden waste, the Indian gut-wounded.

In a blur of time, perhaps just two or three seconds, frightened beyond words, enraged, frantic, John slashed madly at the wounded Indian's upraised arms and scuttled for the cover of the stone wall. As he slithered over the top he glimpsed the boyish figure of Billy locked in combat with a big Indian, the two of them fighting for control of Billy's rifle. Then a section of the mill house roof suddenly caved in with a crash, lighting the scene with a glare that froze the struggle of the figures in the garden and sent an awesome plume of flames and sparks into the night sky. John Albert scrambled along the perimeter of the wall to the scant cover of the willow thicket. There he hugged the firelight shadow of the stone wall. He heard Billy scream, "No! no! no! please, God, no!" and thought he heard the unforgettable tearing sound of the Indian taking Billy's scalp.

John Albert

John Albert made himself as small as possible while the enemy looted and destroyed. Terrified of being discovered, he tried to become one with the icy stones. After a while he began shivering so violently he was afraid he'd give himself away. In the tumult and confusion he thought he heard one of the men from the mill screaming. Then the commotion at last moved to the other end of Turley's compound. He waited a while more, then cautious as a mouse emerging from its hole, he slipped from his hiding place. Crawling on his stomach from shadow to shadow, freezing every few seconds to listen for sounds of pursuit, he made his way past the rocky outcrop and started up the steep slope of the arroyo towards Rio Colorado. After a time he looked back at the burning buildings and saw several obscure shapes of animals and humans lying in the yard. Firelight gleamed on minikin figures of the enemy prancing and whooping in jubilation.

The trail north would take him past Charley's place, but with Charley dead he knew the ranch probably wasn't safe. He hoped now to find help at the house of a French-Canadian in Rio Colorado named LaFôret, another retired fur trapper. For a half-hour or so John Albert slipped off the trail every few minutes to see if he was being followed. He sensed someone was just behind, trying to overtake him. At last, knowing he must try to reach the safety of Rio Colorado before daylight, he risked the trail and kept his feet moving.

From time to time he broke into tears, sometimes with relief that his life was being spared, sometimes with despair at the thought of his abandoned family, sometimes with grief for the deaths of the others. He kept hearing Billy's cry: "No! no! no! please, God, no!" Poor Billy.

He wept too for the impossible journey ahead. But he knew his fate was in his own hands if he just kept moving, if he could keep ahead of whatever danger might be pursuing him. So he jogged along the rough trail until he could jog no more, then walked until he could jog again, then jogged awhile longer, every nerve worn raw by the ordeal of the siege and his escape.

Sensing something ahead, he paused and spotted two obscure figures on the snow-clad trail. In a few moments he heard voices chatting in Spanish. He ducked off the trail and readied his musket. As the party approached his hiding place he

71

thought he recognized the voice of one, a prominent Mexican from Rio Colorado. They were talking about horses. There were two men. They'd drawn almost abreast when John Albert called out in Spanish, "Señor Piño, is that you?"

His voice startled them. Piño swung a weapon in John Albert's direction and cried, "Aiii! *Hola!* Who's there?"

"It's me, señor, John Albert, from Turley's mill. Tell me, señor, is everything quiet in Rio Colorado?"

"What?"

"Is everything quiet in Rio Colorado? Is it safe for me there?"

Without answer Piño conferred in undertones with his companion. Suddenly the two turned their backs to the trail and quickly disappeared into the trees opposite.

John Albert's heart sank. Word of the uprising must have spread as far as Rio Colorado. If he couldn't get help from LaFôret there would be no rest until he left that settlement far behind too.

Even more chary, he waited for a long while until he felt sure the Mexicans had moved on, then sneaked through the woods for some time before venturing onto the trail again.

He jogged and walked for the rest of the night, stopping only to catch his breath on the long, steep hills. The rising sun stained the eastern sky pale pink as he approached the outlying houses of Rio Colorado. He'd covered more than 20 miles of up and down mountain trail. His legs were rubbery. He shivered so badly in the pre-dawn cold that he decided to risk finding relief with LaFôret after all.

On the outskirts of the tiny settlement he heard the muffled crowing of a cock. Then a nearby dog set up a racket, quickly echoed by another, and then another, and then still others more distant until the scattered houses of Rio Colorado were enveloped in a cacophony of barking and howling. Suddenly fearful of being discovered before he reached the safety of LaFôret's home, John Albert cut away from the settlement and hurried toward the brooding mountains, avoiding the nearest house by a good mile. He splashed across the partially frozen Rio Colorado and continued north.

The sun came up, glowing on the mountaintops. He'd lived through the night! He was in the clear now, with nothing ahead of him but mile after mile of empty plain. Better yet, he could look back and see that no one followed. Although half frozen from crossing the river, his mocassins were still in good condition, and the climbing sun offered a little warmth on his face. His spirits improved as he fixed his eye on the pyramidal mass of Mount Blanca some 60 miles distant and decided he could travel a good while yet before stopping to rest.

All morning John Albert jogged and walked toward the impassive presence of Mount Blanca. He scooped snow to moisten his mouth. He felt no hunger. He was a machine. He pictured Turley's millwheel, around and around, ceaseless, untiring - chume, chume, chume - and found himself thinking of Turley and his "Hand of God."

"Look here," Turley like to say as he patted the cover of his *Miller's Guide*, his cherubic smile playful. "Like the Hand of God." He would hold up a hand, his sausage-fingers spread. "Fives, that's all you've got to know. Five-foot millstones at five revolutions a minute gives you five bushel an hour. The Hand of God." He said it often.

So unlike Brushie, who'd become fascinated by the milling side of Turley's enterprise and spent hours poring over the arcane information found in Turley's battered copy of *The Young Mill-wright and Miller's Guide*, 11th edition. He said he found the rules of mechanics and hydraulics and the pitch circles of the cogwheels and the tables of dry measure and the dozens of other complexities of the miller's art profoundly satisfying. He would memorize a column of figures for the pleasure of being able to recite the sequence, as if the words were an incantation for good things to come. At times Brushie hinted to Turley that he'd like to take over Turley's milling operation. But Turley wasn't interested. He had a comfortable life, and saw no reason to change it.

That was the thing about Turley, John thought. He kept things simple. Men like Brushie schemed and plotted and sometimes cheated to get ahead, but Turley just labored on to the hypnotic rhythms of his wheels - chume, chume, chume - grind, grind, grind - his wealth accumulating from a half dozen dull little enterprises like the trickle of flour from his millstones, slow and steady.

Well, that's the way, the miller liked to say: slow and steady wins the race. Yes, John thought, slow and steady.

The former mountain man gave himself small goals - to reach the top of the next swell, to gain the other side of the next

73

gully. He would tell himself he could stop jogging and walk for a while or stop to rest when he reached a certain point, then challenge himself not to stop when he achieved it.

From time to time he thought of his family. By now they would believe him dead, burned to ashes in the inferno of Turley's mill. Turley too, and LeBlanc. Their families would huddle together, crying and saying the rosary. He pictured his wife's face, wasted by her disease. She was barely fourteen years old when they were married, the daughter of a retired American trapper and his Mexican wife, a girl who possessed the rare beauty that sometimes comes from the joining of two bloods. But then the sickness came and dragged on and on and he'd come to resent her illness, her dependency, and there were times when he felt that he no longer loved her, that she had made his life too hard - too many children, the boring drudgery of farm work, her constant coughing, the endless prayers and popish incantations and rattle of beads. Then he would find himself feeling guilty over his resentment, over his smallness of spirit and stingy Christian charity, and he would kneel beside her and hold her hand, wanting to beg forgiveness.

But he could never get words of apology out. Something deep and resentful within always held them back.

He walked and jogged the morning away, then kept going until the light of the foreshortened winter day began to fail.

From early morning the foothills on his right had seemed to sink slowly into the ground as he headed north up a long alluvial flow. To his left the empty plain extended to the horizon, broken only by distant mesas and still more distant mountains. Many miles in that direction lay the Rio Grande.

He reached the landmark of Sangre de Cristo creek and began to retrace its meandering progress northward. As the sun sank below the horizon, its final rays caught the looming mass of Mount Blanca.

At last he reached the waterway's junction with the icebound verges of Indian Creek, a treeless and barren place of rest. The darkness was not yet complete. He stopped and sank to his knees. Since sun-up he had come fifty miles! Before him lay the challenge of the Sangre de Cristo pass, a mountain barrier to shelter and safety. He'd been resting for just a few minutes when he felt his first sudden pangs of hunger and tried to remember when he had last eaten. Yesterday? The day before? There was nothing here to offer sustenence. He had to keep going.

He struggled to pull himself to his feet using his musket as a support. Even after just a brief rest his tortured body had stiffened, and he yelped in pain with his first steps on feet grown as tender as new burns, "Ow! Ow! Ow!" He hobbled onward, his eyes teared with pain.

All day his strategy had been to keep going, steadily, doggedly. Now, out of danger from pursuit, his challenge was to survive the cold, his hunger, his diminished strength, and to reach life-saving shelter and food. He set off following the verges of the watercourse that would lead him to the top of the pass.

A sliver of moon and a million stars revealed his crooked progress in the deepening snow. He pushed up the creek, climbing an endless succession of little mountain meadows though snow that became knee-deep and sometimes waist-deep. Between these alpine meadows he followed a rock-tumbled, tree-fallen mountain path used by animals and men alike. At the edge of a meadow he caught sight of wolf eyes gleaming and saw three or four indistinct forms skulking in the trees. They followed for a long time as he struggled ever upward, his hunger now a constant gnawing.

He climbed the snow-bound Sangre de Cristo pass all night, sometimes having to stop every few feet, his breath rasping and his heart pounding, then forced himself to push on again. He pulled himself ever upward by branches and protruding roots and small tree trunks. His breath made ice of his stubble beard. Sweat froze inside his shirt. His feet and hands turned to wood. And still he climbed. To stop was to die. But a dozen times that night he did not care whether he lived or died. A dozen times, unable to take another step, he wanted to give up the struggle, to fall into the snow and await the bliss of death. But something kept him going, and sometime during the night, too stupefied to notice where their tracks left the trail to seek a more sheltered haven, he passed the overnight camp of two American trappers coming down from Fort Pueblo on their way to Taos with several packs of furs.

An hour or so before dawn John crested the wind-blown pass. He'd made it! Before him stretched the valley of the Arkansas, falling away mile after mile after mile. He stood for several minutes to catch his breath, savoring the sight, leaning back against a steady west wind that wanted to push him forward. Then he gave in and let the wind propel him towards the Arkansas. Before long, now on the leeward side of the pass, he was out of the snow.

A half dozen miles down the trail stood the long-abandoned ruins of an adobe structure that some said was once a small Mexican fort. John stumbled down the mountain pass until he reached the ruins, then took shelter under a nearby cedar. He built a fire with his flint and steel and sat soaking up the warmth of the flames. He rubbed feeling back into his feet and lower legs. He watched the rising sun break a low-lying bank of clouds and followed the swift progress of sunlight down the landscape before him. How beautiful! he thought. I'm alive!

His hunger was a dull ache. He broke off a sprig of the cedar for the taste of something.

He dozed, but it must have been for only a few minutes because the fire was still going when he jerked awake. He shook his head in wonder at his dream of a remarkably antlered deer standing by the trail. When the deer spotted him it had stood on its hind legs and John saw that the animal wore a military coat with shiny brass buttons.

He brushed snow over his fire and with great effort pulled himself to his feet once again. All downhill now. Safe from pursuit and a violent death, he had become a bringer of news, a messenger come to tell of the terror of the uprising.

Not a quarter-mile farther he spotted two deer grazing by the trail. They stood looking at him for a long moment, one of them big-antlered. The other bent again to browse. His heart pounding, John slowly cocked and raised his musket. He remembered his missed shots at Turley's mill and aimed a little over the back of the animal standing stock-still, still looking directly at him, the morning sunlight catching its antlers. His musket woofed, the deer jerked as if stung, took several wobbly steps, then fell heavily, its back broken. An inch or two higher and his ball would have missed.

The next few minutes saw John Albert as close to dying as he'd ever been. Gripped by a sudden spasm of fierce hunger, he rushed forward to slice open the still-twitching deer and snatch out its liver. He gulped the raw, hot flesh in wolfish frenzy, blood and juices streaming from his hands and beard. In moments he had devoured the entire liver.

The reaction was almost immediate - nausea, profuse

sweating, retching, diarrhea. He writhed and retched and shit and groaned and at last lay slumped over the deer's still-warm carcass, his stomach knotted, his bowels fluttering, a headache pounding, so weak he was unable to raise his head. He thought he might die draped like a rag over the dead deer.

But he slowly recovered, and after an hour or so he was able to sit up. He took his time skinning the deer and cut off a small piece from a haunch to put in his pocket. Then he cleaned himself as best he could of his disgusting shit smell. He arranged the deerskin over his shoulders, hair-side in, its protection welcome from the constant west wind.

He knew that some 25 miles distant stood a small trading post on Greenhorn Creek, its proprietor an American. John used his musket to push himself to his feet again and staggered on. His route lay along the fringes of the foothills, Greenhorn his destination.

Returning from a fruitless hunting trip to his home near Greenhorn, Blackhawk spotted a sight in the deep dusk so bizarre that he thought at first he'd come across the Devil. Barely visible in the brush, its form the hue of dead flesh, the monster breathed smoke and bore one huge protruding horn. Blackhawk watched transfixed, his imagination running wild. Then he realized the monster was human and its horn was the stock of a musket.

"Hey!" he called, but the figure gave no notice, and kept its staggering progress through the scrub. "Hey!" he called again. "Hey!"

The figure stopped, weaving and looking about, confused, not seeing the other man. "*Êtes-vous malaise?*" The man looked with an uncomprehending stare in Blackhawk's direction for what seemed an eternity before he half raised a hand in response, then fell flat on his face.

Humming a childhood ditty to himself, Blackhawk knelt to examine the prostrate figure. The man had wrapped his head and shoulders in the fur-side of a fresh deerskin. He looked half frozen, more dead than alive. Blackhawk rummaged in the man's pockets. Finding nothing of value, he sat him up and suddenly recognized the ravaged face of a man he'd trapped with years earlier, before Blackhawk abandoned his white man's name and white man's culture to assume the Indian half of his identity. Now the half-blood hauled John Albert to his feet and flung him like a sack of flour behind his saddle. "Come with Da Da," he said, holding John Albert in place as he turned his horse towards the Greenhorn trading post. For a few moments John Albert struggled to right himself, his protests an incoherent babble. Then he passed out.

The Greenhorn trading post was a small adobe affair. Faint light gleamed through tiny windows covered with scraped hide. When the dogs started barking and John Albert stirred to consciousness, he raised his head to see a half dozen squat Mexicans emerging from the doorway to peer through the darkness at the approaching horseman. At the sight of the serape-draped figures John's heart sank. What a fate, to run and run and run to save his life, only to die in what he assumed would be safe haven! Blackhawk released his hold on John Albert's shirt and the exhausted man fell awkwardly to the ground. "Please!" he begged from his knees, not recognizing Blackhawk. His rescuer towered above, silhouetted against the starry sky like a demi-god, the hawk-wings of his headpiece flaring behind. He looked down at John Albert.

"You safe," he said. "Da Da go now." He handed down John's musket and without further word turned his horse and rode off into the darkness.

John Albert hauled himself upright on his musket to face the staring Mexicans. The last thing he saw before his knees buckled and he keeled over were their shadowy, malevolent forms drawing closer.

When he came to again he found himself on his back near a fireplace under the cover of a blanket. A Mexican girl was bent over a pot in the fireplace of the sparsely stocked trade room, her clay-slathered face catching the firelight. "Señor Brown?" he croaked.

The girl turned to look at him, smiled, and began to dish *posole* from the pot. She swung around to raise his head in the crook of her arm and began spooning in the hot staple, blowing on each spoonful as if cooling it for a baby. He tasted onions and small chunks of meat. Wonderful!

"*Se fue,*" she said at last. When he feigned ignorance she pointed with her mouth towards the door.

Between spoonfuls John looked at his surroundings through a haze of tobacco smoke. The Mexicans lounged on the other side of the room smoking homegrown *punche* in cornshuck wrappers, conversing in undertones. He recognized his trousers hanging on a peg to dry. He raised his blanket covering enough to discover he was naked.

"Señor Brown?" he asked again. Was Brown dead? Were they covering up?

"*Cazando*," she said after a long pause. "*Con los Indios*." He understood then. The American proprietor was out hunting with Indians. He'd heard that a small encampment of Utes was spending the winter nearby. Nonetheless John continued to feign puzzlement. The girl put down her spoon and crooked a trigger finger. John nodded. He felt better.

When he suddenly remembered his earlier sickness after a few more spoonsful he weakly waved off eating any more. The girl scraped the rest of the *posole* back into the pot and awkwardly gained her feet. He saw that she was very pregnant. My God, he realized, she's Brown's wife! Disappearing behind a curtained door, she emerged moments later with another blanket. Almost before she finished spreading the cover over the exhausted man he was falling asleep, a corner of his mind vaguely aware that flight was hopeless. He was too weak to outrun a child. Once during the night he awakened to discover the Mexicans stretched out on every side, surrounding him in sleep.

He spent two days regaining his strength through the charity and ministrations of the trader's child-wife, worried every waking minute that someone would arrive with word of the uprising and the ever-present Mexicans would put him to death. Whenever the dogs started barking or someone came through the door his heart nearly stopped. If the Mexicans tried to engage him he feigned ignorance of their meaning, but he understood from their whispered discussions that they were suspicious. Some said he was crazy.

On the third day John rose shakily to his feet before dawn to slip out the door and be on his way again, draped in his deerskin, his clothes and moccasins in tatters, a final 30 miles to go to reach the safety of Fort Pueblo. He staggered from time to time from dizzy spells.

79

Mormon Town

The Mormons said it was the dogs setting up a racket that sent a couple of men out to investigate. At the fringes of the willow thickets along the Arkansas they found a man they thought was drunk, his head and shoulders draped with a deerskin he wore hair-side in. Staggering and incoherent, the man's clothing was a disgrace. But he was not drunk, and when they helped him to a cabin, shushing his wild words as they wrapped him in a blanket by the fire, the curious gathered.

"Hey!" someone said. "I know him...he's from Turley's mill!"

John Albert roused himself with a mighty effort to his elbow, his squinty eye wide and affirming. His voice was a hoarse whisper and the message that emerged from his cracked lips was unbelievable. Mexicans and Indians were in revolt. Governor Bent was dead. Turley's mill was a burnt ruin.

The Mormons thought he was out of his senses.

In the firelight a woman knelt by the grass-filled tick on which he lay to lift John Albert's head and feed him soup. He stared at her, uncomprehending, and choked on the first spoonful, but when he was able to swallow again and she continued to spoon in soup, his look was that of a grateful dog. Once pretty, in her thirties, she'd been worn by a hard life to leathery skin and deep lines and spare flesh. Such was the price she and other Mormons paid in seeking their new Zion.

John turned his head to kiss her woolen sleeve in gratitude, sighed deeply, and fell asleep in the crook of her arm.

It was not until late next morning, after sleeping some fifteen hours, that John awakened. Briefly disoriented and ravenously hungry, he was able to tell his story in a coherent manner to a curious gathering. He related how Charley Autobees had galloped into Turley's mill to report Governor Bent was dead and that a mob was headed for the mill. Now Turley and his men were also dead and Turley's establishment was destroyed.

The Mormons were still skeptical. Governor Bent murdered? Turley's mill destroyed? An army of rebellious Mexicans and Indians? Hardly believable! How could the insurgents hope to stand up to the Army of the West?

On the other hand, what else could explain why John Albert, coatless and hatless in the dead of winter, had struggled up from Turley's mill to reach the safety of the Arkansas, a distance of some 150 miles? Men from the Mormon Battalion who'd arrived from Santa Fe by way of Taos and Turley's mill just two weeks earlier said the journey was the worst ordeal of their lives. No experienced traveler would take a wintertime crossing of the mountains lightly, especially afoot and alone, but that was how John Albert said he'd plowed across the Sangre de Cristo pass. All the way from Turley's mill!

John Albert started to cry. A woman put an arm around him. Ashamed, he explained his tears by saying he was worried about his family, and cried all the harder.

A couple of elders in the circle of Mormons exchanged looks. Once again God had smiled on them! Earlier that month a dozen Saints had bid good-bye to Turley and John Albert and the other men in the mill. These Saints were the last of the sick from the Mormon Battalion who were ending several weeks of convalescence at Turley's hospitable establishment. A few hadn't wanted to risk the wintertime mountain journey, preferring to wait out the cold weather at Turley's mill. But in the end they'd all struggled across the snow-buried mountains to reach their brethren on the Arkansas. And by God's grace had escaped the massacre! And by God's grace had fulfilled Brigham Young's prophecy that no Mormon who answered the call of the elders to join President Polk's 500-strong Mormon Battalion would suffer harm.

John Albert had found refuge in Mormon Town, a makeshift encampment on the Arkansas River where almost 300 Saints gathered for the winter. They were fed up with the United States. For most of this new religion's 15-year history the government had either ignored them or connived in the abuses heaped upon them. The government did nothing when threats and persecutions drove Joseph Smith and his followers from their new Zion in Ohio. Neither did government act to forestall the armed confrontations that drove them from their next new Zion - Independence, Missouri. Their third new Zion in northern Missouri proved the worst experience. There government-sponsored armed incursions and massacres sent them fleeing back east to find sanctuary in Illinois. But after a few years of relative peace and security in a settlement on the Mississippi River they named Nauvoo, government protection melted away,

Joseph Smith was murdered, their magnificent new temple desecrated, and their communities once again suffered the rampages of hoodlum gangs and armed vigilantes. America would not suffer these fanatic Mormon fools.

Small wonder several thousand fellow Saints now camped on the Missouri River near Council Bluffs, across the river from the new state of Iowa. There they eagerly awaited spring so they might continue their exodus to still another Zion, hopefully their last – this time in California.

Most of the Mormons in the Arkansas camp were sickly soldiers and their families, men of the Mormon Battalion recruited by President Polk to beef up Kearny's Army of the West. Not that Brigham Young and the church elders felt any obligation to help President Polk. Far from it. But the Mormons needed cash to finance their exodus to California, and Army pay answered nicely, thank you. Proof once again of God's beneficence.

On the long summer march to New Mexico, however, God did not smile on those already weakened by the ordeal of their hurried flight from Nauvoo. Along with women and children, three different detachments of sick soldiers from the Mormon Battalion were sent to convalesce at this special encampment on the Arkansas.

They used their convalescence to good advantage. Erecting crude cabins and a makeshift temple, they'd arrived early enough to grow a few late-summer vegetables, and had hunted and trapped and prayed and danced (and even occasionally drilled to honor their Army obligations). When the curious from Fort Pueblo or Bent's Fort came to gawk they tried to trade. The Mormons were sharp traders. Too sharp, some said. Like the loaves and fishes of Biblical times their herds increased miraculously, while just as miraculously any stray cattle in the area disappeared.

But for the most part they got along with their only neighbors, a handful of holdover fur traders and hunters at Fort Pueblo who came and went with the whims of the footloose. Fort Pueblo lay a half-mile across the Arkansas, a trading post in decline, a small fortress of crumbling adobe with a sagging gate. At one time a more important western-trail crossroads, Fort Pueblo's principal reasons for existence now were whiskey and flour and short-term wives for the itinerent. The whiskey and flour came from Taos; the wives came from various Mexican settlements and Indian tribes.

Simeon Turley kept a freight wagon there, for once a year or so Charley or Tom Autobees would haul Turley's whiskey and flour and furs across the mountains by pack mule to Fort Pueblo. Trading the whiskey and flour for more furs, they would then load the freight wagon with Turley's furs and haul them downriver to Bent's Fort and there join some caravan bound for the States.

It was to Fort Pueblo the Mormons soon took John Albert, the proper place for Gentiles. Meanwhile, the Mormon officer in charge of the little colony sent a rider hurrying some eighty miles down to Bent's Fort with news of Charles Bent's murder and rebellion in New Mexico. His message assured the Army there that his Mormon soldiers were ready to fight, and would await orders.

The handful of mountain men wintering at Fort Pueblo were a scruffy lot. With the beaver market collapsed and the great annual trapper rendezvous a thing of the past, most mountain men had moved on to other things. Men like Charley Autobees and John Albert and William LeBlanc and Louis Tolque had become farmers and cattle ranchers and artisans and fetch-its. But for some the freedom and danger of a mountain man's life was as vital as food and drink. How could a man who'd met the challenges of angry bears, hostile Indians, icy rivers and sudden mountain blizzards find satisfaction tending cattle or selling flour or grubbing out a bare living on a hardscrabble farm? Some could not. So with their old lives gone forever, they got by as hunters and guides and Indian traders and interpreters. Some made forays to distant California to steal horses and drive them back to sell, a very profitable enterprise. But mostly they sat around and drank and quarreled. They brooded and told stories about the old days.

They wanted to know if John Albert had run into Mark Head, a mountain man more scarred by encounters with beasts and Indians than an old bull buffalo. "He was going to Taos with some furs, him and a guy named Harwood - you must'a seen 'em."

No, John said, he'd seen nobody. But he didn't realize he'd passed their camp while climbing the Sangre de Cristos pass in a state of near delerium. The fate of the two trappers heading into New Mexico, unaware of the murders in Taos and the attack on Turley's mill, looked ominous.

Within a day or two after the Mormons took John Albert to Fort Pueblo his story had been told and retold so many times that even wide-eyed Mormon children could recite the facts - how Town had galloped up to Turley's mill with news of Governor Bent's murder, how he'd seen the Mexicans cut off Bent's head and kick it around the plaza in Taos - how Turley, wounded in the knee, vowed he would fight to the death to defend his mill - how Charley Autobees fought the good fight at Turley's mill, then made a daring escape to fetch the Army down in Santa Fe - how his brother Tom, a bull of a man, wounded in the groin, fired off his last ball, then charged through a dozen Mexicans, gutting four or five with his Green River before leaping a wall and disappearing into the night - how young Billy shot thirty or forty dead before he finally fell from a ball in the back - how John Albert crossed the Sangre de Cristo mountains in the dead of winter, coatless, hatless, sleepless.

Weeks later John would learn that the squat Mexicans at Greenhorn had decided he was crazy and were afraid of what he might do. They had stuck close to him to safeguard Brown's pregnant child-wife.

Haun's Mill

Nights were worst for John Albert. Nights he dreaded, and he would stay up long past the time when Fort Pueblo quieted, smoking, listening, watching. When at last he retired to the room he shared with several other men, hoping for sleep, he'd be up a dozen times to test the door or peer out the cracks of the shuttered aperture. Sometimes he'd give up and slip outside. Reassuring the dogs, he'd pace the central yard of the small compound and smoke cornshuck *cigarillos*, stopping to listen at the sound of interrupted snoring, the cry of a child, the distant howl of a wolf, the sudden racket of dogs over in Mormon Town. Then he would begin his rounds again, tobacco smoke trailing after him in the winter air, tendrils of memory, wisps of sorrow. He cried silently. He'd grown skinny as a rail.

But darkness would at last give way to dawn. The fort would stir with the first raucous cries of cocks and babies and the muffled morning conversations of women and children in a patois of Spanish and French and English, Arapaho and Cheyenne and Ute. Soon would come the sounds of chopping and firemaking and the bleating and mawing and clucking of the barnyard. Only when life's diurnal rhythms were once again as certain as a heartbeat would John Albert slip through the gate with a blanket to take his place on the bench by the gateway. There he would doze the morning away, exhausted.

He had begun to smoke heavily. Weather permitting, he would spend the entire day on the bench overlooking the Arkansas, fashioning one cornshuck smoke after another, smoking and dozing, smoking and dozing. He craved the firm tug of tobacco smoke in his chest when he inhaled. He relished the bite and bitter aftertaste of the cheap Mexican tobacco. He needed to smoke as much as he needed to tell his story, and the lifeless ground around his perch grew littered with the leavings of his habit. Awake, he stared at the sere expanse of New Mexico across the river, lost in thoughts of chance and circumstance, only vaguely aware of the comings and goings of people from the fort. When visitors came from Mormon Town he would be reminded of their strong, sure faith. The mountain men at Fort Pueblo called them fanatics.

John Albert had never been religious. Quite the opposite. God was to blame for his father's death, killed in the Battle of New Orleans. God was to blame for John being shipped off as a youngster to live with an aunt. If God was All-Good, why had his father died in a needless battle fought six weeks after peace was declared? If God was All-Powerful, why didn't He stop the Battle of New Orleans? Did God want his father to die and his mother to break down with grief? Did God want their family to be sundered? No, to John Albert, all the talk about God's goodness made no sense.

As soon as he was old enough to be on his own John quit going to church. Except for doing what he had to so that he could marry his beautiful New Mexican child-bride, he shunned religion.

But surviving the siege of Turley's mill started him questioning again. Why me? he wondered. Why was he alone spared? Was it God's design? Was it for his family? But Turley had a family. Charley too, and LeBlanc, and Tolque. Why were they not spared? And why was Billy killed - a boy so young and innocent? If they're all dead, he wondered, do I owe some-thing special for my life, something I didn't owe before? Do I owe God?

But God seemed so remote, so aloof. And John Albert was beginning to believe that Simeon Turley's Hand of God didn't show in a single death like his father's or a single horror like the massacre at Turley's mill. Maybe God only kept things going around and around, kept evenhanded the quirks of chance and circumstance, scattered equal measures of happiness and sorrow, pleasure and pain. How else to explain why John had escaped the siege of Turley's mill unscathed, his hat shot off, his shirt holed by musket balls in four or five places, while Louis Tolque died from an errant ball that found its way through a loophole in the loft not much wider than a man's hand? Why?

Perhaps the siege of Turley's mill was one of God's ways of keeping things going around and around. What was the difference between a Christ on the cross and a Simeon Turley wanting to take the blame? "Maybe it's just me they want!" Turley had cried, ready to sacrifice himself to the mob. And how else did one explain Bill Hatfield rising from his bed of agony in the grainbin, his eyes wild: "Gonna pay for my sins, all of you!" And Turley: "No, Bill, that's not so. We all got sins, me too. I'm the most to blame."

A man carrying an expensive double-barreled Wesley-Richards came out the gate and approached John Albert's bench. Dressed in well-worn skins, a slender, small man, he had light blue eyes older than his 20-some years. He wore moccasins and carried a small-bore pistol and a long, bone-handled sheath knife thrust in the belt of his fringed overshirt. His face and small hands were burnished brown by sun and wind. Leaning his long weapon against the adobe, he took a seat beside John on the half-log bench that canted against the wall, their backs supported by the weathered mud bricks. Morning sun cast a faint glow of warmth on their faces and hands.

The man's name was Ruxton, an Englishman who'd come to Fort Pueblo weeks earlier, a lone adventurer who'd spent several months traveling some 1,800 miles up the spine of Mexico, always seeming to be in the right place at the right time to observe the development of the American war with its southern neighbor. Some of the mountain men at Fort Pueblo said he was a man who sat at the edge of the firelight, a slip-away. Some thought he was a British spy. For certain he'd seen plenty. In Vera Cruz he witnessed General Santa Anna's return from exile to take the reins of power of the Mexican government. North of El Paso he spent time with the encamped American army while it gathered itself for the invasion of Chihuahua. In Santa Fe he observed the military occupation of the capital by the Missouri volunteers. In Taos he spent several days enjoying the hospitality of Stephen Lee and his brother Elliott, the man of girth who'd come across the prairies with young Lewis. At Turley's mill he stopped for breakfast just after the departure of the convalescing Mormon soldiers. And there he had met John.

Now, just returned from a hunting trip in the mountains, he'd arrived the previous day to learn of the massacres in Taos and of John Albert's escape.

"You know, ah, I was pretty lucky too," the Englishman said. John Albert glanced over at him. "Mister Lee invited me to spend the winter in Taos. I could've been caught there with the rest of you...just luck I wasn't."

John shrugged. "Maybe so," he said, a corner of his mind tucking that piece of information away for his ruminations on God and chance and circumstance.

The Englishman took out his pipe, charged it with tobacco, and lit up with a glowing brand from the remnants of a small fire at John's feet. He puffed in silence for a minute or two before asking, "I don't suppose, you could tell me about the Englishman?"

John nodded acknowledgement of the question without looking at Ruxton. Although he carried the terror of the seige of Turley's mill in his heart - a nightmare of smoke and darkness and confusion and certain moments as stark in memory as the brilliant snow-capped mountains in the distance - what happened at Turley's mill was changing. Like the greenwood bush, parts of the ordeal shriveled and died while other parts grew, so while his recollections might seem the same, they really were not. Now when someone like Ruxton wanted to hear his story, John was sometimes unsure whether a particular detail was true or something he imagined was true or was just a trick of the telling, something he added so the story made more sense or made the telling better. Maybe even something that might have happened but perhaps didn't. For certain the dead at Turley's mill had become more heroic and the enemy more evil. That was what his listeners wanted. Good needed to triumph over evil. Whites needed to win. Even if the triumph was death. Even if the whites had lost.

He remembered the narrow-faced Englishman huddled in the corner of the distillery with the dogs, withdrawn into white-eyed, wordless terror. He'd never liked the man, who he thought was a whiner and a shirker. But the Englishman was due something in death, just like the others. "Marshall was a good man," he said. "Liked dogs." Ruxton nodded, puffing little clouds.

"I mean, did he, ah, acquit himself well in, ah, you know, battle?"

"Oh, yes...oh, yes," John Albert said, drawing the words out. "Fought with the best of 'em. A good man." The newcomer nodded again, pleased his dead countryman had upheld the honor of the Queen.

"I remember in the distillery," John continued, "when we were wondering what to do, Marshall worried about the dogs. We had to do something about the dogs, you see." Ruxton nodded and puffed as John Albert began fashioning another *cigarillo*.

Perhaps a quarter-mile distant several figures approached on the path that led from the Arkansas. The two on the bench watched the men take definition - slouch hats, patched coats, ill-fitting trousers, sour expressions. The Mormons! What a battalion! The men carried bulging cloth sacks. "Here they come," John Albert said, "trading their Army rations again."

"Morning, Brother John," a gangly man with a patriarchal beard said as they approached the gate. John's head bobbed a greeting. The man detached himself from the group and retrieved a booklet from his side-pocket.

"Found it?" John Albert asked. The Mormon nodded and held the booklet so John could read the title. The Englishmen leaned to see. "The Massacre at Haun's Mill," he read, and a subtitle of many words.

"God works in mysterious ways," the Mormon said, leafing through the pages. "Turned out one of our young men had it among his things." He found what he was looking for and held the booklet near, pointing to a name in a long list of names. His fingernail was rough and split. "This one's brother had it. Only he's dead too now. Last November. And his poor mother a widow, bless her."

John Albert put his cigarette in the corner of his mouth and took the proffered booklet. Squinting through tobacco smoke at the column of names, he asked, "All killed?" He ended his brief question with a little tobacco cough.

"Murdered like dogs! Even boys! See this," the Mormon said. "And this?" He pointed to a couple of the names. A crescent of black under his fingernail trembled near the print. "Boys! One of 'em was nine years old!" The other Mormons stood in a semicircle and watched the reactions of the Gentiles.

The Englishman, still leaning over, was looking for something on the page he did not see. "Who was Haun," he asked finally.

"Jacob...Jacob Haun," the Mormon said abruptly. "Owned the mill."

"Back in Missouri," one of the other Mormons offered.

"He, ah, wasn't killed?"

"Wounded." The Mormon took the booklet back and turned the page. He showed them another long column listing the names of the wounded. One entry jumped out at the Englishman. Alma Smith, age 7.

The Mormon fixed Ruxton with a glare, "Jacob Haun. It was his mill and his blacksmith shop. That's where they murdered most of 'em, in the blacksmith shop. Poked their guns in and shot 'em like dogs. Dragged one of the little boys out from un-

89

der the bellows and shot his face off. Cut 'em up with corn knives."

"Who?" the Englishman asked. "Indians?"

"Indians!" the Mormon spokesman said as he spat with contempt and exchanged bitter looks with his companions. "You think the Devil's work is all Indians? No, by God, white men! A mob of Missouri men! Worse'n Indians!"

The Englishman looked nonplussed.

"Our kind," John Albert said sadly. He sighed, a huge sigh that lifted his shoulders and dropped them heavily. "I was trying to figure something out," he said, gesturing with the booklet, "something from Turley's mill, something one of the men said. This is what he was talking about...Haun's mill." He looked at the booklet. "He was shot and was going to die and he told us it was because of what he did at Haun's mill. I'd never heard of Haun's mill."

The Englishman nodded as if he understood, but he was ignorant of what had happened at Haun's mill.

"'Vengeance is mine, saith the Lord,'" the Mormon intoned. His companions nodded. The Englishman looked from the Mormons to John Albert, not following their meaning. Not until he read about the massacre at Haun's mill.

Perhaps 20 Mormon families were gathered in the vicinity of Jacob Haun's establishment on that uncommonly warm fall day just eight years earlier, October 30, 1838. Most shared a half dozen log houses scattered along either side of Shoal Creek, but some who were on the move lived in tents and covered wagons near the blacksmith shop. Weeks of ugly confrontations with both civil authorities and hoodlums had them all scared. Armed gangs had bullied new arrivals from the east on the road to the Mormon settlements. News from the main settlement at Far West some 30 miles distant told of an advancing army of militia determined to drive the Mormons from Missouri.

Haun's mill could muster about 30 men in arms, but their weapons were mostly shotguns and small-bores. Nonetheless, because of the threat of violence they'd elected a war-captain to direct their defense, a man named Evans. For several days they had kept a watch-guard stationed at the edge of a thin woods to the north, the only practical approach to Haun's mill, but with

90

assurances from neighbors that they really had nothing to fear they withdrew the guard and went about their fall chores, apprehensive but hopeful of continued calm.

About four o'clock in the afternoon more than 200 horsemen suddenly burst from the woods and charged across a cornfield towards the settlement. Evans ran towards them waving his hat. "Peace!" he cried. "We want peace." The riders halted. Behind Evans the Mormon men grabbed weapons and ran for the blacksmith shop, their "blockhouse," a solid structure built of logs but left unchinked. Wide gaps between the logs let in light and air. Evans stood facing the ranks of horsemen, his hat held out with both hands as if he were taking up a Sunday collection. "Peace," he cried again. The horses panted and pawed. The riders sat impassive. Then the leader raised a pistol and fired a single shot in the general direction of the mill. A puzzled silence. Then a ragged racket of pistol and musket shots sounded and the horsemen kicked their mounts into motion, yowling like maniacs.

Evans turned and fled. A couple of latecomers making for the blacksmith shop fired at the charging horsemen as they ran. One of them fell wounded from the rattle of returned gunfire. Evans slid shut the wagon-door of the blacksmith shop. Inside, a few men fired through the gaps at the swirl of horsemen outside. One of the riders grabbed a leg and fell wounded from his mount. Horsemen rode up to the blockhouse and poked the muzzles of their weapons through to fire. The blockhouse men screamed with surprise and pain as lead tore through flesh. Several huddled together in a mass, petrified with fear, unable to discharge their guns. Only a few had enough presence of mind to reload and return the fire that poured in.

At the first shots of the charging horsemen the settlement had panicked. Women and children struggled across the steep-banked creek and sought safety in the abrupt, woodsy hillside opposite. Others snatched up children and retreated into their houses. Within moments horsemen were galloping through the settlement, shooting at anything that moved, even the shadowy shapes of women and children clawing their way up the hillside across the creek.

After just a few minutes of ferocious gunfire around the blacksmith shop, seeing disaster in the making, Evans cried "Every man for himself!" and threw open the door and bolted for the footbridge across the milldam. Those who could still run followed his lead, but Evans was the only one fleeing the blacksmith shop not cut down. An old man fell groaning, shot in the leg, his long-barreled musket beside him unfired, a relic of the War of Revolution. "Take it," he croaked to a wild-eyed horseman looming over him. The young man jumped down from his horse, snatched up the weapon, placed the muzzle against the old man's chest, and pulled the trigger. Whoomp! Then he hacked at the writhing victim with his corn knife.

Horsemen rode up to the open doorway of the blacksmith shop and fired into the dim, smoky interior, then reloaded to fire again and again. Two whimpering boys inside, one badly wounded, crowded into a hiding place beneath the bellows.

Dismounted riders now broke down cabin doors and helped themselves to clothing and bedding and foodstuffs. They yipped and hooted like wildmen, scattered belongings, threw dishes and cookware and household objects through shattered windows. One put on a bonnet and pranced around for the amusement of his fellows. Others stuffed chickens and other barnyard fowl into their shirts. One captured and trussed up a pig, but when the animal would not stay put in front of his saddle he pushed it off and shot it and left it squealing and bleedingand crabbing in a circle, its back broken, its hind legs useless.

Inside the blacksmith shop a vigilante noticed a boy hiding under the bellows and pulled him out by a foot. The boy's chest was red with blood. His face was blackened by soot and his trousers dark in the crotch where he'd wet himself. He tried weakly to scrabble back under the bellows, his bare feet working at the dirt, his hands raised as if to ward off a blow. Hatfield cackled and dragged him outside and put a foot on the boy's head to hold him still. As men stood gawking at his little prisoner the boy fluttered briefly and then lay still, dead.

Another of the vigilantes discovered the other boy under the bellows, poked his musket into the space and fired. When they dragged the body out the boy's face and the top of his head were missing. A few of the men were shaken by the sight, but Slim spit tobacco juice and explained his deed. "Nits make lice," he said, and challenged his comrades with a wolfish grin.

That boy was the last casualty. Every male who had not fled into the woods was either dead or wounded.

With twilight the vigilantes regrouped and departed, appropriating a horse and wagon for their casualties, three wounded, none seriously. As evening thickened, women and children began to emerge from hiding. One had sheltered her wounded daughter with her body while musket balls hissed and rattled through the foliage where they hid. Another woman, hit as she lay cowering behind a log, came out with her bleeding hand wrapped in her apron. The women called in low voices to one another, fearful their voices might bring the raiders back. At the sounds of their voices one man who'd fled for the creek rather than the blockhouse crept cautiously from his burrow in a thicket, his side bleeding from a gunshot wound.

Survivors lit lanterns and searched through the darkness as others tried to comfort the terrified children. Untended milk cows began to bellow for attention. Nervous, growling dogs roamed the carnage, sometimes stopping to yowl piteously. Scattered in the darkness like storm-tossed debris were dead and wounded husbands and fathers and brothers. Nine lay dead just around the blacksmith's shop. Some were so badly mutilated as to be scarcely recognizable. The women found the wounded by their groaning.

All night they gathered the dead and tended the wounded. By noon the next day two more had died, and the unseasonable warmth began to corrupt the bodies.

Not far from his house Jacob Haun had been digging a well. A pulley on a tripod straddled the hole, now more than ten feet deep. The survivors dragged the bloating bodies over to the well on a broken door and slid them into the mass grave, pausing to offer brief prayers for each victim before sending him down. When the seventeen dead had been dumped into the unfinished well, they threw down straw and a few barrows of dirt.

By mid-afternoon that day a contingent of twenty or thirty horsemen cantered across the cornfield as the survivors finished their gruesome task. The riders stayed at a distance, watching the survivors gather up the wreckage of their lives. One of the women went towards them. "What more do ye want?" she cried. "Ye've killed us all! Git out of here!"

One of the horsemen started to speak, then shrugged and turned his mount away. Then he turned back again. "You know what's good for you, old woman, you be the ones git out!" The horsemen rode away through the woods. Later the survivors heard of the story the horsemen told, that they had returned to help bury the dead.

"But why?"

It was next day, and John and the Englishman were seated on the bench again. John shrugged off the Englishman's question. To John the question wasn't "why." There was always a "why." Greed. Revenge. Jealousy. Hate. For John it was "how."

After both men had read the little pamphlet entitled "The Massacre at Haun's Mill," John still had trouble picturing Hatfield and Slim among the vigilantes. Hatfield putting his foot on the boy's head, Slim hacking at the old man with a corn-knife. Not Hatfield and Slim! He'd sat at the table with them, shared food and liquor and stories! And yet....

Slim had been so scared in the distillery, afraid of being found out, like a schoolboy caught cheating: "Ain't so, Bill, ain't so!" Yet, John Albert knew deep down that he could see Slim that way. And Hatfield. And even Billy. Men out of control, the beast in them let loose. Did every man have a beast inside? Even him? How else could he explain slashing like a madman at the wounded Indian in the old hog pen? Out of control with panic and fear and anger and hate. Slashing and slashing past the point of killing. Yes, John Albert thought, feeling so weary and sad he felt like sinking into the ground, even me. Ruxton looked over to see John Albert crying again.

Simeon Turley

At first Brushie insisted Turley lead the other party out the escape hole in the foundation. In the darkness his whisper was harsh and accusatory. "This ain't my fight," he told Turley. "It's you they want, your head! You go out!" But when the time came for Turley to slither out, Brushie suddenly changed his mind and said that he wanted to go first. He positioned himself at the mouth of the hole, breathing heavily. Then he lost his nerve and backed away. "No, you!" he ordered LeBlanc. "You're the big mountain man! You see what's out there!"

LeBlanc said they had to silence the dogs first. The animals might betray them. Huddled with the two animals, Marshall heard LeBlanc draw his knife and made a whimpering sound and locked the dogs in a desperate embrace and said that Le-Blanc would have to kill him first. Determined, LeBlanc made a move towards the Englishman in the dark, but Turley's hand restrained him.

"Just go," Turley said. "Just go. We'll keep the dogs quiet."

Without another word LeBlanc quickly scrabbled part of the way through the hole, paused to look and listen, then disappeared.

"Keep 'em quiet then," Turley said to Marshall, and quickly followed after LeBlanc. Their hearts pounding, the two men belly-crawled undiscovered to the other side of the narrow cart track skirting Turley's compound and reached the cover of the scattered piñons. Silently praying for invisibility, they hugged the ground among the fireshadows of the piñons. Suddenly they heard the crash of the collapsing roof of the mill and then a hideous scream. They waited, every nerve taut. Then, after a time, scarcely breathing, seeking the shadows, they belly-crawled higher up the hillside. Several times they stopped to peer behind. Smoke-blackened skin and clothing disguised their presence in the murky night. They heard the crackle and hiss of the fires, sounds of smashing and looting and drunken celebration. They glimpsed figures passing on the cart track below, but none took note of the obscure escape hole in the foundation or raised an alarm. But where were Brushie and Marshall?

They waited until LeBlanc at last signaled that they needed move on, then LeBlanc led Turley inch by inch up the hill. Finally, some two hours after their escape from the cellar, perhaps two hundred yards from the arroyo floor, they risked progress afoot among the piñons.

Cresting the hill at last, they sneaked through the trees for a half-mile or more before cutting over to join the trail to Rio Colorado. The going was easier then, although in the darkness Turley fell several times when his weak knee gave way. It helped him to put an arm on LeBlanc's shoulder so he could take some of the weight off, but he still stumbled frequently and his knee soon felt afire. Every time his footing failed on the rocky trail a hot blade-thrust of pain shot up his leg. He was scarcely able to keep from crying out. Once they heard voices and hid by the trail as two men passed conversing volubly in Spanish. In what he later thought was a trick of his imagination, Turley believed they had been talking about him.

With the growing light of dawn LeBlanc discovered a set of fresh footprints going in their direction, a man in a hurry wearing Cheyenne moccasins. John Albert had been fond of Cheyenne footware! But LeBlanc was unable to tell for sure the footprints belonged to John Albert, and he racked his brain trying to remember some detail of John's moccasins that would indicate the tracks were his. "Maybe it's John," he said at last. The odds were impossible, but both men privately imagined the joy of finding John Albert somewhere ahead resting by the trail.

By mid-morning Turley said he could go no farther. With each step the pain in his left knee was excruciating. "Go on without me," he told LeBlanc. "Save yourself. I'm just slowing you down." LeBlanc knew every minute he stayed with Turley increased the chances of his own death. Traveling alone, LeBlanc was a French-Canadian, a *voyageur* with a Mexican wife, a man born into the True Faith. But so long as he remained with Turley he was an ally of the Americans and a target for death. The smart thing for LeBlanc to do was to get away from Turley as soon as possible and to find refuge with his own people.

LeBlanc shrugged. He told Turley he would stop at Charley's ranch and send back help, or would return himself with a horse to get Turley to safety.

He half carried the gimpy man to a thick growth of trees some distance from the trail and used his skinning knife to cut a few pine boughs for a place of rest. They shook hands. At the last moment Turley pulled LeBlanc into a powerful embrace.

"*Merci*," he said. "Thank you, William LeBlanc, for all that you have done." His words had a tone of finality that brought a lump to LeBlanc's throat.

Turley lowered himself onto his bed of boughs with a sigh of relief. He massaged his knee, his expression showing a mixture of pain and and weariness and resignation. LeBlanc nodded and waved a brief farewell, and as he made his way back to the trail he swished a pine branch over their tracks. Despite his efforts he knew that an alert eye would discover the way to Turley's hiding place.

For a time, unimpeded by Turley, LeBlanc's progress was good, and he felt hopeful. He thought of reunion with his family, of encircling all of his children at once with his arms, of gathering them as he had seen in a picture of Jesus with a flock of children, "Laissez venir à moi...." Then he remembered Louis Tolque and began to weep at the loss of his good friend. He began saying prayers for the safety and well-being of his family and Louis's family and promised Jesus and the Blessed Virgin that if he survived this awful ordeal he would be an upright man for the rest of his days. The prayers made him feel better, and for a time he even considered doubling back and trying to sneak back down to his little farm in the arroyo. But before long weariness weighed like dead weight on every limb. He began stumbling over half-hidden roots and rocks on the narrow trail and once or twice went sprawling. He realized he had no choice but to find succor with LaFôret in Rio Colorado.

LeBlanc had never been to Charley and Tom's ranch, but three or four miles from where he left Turley he found the turn-off on Llama Creek and followed it towards the mountains until he reached the small clearing containing the Autobees' crude house. Suddenly Charley's big yellow dog charged at him with bared teeth, barking viciously. LeBlanc kept the determined animal at bay with the barrel of his musket until the women in the house called off the animal. Through a raised corner of the scrapped hide that covered the front window the muzzle of a musket pointed at LeBlanc. He stood rooted in place as he asked if Charley's brother-in-law Jose was home. The women told him to go away. They said they had many guns and that their men were returning soon. Understanding little of their excited rattle of Spanish, LeBlanc nodded dumbly. He wondered if Charley's body lay inside.

LeBlanc tried to communicate his identity and his acquaintance with Charley and Tom. Then he tried to explain Simeon

Turley's situation. His speech was an amalgam of French and Spanish and English that the women received in silence. Finally he asked if Jose could ride down the trail with a horse to bring Turley back. He waited for a response. He repeated his request, his hands folded in supplication. With no response forthcoming he at last turned away to seek the main trail again, not knowing if the women had understood anything at all of what he'd tried to communicate. He felt defeated by their suspicion and fear and hostility. The idea of going back for Turley himself was out of the question. It was far too risky. With a saddened heart LeBlanc thought, I've done all I can.

Towards evening, on the verge of collapse, he reached the home of Francisco LaFôret. His heart sank when he learned that LaFôret and his eldest son were out hunting. But they were expected back anytime, LaFôret's younger son said, reading LeBlanc's disappointed expression. The boy invited LeBlanc into the house to warm himself by the fire. Not knowing whether news of the rebellion had reached Rio Colorado, or even where the loyalties of the half-Mexican boy might lie, Le-Blanc remained silent about the events at Turley's mill. Seated cross-legged by the fireplace, mirroring the boy on the other side, he attempted small talk in French about hunting and horses. Soon, despite his best efforts to stay alert, he found himself dozing off. Finally, as LaFôret's wife began stirring between them to prepare the evening meal, he gave up and let his head sink to his chest. His last thoughts were that he hardly cared what happened to him, if only he could sleep.

Soon after LeBlanc turned off the trail to seek Charley's place, a man named Lucero rode by from the direction of Rio Colorado. Farther down the trail he was surprised to hear the sound of snoring from somewhere off the trail. Curious, Lucero dismounted and followed the sound, and quickly discovered LeBlanc's hasty efforts to conceal Turley's hiding place. When Lucero found Turley, a man he had known for years, he called him by name with a gentle voice. "Señor Turley?" Startled from his exhausted sleep, scrambling to sit upright, Turley quickly regained his composure, and after a few pleasantries told the Mexican that he had been on his way to Rio Colorado when his horse shied and threw him, injuring his bum knee. The damned animal had run off, he said, and here he sat, horseless and unable to walk.

"Yes, yes, I understand," Lucero said. Such a sad twist of

fortune to be left in such a predicament, he added. One moment you're riding along like king and the next you're sitting on your backside looking like a fool. He half laughed as he said the situation of the miller reminded him of something from Cervantes, and the men laughed together.

If Lucero thought Turley's appearance was strange he failed to let on. The miller's face and hands were dark with soot and dirt. His filthy, ragged clothes were reeked of smoke. Turley looked like a desperate man on the run, and his efforts to explain away his situation were ridiculous. If Turley's horse had run off, it must have flown like a bird, because Lucero had not seen hoofprints. And Turley must have had his *escopeta* in hand when his horse threw him, because it leaned against a nearby tree. But the two men played the scene through.

Turley asked if the Mexican might take him on horseback as far as the Autobees ranch, where he could perhaps procure another mount.

No, Lucero said, he was very sorry, but he was on his way home from important business in Rio Colorado and could not reverse his course. He would end up travelling in the dark if he did. But perhaps he could take Turley back to his mill riding double? Lucero would be happy to carry him back because it was on his way. That would be no trouble at all.

No, no, Turley said, he appreciated the offer, but he really had to get to Rio Colorado because his business was also very pressing. But perhaps Señor Lucero would allow him the use of his horse for a small consideration? Unfortunately, in his haste Turley had forgotten to take his purse but he had his pocketwatch, a fine instrument in a case of gold. He would happily exchange his watch for the use of Señor Lucero's horse, which he would be sure to return as well-cared for as if it were his own. Again Lucero demurred.

After more fruitless negotiation Lucero said he really had to be on his way but would stop at Turley's mill and send back help. The two men shook hands, and as Lucero mounted again he looked down at Turley with a low laugh. "Forgive me, señor, but I must tell you of that little something from Cervantes, the thing that made me laugh, something he says about misfortune. Do you know the great Cervantes?"

Turley shook his head. "Just the name," he answered.

"Yes, well, that's the way of the world, isn't it? We each have our own heroes, you Americans, we Mexicans. Anyway, it is a saying from *Don Quixote*, and the saying goes like this: 'The wheel of fortune turns faster than a millwheel.' Imagine, the wheel of fortune, like a millwheel! And you being a miller! Very true, don't you think, Señor Turley?"

Turley laughed politely. "Yes," he said. "Very true."

"Well, *adios* then, Señor Turley."

"Yes, *adios*, Señor Lucero." As the Mexican turned his mount and started through the trees for the trail Turley thought of lunging for his shotgun. He knew Lucero would betray him. But then he decided, No, I could never bring myself to shoot a man in the back, even my enemy.

When he reached Turley's mill Lucero told the rebels still hanging around where the American was hiding. A dozen or more hurried back on horseback to run Turley down before dark. By the time they found Turley he'd cut a crutch and had managed to limp along for another mile or so towards the Autobees ranch. But he was still some distance from that dubious refuge when the riders caught up with him. Giving up without a word, he fell to his knees and began to pray. The rebels shot him with arrows, then scalped him and stripped him of his clothes. Before leaving, they cut off his head and left his body for the wolves.

The Pueblo

About two miles from the central plaza of San Fernando de Taos lies the Taos pueblo. Long before the first Europeans arrived to settle the New World, Indians of the Tanoan culture populated an adobe fortress here, raising corn and vegetables in the rich valley surrounds and hunting for deer and bear in the nearby mountains to the east. After the arrival of the Spanish conquistadors the people of the pueblo continued to carry on the rudiments of their ancient ways of life as generation after generation rubbed up against the new ritualistic religion of Spain and the ill-managed government of this far-north outpost of Spanish authority. Not much changed after Mexico won its independence. Sometimes the people of this close-knit pueblo (a word in Spanish meaning town or village) found common cause with their neighbors in San Fernando de Taos; most times they shut them out.

On the sunrise side of the pueblo lay an extensive horse meadow that reached to the foothills of the mountains, sprinkled with leafy trees and fragrant in summer with knee-high grass. There, just a few months before the uprising in Taos (the familiar name for San Fernando de Taos), above an embankment of the creek that ran through the meadow, the rising moon had cast leafy shadows from willows and cottonwoods on two naked, conjoined people. The Delaware lay on his back with Red Willows astraddle. She tickled him under the nose with a grass stem and he wrinkled his face and laughed a great exuberant laugh of pleasure and happiness. Red Willows laughed too, and drew a handwoven blanket over the two of them against the gathering evening chill. She kissed the Delaware with love.

Now, under those same trees, stark and leafless on a moonless night, the Delaware stared unseeing at a gurgle of black water that ran between ledges of ice. He sat alone, his heart an ache of loss and grief and rage. Red Willows was dead.

The ball that killed her came from Turley's mill. Another ball meant for him had been a swift hissing, the missile passing under Charley's mule and skipping off the frozen ground a dozen yards beyond. Why was just Red Willows killed? Why not him?

101

His favorite memory of her came to him again, an image from months earlier that freshened the ache in his heart: Red Willows strolling to this same creek where it ran through the pueblo, waterpot on her head, her hips swaying gracefully beneath a fringed skirt, her soft, knee-high pueblo boots oddly exciting. At the time he thought the small boy at her side meant she was married, and he'd been surprised by her smile. Perhaps she had already learned who he was, a Delaware hunter asking the elders for permission to spend the winter in the pueblo.

Soon after that encounter came a day when his heart hammered at the sight of Red Willows' father advancing deliberately over the rough bridge that spanned the creek. Sun Runner's graying hair was long and loose in the fashion of the pueblo, partially captured by a blue-banded trade blanket he wore against the late afternoon chill. He'd been pleased with the Delaware's presents - two horses and a grizzly pelt that Sun Runner kept in his quarters to spread for guests. And some peppermint candy from the Greenhorn trading post near the Wet Mountains to the north where the Delaware hunted. Sun Runner had loved the peppermint candy.

The Delaware was certain Sun Runner would give him permission to marry Red Willows and this next step was just a formality, but the young hunter could scarcely keep his hands from fidgeting in nervous excitement.

Sun Runner signed a greeting, offered his hand, and indicated a wall where the late sun promised warmth for a little longer. The two men sat facing each other in silence while several elders settled around to observe their dealings. After Tomasito came, the principal chief, they all smoked a common pipe in silence, each following the ritual of his own medicine. The tobacco spent, communication proceeded by sign language, for the Delaware's Tiwa was rudimentary and the Pueblos knew the silent language of the plains from their annual forays across the mountains to hunt buffalo. The conversation of the Delaware and Sun Runner was echoed in shadows on the wall.

Sun Runner nodded respectfully to Tomasito, then addressed the young hunter. "The elders want to know if you will share all things with us."

"Sun Runner, I promise you that everything I possess belongs to the pueblo." Like Sun Runner's question, the Delaware's answer was rehearsed, for he had already spent much time explaining why he sought a pueblo wife. He had talked with Red Willows' brothers and with various elders and captains. On one special occasion he had been invited to a long session to recount the history of his people, the "Lenni Lenâpé," the first people, his tribe's name before the whites began calling his people the Delaware. "My Lenni Lenâpé name is En-di-ond," he'd explained, "He-who-was-seen, for I have been seen in many places. Only my white man's name is Big Nigger. I think the whites call me 'Big Nigger' because I am strong."

"The elders want to know if you will fight our enemies."

"Your enemies are my enemies," En-di-ond said.

"The elders want to know if you will respect our ways."

"I will always respect the ways of my grandfathers, the Tiwa."

"You will be the new father of my grandson, Nicholas."

"I will watch over Nicholas and teach him like my own son. I will teach him to respect his grandfather and grandmother and all elders and to learn the ways of the pueblo."

"You will be the new husband of my daughter."

"I will be a good husband to Red Willows. I will provide for her and give you many grandsons."

Sun Runner smiled slightly and gathered his blanket more snugly about his middle. He sat in silence for several minutes, glanced at Tomasito, then said, "I am pleased with what you say. I have thought a lot about your request and have talked with many others in the pueblo. You brought me good presents and say good things. I am inclined to grant your request.

"But listen carefully. You come from far away. Red Willows is my only daughter. Nicholas is my grandson. If you go back to your people and take them with you my wife, I will have no daughter to look after us when we are old."

After Sun Runner had sat silent for several moments, En-di-ond nodded gravely. "I understand what you say and respect your concern, but I have no intention of returning to my people. My people live in log houses like whites and keep cows and hogs and sheep. But now the whites want our land again. In the old days they got my people drunk and made them do foolish things. I think it will soon be the same again. The whites will give my people whiskey-money and presents and make us move again. The thought of this makes me sad and angry. I will

103

not move again, ever.

"Sun Runner, when I was a boy I saw few whites. Then I saw more and more. Now they are everywhere. In the mountains there are not so many, and that is why my heart was full when I hunted there with my Delaware brothers. But now there are just a few of my Delaware brothers left. The beaver are almost rubbed out and are not worth much anymore. I must find a new life, and the buffalo road is not my road.

"Sun Runner, when I look at this place I see a home that is older than my oldest grandfathers. If my people had lived in this place we would not have given our land away for whiskey and trinkets.

"Sun Runner, I respect you as I respected my own father. Your people have welcomed me and treated me well and I thank you for that. I thank all of you for that. I respect your daughter Red Willows and your grandson. I respect the ways of the pueblo and want to live in this place. This is where I want to live and grow old, forever."

Sun Runner sat quietly as he studied the Delaware suitor. Then his eyes found Red Willows, who had dawdled nearby with Nicholas the entire time. He smiled at her and nodded. "Good, En-di-ond," he said. "You have spoken well. You may have my daughter Red Willows. Now we will smoke on it."

Yes, En-di-ond realized as he brooded by the gushing stream, even with Red Willows dead he would fight for the pueblo. He'd already taken one scalp at Turley's mill to avenge her death. But was one scalp enough? And who was his enemy now? Turley's mill was a smoking ruin, the men inside all dead. Perhaps it made no difference. He'd pledged to fight the enemies of the pueblo, and word had gone forth that Mexicans and Indians would march together on Santa Fe to take back their land from the Americans. From a handful of aggrieved Indians confronting Governor Bent about the new laws, the people's smoldering resentment and grievances had blossomed into a full-fledged uprising against the Americans and anyone who sided with them. Growing ranks of Mexicans and Indians would carry the fight to Santa Fe and across the mountains to the east.

From the pueblo the Delaware heard sounds of drumming and shouts and singing as warriors prepared for the march on Santa Fe. Tomorrow they would set off, their strength growing as fighters joined from every pueblo and town they passed. And tomorrow En-di-ond would be among them. But who were his enemies now? Any white? Any American? Even Charley Autobees, a thick-headed man with a good heart? Did they all have to die? Was the road of bloodshed the only road to follow?

The Delaware was unable to shake his sense of futility and utter loss, his feeling of being betrayed by some dark force. The One Below? Suddenly in the black water of the creek he saw a familiar, unbidden vision, the doleful procession of his people - women with papooses plodding along a muddy trace, shuffling grandmothers and grandfathers keeping watch over the small ones, some with burdens, the older children herding livestock that stopped to browse and wanted to stray. He saw old, blind Black Turtle, staff in hand, being led by one of his grandchildren, and tiny, wise Two Owls, bundled to her wrinkled chin in a blanket, riding atop a high-piled rickety wagon pulled by weary oxen. He saw himself astride his father's horse looking down at the dazed faces, carrying across his back the musket that was his only legacy from his father, its broken stock bound with rawhide, the repair an unlikely conjoining of white culture and Indian culture that seemed a metaphor for the Delaware's fate. Even now the vision of his people's trek evoked rage. That journey was only the most recent removal - from a thin-soiled, rocky refuge in the hills along the James Fork in Missouri where they'd survived floods and hunger and harassment by white settlers before being squeezed from that place too. Before that they were removed from Indiana where En-di-ond was born, and before that from Ohio where his parents were born, and before that from their tribal homeland far to the east on the Delaware River where countless generations had lived in a time of storied peace and plenty before squandering their birthright for rusty hatchets and thin blankets and watered rum and broken promises.

When would it end? When would the whites have enough? When would his people have a home? Even now, with his tribe barely re-settled once again, whites tramped through Delaware land on their way to Oregon and Santa Fe, helping themselves to Delaware timber, making off with any stray horses and cattle, contemptuous of protest. The white man's justice was a mockery.

The Delaware hunter raised eyes saddened by the flood of memories. He suddenly knew he needed to cleanse his spirit of the pain and invoke the strength of the One Above. He needed to give himself a vision for battle.

He shrugged off his blanket, shed his clothes, and stepped naked onto the ice of the creek. He thought of how the little stream wended its way through the pueblo to join the Rio Grande on its long journey to the salty sea and the morning sun. From the sea the One Above would take this water back into the sky and return it to the earth, sweet again. Perhaps the water would return to this very land, perhaps to the sacred, snow-capped mountain of the pueblo. A circle of life. He stepped into the knee-high coursing stream and stood for some time, his feet and legs growing numb from the icey water. "Perhaps," Endi-ond thought, "in another life I will cleanse my spirit in this same water again." He made himself fall to his knees, then pitched forward full-length into the frigid water.

The shock and ache were greater than the pain in his heart. His head immersed, he anchored himself to the rocky bottom until he desperately needed to breathe. He raised up to take several gasping breaths, then plunged in again. Feeling began to leave his hands and arms and legs. His diaphragm pumped fruitlessly for air as he fought the urge to raise his head. He felt himself become one with the water. A pleasant warmth began to gather close around his heart, which seemed to shrink smaller and smaller and yet grew warmer as he felt himself slipping away in the bubbles that escaped his nose. His spirit was leaving his body. He was enveloped by peace and well-being. In a dreamlike way he suddenly realized why his people always left a place for a dead person's spirit to escape the grave.

He pushed himself to his knees with a mighty effort, gasping for air, water pouring from his head and shoulders, giddy from his ordeal. Recovering for a few moments, still tingling, he scooped a mouthful of water and awkwardly regained his feet. He held the mouthful of water to warm it with his spirit. He stumbled to his clothes to fetch a pinch of tobacco from his pouch, shaking so violently that he spilled much of the pouch, but he succeeded in squirting water from his mouth and making a tobacco offering for each of the four winds, and a final, impromptu offering for the One Above.

Shivering, his teeth chattering, he rubbed himself so vigorously with his blanket that his legs and arms would later feel raw, but his heart no longer ached as he donned his clothes, his chilled muscles making his movements awkward and jerky. Then he stood wrapped in his blanket until the shivering subsided. Yes, he had to fight, but not just to avenge Red Willows' death or for anger at his people's fate. He had to fight for the living, for Nicholas and for Sun Runner and for Tomasito and all those who befriended him in the pueblo. He had to fight for those who had gone before and kept this place near the sacred mountain for him to enjoy.

He sensed movement and looked up to see the ghostly shape of a white owl glide overhead. He watched it flap and glide, flap and glide up the course of the stream until it disappeared in the darkness. So effortless. So pure. He took a deep, shivery breath of the crisp night air, knowing that in the owl he had just seen something holy.

Oh, how he loved this land! So vast, so rich with game, its people rooted like trees. I want this place to be here, forever, he thought. I want to enjoy this land until I'm old. And then I want to come back as an eagle or a cloud and enjoy it again and again. That is what I truly want. This land is what I fight for.

Suppression

Santa Fe

So you didn't really see anything, any fighting? What you're telling us is all the word of some Mexican?" With his tunic unbuttoned and a nightshirt tucked into his trousers, Colonel Sterling Price sat in candlelight behind a bare table in the Governor's Palace in Santa Fe, his irritation at being roused in the middle of a cold night plain for all to see.

Thick-tongued, swaying with weariness, Town stood before the grumpy colonel at a loss, wishing he hadn't guzzled whiskey at Beckwourth's tavern. Unable to go beyond what he'd already reported, he nodded dumbly. Behind him he heard someone yawn.

"But why would he ride all day and half the night if there wasn't something to it?" Beckwourth asked. "You've got to give him that!" The colonel dismissed Beckwourth with a glance. The counsel of a Negro half-blood clearly bore little weight with Colonel Price, a Missouri congressman who'd resigned his seat for an officer's commission in the Mexican war and now commanded the 2nd Missouri Volunteers.

"Look, Town," the colonel said, pointedly ignoring Beckwourth, "if I jumped at every rumor we've heard in the last two months I'd have this regiment spread from here to Kingdom Come. We're too thin as it is. I need more proof than some secondhand story started by some Mexican."

"But the screams - I...." Town stopped, defeated by his own muddled thoughts. He turned to Beckwourth for help, his look pleading. Beckwourth wondered if he should tell how Town had pounded desperately on his tavern door and burst into tears of relief when the door opened. The exhausted rider hadn't even noticed the cocked pistol in Beckwourth's hand, a precaution for the late night disturbance. But what was the use of saying more? Price wanted proof of an uprising in Taos, something more than even a white man's word. The half-blood tavern-keeper shrug-ged. Let Price find out for himself, the arrogant fool!

"But perhaps the Colonel would consider a reconnaissance," someone offered. "Show the flag, so to speak."

"On what?" Price snapped. "Goddamned burros? We can barely keep our Goddamned couriers in saddle!"

111

True. Kearny's horse-heavy Army of the West had so ravaged the fragile grazing grounds around Santa Fe that Colonel
Price had sent most of his horses and draft animals to forage on
the other side of the Sangre de Cristos mountains. Virtually his
entire regiment was afoot. He now commanded a force that was
reduced to hobbling about like infantry.

Colonel Price stood. "Proof! gentlemen, get me proof and I'll
act!" And with that dictum he stomped off to bed.

Charley Autobees brought proof just a day later, a tightly
rolled, hand-written paper and a sullen Pueblo Indian prisoner.
"It's a call to arms," an American trader said, skimming the
first few lines of the paper. He'd been summoned by Price to
decipher the document because not a single officer in Price's
command could read more than a few words of Spanish.

"A call to arms!" Price said.

"What they call a *pronunciamento*."

"I don't give a good God...I don't care what the hell they call
it! What does it say!"

The trader continued reading, summarizing aloud. "Well,
the usual - you know, loyal sons, mother Mexico - ah, here...*la
hora está aqui*...the hour has come to raise the bloody banner of
liberty and..." He heard the irritation in Price's sharp intake of
breath and hurried on. "...but it basically says they're going to
drive us Americans out of New Mexico."

"That bullshit again! What else? Does it say when, or how?"

The translator scanned the document. "I, ah, I don't see it
right off. Might be buried in all this foofaraw."

"Maybe it's in code, or invisible ink," an officer suggested.

"You think the Indian prisoner knows?" another asked.

Price looked exasperated. "Well, write out a full translation.
See what the hell else you can get out of it. We'll deal with the
Indian later."

He returned his attention to Charley, sizing him up. He saw
a large, grimy, bleary-eyed, ugly man, clearly ill at ease in the
bustle of words.

"All right, Otterbee, what else."

112

"Autobees," an aide corrected, "Charley Autobees."

Price flicked an impatient glance at the aide. "All right, Autobees," he said with elaborate care, "tell me how you came by that paper."

Charley hardly knew where to begin. Bone-weary after more than two days of scant sleep, his memory of events was blurred. It was Turley's mill that he wanted to talk about, the fires around Turley's mill.

Charley and the Delaware had set out from Charley's ranch in the dark, after Charley led the Indian out of earshot of the women to tell him about meeting up with Town and learning of Bent's murder. He told about seeing the mob making for Turley's mill. "They'll want my hair too, hamigo," Charley said. "If there's fighting they'll be coming here too, so I'm heading for the Arkansas first thing in the morning, after I find Jose and my boy and get a couple of fresh horses."

The Indian remained silent for a long time, then said he didn't think Charley should go north. The Arkansas was five days distant, on the other side of winter mountains. Charley would be alone on the trail. He might get snowbound and trouble catch up with him. Or maybe Turley would talk things out and settle matters peacefully.

No, a better plan would be for Charley to go back to Turley's place and see what was going on. If there was fighting at Turley's, then Charley should set off for Santa Fe. He could avoid Taos and the pueblos and get to the safety of Santa Fe before the trouble spread. And even if he ran into trouble on his way south at least he'd be headed towards help.

Charley was persuaded by the Delaware's reasoning, then had to be talked out of waiting until morning to find Jose and securing a fresh horse. "You better move and move fast," the Indian said. "I'll go down with you to Turley's."

So Charley saddled up his mule again, said brief good-byes, and climbed aboard. He made his kids hold the dog back as the Indians also got their mounts in motion. The two wives stood silhouted in the doorway wrapped in their *rebosas* against the cold. They were sullen, their displeasure evident at being left alone again in this isolated corner of the foothills.

Charley and the Indians rode back to Turley's mill in silence, Charley letting his stumble-weary mule find the way. Nicholas perched behind his mother on one of the ponies. It was perhaps nine o'clock when they reached a point of vantage where they could look down into Turley's compound. Below they saw figures moving across the light of a dozen bonfires. The night was nearly moonless, but through a haze of clouds the starshine gave shape to the buildings below. The still, damp air carried smells of woodsmoke and cooking meat. "Beef," the Delaware said.

"Maybe Turley's seed stock," Charley sighed. "A couple of black cattle he brought out last spring for breeding. He treated 'em like pets."

They watched the scene for several minutes, seeing the brief flash of a musket and later hearing its muffled pop and an answering flash and later pop from the mill. They heard faint whoops and occasional laughter. Charley felt an immense sadness overtake him. Here he stood on the rim of the arroyo above the fray, seeing the inevitable doom of his friends in the mill. And suddenly he thought of the man who'd stood helpless while Charley's father drowned, an image Charley had carried like a curse since very early boyhood - of his father's arm raised in a plea for help as a raging river-current swept him away.

The abject witness had come to see Charley's mother. He told her he was sorry but he'd been helpless to do anything. "Why?" Charley cried, his tears hot, his question an accusation. "Why didn't you? You didn't even try!" The man looked down at Charley with the most sorrowful face Charley had ever seen. Tears streaked his leathery cheeks as he stood dumbly, unable to say more. Now Charley knew how the man felt.

Charley tried to swallow the lump in his throat as he made ready to leave. "There's a trail up here runs west," he said, his raspy voice strained. "Down to Dolores. I can go that way." He patted the neck of his exhausted mule.

But he didn't want to go to Dolores. He didn't want to go anywhere. He wanted to hide - in a cave or a bear den. He wanted to wrap himself in a blanket and not emerge until spring, until after this sudden madness was done. To reach Santa Fe seemed an impossible goal.

The Indian slid off his horse. "Get off that mule," the Delaware said.

"What?"

114

"Get off that mule. Take my horse."

"Whirlwind?"

"He'll outrun anything. That sorry mule's going to quit before sun-up and we're staying up here until morning anyway. I'm not going down there in the dark and get shot."

Charley dismounted, instantly relieved. With a fresher mount he might make it safely to Santa Fe. Silently he blessed the Indian.

He felt as if he should make a joke to lighten the moment, perhaps say something about having to ride Whirlwind Indian-style, knowing he'd never be able to put his saddle on the Delaware's horse.

But he could think of no words, and as the men exchanged their reins he felt the lump in his throat grow. "Obliged, hamigo," he managed to say, his voice even huskier than normal. He did not risk saying more for fear he'd start to cry. The Indian seemed impassive.

Charley handed his musket to the young hunter, jumped to get a leg over the big sorrel's back, and hauled himself up. He waited until the horse got used to him, then leaned for his musket. He shook the Delaware's hand for a long time. Finally he signed a farewell to Red Willows and Nicholas and turned Whirlwind to seek out the trail to Dolores. "You bring my horse back, Charley, you hear?" the Delaware said. Charley waved without turning around, his gesture almost lost in the darkness.

"Charley! Charley!"

Colonel Price's aide was shaking Charley's shoulder. "You said you got the *pronunciamento* off an Indian who hid it in his quiver."

Charley collected himself. He was numb with fatigue. He nodded.

"But you couldn't read it," the aide prompted again. Charley had already told his disjointed story to the officer of the day. He shook his head. "But you knew it was important so you took the Indian prisoner." Charley nodded. "And then you went to this Frenchman's place and he went and got someone who could read what the paper said, a priest." Charley nodded again.

115

Maybe not a priest, but someone who could read, a Mexican he didn't know up at Embudo. Charley's memory was blurred. By the time he reached Baptiste Chalifoux's crude little house with his Indian prisoner he had gone without sleep for a day and a half and ridden 80 or 90 miles. He'd crossed Picuris Mountain twice. Exhausted, he could scarcely follow the tortured conversation between Baptiste and the Mexican as the Mexican tried to explain with his Spanish-English pidgin what the paper said and Baptiste with his French-English pidgin tried to understand.

After the Mexican left for home Baptiste had ridden up the Taos trail for a distance to keep a lookout in case an enemy force appeared while Charley tried to get an hour or two of rest. But although he was too tired to take another step he found himself unable to sleep. After a time he rose to pace Chalifoux's crude adobe house, lay down again, got up to pace, and finally in mid-afternoon fell into a fitful doze.

"And last night the two of you brought your prisoner down here." Charley nodded. They had started at dusk after tying their prisoner's feet under one of Baptiste's burros.

The first part of the trail was difficult in the darkness. They had cautiously skirted the scattered settlements - La Joya, Los Luceros, San Juan, La Cañada, Pojoque. Pushing hard, they passed Teseque in the predawn and reached the first houses of Santa Fe just after sun-up, startling a sentry post on the road by the new fort.

"Who's the prisoner?" Price asked. "What made you suspicious of him?"

Charley half shrugged. He tried to think. They had spotted each other at about the same time on Picurus Mountain. The Indian was afoot on the trail headed south, maybe a hundred yards ahead. Seeing Charley, he'd bolted from the trail and started scrabbling up the detritus to get away. Charley fired a shot to bring him to a halt, the ball whining off a rock near the Indian's head. Maybe it was anger that had made him shoot at the frightened Indian, a young man of perhaps twenty. "I don't know. I was mad, I guess. I just wanted to know why he was running, why he was trying to get away."

"And a damned good thing too, Charley," the aide said, prompting Price. The Colonel nodded agreement and gave Charley a small smile.

116

"And what about Governor Bent?" Price asked. "What do you know about that?"

Charley shook his head. "Just what Town told me, that a mob killed him."

"Anybody else? Did you hear about them killing anybody else?"

Charley looked blank.

"Did they kill anybody else in Taos?"

Charley shrugged. "Don't know," he said.

"Tell the colonel what you saw when you got back to Turley's mill," the aide said.

"Fires," Charley answered.

"Fires?"

"Siege fires, Colonel," the aide said. "By the time he got back to Turley's that night he saw maybe two or three hundred men camped out around the mill."

"Jesus! Two or three hundred! How many men are in the mill? Are the Mormons still up there? How many Americans?"

Charley looked blank, then began to count slowly on his fingers. "Nine, maybe ten," he said. "I guess the Mormons left. They weren't there. A couple of Turley's men are Frenchmen - LeBlanc and Tolque. And a foreign guy named Marshall."

"Jesus! Can they hold out?" Price asked. "Do you think they can hold out?"

Charley studied the floor. So much had happened, so much he didn't understand. How was it that things had suddenly gone so bad? How was it that all of a sudden his whole life was turned upside down? Hell, the whole world turned upside down!

When at last he raised his eyes to regard the impatient colonel his face was a map of sorrow and fatigue. "How soon can you get there?" he rasped, the tone of his utterance betraying an exhausted, abject hopelessness.

The Volunteers

Yow! We're gonna fight!" one of Colonel Price's men cried. Word had come down that they were going to meet the enemy, a rebel army of hundreds marching on Santa Fe from the direction of Taos.

The Americans were ready for a fight, all right! Nearly six months after enlisting, the disgruntled volunteers of the 2nd Missouri had no more to show for their soldiering than a long, hot march across the desert and weeks of boring garrison duty in the dusty little capital of Santa Fe. They drilled and stood inspections and pulled guard duty and choked down Army fare and worked like mules on the new fort overlooking the town. And they had yet to fire a shot in battle. A fine lot for a soldier! Meanwhile their brothers in the 1st Missouri had marched south to score a lop-sided victory over the Mexicans near El Paso. Oh, the men of the 2nd were ready for a fight all right, any kind of fight!

But Colonel Price had a few problems in going to meet the enemy. For one thing, the 2nd had no horses. Most of its animals wintered at grazing camps on the other side of the Sangre de Cristos, inaccessible on short notice. For another, an epidemic of measles had swept through northern New Mexico that winter and killed or sickened hundreds, including many of his men.

But Colonel Price couldn't afford to wait. With the enemy on the march from Taos he had to act, and he scrambled to put together a fighting force from his Santa Fe companies.

It wasn't much. The only artillery he could spare was a battery of four stubby mountain howitzers from a St. Louis company, twelve-pounders that barely outranged a musket, good for lobbing bombs but little else. The rest of his artillery he needed to hold back in case of a flanking attack on Santa Fe. As for troops, he could go forth with just seven companies - companies thinned by sickness and death and resignations and desertions, each able to muster only about forty men.

Desperate for help, Price sent word to Albuquerque to bring up reinforcements and called on the civilians in Santa Fe to raise a mounted volunteer company.

Some called this volunteer company the "mountain men" company. While it was true that many of the 68 Americans and

118

French-Canadians and Mexicans who signed up were former-mountain men, many were simply teamsters and miners and traders and store clerks. Indeed, other than their anger over the news of Governor Bent's murder and the attack on Turley's mill, their only common bonds were their horses. Each man could provide a horse to ride into battle, and these volunteers would give Price his only mounted fighters. But they never called themselves the "mountain men" company. They were "St. Vrain's men." With the body of Charles Bent a-moldering in Taos, Ceran St. Vrain wanted revenge for his partner's death, and it was the blood in his eye as much as his wealth and station that inspired Colonel Price to commission the patriarchal merchant as captain of the Santa Fe volunteers.

St. Vrain's volunteers mirrored the composition of the trader-trapper-merchant class of the American West. Privates all, Charley and Tom Autobees and Town were Americans, Baptiste Chalifoux and the Leroux brothers were French-Canadians, the Esquival brothers were New Mexicans. Dick Green, the dead governor's servant-slave, was also one of St. Vrain's men, but he was unofficial and not carried on the muster rolls. Neither did he own a horse. Sent down from Bent's Fort to Santa Fe after Charles Bent assumed his responsibilities as governor, Dick Green's status as a slave in New Mexico was a sticky legal issue. Was a Missouri slave legal in the new American territory? Probably not. But America's conquest of New Mexico had bubbled up so many sticky legal issues that Green's slave status hardly stood out.

Nonetheless, Green approached St. Vrain and asked if he too could join the Santa Fe company. St. Vrain rummaged among his own possessions to equip Green with a musket and accoutrements and found a place for Bent's servant as a teamster on one of the quartermaster wagons.

Three days after Charley brought in the *pronunciamento,* Price's diminutive army got under way on Saturday, January 23, a cold, overcast day that promised snow.

The Americans knew little about the enemy they were about to confront. Those familiar with the area's often violent political past recognized some of the men who'd attached their names to the *pronunciamento.* Troublemakers of old, did they lead the insurgent army? Colonel Price wasn't sure. Indeed, except for rumor and speculation Price knew nothing more about the situation in the distant Taos valley than what he'd learned from Town and Charley. Was Turley's mill still holding out?

119

Had the uprising spread east across the Sangre de Cristos to threaten the Army's supply lines? What kind of fighting force would they meet, and where?

Keeping some of St. Vrain's men in front of his regiment as scouts, Price marched on foot at the head of a column that stretched almost two miles on a narrow, rock-strewn trail, a trail that had never seen so many massed wheels as the mule-powered supply train bumping along at the rear. The trail would take him past the Teseque pueblo and to the Pojuaque pueblo by nightfall, some thirteen miles distant. There, absent the enemy, they would bed down for the night. Next day he'd march his men through the village of La Cañada until he struck the Rio Grande, then follow the river north though several small towns to Embudo. If he didn't meet the rebels sooner he expected to confront them at a narrow pass just south of Embudo. One of the Army's topographical engineers had called it "a damned Thermopylae," a perfect place to hold off an army. Of course, he'd been thinking of Americans holding off Mexicans.

Price and his men met the enemy sooner rather than later. In the early afternoon next day about twenty of St. Vrain's men came thundering back up the track to meet the van of the column. Yipping and waving their hats, they shouted, "We found 'em! We found 'em!" A man named Metcalfe, a tall, affable fur trader the volunteers elected as St. Vrain's 1st lieutenant, reined in his horse with great drama. Metcalfe's eyes glittered. "We found 'em!" he announced proudly.

"Where?" Price asked the novice officer. "How many?"

Metcalfe struggled to control his panting, lathered horse. "What?"

"Where are they, man, how many? How many are there?"

Metcalfe looked at Price with a dumbfounded expression. The blood drained from his face. How was he supposed to know? In the distance they looked like a swarm of ants. St. Vrain, who'd been keeping Price company, gave Metcalfe an encouraging nod. Metcalfe swallowed. "Just this side of the river, in the valley," he said. Price exchanged looks with St. Vrain. Oh, if only they could blast them from the heights with field guns!

"And they're headed this way!"

120

"Damn!" Price said. "How many?"

"Well, Jesus," Metcalfe said, his voice uncertain, "I don't know. Hard to say...." Price sent St. Vrain another look, his exasperation with the volunteer officer plain. Metcalfe looked from one man to the other, at a loss. "Well, Christ!" he cried finally, "the buggers are all over the place! Maybe twelve, fifteen hundred. They're all over the place!"

Price ordered his command forward in quick march. If the enemy was coming to meet him he wanted to fight from the high ground. Better yet, he wanted to get control of La Cañada, a fortified village some five miles distant.

Too late. When his winded, sweaty troops reached a small stream that skirted La Cañada they found the enemy ensconced on the opposite side. The rebels occupied several scattered adobe houses but seemed to be concentrated in a cluster of three buildings that formed the heart of a rancho. Behind the rancho an adobe wall enclosed a large orchard that also teemed with enemy. Hundreds more, mounted and afoot, were drawn up in formation on a hill behind the orchard and on several finger-like hills to the east. As the Price and his principal officers regarded the enemy, another large mounted force suddenly materialized on a long hill to the west, somewhat to his rear. The Americans stood awestruck. So many! After a quick survey Price concluded Metcalfe's estimate was not far off. He might be outnumbered four-to-one. But he saw no artillery.

In his hurry to command the high ground Price had left his ammunition wagons far behind. Nonetheless he decided to engage at once. Keeping his footsoldiers safely out of musket range, he sent the four howitzers across the little stream to open fire on the houses and the finger-like hills to the east. Soon three of the stubby guns were blasting away at the adobe houses near the orchard, while the fourth fired on another house on the right flank. But they didn't fire with impunity. Enemy musketballs whizzed. They ricocheted off the guns and carriages and holed the artillerymen's hats and clothing. A gunner fell wounded with a gaping wound in his throat. Another screamed when he took a ball in his leg. The twelve-pounders boomed away.

"They're after the wagons, Colonel!" one of Price's officers cried. Price looked back to see the enemy horsemen on his west flank pouring down the hill. If they got between him and his supply wagons they would cut off the ammunition reserves for his artillery!

"Ceran! Get back there and keep those sons-a-bitches away from our wagons!"

St. Vrain's company raced back to confront the enemy in a wild, undisciplined charge that saw every man for himself and Charley pushing Whirlwind to the very front of the pack. He had broken Whirlwind to a borrowed saddle, and with his back arched to keep his weight behind on the big pounding horse Charley's hair streamed behind like a battle pennant. In the distance the wagons jumped and careened as whip-driven mules flew over the rough ground towards the safety of the Americans.

"Cut 'em off, Charley, cut 'em off!" St. Vrain cried, his words unintelligible in the thunder of hooves. Charley glanced back to see St. Vrain gesturing desperately with his sword. He wanted Charley and the lead riders to swing behind the attackers. Gesturing for Tom, Charley steered Whirlwind in that direction and was followed by two dozen yowling, whooping riders, while St. Vrain managed to direct Metcalfe and the rest of the horsemen straight ahead to the wagons. Within a minute the two-pronged rescue neared the first of the wagons and threatened to envelop the attackers.

Seeing they might be surrounded, the enemy broke off their attack and scattered toward the Rio Grande. Except for two hapless men who'd climbed into a wagon abandoned by its driver. Intent on pilfering the still rolling vehicle, they didn't notice the arrival of St. Vrain's men. As horsemen got the wagon's team under control and brought the vehicle to a halt the looters emerged from beneath the arch of the canvas to look about with wild surprise. The last thing they saw was the smokey blast of a half dozen muskets.

After St. Vrain's men herded the supply wagons to the safety of the main force, Price ordered a charge on the lone house on the right flank. Standing at the base of the hills, the house poured forth an incessant rattle of musketfire that was giving the artillery a hard time. Two companies of volunteer infantry charged down the canyon slope through a fringe of leafless willows to splash across the icy stream. Formerly with the 1st Missouri, now deployed in Mexico, the two attacking companies had been left behind because they were footsoldiers, the clean-up guys. Today these "clean up guys" were determined to show their worth. After all, had not Colonel Kearny himself opined that infantry with bayonets was the backbone of an army? Now, their bayonets flashing in the weak gleam of late afternoon sun, their voices raised in a shrill, inchoate cry of animal passion, the two companies charged the house. Shocked by the ferocity of the American assault, the enemy fled after a brief fusillade and retreated up the finger-like hills, but not before one of the Missouri men caught a ball between his eyes that blew his brains out the back of his head.

The troublesome house under control, Price sent down a third company as reinforcements and ordered St. Vrain's men to sweep behind the rebels on the hills. He wanted to cut off their retreat. Simultaneously he sent three of the four remaining companies ahead to attack the rancho and the orchard stronghold, which now received the punishment of all four howitzers.

The combined assault broke the enemy. Committing the last of his reserves, Price sent his final company up the four finger-like hills. Assaulted from the front and threatened by St. Vrain's men in the rear, the enemy fled from the hills toward La Cañada, soon joined by hundreds more streaming in panic from the protection of the rancho and the walled orchard. With the enemy in full retreat, Price ordered his artillery to a hill behind the orchard where he could command the town of La Cañada.

But the enemy forces didn't retreat to the protection of La Cañada. Many fled straight through the little town toward the Rio Grande. Others scattered north through the hills, and as the sun sank in the late winter afternoon hundreds of tiny, fleeing figures disappeared into the gathering gloom.

That night the American troops bivouacked in La Cañada, whose principal feature was a large church, a cross-shaped structure of unfinished adobe some 150 feet in length, *La Iglesia Nuestra Señora de Carmel y San Francisco*. Crude and cavernous, dirt-floored, devoid of furnishings except for the altar area and the two side chapels, its only decorations were several crudely painted *retablos* behind the altar and a life-size, carved Jesus lying in state in a niche with one nail-holed hand raised in blessing. The hand was missing parts of two fingers.

Giggling nervously, the parish priest fidgeted, then finally folded both hands over his paunch to disguise their trembling. Like other New Mexico clergy he'd journeyed to Santa Fe to pledge allegiance to the new American government, never imagining his true allegiance would be tested. Now he found himself compelled to deal with a government he bitterly resented. Appealing to St. Vrain to respect the sanctity of the church, he assured him the townspeople were innocent bystanders to the turmoil.

St. Vrain waved aside the priest's appeal. One of the few Americans with Price who was fluent in Spanish, St. Vrain told the priest that American soldiers would bed down in the church. The cleric blanched at St. Vrain's pronouncement, but with the Americans already positioning their howitzers just outside the church grounds, he giggled and said, of course. Then at a word-to-the-wise suggestion from St. Vrain, the priest scurried off to see that some of the populace doubled up with relatives to make their houses available for the wounded and American officers. Thus far almost forty wounded Mexicans and Indians had been carried into La Cañada. By the time darkness fell, just five hours after Metcalfe galloped up with word of the enemy's number, the Americans were settling into the best La Cañada had to offer, firmly in control.

In one of the side chapels of the church several nuns from the *convento* tended the six American wounded, four of them artillerymen. On the other side of the transept nuns also prepared two Americans for burial - the soldier who had his brains blown out in the charge on the house and another killed in the charge on the hills, a civilian teamster who'd volunteered to help fill out one of the under-strength Missouri companies, a mere youth.

That evening Baptiste Chalifoux approached Charley. Grizzled and barrel-shaped, Baptiste had spent much of his life roaming the west as a trapper before settling down in Embudo. He pronounced Charley's name "Shawlee." Now in his French-English pidgin he said, "Shawlee, Big Nigger give you big horse, *n'est-ce pas? Mais* I tink I see him out dere, big as bear, *chapeau rouge, n'est-ce pas?* He fight, Shawlee, he fight wi' dese dam Mesican! Why you tink, Shawlee? Why you tink he fight dis time?"

Charley gave Baptiste a blank look. Big Nigger fighting with the rebels? Why? The Indian told him that he was going to stay out of the fray. What in the world had turned him?

Early next day the American lookout in the church belfry spotted a mounted enemy force on a distant hill. Bugles and drums called the weary American troops into formation once again, and within minutes Price had them marching out to confront the foe. But the enemy sank from sight behind the hill, and by the time St. Vrain's horsemen reached the summit where the enemy had appeared the entire force had vanished.

For the rest of the day townspeople and Americans scoured the battlefield to find any remaining wounded and to pick up the dead. By noon they'd brought in 36 enemy corpses. They laid the bodies in a row on the little plaza for identification. "Look at those mongrels!" one of Missouri men said. "Every damned color! Bastards must breed like dogs!"

The priest identified one of the dead, a compact, swarthy man with long, glossy black hair. He was Jesus Tafoya, a rebel "general." Tafoya had dressed for battle in the green uniform coat of the Mexican militia. Sometime during the day someone among Price's men cut off one of Tafoya's ears.

La Cañada

Charley slouched against the wall by the rectory door and listened to St. Vrain hold forth. The wealthy trader had a dandy side, Charley thought. The folds of his white, fancy-front shirt looked alive in the firelight, and even in this room packed with unwashed men and thick with tobacco smoke Charley caught an occasional whiff of St. Vrain's cologne. Among his unkempt audience St. Vrain stood out like a big-city preacher. He refreshed his incongruious stemmed glass from a bottle of claret on the floor by his side.

Word had gotten out. The evening before, relieved to learn from locals that the wives and children of Americans living in Taos had been spared from the violence, St. Vrain had sat by this same fireplace sipping claret and keeping a dozen men of the 2nd entralled as he told story after story about Charles Bent. But tonight he was talking about New Mexico, and perhaps 40 men were crowded into the church rectory to be entertained.

The Missouri 2nd was a cocky bunch, reflecting Price's own new confidence. Having routed a superior force in the battle of La Cañada, Price had seen enough to know the rebels were poorly led, undisciplined, and badly out-gunned. With Santa Fe safe from rebel attack, Price could afford to wait for reinforcements for his push north. Already enough horses had come in from across the mountains for Price to mount half a company. With St. Vrain's volunteers the 2nd now had more than 90 horsemen, and Price expected reinforcements from Albuquerque any day. But no need to hurry. In Taos the dead were dead.

"Sometimes we just seem to go in circles," St. Vrain mused as he stared into the crackling fireplace. "Ten years ago it was just like now. 1837. Word came down to Santa Fe that La Cañada was up in arms and a bunch of rebels were setting up their own government."

Charley vaguely remembered the time. Men from La Cañada had come up to Taos and made speeches on the plaza about a new government - of the people and for the people. They promised no one would pay taxes under the new government. To Charley the speeches were gibberish but he'd drunk the free liquor and pretended to cheer with the rest.

"The rebels back then were riled up about taxes just like

now," St. Vrain continued. "They said the government in Santa Fe was going to make you pay a tax to do it with your wife." His audience burst into laughter. "And the people believed them." Now the rectory rocked. *"Vraiment!"* St. Vrain cried, wearing a broad grin. *"Vraiment!"*

As the laughter died he shook his head and licked a fresh cigar, a small smile playing above his bearded chin. "But you'll throw a lot of rocks in this country before you hit a man who can read and write. Fact is, nobody paid taxes anyway. That's why they taxed us traders. We paid our duties in cash, practically the only cash the government got. Fact is, people around here can barely scrape up enough to pay a priest to get married and buried, let alone pay taxes. Except for us traders, all the government gets is labor, so many days of a man's time to fix roads and such."

"Some roads!" The room laughed again.

"Well, that's right," St. Vrain said, acknowledging the wisecrack with a wry smile. "But when rumors got started about those new taxes the people believed them. There were already stories about the new governor down in Santa Fe, one of those *grandee* fellas sent up from way down in Mexico - how he ate off gold and silver dishes and had orgies in the Governor's Palace. Oh, the rumors flew thick and fast, all right."

"Sounds like Missouri, Captain," someone called out. The room laughed again and St. Vrain joined them. Then he seemed to be back in his memories as he took time to bite the end off his cigar and get his smoke going from a fireplace brand.

Something in St. Vrain's reflective mood caused Charley's own thoughts to turn inward, and he suddenly remembered that time as being the low point in his life. He'd just spent another miserable winter trapping beaver in the Rockies, had come down to Taos to sell his disappointing take of furs, and had started drinking.

A good binge was nothing new for a trapper after a long thirst, but there was something different about Charley's drinking that spring. After having lived several years of a fur trapper's life with a Cheyenne wife and then a Flathead wife and some other Indian wives between, Charley was starting to feel he wanted no more icy streams and hard winters and Indian wives. Enough dugouts and teepees! He wanted an easier life. Besides, if he never went back to his Flathead wife she'd just take up with somebody else anyway.

But as matters turned out it was impossible for him to get back unless he'd hoofed it. Even now Charley was unsure how he'd managed to drink and gamble away a year's earnings in a month's time. Almost two hundred dollars. Even his horses.

Oh! that drunk was a buster, all right! Old-timers still remembered Charley's drunk as one of the best, and the old-timers in Taos had seen some mighty wicked drunks. Finally, when Charley waked one morning with still another massive hangover and possessing little more than the clothes he wore he began to realize that he looked and stunk like a derelict and felt like he was at the bottom of a deep, dark well looking up. The people in Taos avoided his eyes. The world he once enjoyed looked impossible to reclaim.

He began to brood, and in the depth of his self-pity he realized that for the first time since setting out on his own from St. Louis as a youth he was not able to send a few dollars back to his mother for her birthday. After that realization, Charley swore off drinking, cleaned himself up, and went to work for Turley.

"So this Mexican grandee comes up from Santa Fe," St. Vrain continued. "Figures he'll talk to the rebels. He met up with them just downriver, near that big butte, the one we call Black Mesa." St. Vrain told how the Mexican governor had mustered a few presidial soldiers and some militia as protection, but no sooner did he meet the rebels for negotiation than the shooting started and most of his badly outnumbered troops deserted to the other side. The governor fled back to Santa Fe, then lit out for the safety of Albuquerque. But after a few miles his party was cut off by the rebels and massacred.

"He fought to the death, they say, but he got his head kicked around the plaza in Santa Fe for his trouble." The rectory was quiet. Americans were unused to the idea of cutting off an enemy's head and kicking it around like a ball. Rumors of Charles Bent's own decapitation had horrified Price's men.

"There was a great bunch of us American traders in Santa Fe at the time, most of us just passing through in a big caravan going down to the fair in Chihuahua. So when we heard the rebels were coming down to take over Santa Fe we got ready to defend ourselves. Well, let me tell you, we had guns like porcupine quills on the plaza, maybe five or six hundred all told. Every one of us had maybe a half dozen.

"But the Mexicans never bothered us. They came to town

and set up their new government and we went our separate ways." St. Vrain puffed his cigar, contemplative.

"After a while some of the rebels made a trip to Missouri to see if the United States would take in New Mexico as a new territory. They figured they got nothing but abuse from the government down in Mexico anyway, so why not? But nothing came of it."

"So what happened," someone asked. "Did Mexico just let the rebels be?"

St. Vrain snorted. "Oh, no! No, sirree! That's when Armijo came up from Albuquerque."

The Missouri men knew of Armijo, the Mexican governor who'd fled Kearny's Army of the West and abandoned his land to the Americans, a man they considered a fat, slippery coward. "Armijo didn't want to come up," St. Vrain continued, "but the people down in Albuquerque made him. After all, he was in charge of the militia and needed to restore order. So he marches up with a couple hundred militiamen and negotiates. 'Give me your leader to bring to justice,' he says, 'And we'll forget the whole thing.' Well, by this time the rebels had gotten to squabling among themselves anyway, so they convinced the rebel governor to turn himself in and Armijo shot him on the spot. After a priest confessed him, of course. Then Armijo made himself governor."

Charley remembered the story that had come up to Taos. Armijo and the rebel governor had greeted each other and shook hands, exchanging brief pleasantries. Then Armijo said, "Confess him, padre," indicating the rebel leader with a brief pursing of his lips. A priest heard his confession. Minutes later a firing squad shot the man dead. That incident did not do much to help the priest's reputation, a well-known community figure from Taos.

"The priest was from Taos," St. Vrain said, "Antonio Martinez. Some say he cooked up the surrender of the rebel governor just to get in good with Armijo because he knew the rebellion was finished anyway. Maybe that's true. I know Charles never trusted Martinez. 'How can you trust a rich priest?' he always said. No love lost between those two, I tell you. Part of it was that Martinez resented every dollar Charles ever made in this country. Actually, I wouldn't be surprised if the bastard didn't have his hand in this business too, the son of a bitch."

129

"That's not the way it was!" one of the Esquival brothers hissed later. Sprawled around the two brothers on the earthen floor of the church a couple hundred men slept the noisy sleep of soldiers.

"I know," his brother whispered back, "but how can we say that St. Vrain is wrong? He is the captain?"

"But it's not right that we don't speak up. Why is it so hard for us to speak up? Why don't we say, 'No, Señor St. Vrain, that's not the way it was? That's not what Governor Armijo did."

"I know, I know. It's hard to sit quiet." The brothers remained for some moments, each lost in his own throughts.

For several years the two young New Mexicans had worked the Missouri-Santa Fe trade alongside Americans. They'd seen the wealth and energy of bustling St. Louis and the promise of American enterprise and invention. In the enthusiasm of the hour they'd proudly joined St. Vrain's company to bring the murderers of Governor Bent to justice. But the mutilation of their dead countrymen and the open contempt of the Missouri volunteers for their two swarthy comrades-in-arms had tarnished the Esquival brothers' enthusiasm.

Breaking the silence the younger one whispered, "But if truth suffers, it doesn't die."

The older one snorted. "Pah! Old words! And who's going to end truth's suffering? You? Who's going to stand up and tell our stories true? Pah! St. Vrain scrambles our history and we sit like stones. We're too polite, we Mexicans, too respectful!"

Another long silence followed before the older brother continued. "Are we going to let these pushy Americans take our history too? Are we going to let them take our stories? And what about our children? What will they learn of our past? Have we no pride? Mexico is an independent country," he hissed. "A sovereign nation! Where is our pride?"

The younger brother didn't answer.

"Tell me, brother, how long are we going to let the truth suffer, eh? how long?"

Price marched out of La Cañada with a new fighting man, Dick Green, Charles Bent's servant-slave. Green had shot an enemy rider trying to grab the harness of his lead mules in the La Cañada conflict and saved his wagon from capture, an act of derring-do witnessed by several of St. Vrain's men. In recognition of his feat the men presented Green with a captured horse and invited him to join their company. He proudly rode out of La Cañada as a full-fledged soldier among the Santa Fe volunteers.

A mile or so from La Cañada, Price struck the Rio Grande. Here the trail branched west and north. Westward was the Old Spanish Trail, neither old nor Spanish nor much of a trail, but a general route that after 1,200 difficult miles led the intrepid traveler to the settlement of Los Angeles in California. Price followed the north branch. Sixty miles distant lay Taos.

All day Price followed the Rio Grande through a succession of small riverside flats and gravelly hills, land cultivated by Indians for generations. The soldiers passed winter-dead orchards of peach and apricot trees, stubble-fields of corn and wheat, and small dormant gardens. That night they bivouacked near a non-descript collection of houses called Los Luceros. Like every other house in New Mexico, the vigas of each abode were festooned with garlands of red chili peppers.

"What's the name of this place?" one of the Missouri men asked no one in particular.

"Los Luceros," another answered.

"What?"

"Los Luceros."

"What's that mean?"

"Lights. Los lights."

"What'd he say?

"Lost Lights."

"Lost Lights...wonder why they call it that?"

So Los Luceros became Lost Lights, just as the Purgatorio River became the Picketwire River, and a local brandy called *aguardiente* became "the ingredient" and dozens of other places and things in New Mexico assumed new identities in the minds of the dead-ear Americans invaders.

131

Next day, Thursday, January 28, reinforcements arrived, a road-weary company from Albuquerque commanded by Captain John Burgwin, a West Point graduate who'd served with Kearny's 1st Dragoons for a dozen years. But Dragoon captain or not, the horses in Burgwin's company had also gone with those units intending battle in lower Mexico, leaving his company afoot. Burgwin and his men had quick-marched more than 100 miles to Price's aid - U.S. Dragoons hurrying over the sand and rocks along the Rio Grande like infantry. Such was Army life!

Arriving with Burgwin's Dragoons was another company of Price's 2nd Missouri and a 6-pounder field gun with almost twice the range of the howitzers. The American force now numbered almost 500. To a fife and drum rendition of "The Girl I Left Behind Me" they set forth from Lost Lights in good spirits.

Embudo

Wal, Fitz," a messmate drawled, "I'll say this...I never seen a meaner place for fightin'." Fitz nodded and shifted the weight of his musket. Goddamned New Mexico, he thought. Boiling hot or freezing cold! Miserable Goddamn worthless pile of frozen shit!

A round-shouldered Dragoon of twenty-something, Fitz was a private who'd come up from Albuquerque in Captain Burgwin's company. Like many of the swaggering American soldiers, he was contemptous of everything Mexican. He derided the mud-brick houses, the simple daily fare of the people, the cookie-cutter clothing of the poor. He growled at street vendors who proferred their meagre wares and sneered at the constant religious processions that wended through the narrow, dusty streets. He would not even acknowledge the long-lashed, dark-eyed beauty of the señoritas.

He was a good soldier otherwise. Indeed, better than most. Meticulous about keeping his weaponry and equipment in good condition, he did his duty well and without complaint. Around his neck on a leather thong he wore a heavy silver cross. Badly battered, the cross seemed an oddity to those who knew anything about Fitz, an irreverent loner. But Fitz never explained his silver talisman. If asked why he wore such a big heavy cross he would just compress his lips and shake his head. It was a private matter.

Like others, Fitz had chaffed at the confusion and delays and sour luck that kept him from battle in New Mexico. He was nearly beside himself with frustration when his company had to give up their mounts and go on garrison duty in Albuquerque. Now, thanks to the rebellion, he had his chance to see some action.

That morning the column had turned away from the Rio Grande to follow a dry, rocky streambed up a long draw until it reached the top of a divide. Now they followed another streambed down the other side. The going was hard, and despite the sharp January air, sweat beaded the soldiers' foreheads. They stumbled and tripped over half-hidden rocks, avoided the steaming dung left by the horses ahead, slipped in the greasy residue of snowmelt, turned their ankles on the rocks and wagon ruts, and complained and cursed. Overhead, luminescent behind low, gray clouds, the sun hung like a fog-bound paper lantern. Drifts of brownish-gray snow cowered in the shade where slabs of upthrust rock blocked the sun's pale warmth. Ashy with windblown dust, barely sustaining life, forlorn mesquite, juniper, and piñon struggled for life in the detritus. So sere and depressing. The idea of shedding human blood over possession of such a place was ridiculous.

To the left a brooding monolith of fractured lava a couple of hundred feet tall now paralleled their route. To the right rose steep-sided hills of broken rock. In many places the track the column followed was scarcely wide enough for three men abreast. Beyond this ugly passageway lay Embudo, a small settlement strewn along a brief, abrupt-sided valley where Baptiste Chalifoux made his home. The dry streambeds the soldiers followed were the only practical route to Embudo; the Rio Grande now rushed through a deep gorge that made passage along its course impossible.

The men had been on the march for several hours when Metcalfe and his scouts brought word that 60 or 70 enemy waited in ambush ahead. Colonel Price ordered St. Vrain's men, Fitz's company, and elements of the 2nd Missouri under the command of Captain Burgwin to flush them out. Meanwhile, Price split off the supply train and the main body of his troops to lead them towards Taos on a route that avoided Embudo.

Soon a ripple of cries worked down the line of Burgwin's troops. "There they are!" "There they are!" Bits of color and movement barely visible among the rocks betrayed the enemy.

The opposing force had chosen the chokepoint of a gorge to block the Americans, a place where enormous boulders constricted the twisting track to a passageway barely six feet wide. Small wonder one of the Army engineers had called this chokepoint "a damned Thermopylae." The task for the Americans was clear - rout the enemy from their blockade, or be denied the road to Embudo. Either drive them out and keep them moving north, or risk attack on Price's main body from behind.

But Metcalfe and his scouts had badly underestimated the strength of the ambush. As Captain Burgwin surveyed the scene through his telescope he saw that the terrain crawled with enemy fighters. On both sides of the pass they moved among the rocks like ants, three or four hundred, perhaps more. His own command numbered less than two hundred. He snapped shut his telescope. "Dismount your men," he ordered St. Vrain. "We'll set up skirmish lines. You and your mountain men take the left. Lieutenant, you take the right. Get up these hills as highas you can and start moving forward at my signal. Open fire as soon as you see fit."

"And make sure they don't get behind us," St. Vrain said.

"And make sure they don't get behind you," Burgwin laughed.

The Delaware had hidden himself in a shallow cleft that gave root-space to three or four small piñons. He lay chin on hands behind a little barricade of rocks and watched the Americans dismount a half mile distant. The enemy began toiling up the steep hillsides. Their progress slowed by treacherous footing on the icy rocks, they took some time to reach the near-vertical cliffs and rough slides that offered no further upward advance. Then a bugle call sounded from the draw, quickly answered by another and then another. The small figures began moving forward in a ragged line. A column of soldiers in the center kept to the trail. On his side of the gorge the Delaware could see the Americans slipping and sliding and grabbing at rocks and vegetation to keep their balance. Some lost their footing and fell, their curses audible over the distance. Those on the other side of the gorge were dressed in the telltale blue of Army soldiers, but those on his side wore a hodge-podge of dress. A racket of bugle calls echoed and re-echoed off the rocky chasm.

When the Americans were still a quarter mile distant several Pueblo Indians broke from their cover to run out and taunt the enemy. They discharged their muskets in a quick staccato of pops, and one bent over to present his bare backside to the Americans. As a Mexican in militia green shouted angrily at the Indians, they scampered back, yipping and shaking their weapons above their heads in triumph. Among the rocks other Indians stood to dance and yip their approval.

In a few minutes the distance between the fighting forces had shrunk to perhaps three hundred yards. Across the draw the Delaware could see some of the soldiers sitting down to rest behind the cover of rocks and brush. A few sat with their heads sunk towards their knees in exhaustion. Others tipped their canteens to drink. The torturous terrain was taking its toll. On his own side of the gorge, some of the Americans high up settled into position behind rocks and outcrops. They sent musketballs whistling and zinging among exposed Mexicans and Pueblo Indians. The Delaware lay quietly, just a foot or so of his musket poking through an opening in his rock barricade.

Suddenly something caught his eye. A red blanket coat emerging from behind an outcrop. Charley! Fighting with the enemy and headed straight toward him. The Delaware shifted his weapon so that it pointed in Charley's direction.

Charley was having a difficult time maneuvering across a steep slope of gray shale. The Indian watched him slip and fall and saw another man reach down to help him up, a black white man. Then he heard an American farther down the slope laugh and shout something to Charley.

The enemy skirmish line drew steadily closer, half hidden by puffs and wreaths of gunsmoke as more of them stopped to kneel and fire and reload and advance again, their musket-fire a noisy rattle. Behind, the Delaware heard Mexicans and Pueblo Indians already begin to slip back to safer ground, the firepower of the Americans overwhelming the forty or fifty muskets of the blocking force. The arrows of the Indians were ineffective, their tomahawks and clubs and spears useless. Amid the noise of gunfire and war-whoops he heard a few cries of pain and the "Ufff" of someone nearby hit by a ball. He glanced back to see a Pueblo with a musket trying to gain higher ground suddenly sprawl as if struck by a giant warclub. A youngster dashed out to grab his weapon. Deadly balls hissed and whirred. They skipped off the rock and flitted through the sparse foliage.

His heart pounding so hard that his vision jumped too, the Delaware lay hidden until Charley had advanced to within a hundred yards. Then he sighted on the red coat. He tracked the whiskey man in his sights for a minute or more, wondering if Whirlwind was among the enemy's horses at the far end of the draw and if he would ever ride his wonderful horse again. He thought of Charley's woman and the new baby at Charley's ranch. He recalled the catch in Charley's voice when the two men had said good-bye on the hill overlooking Turley's mill. Suddenly the Delaware shifted his sights to the chest of the black white man and fired and through the cloud of smoke from his musket he watched his target fling his musket as he was spun violently around by the Indian's ball. The Indian saw the black white man teeter awkwardly as he struggled for balance, then saw him fall and begin sliding headfirst on his back down the steep slope. Charley reached out a foot to stop the man's progress on the shale, throwing a look of surprise toward the smoke drifting up from the Indian's hiding place. The Delaware heard somebody cry, "Dick! Dick!" Then the Indian scrabbled backwards, gained his feet, and made a dash for safety, leaping and dodging on the rocky slope like a mountain goat fleeing wolves.

On the other side of the gorge Fitz fired at several figures scampering among the rocks ahead. Missed!

"Damn buzzards won't stand still, will they, Fitz? By God they scoot!" Fitz wiped sweat and powder-grime from his face with a sleeve and crouched behind a bush to reload, swearing softly to himself. He tore the paper of a cartridge with his teeth and dumped the powder down the maw of his musket as he looked ahead for other targets, the barrel of his weapon almost too hot to hold. His breath rasped. His throat felt like sandpaper. Although the rough frozen landscape ahead crawled with enemy, so far he'd blasted away at least a dozen times with no effect. He wanted a hit, dammit! Why couldn't he get a hit! Already soldiers were coming upon dead bodies among the rocks as they steadily pushed the enemy back through the pass to Embudo.

He stuffed cartridge-paper and a ball into the orifice and rammed them home with his wiping stick. He released a percussion cap and fitted it with trembling fingers in the nipple of the firing mechanism and set his musket to half cock. "Goddammit!" he said aloud as he stood again.

Down in the draw he saw reinforcements coming up the hill towards his outfit. They'd just ridden in, two dozen tiny figures in blue, their bugle blowing, their guidon fluttering. Well, they'd see soon enough how hard it was to fight on this Goddamn worthless pile of rock!

"Keep moving, keep moving!" the lieutenant called to those gawking at the newcomers, gesturing with his sword towards the pass. "They'll catch up!"

Fitz pushed on, his company a wearied thin line of blue spread along the side of the steep, boulder-strewn hill. Patches of ice and snow in the shadows made the footing treacherous. The soldiers fired at will at anything that moved and occasionally dodged the flight of an arrow from some determined fighter who hid until the Americans came within range. Down in the draw, near the chokepoint, a couple dozen muskets still popped away at the advancing Americans but it was becoming clear the enemy was being routed. Fitz saw enemy figures scampering back up the draw and taking to the hillsides, some of them helping wounded comrades out of range of the American guns. On the skyline of a saddle in the hills ahead, tiny figures fled to safety on a shortcut to Embudo.

Suddenly a figure emerged from behind some nearby rocks to loose an arrow that took the hat off an amazed soldier not a dozen yards away. At least half of Fitz's troop sent lead balls chasing after the Indian as he ducked and dodged among the rocks and brush to safety.

"Goddamnit!" Fitz complained as he crouched to reload again. "Thought I had him!"

That night the Americans under St. Vrain and Captain Burgwin slept in Embudo.

"Who was he?" Captain Burgwin asked, bending to look at the boyish face of one of St. Vrain's men. Covered by a blanket, the young soldier looked asleep. His expression was peaceful, his slightly upturned lips suggesting a smile. He might have been dreaming of something pleasurable, perhaps of exchanging smiles with a beautiful girl. A small dark hole just below his breastbone was the only hint of his violent death.

"Papin," St. Vrain said, giving the French pronunciation, "Gervaise Papin. This was his first trip west. He was working for his uncle in the Santa Fe trade." St. Vrain's eyes were wet with tears. The corpse of the young volunteer lay on the altar table in Embudo's little chapel, a crude structure of unfinished adobes with a weathered, wooden cross over the entryway and a few small, handpainted *santos* set in niches near the altar.

Captain Burgwin glanced up at the primitive carving of a gaunt Christ-figure on a cross that hung on the wall behind the altar. "Catholic?"

St. Vrain shrugged. "Papin." he said again with the French pronunciation. "We're all Catholic."

Captain Burgwin nodded and reached out to touch the young man's cold cheek. Papin must have shaved that morning, because Burgwin could feel the short bristles of early growth. He ran the backs of his fingers gently up and down the cheek against the bristles. So young. His was their only death in the battle of Embudo pass. Why him?

A draft of cold air through the open doorway stirred the dead man's soft, dark hair. "We'll bury him tomorrow with full military honors," Captain Burgwin said. St. Vrain nodded and leaned to pull the blanket over the young face.

"We'll set up a watch here for the night," Burgwin said.

St. Vrain nodded again.

"To keep away the rats," Burgwin added unnecessarily. Outside the chapel Captain Burgwin asked somewhat off-handedly, "How about the nigger?"

"You mean Dick!" St. Vrain said with sudden feeling. "His name is Dick Green. I've known him for a long time and he's a good man."

Captain Burgwin shrugged a small apology. Large, feather-like snowflakes had begun drifting down while they were in the chapel, and the ground now lay under a thin, soft blanket of white. The big flakes settled on their hats and shoulders as they headed towards the priest's house where they would spend the night, their footprints corrupting the pure whiteness of the new-fallen snow. Sounds of laughter and loud talk mingled in the cold night air as Burgwin's command bedded down in houses and sheds scattered along the steep-sided valley. The day had been good for the soldiers and Santa Fe volunteers. They had routed the enemy once again and counted some twenty dead Mexicans and Pueblo Indians.

"Well, is Green going to make it?" Burgwin asked.

St. Vrain also shrugged. "Got him right here," he said, pausing to poke a finger rather roughly at Captain Burgwin's right breast. "He lost a lot of blood because they had to take the ball out through his back."

Captain Burgwin whistled softly.

St. Vrain sighed deeply. "He was with Charles a long time, and he wanted to fight for revenge. He's got a wife down in Santa Fe."

Captain Burgwin nodded, aware of St. Vrain's emotions. "Well, your men did a fine job today, Captain. This whole command did, but you and your men deserve much credit and you can all be proud of yourselves, very proud. We couldn't have asked for more."

"Dick Green deserves to be free, sir, as free as you or me! Especially after today! He's a good man."

Captain Burgwin nodded. He wondered why St. Vrain was so touchy. They walked in silence for some time.

"I just hope he makes it," St. Vrain said softly, his voice choked. "I just hope to God he makes it."

Taos

St. Vrain had expected Taos to look different, perhaps more alien. But under a vault of blue sky the little town clustered in the valley as before, looking in the distance like child-size bricks abandoned in the snow. Still more distant stood the piled bricks of the pueblo. Only a wicked, cold wind betrayed the tranquility of the winter scene, a wind that tore shreds of smoke from the town's chimneys and sent small swirls of fine-grained snow chasing each other over the drifts.

St. Vrain rode with his chin buried in his collar, his hat pulled low to break the bite of the wind. Home, he thought. We called this place home for years but we took too much for granted. We thought we could pretend to be Mexicans and have things our way. We thought the land was ours for the taking.

"Ceran!" Metcalfe called from behind. St. Vrain glanced back to see Metcalfe gesturing toward the town. From the broad, shallow dish of a draw a handful of horsemen had come into view, heading their way. They carried a white flag, barely discernible against the backdrop of the snowscape. St. Vrain pulled his musket from its scabbard and breathed in the trigger slit in his thick mitton to warm his fingers. He put his musket on half-cock and laid it across his saddle. Behind him, he heard the men of his advance party follow suit.

As the horsemen drew near, St. Vrain recognized the priest's black hat and sheepskin coat. He held up his mittened hand. "Looks like they want to talk," he said to Metcalfe, who had pulled up alongside. Metcalfe wiped his runny nose with a sleeve. His cheeks were bright red from the cold. Usually a dapper dresser, he looked rather silly with a piece of old wagon canvas tied over his hat and under his chin to protect his ears from the bitter northwest wind.

When the horsemen were within a hundred yards St. Vrain exclaimed, "Well, I'll be Goddamned! That's Elliott Lee's big gray. I think that's Elliott Lee." He kicked his mount into motion again, its hooves sending up snow-tails. "Elliott!" he called to the heavy-set man. "By God, we thought you were dead! Is my family all right?" St. Vrain rode up extending a bare hand, Metcalfe right behind.

Smiling bravely, Elliott Lee shook St. Vrain's hand, struggling with his emotions. Finally he answered, "Yeah, they're fine, Ceran."

"They're all right? You sure?"

"Yeah, they're fine, really. Jesus, Ceran, I was almost killed. The priest here saved me." He gestured toward the cleric.

"Saved you?" St. Vrain stared at the priest with a look of disbelief, then at the other riders, several older Mexican townsmen with familiar faces. They removed their big-brimmed hats to hold them across their chests in a gesture of politeness. The icey wind ruffled their gray hair. "Was anybody else saved?" St. Vrain asked.

"No," Elliott Lee answered with a strangled voice. He took a big breath. "I thought I was a goner too." Again he struggled with his composure. "Jesus, I'm glad to see you," he said, his voice strained. Then suddenly he bowed his head and covered his face with his free hand. His shoulders shook for a few long moments before he took several big breaths.

When he looked up again he said, "But Padre here took me to his house and stood in the door against the mob. He wouldn't let them hurt me." He lifted his ample left leg to show St. Vrain a bootless, bundled foot protected by a thick knit sock. "I was running for my life and got shot in the foot and the priest pulled me into his house."

"Well, I'll be Goddamned," St. Vrain said, shifting his gaze again to the priest. Antonio Martinez was a large, lantern-jawed man whom St. Vrain had known and distrusted for years. The priest had evidently come in a hurry. Under his long sheepskin coat he still wore a black cassock hiked up around his thighs, exposing heavy woolen trousers and high-heeled boots with big-roweled spurs of the Mexican style. St. Vrain noticed Martinez and the other Mexicans kept eying the long retinue of Price's army perhaps two miles to the south. Not knowing English, none of the Mexican party understood the conversation between the Americans.

"We heard they killed you all," Metcalfe said.

"Are the rest of the families all right?" St. Vrain asked.

"Yeah, they left the families alone, thank God. Everybody's all right - Stephen's wife, Bent's wife, the others, but they killed Bent's brother-in-law and Carlo Beaubien's boy. And everybody else is dead."

142

"Beaubien's boy! Narcisse? They killed Narcisse?"

Elliott nodded as he fished out a big handkerchief and wiped his eyes. "If Padre here hadn't...Ceran, he went and got Stephen's body after they threw it off the store into the street." Elliott bowed his head, his shoulders shaking, "He was...they...." St. Vrain leaned over to put a hand on the man's arm. Elliott collected himself, sighed hugely, and straightened a little. "They think some might have gotten away up at Turley's place. I don't know. I didn't know anybody up there. I guess they got two Americans up at Rio Colorado too."

"Rio Colorado?" St. Vrain said. "Who the hell was that? There aren't Americans up at Rio Colorado, are there?" He turned to Metcalfe. "Who's up at Rio Colorado?" Metcalfe shrugged and made a face.

The priest said to Elliott, "Señor...."

Elliott acknowledged the cleric and turned to St. Vrain. "Listen, Ceran, they want to talk. They want you to spare the town."

"Spare the town? Where the hell are the rebels?"

"The pueblo. But there's not many now. Most of 'em went back home, dropped off at the other pueblos."

"That true, Padre?" St. Vrain asked the priest in English, then repeated the question in Spanish. "Have most of the rebels gone home?" The priest rattled off a long reply, the Mexicans behind him nodding agreement as he reported that almost all the Indians from the pueblos to the south had gone back to their homes. The leaders of the insurrection (a disturbance, he called it, *el tumulto*) had retreated to the Taos pueblo. But the townspeople in Taos were peaceful. They had wanted nothing to do with the trouble in the first place and wanted no part in any fighting now. In fact they asked the priest to come out and beg the army not take revenge on innocents. As Martinez talked he kept his gloved hands clamped on the pommel of his saddle as if afraid to gesticulate.

Goddamned liar! St. Vrain thought as he turned to measure the progress of Colonel Price. *El tumulto!* St. Vrain was dead certain the priest had been in the thick of the plotting. Plenty of people were saying as much. And now the son of a bitch sat on his horse trying to cover his ass! But why had he saved Elliott Lee?

143

Price's little army had drawn visibly closer. The van was moving fast, determined to shelter that night in Taos even if they had to fight the Devil himself to kick the rebels out of town. Picuris Mountain had beaten them up. After Burgwin's command rejoined Colonel Price following the battle of Embudo, the American force spent four miserable days reaching the valley of Taos. Knee-deep snow had them trampling down miles of mountain track to make a passage for the new six-pounder and the supply wagons. They spent two sleepless nights in temperatures hovering near zero. Many suffered frostbite from sleeping in the open. If ever an army was ready to make the enemy pay for its miseries it was the American column slogging towards Taos.

"We'll have to see what the colonel says," St. Vrain said to the priest. "Follow me." He wheeled his mount around and headed back toward Colonel Price.

Taos was terrified as the weary, chilled American soldiers hobbled into town at mid-day. Padre Martinez and his delegation had hurried back to spread the word: Colonel Price offered his personal assurance the Americans would bring no harm to a household that kept its door open as a sign of peace. Despite this promise, the people cowered in their houses and listened nervously for the inevitable appearance of the American soldiers. For most of them it would be their first view of the *gringos*.

Soon they came. With loud voices and shouts of discovery a company of the 2nd flooded a dozen twisty lanes, stomping into every house, sizing up the inhabitants, poking and prodding the family's furnishings and belongings. A few townspeople gestured for the soldiers to help themselves to bread and simmering beans they had set out for the soldiers' appeasement. The soldiers discovered no doors to kick down. Every house in town stood open to the winter day.

They found evidence of looting at Stephen Lee's store on the plaza and at Beaubien's store and at one of Charles Bent's stores. Turley's Taos warehouse and several other businesses and homes belonging to absent Americans had been ransacked too. Rebels had also battered at the door of St. Vrain's home, but his wife reported the *insurrectos* took only guns, ammunition, and whiskey and had left them alone. Several cases of his claret stood undisturbed.

Meanwhile, Price marched the bulk of his force out to the pueblo, two miles distant. His plan was simple. He would show the rebels his army of 500 and his five pieces of artillery and give them a chance to surrender. With luck they'd have the leaders in hand by nightfall and a quick, bloodless victory. Even the weather seemed auspicious. The wind died. The air was crisp and bright, and when the pueblo's twin church bells began to clang the alarm they sounded just a stone's throw away.

Even Fitz was impressed with his first close-up view of the pueblo - a huge adobe church and two stair-stepped pueblo structures of five or six stories, one on the north side of the compound, the other on the south. Against a backdrop of blue sky and purplish snow-peaked mountains to the east, afternoon sun suffused the adobe fortress with a warm, pale brown glow, setting off the bright colors and glitter of its defenders. Had the scene not been warlike it might have been festive.

Arrayed on the upper stories with their firearms and bows and arrows and spears and lances, the *pueblanos* observed the approach of the Americans.

The enemy fortress was formidable. Enclosing about ten acres, home to several hundred people, almost the entire compound was surrounded by a wall some eight feet high. This defensive perimeter was a combination of mud-mortared rock, upright logs that formed palisades, and adobe bricks that over the centuries had been slathered with layer after layer of protective mud. In some places the walls stood three to four feet thick.

In one corner of the compound the huge church with its twin belfries stood like a fortress within a fortress. Even the main pueblo buildings were ideal for defense, their roofs rimmed with low parapets offering protection from enemy fire. While two or three small gates in the perimeter walls permitted entry to the interior, anyone entering would be exposed to a deadly crossfire from the pueblo buildings.

Price soon learned the rebels had no thoughts of accommodation or surrender. Few of those in the pueblo had ever seen the power of artillery, and the Indians considered the fortress impregnable. As soon as the American soldiers came within range, the roof and belfries of the church began venting telltale puffs of gunsmoke. Musket balls skipped off snowbare patches of frozen ground near the van of the American column.

145

"Damn!" Price said, and kept his troops out of range. Along with several officers, he mounted a horse to circle the fortress, looking for a point of attack. On the south and east sides, a few corrals outside the palisade opened onto a meadow that extended for several hundred yards before giving way to chaparral and then to cedar forests blanketing the low hills. The corrals stood empty, the animals apparently driven to hidden retreats. He saw no advantage for attack on the meadow side. Indeed, the entire palisade was loopholed, and several buildings protruded like blockhouses. Even if he kept his artillery out of musket range on the meadow side, his stubby howitzers could do little damage to the church stronghold on the opposite corner of the pueblo.

The north side offered some promise. A centuries-old trash mound several feet high rose just outside the wall on the northeast corner, offering possible cover for an infantry assault. At the opposite corner reared the massive walls of the Church of San Geronimo, as solid as a mountain. Gunfire from its belfries and roof and loopholes would cause real problems.

But Price decided the church was his best point of attack. If he got control of the church and could breach the gate near the dump at the opposite corner he would have the north pueblo in a pincer.

But then what? Once his troops entered the compound the north buildings would be a bloody business to invest. With neither windows nor doors, the bottom story was like another fort, with loopholes for weapons everywhere. And the enemy would have the advantage of knowing the interior warrens. If they fought from room to room and level to level they would spring on his troops with knives and hatchets. Colonel Price shook his head. He hoped to God the fighting wouldn't come to that.

He decided that for the rest of the afternoon he'd pound away with his artillery and give the enemy a taste of what was to come. Maybe, seeing the damage his big guns could do, they would surrender after all.

Just after two o'clock in the afternoon the four howitzers and the 6-pounder began blasting the enemy's defenses from three hundred yards, a distance beyond the range of effective enemy musket fire. The artillery concentrated on the church's western wall.

Boom! The first howitzer shot skipped off the ground in front of the wall, bounced back off the adobe, and exploded on

146

the ground a dozen yards from the church with an eruption of dirt and smoke and iron shards. The troops cheered. *Boom!* And the troops cheered again. *Boom!* "Give it to 'em, boys! Show 'em how a real army fights!" *Boom! Boom!* Balls aimed high buried themselves in the wall of the church, exploded, and sent up clouds of smoke and billowing dust. Many bounced off. The troops cheered each explosion as their comrades sent round after round towards the enemy fortress. *Boom! Boom! Boom! Boom! Boom!* as regular as clockwork. The sounds of cannon fire bounded up the distant canyon walls and echoed in the hills. Children cowering in the pueblo apartments shook in terror. And not just the children. The rag-tag rebels had never seen such explosive power. What fortress could withstand such punishment?

But the adobe was Indian magic. And if the pueblo had never seen the power of artillery, Colonel Price had never seen the power of adobe. The mud structures seemed to suck up the force of the shells. At three hundred yards his howitzers were no more effective than ancient catapults heaving rocks, and his six-pounder not much better. After two and a half hours of continuous bombardment - more than a hundred rounds - the church wall stood bruised but unbreached, and harassing fire from its inhabitants continued to skip off the frozen ground around his artillery.

Colonel Price scratched his head. His caissons were empty. The ammunition wagons had still not arrived. His troops jiggled and jumped, chilled from standing around and watching. Cold and tired and hungry, they had long since stopped cheering.

Price called it quits. To the jeers and taunts of the enemy, he hitched up his artillery and marched his army back to Taos. So much for quick victory.

147

Casa Martinez

A dozen American officers sat around the priest's dining table – actually two tables placed end to end, one of them a borrowed table several inches lower than the priest's own. Above the tables the smoke-darkened wood of the ceiling soaked up light from a dozen candles on the table and in wall sconces. A reddish boltcloth skirt that covered the lower parts of the whitewashed walls looked the color of dried blood in the funeral gloom.

But despite their gloomy surroundings the Americans were merry. Having started drinking "the ingredient" before they arrived at the priest's house for dinner, they were not only merry, but cocky. Despite the failure of their artillery to cow the pueblo that afternoon they were certain the following day would bring the rebels to justice. They chuckled at someone's remark about "a good drubbing." Oh, yes, a good drubbing, that's what the bastards needed! Show 'em who's boss for once and for all!

From his place of honor at the head of the priest's ponderous, Spanish-style table, Price tinkled his glass with a spoon. When the room quieted he asked the priest for a blessing. Padre Martinez met the colonel's eyes and intuited his meaning and bowed his head, hiding his frustration at St. Vrain's absence. The priest knew just a smattering of English, about as much as the Americans gathered in his house knew of his own native tongue, a few essentials and a few pleasantries. For those around the priest's table to hear a normal conversation in the other's language was to hear gibberish. Without St. Vrain as a translator the priest was tongue-tied, and at some point during the evening he knew Elliott Lee, sitting across the table, would be asked about the killings. And there Martinez would sit, ignorant of what Elliott Lee might say. Would the man be fair? Not only to Martinez but to all the other Mexicans who had been surprised by the sudden violence? Would Elliott exaggerate the horrors and the savage cruelties and inflame his listeners?

Antonio Martinez was a Mexican patriot, but despite St. Vrain's suspicions the priest had not been involved in the uprising. Although he and many other townspeople had heard rumors about impending trouble, he'd been as shocked as the Americans at the outbreak that fateful morning three weeks

148

earlier. Now, with the rebellion obviously failed and every Mexican a suspect, he saw himself thrust to the front as his people's protector, as a shepherd guarding his flock. Fearful the Americans would wreak retribution on the weak, he felt no shame in playing the supplicant to Colonel Price. Indeed, the closer he kept to the American commander, he reasoned, the better his chances of tempering the Americans. He'd used the parley on the outskirts of Taos to offer his house to the colonel. After all, *Casa Martinez* was one of the best abodes in town.

And Colonel Price, part of him wanting to accept the priest's overtures as genuine, and a larger part sensing good local politics, had accepted the invitation.

Martinez crossed himself and in a rather wordy preamble to his blessing asked for God's mercy on all His children, on both the upright and the misguided, and for tolerance and forgiveness among men. Then he paused briefly and asked the regular blessing for the food. He crossed himself again.

Elliott Lee followed suit. "Amen," Elliott said, and the Americans echoed him in a ragged chorus, ignorant of the meaning of the priest's invocation.

They began to pile into the abundant food with noisy gusto, the main course a peppery beef stew made with potatoes and carrots and onions (vegetable rarities for the soldiers since leaving Missouri). Fragrant baked beans and boiled rice steamed in big bowls. The priest also supplied American-style bread with a tub of butter and pots of red and green pepper sauce for braver palates. As the meal progressed, Martinez sent subtle signals to his servants to fill an empty glass, to offer more stew, more beans, more bread. Emerging from the shadowed obscurity of an open doorway, his staff came forward to serve the guests with deference, then melted into the shadows again.

At the lower table the officers told stories on one another with a good deal of laughing. Not understanding the reasons for their laughter, the priest tried to mask his uneasiness. He would have appreciated assurances that their merriment was not directed at him and the looks he sometimes caught from the lower table were simple curiosity aroused in part by the priest's reputation. Was Martinez really a scoundrel? A conspirator? A rapacious wolf in cleric's clothing?

Colonel Price ate moderately, conversing quietly with Captain Burgwin. He wanted Burgwin to understand why the men of the Price's own 2nd Missouri would be held back and why Captain Burgwin's Dragoons would bear the brunt of the morrow's attack. Privately pleased that he would lead the assault, Burgwin assured Price that his Dragoons would give a good account of themselves. Then, after several minutes of discussion with Burgwin, Price caught Martinez looking at him with an odd expression, as if he wanted to speak. The colonel acknowledged the priest with a small smile and a polite nod and a raised glass.

A commotion at the street door interrupted the dinner conversations. St. Vrain was ushered in. As Martinez stood to welcome the newcomer, relieved the trader had arrived at last, St. Vrain announced he'd just come from seeing Charles Bent's widow. "Jesus, she saw the whole thing!" he announced to the assembly. "The bastards scalped him right in front of her eyes!" A perceptible ripple of outrage ran around the table. St. Vrain took his seat, ignoring the priest's proffered hand and drained a half glass of wine in one draught, not even noticing it was not claret. "Sons a bitches!" he said, spooning stew. "They're gonna pay!" There were loud murmurs of assent, and some of the officers rapped the tabletop with their utensils in approval.

As a half dozen conversations gradually picked up again, Elliott Lee suddenly blurted above the voices, "Well, at least they didn't cut off his head!" Faces turned.

"What?" St. Vrain asked rather sharply. The room quieted. Elliott's large face reddened. His eyes sought the priest's.

"Well, I mean the rumors, that they cut off his head and carried it around the plaza on a pole. None of that's true!"

St. Vrain shot back. "No? Well, it's bad enough, what they did! Jesus, Elliott, you aren't sticking up for 'em, are you? Christ, they killed your brother!"

Elliott reddened even more, writhing as if someone had poured something cold down his back. He swallowed several times, the workings of his throat audible in the dead quiet. His eyes glistened when he responded in a strained voice, "I know they killed my brother, Ceran. You don't need to remind me of that. I know they killed the others too, and they would've killed me. But it was a mob, a bloodthirsty mob that got out of control! And a lot of the people had no part! Good people! And if it wasn't for the priest here I'd be dead. I...I...I just think we need to be careful about who we blame, is all."

Price broke a long, awkward silence. "Of course, Mister Lee, we must always remember our responsibilities, especially as military men." He paused. "But we certainly need to get to the bottom of this mess. I mean, you don't believe this uprising just happened, do you? That there was no conspiracy, no planning? Christ, we've all seen that thing, that *pronuncia*-whatchamacallit thing. Surely you don't believe there was no conspiracy?"

Elliott shrugged uncomfortably and made a stubborn face of downturned lips. He would not raise his eyes, and when he answered his voice was grudging. "No, there was probably a conspiracy." But after a silence and as the table began to stir again, he suddenly exclaimed, "But, Christ! Don't you see? My brother saw the trouble coming weeks ago! He tried to tell Charles Bent! He tried to tell all of you. That's why he went down to Santa Fe. But you wouldn't listen. That's what gets me. If you would've listened, if you all hadn't been so cocksure about everything, if you'd sent soldiers up here like he asked, well, then maybe we could have avoided all this. And maybe my brother'd still be alive. Maybe they all would!"

Coloring deeply, St. Vrain half rose in protest at Elliott Lee's final words, then sank again as Price put up a calming hand.

Elliott's brother Stephen had lived in Taos for almost twenty years, so when his friend Charles Bent returned to New Mexico as the new American governor it came as no surprise that Bent appointed Stephen Lee as sheriff of Taos. Stephen had already begun worrying about the mood of the town. "Something's in the air," he told Elliott after his brother's arrival with St. Vrain's party. "Something's going on. Some of the folks won't look me in the eye. I don't know what it is, but something's going on."

He told about a recent run-in with some Indians. As he crossed the plaza early one morning he saw a half dozen Pueblos hunkered against the wall of his store. When the Indians saw him a couple of them got to their feet and one moved off a few feet to piss against the wall. "Hey!" Stephen Lee called. "Stop that!" The Indian half turned, his stream of piss steaming in the cold. "Get away from there!" Stephen said in Spanish. Another of the Pueblos weaved towards the American making a pawing gesture that meant, "come forward."

"Whiskey," he said as they neared one another. "Whiskey."

151

"No, no whiskey. You've had enough whiskey. Go home. No whiskey."

"Whiskey," the Indian said, reaching under his blanket to produce the carcass of a jackrabbit.

"No, no trade! No whiskey!"

"Whiskey!" the Indian said, thrusting the dead animal at Stephen. "Whiskey!"

"No, Goddamnit! No whiskey! Go home! You're drunk! You're all drunk!"

"Whiskey! whiskey!" the Indian repeated as he pushed the rabbit against Stephen's chest. The storekeeper made no effort to take the offering, and when the Indian let go of the rabbit it fell between them and hitt the frozen ground with a plop. A smear of pinkish fluid from the carcass stained the American's coat.

"Goddamnit! No whiskey! Go home!" He stepped over the rabbit with a booted foot as he made for the door of his store. He'd gone only a short way when the rabbit struck him in the back. He turned angrily to see the Indian stalking off. He picked up the rabbit and threw it after the Indian, who did not deign even to glance down when the badly thrown carcass landed near his feet.

That incident was just one in a series of escalating confrontations between Stephen Lee and the pueblo-dwellers, but for some reason it stuck in his mind. Perhaps it was the Indian's aloof disdain or perhaps the drunken meanness, because after Stephen threw the rabbit after the Indian the rest of them stood to piss against his wall also.

As much from frustration as anything, Stephen Lee was soon putting some of the troublemakers in the town's little *calabaza* to cool off. But matters got worse. By the time he had a dozen Mexicans and Indians behind bars, rumors of trouble were all over town. A couple of weeks before the uprising he and a few others rode down to Santa Fe so he could talk over the situation with Charles Bent. He ended up asking Bent if he couldn't convince Colonel Price to send a detachment of soldiers up to Taos. "We're going to have trouble if we don't," Stephen Lee said. "The town's getting ugly."

But Charles Bent made a show of pooh-poohing his friend's concerns. "It's all talk!" he said. "Listen, they'll get used to our way of doing things and end up thanking us. It's just a matter of time. You know how it is out here, you change any little thing and they think the sky is falling."

But Bent was already aware of widespread agitation about the new American system of taxes, and he planned to issue a proclamation in an effort to calm some of the unrest. In addition to dispelling the more outrageous rumors about the new taxes, he wanted to ask for the people's patience. He'd already he planned a visit to Taos to bring his family down to his new home in the Governor's Palace anyway, so he decided he'd join Stephen Lee on his return, take the proclamation with him, and deliver it in person on the plaza in Taos. He was sure that would set things right.

Just outside Taos, however, they had a run-in with a dozen Pueblo Indians who galloped up to the tired travelers. In an unusual breach of Indian ettiquette, Tomasito, the principal chief of the pueblo, didn't offer to shake hands. Instead, in a mixture of Tiwa and Spanish he immediately demanded Bent free the men Stephen Lee held in the jail. Bent held up a mollifying hand. He said the law was the law and he couldn't let the troublemakers out of jail without due process, even as governor. He mentioned the proclamation he planned to give in a day or two. Have patience, he asked.

Tomasito shouted at Bent, saying Americans were worse than the greedy Mexican *ricos* and the proclamation was worthless. He used a Tiwa word to describe Bent's promises, "fart-wind." The Indians bullied the travelers' horses with their mounts and made threats about taking hair.

"I'm glad Bent got to see it for himself," Stephen Lee told Elliott that night. "I pulled out my pistol and told 'em to get the hell home or I'd run the whole lot of 'em into jail. Well, they backed off then. They turned tail and galloped off howling like a pack of coon dogs. But at least Bent saw what I was talking about. Maybe now we'll get some soldiers up here."

That evening was the last time that Elliott Lee saw his brother Stephen alive.

Colonel Price didn't want the priest's dinner sullied by tales of gore. There would be gore enough in battle next day. But he was intensely interested in something about the uprising that so far the Americans could only guess at. "Why the rebellion?"

he asked Antonio Martinez. He indicated to St. Vrain that he wanted him to translate, as if the matter were official business.

After St. Vrain translated Price's question, the priest sighed heavily. Why should he try to explain? he thought. All evening he'd felt the condescension of his guests, as if he hardly deserved a place at his own table. No, it was worse than condescension; it was almost contempt! As cutting as a cruel winter wind. But he knew he had to try, even though he didn't completely understand the reasons for the uprising. Perhaps helping Colonel Price and the Americans understand would temper their retribution.

Martinez folded his large hands on the well-worn table covering. He spoke with his eyes fixed on a guttering candle, as though visualizing the history of events in the erratic flame. Hoping he could trust St. Vrain to convey his meaning, he paused every few moments for his fellow townsman to render his words into English, all the while resenting his dependence on the trader. Except for the voices of the two men, the room was eerily quiet.

Too much change, Martinez told them, too much change too soon. Especially after Kearny broke his word and annexed the whole of New Mexico. After all, when he marched into Santa Fe had not Kearny assured the Mexican people he had come only to make good on America's rightful claim to the eastern half of New Mexico? Even Mexicans saw the Americans had a case for that, a document signed by General Santa Anna himself, although it had been signed under duress after Santa Anna's defeat in the battle of San Jacinto. But when Kearny grabbed the whole of New Mexico and marched off to conquer California the people felt betrayed.

"Then stories began coming up to Taos from Santa Fe of American soldiers not respecting the Church or the women or the people's traditions. American officials brushed aside Mexican ways - now there would be no gambling on Sundays, no Sunday markets. Now everyone would need a license for this and a permit for that. Then came page after page of new American laws, very different from Mexican law. And new taxes. Especially new taxes! Dozens of new taxes and fees. And meanwhile the demanding stomachs of the occupying American army drove prices up until the poor could scarcely afford a mouthful of beans. Secretly the people wished Mexico would send an army to drive the Americans away and give them back their birthright.

154

But that was the stuff of dreams, and the people suffered in silence.

Certain men looked for trouble. With Mexico fighting for its soul in the south, they knew the government would never send an army north to recapture this faraway land. So men of rank, used to lives of privilege, made plans to overthrow the Americans and return themselves to power. They saw themselves as patriots. Secretly they visited every town and pueblo to stir up the people - Pojoque, La Cañada, Abiquque, Mora, Embudo, Las Vegas, San Miguel, Albuquerque, many, many places. Taos too. "We must drive the Americans out!" they said. But behind their backs the people rolled their eyes. They remembered how these *ricos,* these rich men, had treated them before, how a common man would slave for years to pay back money borrowed for a wedding or a funeral, how sons and daughters grew up in bondage to their family's never-ending indebtedness. Now these same men appealed to the people and made big promises about freedom! Behind their backs the people snickered at them. The Pueblo Indians the same. They asked, "Why should we spill our blood to give these *ricos* back what they took from us?"

So only a few would follow these men, and when the Americans uncovered their plans for the Christmas Eve massacre their designs all came to nothing anyway. After the Americans administered a few floggings, the culprits slunk away. But life got worse and the common people lost their way in the new laws.

Martinez paused to take a drink of wine, surveying the faces at the table as he did. His listeners were rapt. "We have a different way of doing things, you see." He smiled a small smile. "We have a saying: The best law is a rusty tool." Then he told how the village *alcalde* would usually try to settle disputes by common sense. The *alcalde* would listen to this side and that side and would make suggestions. The parties tried talking things out. Sometimes even Martinez would be invited to offer his counsel. And often as not the quarrels simply disappeared, like water into the ground.

"We have laws also, you see, but we seldom use them. That's why we say the best law is a rusty tool. But with you Americans everything is the law! The law is a shiny, sharp tool. Everything has to be looked up in books. Everything must be written down. And when Señor Lee became the sheriff, of course he said everybody had to follow these new laws. What else could he do, even though he lived here for many, many years where the law is a rusty tool?"

Yes, St. Vrain thought, waiting as the priest paused to drink again, and I'd bet you were right in there with the rest of them, yammering about the good old days.

But the worst thing, the priest continued, was an insult to the people. The American government said everyone had to prove they owned the fields they farmed and the houses they lived in. Everybody! Respected families! Families who had lived on the same land for generations! In our land of rusty laws the Americans now said all the people had to bring papers to prove that they had a right to their own land. And the people were afraid. They thought the Americans were going to steal their land. They thought the Americans were going to say, "This paper is no good, señor. You do not own your land!" Or they would say, "What! You have no paper? Then I'm sorry, señor, but you must give up your land. You have no right to live there."

Martinez had grown animated, and he implored Colonel Price with extended hands. "And now I beg forgiveness, Excellency, but I must speak plainly. These men in the government, these men who made the new laws, these men who wanted to see papers, these were the very same men who grabbed thousands and thousands of *hectares* of land from my people through the corruption of our former governor."

St. Vrain's intake of breath was so sharp Price looked at him. Martinez hurried on. "But not just foreigners, Excellency. I cannot blame just them, men like Señor Bent and Señor St. Vrain, even Señor Lee's dead brother, God rest his soul! But my countrymen too. These foreigners grabbed our land with the connivance of my own countrymen!"

St. Vrain bristled, flushing deeply. You son of a bitch! he mouthed.

Colonel Price had watched St. Vrain's agitation grow. Now he waited for a translation that was not forthcoming. "What?" he asked. "What was that? What'd he say?" St. Vrain remained silent. He glowered at the priest, who sat with downcast eyes awaiting St. Vrain's translation. Colonel Price said, "Ceran, what's going on?"

You bastard! St. Vrain thought, his face dark, his eyes smoldering, you and your family have grabbed more land around here than anybody, and you just can't stand seeing anyone else getting ahead, can you?

"Captain?" Colonel Price said, his irritation showing.

St. Vrain at last broke off his dark look and made a show of settling back in his chair. He waved the matter aside with his cigar. "Oh, nothing much, Colonel!" he said. "Gossip is all. Some folks think that Governor Armijo gave too much land away."

"The Mexican governor?" Price asked. "Father Martinez is bad-mouthing Governor Armijo?" Of course Colonel Price had heard Armijo could be bought and that Charles Bent and St. Vrain had paid off Armijo plenty of times. Charles Bent especially was known as an empire-builder with a finger in every pie. Talk was that he'd even bought the governorship back in Washington.

"Yeah," St. Vrain said, "but these days everybody bad-mouths Armijo. That's nothing new."

"But what else? He said more than that, didn't he?"

St. Vrain sent a sarcastic smile towards Martinez. "Yeah, well, there's plenty of gossip around town. Some folks don't have anything better to do, do they, *padre*? and we can't help if they're busybodies!

"But I think...," St. Vrain said as he turned to address Colonel Price, "...I think what we've got to remember is that these devils murdered and scalped Charles Bent and Stephen Lee and Jim Leal and Cornelio Vigil and Pablo Jaramillo and Narcisse Beaubien and Simeon Turley and John Albert and all those men up at Turley's mill. And now just tonight I heard they murdered Mark Head and another man up at Rio Colorado and I tell you they're sure as hell gonna pay for it, every damned one of them!" As St. Vrain finished his voice rose, his face turned red, and he struck the table with a fist.

The officers at the lower end of the table applauded. Martinez and Elliott Lee looked at each other with embarrassed expressions.

"Well," Price said at last, "there's no accounting for talk, is there?" He fingered his glass, one of three among the head-table diners with a stem. The Americans waited on his words. "But at least Armijo avoided bloodshed, didn't he? Unnecessary bloodshed. At least he saved lives." He raised his glass toward the priest in a gesture that could have been a toast, but as he said nothing Martinez was confused and nearly knocked over

157

his own glass before clumsily responding. They drank looking into each other's eyes, Martinez showing anxiety mingled with gratitude.

Putting down his empty glass, Colonel Price smiled and pushed back his chair. "Well, gentlemen, we've got an early day tomorrow." He let the implication dangle. Heads nodded. Men followed Price in pushing back their chairs (or what passed for chairs, for several at the lower table perched on two benches brought in from the portico). Martinez got quickly to his feet.

"Ceran," Price said, as he rose, "give *Padre* our thanks. We're all indebted for his generous hospitality and his most interesting history. He strikes me as a worthy man of the cloth," he said as he inclined a slight bow towards the priest. St. Vrain addressed Martinez wearing a half smirk. He relayed the colonel's thanks.

As an aide helped Colonel Price into his coat for his evening rounds, Martinez panicked. From St. Vrain's abrupt translation Martinez thought he had offended the colonel and Price had decided to leave his house because he felt insulted. Had Martinez presumed too much in speaking so frankly? The priest fluttered his hands, apologizing in rapid Spanish for any offense, appealing for the colonel's forgiveness. Price looked at him in puzzlement, then smiled and stepped forward to shake the priest's hand. *Muchas gracias*, he said. Martinez bowed deeply, more confused than ever.

Following the colonel into the night St. Vrain muttered, "What a Goddamn liar!" Price glanced at him.

"Well, maybe, but I don't think he lies all the time." Colonel Price paused. In the distance he heard the faint sounds of drums and singing from the pueblo. He looked up into a brilliant night sky, his gaze followed by the others.

"Beautiful!" Captain Burgwin said as he regarded the myriad stars. "Makes you want to live forever."

Price nodded. He was thoughtful for a moment, then said, "Actually, gentlemen, what the priest said about all those rumors and fears - I wonder if that's true, if we'll ever know for sure why we had a rebellion to put down."

Someone else said, "And I wonder if anyone back home really cares."

The Pueblo

The artillery had terrified the pueblo. The thunder of cannonfire and the deadly explosions sent women and children and even some of the fighting men fleeing in panic to hide in the bowels of their buildings. But at a distance of three hundred yards the howitzers did little damage to the fortress church. For his attack the following morning Price moved the big guns a hundred yards closer, still beyond arrow range, even beyond accurate musket range. Once again the bombardment sent *pueblanos* scurrying for cover. A howitzer would belch, spewing fire and smoke, and a moment later adobe would erupt with deadly shards of broken iron and hissing chunks of dried mud. Colonel Price again concentrated his fire on the church.

All morning the fighters in the pueblo endured this point-blank pounding, their popping muskets a puny response. Once or twice they whooped and celebrated at the sight of a wounded artilleryman being dragged to safety, the victim of a lucky shot, but cannonfire took a steady toll on the pueblo. Those behind the parapets and at loopholes suffered shrapnel injuries from airbursts and hissing chunks of hardened mud. By late morning the constant shelling at last breached the wall by the western flank of the church; the barrier lay a tangled, partially collapsed ruin of splintered logs and broken adobe.

"Fight like men!" a muscular rebel cried in English from the church roof. He shook his musket at the Americans. It was the Delaware. He ducked below the parapet as a howitzer huffed smoke and fire, then was jolted by the impact of the missile on the upper wall. The explosion rained adobe debris on two dozen defenders remaining on the roof. Another howitzer huffed, and an earshattering airburst above the church mangled three or four defenders. Then a quick succession of airbursts drove the men from the rooftop and the belfries into the church. When at last the bombardment paused, those peering through loopholes in the upper walls of the church saw the Americans moving their big guns even closer. Others manhandled a long ladder that would reach the roof.

On the opposite side of the pueblo, scattered in a rough line in the chapparal beyond the horse meadow, St. Vrain's mounted men formed a blocking force in case the rebels made a break for the mountains. From the pueblo the men heard a continuous faint cacophony of defiant war cries, a ragged counter-point to the steady *boom! boom! boom!* of the howitzers and the flatter, sharper sound of the six-pounder.

"We should find a way out," the older Esquival brother muttered, his eyes fixed in the direction of the pueblo, his words just loud enough for his brother to hear.

"A way out? Why?"

"This isn't fighting! It's murder!"

"But we haven't hurt anybody yet, you and me! And besides, maybe they'll give up pretty soon."

"You fool!" The older one spat. "Those big guns have been killing the *pueblanos* all morning! Does it look like they're giving up?"

"I'm no fool, Julio! You've no right to call me a fool! And remember! this was all your idea. You're the one who wanted us to join!"

The older brother didn't answer except to curse under his breath, and when his horse lowered its head to nibble at a few frozen stems poking through the snow he jerked the reins so sharply the animal recoiled with a grunt. The younger one looked at his brother with disapproval.

"All right, all right, you're not a fool!" the older one said at last. "It's me. I was the fool!"

The brothers remained unspeaking, unwilling even to look at each other. When the older one finally broke the silence his voice was reflective. "I thought we could do this without so much killing - that these people would see reason and give up. I thought we could bring a few of the bad ones to justice and go home and be in good with the Americans. As God is my witness that's what I thought! But these fools don't give up! And you know what's going to happen? They're going to die like rabbits! When they can't hold on in the pueblo any longer they'll run for the hills and these wild men will chase them down and kill them like rabbits. They're all going to die, Raphael, and I want no part of it."

"Me neither," the younger one said at last, his voice so choked and sad that his brother turned to look at him. The youth's face was pinched. He looked like a little boy ready to cry. "I don't want to fight anymore either, Julio. They're our own people!"

160

As the morning's battle was joined St. Vrain's men had at first kept in the saddle, ready to give chase to the enemy. But after a time they began dismounting to relieve themselves and stamp their feet and swing their arms and clap their mittened hands to restore feeling from the numbing cold. They might find a neighbor and say, "Some go, eh?" or "What'cha think?"

Smelling woodsmoke, Charley and his brother Tom led their horses to a tiny glade in a clump of cedars where a half dozen French-Canadians had built a fire. Baptiste Chalifoux squatted by the flames, his hands extended to the warmth.

"Shawlee!" he greeted Charley, moving to make room. "What'chu tink? *Il fait froid, n'est-ce pas?*"

Charley nodded and tied Whirlwind to a cedar branch and bent to stretch his hands towards the fire. "What'chu tink, Tom?" Baptiste said as he rubbed his thick, paw-like hands, winking at the younger man. "*Il fait froid, n'est-ce pas?*"

Tom nodded. Then, as if the affirmations of the newcomers proved his point, Baptiste repeated the observation that he had already made several times to the others, "*Oui, il fait froid, trés froid.*"

Sunk into their high-collared coats, the men around the fire seemed mesmerized by the protean coals as they half-listened to booming artillery and the tumult from the pueblo. Charley stared at the hypnotic changes in the coals, lost in his thoughts. The night before someone had told him the rebels had killed Turley up at Charley's place.

At first Charley was disbelieving. How could the bum-kneed miller have gotten through the enemy seige? And how did Turley manage the miles of snow-covered up-and-down to Charley's place?

Now, as he hunkered by the fire and pondered the miller's death, Charley kept seeing the look on his wife's face the night he'd left her to go with the Delaware. She'd been ornery as settin' hen, for sure! Could she have been mad enough to egg on her brother Jose? Was Jose in on killing Turley? And if he was, could Charley bring himself to turn Jose in?

Jesus! Charley suddenly realized, this rotten business has got me thinking of family going against family.

161

"Shawlee," Baptiste said with a nudge that broke Charley's introspection, "LeBlanc, *c'est bon, n'est-ce pas?*"

Charley nodded and returned a small smile. They'd also learned LeBlanc was alive and had made his way to the safety of LaFôret's home in Rio Colorado. Yes, LeBlanc alive - that was something. Maybe LeBlanc and Turley had escaped the mill together.

Charley had always liked LeBlanc. Somehow the French-Canadian seemed to find contentment with his wife and family and his little farm that eluded Charley. At times Charley had found himself envying LeBlanc's simple faith and stay-at-home life. Maybe, Charley thought, I should quit trying so hard to get ahead and...

Suddenly the men heard a shot from down the line that sent them swearing and scrambling for their weapons, fumbling with gunlocks stiff from the cold. They froze in postures of readiness, their hearts in their throats as they peered through the thick growth towards the pueblo. The artillery had suddenly fallen silent.

"Don't shoot! Don't shoot!" someone cried above the muffled hoofbeats of a galloping horse. "Don't shoot! Don't shoot!" a grinning, red-faced Town cried as he pounded by on his father-in-law's good-looking black horse, kicking up spurts of snow and waving a paper at the half hidden volunteers. "Orders! I got orders! Don't shoot!"

"*Sacredieu!* I shoot dat Town!" Baptiste exclaimed after Town had passed. He rapidly beat his chest with his hand to simulate a racing heart. Then he rolled his eyes and laughed. Charley and Tom exchanged amused looks and shook their heads with suppressed smiles while the French-Canadians joined Baptiste's laughter. That Town!

In a few minutes St. Vrain relayed the news from Colonel Price. The wall was breached and Price was ordering a direct assault to take the church. At the colonel's signal the half-company of mounted Missouri 2nd waiting in the chapparel with St. Vrain's company would create a diversion by simulating an attack from the meadow side of the pueblo. St. Vrain's men were to continue holding their positions in case of a breakout.

Once again Charley and Tom took to their mounts to find their places in the ragged line of volunteers. They heard bugle calls and drumbeats and saw the gleam of the bayonets of distant footsoldiers forming into ranks. As cannonfire resumed and reached a crescendo, a bugler called the half-company of the 2nd to horse.

Colonel Price gave the order to charge. Gunfire from the north pueblo and the interior of the church felled several Americans as bugles and cheers sent five companies dashing across the snow-covered garden plots and pasturage. Three companies of the Missouri 2nd attacked the long north wall. Captain Burgwin's Dragoons and another company rushed the west wall of the church. There they hugged the wall while some of their number raised the ladder to scramble up with axes and chop through the church roof.

But the attack stalled. Chopping a hole large enough to shoot through was taking forever and soldiers peering over the parapets on the roof found few targets in the pueblo compound. The enemy was little more than gunbarrels poked through loopholes or fleet figures that dashed around corners, but any exposure by the soldiers beyond the protective angles of the church drew instant fire. Already two more of Burwin's Dragoons lay wounded. The beleaguered men huddled by the perimeter walls looked at their officers as if to ask, "What've you gotten us into?"

Pinned down, knowing he had to act, Burgwin decided to force the front door of the church. Once inside the church they would outflank the north pueblo.

With a half dozen men hoisting a salvaged timber as a makeshift battering ram, Burgwin drew his sword and led his small party of volunteers around the corner of the church, through the remains of a gate, and up some steps.

At the top of the steps Burgwin was gesturing with his sword when he went sprawling with a musketball in his back. He was already losing consciousness as his troops dragged him to safety. The battering ram lay abandoned on the steps.

One of the fighters in the church grabbed the Delaware by the shoulder and pointed to the opposite wall, indicating he should go look. Through a loophole the Delaware saw Sun Runner in finery, his head wrapped with a bloody rag, making his deliberate way to one of the crude log bridges over the pueblo's stream, seemingly oblivious to the noise and confusion.

163

In his arms he carried a limp, human form. When Sun Runner reached the stream he laid his wife's body in the middle of the bridge and sat cross-legged beside it to face the late-morning sun. Even in the tumult, shreds of Sun Runner's death song reached the Delaware's ears.

"No!" the Delaware cried. He knew he should respect the right of a man to die, that a man's death was his own affair, but Sun Runner was like a father, and his age and wisdom and gentle ways had given hope and something healing for the spirit to the Delaware. Indeed, after the older man consoled him over the loss of Red Willows, the Delaware carried Sun Runner's healing in his heart like a medicinal balm.

They had been sitting in Sun Runner's pueblo apartment, Nicholas in the nest of his grandfather's legs. The Delaware had signed his sorrow, his hands making a breaking motion, then rubbing his heart with one hand. "You must not take the blame on yourself," Sun Runner signed in reply. "Sometimes we can do nothing but give thanks for our lives." Suddenly several twittering sparrows flew into the pueblo apartment, fluttering and swooping in confused chasing flight around and around the small room before shooting up again to disappear through the roof-door. The consternation on the face of Red Willows' mother was immediate, and she and Sun Runner exchanged looks. "That was a bad sign," Sun Runner explained after a long moment. "More bad things are coming." The older man looked reflective for a long while. Then he said, "But we can be happy for today, and for our many days." He talked of how one can draw power from the beauty of the world and keep lost loved ones with them forever in sacred places and in the heart and can live with them forever in these places even after death.

"You will have Red Willows with you forever if you make room in your heart for the beauty of the world," he said. He thought again for several moments before he continued, "And you will make Nicholas proud when you go to fight the Americans."

"Nothing lives forever," Sun Runner sang on the bridge, his song barely audible to the Delaware peering out the loophole. *"Only the mountains and the rivers and the sun. I am but a shadow. I am ready for my long sleep."*

The Delaware saw Sun Runner slowly unwrap his bandaged head and raise both arms to the sun in an invocation. A badly fused shell burst in the creek, sending up a fountain of water near the Indian and showering him with spray.

164

"Nothing lives forever. Only the mountains and the rivers and the sun. I am but a shadow. Thank you for my life."

"No!" the Delaware cried, as another shellburst near the bridge lifted Sun Runner from his place, sent him sprawling, and tossed the woman's body into the stream. Blood spouted from the stump of Sun Runner's awkwardly upraised arm. His hand was blown off. Then the Delaware saw Nicholas running towards his grandfather from the south pueblo. "No, Nicholas!" he cried. The boy disappeared in another fiery cloud.

Furious at the wounding of their captain, Burwin's Dragoons began hacking at the wall of the church with axes, a man on each side of their point of attack. They chopped out chunks of the dried mud until their arms grew too weak to continue, then gave up their axes to others. As the hole in the wall deepened, their axe-work became more awkward, and men crawled into the cavity to gouge at the adobe with bayonets and knives. Price meanwhile ordered the howitzers to lob bombs into the compound. He had blood in his eye now. The rebels would pay a dear price for Captain Burgwin. All these heathen bastards would pay!

The Dragoons finally broke a small hole through the church wall at the end of a cone-shaped tunnel almost five feet deep. As Price moved the six-pounder to within 60 yards of their breach, an intrepid Dragoon held a howitzer shell until its fuse burned nearly to the plug, then pushed the bomb through the hole. WHOOMP! the soldiers heard as they crouched out of harm's way. Thick tendrils of smoke snaked back from the hole. They cheered and pounded each other on the back.

They threw in three more bombs, each producing a satisfying WHOOMP! Then they took cover as the six-pounder blasted at their handiwork to widen their hole. Several rounds later the cavity gaped wide enough for men to scramble through. Gunfire from inside the church had ceased.

Price ordered the six-pounder to a point-blank range of ten yards. The gun blasted three rounds of grape into the interior of the church. Then, their bayonets fixed, Dragoons followed through the hole, Fitz among the first.

The interior was opaque with smoke and dust. Suddenly several figures fell on the Dragoons with knives and tomahawks. War cries and grunts and the sounds of clashing steel

165

reached a quick crescendo. And then there was silence, except for the panting Dragoons and scampering moccasins across the rubble as the last of the defenders retreated through the vestibule.

After the fortress-church fell, Price concentrated his forces on the north buildings. Soon he had a breach in the gate by the trash mound. Soldiers poured through the gate and into the compound. The pueblo fighters in the north pueblo now found themselves out-flanked and out-gunned, and when Price ordered a charge by several more companies on the north wall, resistance collapsed. A couple hundred rebels broke for the south buildings, but in their flight more than a dozen fell to American guns.

Perhaps sixty more dashed for the opening in the perimeter wall where the creek entered the pueblo from the horse meadow. Abandoning the promise of security in the south pueblo, they chose to seek the safety of the mountains. Some ran for the cover of the trees and brush along the creek. Others ran to reach the chaparral beyond the horse meadow.

Bursting from their hiding place in the chapparal, St. Vrain's men rode them down. They shot and clubbed and hacked and killed without distinction. They slaughtered men in the prime of life and terrified youths and old men and even women who had fought alongside their men. Determined that none would escape their revenge, that anyone attempting to flee would pay the ultimate price, they killed in a wild, blood-soaked frenzy.

Charley too. He spurred Whirlwind to run down a fleeing Indian as if chasing a buffalo, put the muzzle of his musket within a foot of the man's back, and pulled the trigger. He tomahawked another wide-shouldered youth darting and dodging like a spooked deer. The boy went sprawling, his outstretched hand still clutching his bow. By the time Charley could turn his horse another rider had shot the boy with his pistol. Nearby Charley glimpsed Baptiste Chalifoux on his knees taking a scalp.

At some point during the frenzy St. Vrain saw the Esquival brothers pick up the pursuit of a rider who'd broken from the pueblo on a pinto. "Get 'im, boys, get 'im!" St. Vrain cried "Don't let the son of a bitch get away!" Urging their mounts to speed, their big Mexican hats dancing behind, the brothers pounded after the fleeing rider.

Within minutes the massacre in the horse meadow and on the verges of the creek was over. The battleground lay littered with bodies, so many they could have been sheaves of grain in a harvest field.

Inside the pueblo the two forces were stalemated. The Americans occupied the now-burning church and the north pueblo, and the Indians and Mexicans occupied the south pueblo. Between lay a killing field. As dusk gathered, shooting grew desultory, then ceased.

Just before dark the Esquival brothers returned to the horse meadow empty-handed. They looked in horror at the carnage. That morning the meadow had lain pristine with new snow. Now it was churned dark with blood and gore, ugly with horse dung and uprooted clumps of lifeless grass. They stared at the shallow, blood-smeared troughs where soldiers had dragged the bodies of the dead to wagons.

The brothers searched out St. Vrain and found him hunkered by his horse under a big willow near the creek, staring with unseeing eyes at the scene of death. The older brother displayed his big Mexican hat holed by a ball. "He got to the trees and started taking pot shots," he explained, waggling his little finger through one of the holes. St. Vrain barely glanced up, his thoughts and emotions still roiling from the massacre. He'd killed an Indian he had known for years in hand-to-hand fighting, a man about his own age. In the heat and terror of the moment he had fought with a mindless fury, his rage and primal urge for survival and revenge fueling him with extraordinary strength. But after wrestling his opponent to the ground and gaining the upper hand, after he knelt astraddle the man's back and had his long hair in gripped in one hand and his upraised tomahawk in the other, when he could have spared his opponent's life, he did not. In that brief instant of hesitation with his weapon raised to strike the fatal blow, when he knew that he had won, something in him said, Kill! And he had killed. In the heat of the moment he had murdered a helpless enemy. Why?

With a distracted motion St. Vrain waved off the explanations and apologies of the Esquival brothers. "Sure, boys," he said, his affect flat. "No sense taking foolish chances."

167

But that evening, back in Taos at a place known as Asa's Tavern, as St. Vrain's men relived their exploits in the horse meadow, Town announced it was one of the principal rebel leaders who'd gotten away from the Esquival brothers. Town had recognized Pablo Montoya on the pinto as he bolted by within a dozen yards. Town said he would have joined the Esquival brothers in pursuit but he was tied up by a "danged purblow" trying to unhorse him in a tug-o-war over Town's discharged musket. "Purblow" was mountain man talk for a Pueblo Indian.

News that the Esquival brothers had chased Montoya into the mountains caused some excitement, and quite a few more fingers waggled through the holes in the young Mexican's hat. Waugh! That was a close one!

But when Colonel Price stopped by to congratulate the Santa Fe volunteers and learned Montoya had slipped away he exploded. "Jesus Christ! you let him get away? You let Montoya get away?" He face purple with rage, he looked ready to fall on the Mexican brothers with his fists. They paled and shrank before the colonel's onslaught.

"That's enough!" St. Vrain shouted after more of Price's sputtering invective. St. Vrain shouldered his way through to get between Price and the Mexicans. Someone handed St. Vrain the holed hat, and as he showed Price the hat English and Spanish tumbled from the Esquival brothers like water flowing down a mountain course, words of apology, of explanation, of denial. St. Vrain held up a calming hand.

Price also calmed down. "All right," he said at last, putting his own little finger through one of the holes. "All right."

Sometime later, after huddling with St. Vrain in a corner and shaking hands with the burly trader, Price rapped on a table to announce a cash reward of $100 to the man or men who brought Montoya back to face justice. The mountain men cheered and Price shook hands with the Esquival brothers and slapped some of the others on the back as he left. When he recognized Charley off to the side he nodded a greeting. "Otterbun," he said half aloud, still unsure of Charley's name. In salute Charley raised an index finger in the direction of his eyebrow.

That cold winter night, while the American soldiers sheltered in the north pueblo, many of St. Vrain's men camped for the night in Asa's Tavern. And that night Charley came down with a bad cold.

Taos Mountain

Next morning Charley waked early with a headache and a sore throat. As soon as he raised up he sneezed and his nose started gushing. The darkened main room of Asa's Tavern was carpeted with snoring men. Some sprawled in sleep atop tables. They lay wrapped in trade blankets and buffalo robes and their great coats in the oblivion of their dreams.

Charley untangled himself from his blanket and coat and maneuvered his way to the back door and into the gloomy pre-dawn. The day looked to be overcast. In the kitchen hut he found a couple women already busy with their morning chores. Wordless, they poured him a cup of coffee that eased his throat, and while he went to the stables and saddled Whirlwind one of the women warmed beans from the previous night's supper. Wincing at each swallow, Charley ate standing near their fire as he recalled scraps of the evening.

Asa's Tavern had been a scene of noisy, boastful stories and exaggerations and several near fights, all part of getting over the massacre in the horse meadow. They had killed 51. Some of the men felt small at what they'd done and chose to sit quietly or had gone off to be alone. Others, even some of the most hardened of St. Vrain's men, had drunk too much whiskey. So much killing did not go down easy. Charley had seen the same thing even with buffalo. Something in a man went against so much killing, and in the horse meadow there had been way too much. Things had gotten out of hand.

After Charley finished the warmed-over beans and slurped a second cup of coffee the women gave him two small loaves of fresh-baked Mexican bread, their crusts hard as rock. He put them inside his blanket coat to keep them from freezing and gave the women each a dime.

The cart track to the pueblo lay deserted in the dawning. The pueblo itself looked as lifeless as a sarcophagus. The only signs of human habitation were a few wispy plumes of cooking smoke. Surly American pickets guarded their fires near the pueblo and looked at Charley with suspicion, but no one raised a challenge.

Charley skirted the south side. Atop the Indian stronghold he noticed a white flag he hadn't seen the evening before. Well, maybe they've had enough, he thought. Maybe we've all had enough.

Beyond the horse meadow he picked up the tracks of Montoya and the Esquival brothers. He was pondering how far the brothers had followed when he noticed in the brightening day another set of tracks made by the moccasins of a pueblo man. The moccasin tracks were fresher. Someone besides Montoya had escaped from the pueblo, perhaps during the night.

After a time Charley found where the Esquival brothers had caught up with Montoya. Then he discovered the rebel leader had turned his horse to face them. Jesus, they had talked! The hoof-trampled snow indicated a lengthy conversation. Then the tracks showed Montoya had continued up the stream and the Esquival brothers headed back to the pueblo.

So the Mexicans brothers had lied! The holed hat was probably from their own musketball!

Charley kept on Montoya's trail. The moccasined man's tracks also continued following Montoya. Soon Charley recognized Montoya's horse was lame in its left rear quarter and the pueblo man was also hurt. Here and there he saw faint pinkish spatters in the snow.

The trail followed the stream, climbing steadily through increasingly steep-sided gorges relieved from time to time by little meadows. The sacred mountain of the pueblo loomed above like a foreboding, blue-black storm. It stood brooding, its summit lost in morning clouds. The pueblo believed their sacred mountain was forbidden to outsiders.

Where the snow was deep Charley noticed Montoya had kept to the saddle. That was foolish, Charley thought. Better Montoya should break the trail and save his horse. But Montoya was getting old. Maybe he was too tired also. How many days since the rebels had killed Bent? Two weeks at least, and all that time Montoya would have been snatching food and sleep as he tried to keep the rebellion going. Maybe by now he was as sick of the killing as Charley was. Maybe by now nothing much mattered except to get back to regular life. Maybe by now, like Charley, Montoya had lost too much.

At a fork in the trail Charley saw the rebel leader had taken the wrong track.

Charley dismounted to lead Whirlwind, puffing as he climbed a switchback that rose quickly. The sharp air hurt his throat. His headache throbbed. He raised his scarf to his mouth so the air warmed a bit before assaulting his throat. Then the realization came to him that the moccasin man must also be trying to catch Montoya, because he too had followed what any man from the pueblo would know was the wrong turn.

The climb afoot got Charley sweating. He took the scarf from around his neck and stuffed it in his pocket and breathed through his mittened hand. He wondered how long Montoya had kept moving. Maybe not long. The gimpy horse would have been balky, especially on the poor trail.

Where was the Mexican headed? They said this branch of the trail led to a wispy waterfall, to a wall of rock that offered no farther progress. It was the end of the trail. Didn't Montoya know that?

After an hour or so Charley saw where the moccasin man left the trail. Tying Whirlwind, Charley stalked the tracks, his musket ready. A short way off the trail he found the remains of a small fire in a shallow cavity of a rock-face. A few crushed boughs showed where the man had sat. The ground under the coals still held a little warmth. Moccasin-man had taken a different way back down to the trail.

Charley climbed for another half-hour and was leading Whirlwind again when he stopped on a level to blow his nose with a finger alongside each nostril. His head pounded and he wondered why he kept going. The throbbing of his head made the $100 reward Price put on Montoya's head seem hardly worth the pain. Besides, what was so important about Montoya? If he got away he'd turn up again, probably right back in the Taos valley.

Charley imagined Montoya's return years hence, how he would protest his innocence: "Oh, no, señores, I knew nothing of the trouble in Taos, nothing. I was away, you see." Then what would Charley do? What would any of them do? Time had a way of healing the wounds of most hurts.

The Delaware's voice seemed to come from right behind. "You bringing my horse back, Charley?"

Charley turned slowly. The moccasin man was Big Nigger! The Indian was probably hidden in a thicket of little pines thirty yards up the steep slope. He must have slipped off the trail around the bend and doubled back. Charley wondered how long he'd waited in ambush. The Indian spoke again. "Since you gave me a white man's word, I wondered."

"You hurt?"

The Delaware did not answer.

"You gonna shoot me?"

The Indian's laugh was a grunt. "I could've shot you at Embudo."

"Didn't try?"

"Shot the black white man instead."

Charley made a face. "Well, you didn't kill 'im," he said after a pause. In the mountain stillness their words carried with unusual clarity.

"That's all right."

They were silent, Charley looking for the Indian without wanting to seem too obvious. He could see a portion of the trail some way down the mountain where the Delaware must have first spotted him.

Charley's musket was sheathed on the horse. He could try to grab it and take cover behind Whirlwind, but the track was narrow and the downslope fell away like a cliff. If the horse shied Charley might find himself entangled in windfalls halfway to hell, an easy target for the Indian.

When Charley finally spotted the dull gleam of the Delaware's musket and his darker shadow in the pines he was surprised he'd failed to see them earlier.

"They shot her, Charley."

"Who?"

"Red Willows."

"Who? the Army?"

"No, Turley's. Somebody at Turley's."

Charley's shoulders sagged. "I'm sorry, hamigo, I'm sorry they did that."

"Little Nicholas is dead too."

"The boy?"

There was a long silence. When the Delaware spoke his

173

voice was strained. "Those big guns, Charley. Those big guns killed him at the pueblo. After dark I went out and got him. He was so small...so small."

Charley slowly shook his head. He could think of nothing to say. He made a sound at the side of his mouth, a *chik,* and shook his head. "It was ugly," he said at last, scenes of the massacre in horse meadow vivid in his mind's eye. "The whole damned business, it's just too damned ugly."

The Indian didn't say anything for a long while. Then he stood, an obscure looming figure in the darkness of the little pines. "You after me?" he asked Charley, parting boughs and stepping into full view, his musket in his right hand, a bow and quiver on his back. His other arm was hidden beneath a blanket over his shoulder. His hair was loose and spread over his shoulders in the pueblo style. Charley saw a dark blood stain on the blanket.

"Didn't know it was you," Charley said. "Thought you was a Pueblo." The Indian half laughed as he picked his way carefully down the slope. A few feet from the trail his foot caught on something covered by snow and he pitched forward, saving himself from tumbling down the slope by grabbing the top spire of a little pine with his blanket hand. He sat heavily in the snow by the trail, barely suppressing a groan. He packed down a place for his feet and propped his musket upright between his legs, the blanket fallen away. He looked worn out.

"Me, too," he said, regarding his moccasins. "I thought I was a pueblo too." Then after a long pause said, "But I'm going home now, before you people hang me."

"They say you're already dead, that you got all shot up in the church."

The Delaware snorted. "That's why you'll hang me. You can't have me alive if I'm already dead."

Town had said in Asa's Tavern that Big Nigger was seen on the church roof taking pot shots at the Americans and even Price had wondered who the powerful-looking Indian was who taunted the Americans in their own tongue. Some swore it was Big Nigger who shot Captain Burgwin and that he had killed three or four more soldiers in the church. In Asa's tavern the stories and exaggerations of the familiar Indian's feats were already beginning to represent the faceless, vanquished enemy, his white man's name capturing both the grudging awe and the

174

thinly veiled contempt most Americans felt for those who had risen up against the new American government. Dead, the Indian would become larger than life, a fairytale monster slain to save the kingdom.

"I hid in the south pueblo and sneaked out last night along the creek to get across the mountains. Then I saw these tracks."

"You know who it is?"

The Delaware shrugged. "Don't need to. I need a horse. I didn't see until daylight that the damned thing's lame." He regarded Whirlwind, a much thinner horse than when he'd given him over to Charley on rim of the arroyo above Turley's mill. "You trying to kill my horse too?"

Charley eased his way around Whirlwind and hunkered. The Indian wore a blood-encrusted bandage on his left forearm. A little fresh blood still seeped. "Hurt bad?" Charley asked.

The Indian shrugged his good shoulder. By way of reply he asked Charley, "You got tobacco?" Charley reached beneath his coat and drew a plug from his shirt-pocket. He seated himself beside the Indian and cut off a good-size chunk and offered it on the blade of his knife, then cut another chunk for himself. The two men worked their tobacco in silence as they looked past the long gorge they'd come up, Charley regretful of his sore throat whenever he had to swallow. In the distance variegated striations of washed-out browns and gray whites stretched forever, the dark sides of far-away mesas barely visible in the ghostly air.

Picking up their conversation from when it had been interrupted by the tobacco ceremony, Charley said, "It's Montoya. A couple of our Mexican boys let him get away."

Charley was silent for a long minute, then suddenly said with some feeling, "They say Turley was killed up at my place." Charley shook his head at the thought. "And now I keep wondering about my wife and Jose, about whether they had anything to do with it." Neither man said anything for some time, then Charley said, "I don't know what I'd do if they did. I'm sick of all this killing. Maybe it's for the law to decide."

The Indian didn't respond. Instead he removed the messy tobacco cud from his mouth and pulled down the top of his bloody bandage with a finger.

"Ball?" Charley asked.

"Long knife." The Indian squished the tobacco onto his wound and straightened the bandage he'd fashioned from the red bandanna he usually wore as a headdress. "It got pretty hot in the church before we got run out."

Charley nodded. He saw himself tomahawking the boy in the horse meadow. He remembered seeing St. Vrain struggling hand-to-hand with an Indian.

"There's a one hundred dollar reward for bringing Montoya in," he said. After a long silence he said, "But it's not the money."

"You going to shoot him?"

"I told you, I'm sick of the killing."

"I was thinking of what Montoya might want. At least a ball is quicker than hanging." The Delaware offered a small smile.

Charley didn't smile back. "I don't know. I guess I just wanted to get away from all the killing...all the bragging."

A light snow had begun to fall. Charley twisted on his perch to regard the trail ahead. His headache was suddenly better, almost gone, but he still winced at each swallow. "How far you figure he is? This trail don't go nowhere."

The Delaware didn't look at Charley and waited for some time before he replied. "Wouldn't surprise me if we got him before long."

They caught up with Montoya at the dead-end. Perhaps an inch of fresh snow had fallen by the time they found him sitting on a meagre cushion of pine boughs, one boot off, his foot bare, his ankle resting on his other booted foot near a smoldering fire. At their approach the Mexican rebel leader barely raised his head. The pinto stood nearby, a smallish horse with its nose and left rear hoof inches from the ground. Montoya had pulled down some moss and a few clumps of dead grass that found life in the fractured rock-face near the waterfall, but the animal seemed disinterested. The waterfall itself was ice. Cycles of freezing and melting had created grotesque shapes that swirled up the dark granite like a sculpture of vaguely humanoid figures trapped in myriad postures of torment. The towering wall of rock and ice seemed to give off a damp coldness that was perceptible even in the winter air.

"Señores," Montoya said at last. Charley was uncertain whether Montoya recognized him as a longtime Taos man. Gray-haired, in his fifties, Montoya's once-handsome face sagged with fatigue. His eyes were distant and mournful.

The rebel leader was dressed in leather pants of the Spanish style that once were probably elegant, but now, like his high-heeled, thick-soled boots, the leather was scuffed and cut and soiled. A soiled trade blanket covered his neck and shoulders. In the poor light his green tunic beneath looked almost black. He was hatless, and snow had settled on his hair and shoulders. His hands were bare. His musket, an expensive weapon prettied with embossed silver, leaned against a nearby tree, where his sword and powderhorn and bullet pouch hung from the stub of a broken branch. He made no effort to rouse himself, but remained seated on the ground massaging the ankle of his bootless foot. He seemed almost disinterested in the newcomers.

"Perhaps this is where I'll die," he said in Spanish, not raising his eyes from the struggling fire. Charley understood Montoya had probably said something about death but was unsure of Montoya's meaning.

"What'd he say?" the Indian asked.

"I guess he thinks I'm gonna kill him."

"Well?"

Charley shook his head once and walked over to get Montoya's musket, an older-model flintlock. He examined the pretty silverwork and made a point of turning away before he raised the weapon to his shoulder a couple of times to test its feel. He admired the silverwork again before he removed the flint and placed the weapon against the tree, aware the Indian watched his movements with a close eye. Then Charley examined Montoya's horse. He concluded it must have had pulled a hamstring when the Mexican made his dash for the mountains. "I was wondering," Charley said as if to no one in particular, "Where's my mule?" He hunkered by the fire.

"Got shot."

"Got shot?" Charley looked surprised.

"At Turley's. Somebody in the mill at Turley's that was a good shot."

177

Charley shook his head. "Damn!" he said regretfully. "That was a good mule." He sighed. Well, maybe the $100 was all right after all, he thought. He'd need another riding mule. After years of getting around on horses he'd come to like the sure-footedness of a mule.

He squatted across the fire from Montoya. "You know English?" he asked. "Hobble English?" Montoya glanced up, then shrugged with downturned lips. "You know sign?" Charley asked, and waggled a forefinger away from his mouth, Indian sign language for speaking. Montoya shook his head.

"Why don't you try two fingers, white man," the Indian said.

Charley looked around at the Indian, puzzlement on his face, then smiled a little when he caught on to the Indian's joke about a white man's forked tongue. "Well, this is a fix," Charley said, stirring the fire with a stick. "We can't talk." He succeeded in coaxing a few more flames, but then the smoke made him sneeze, so he rose to break off dead branches to make a better fire, snapping the branches over his thigh into smaller pieces with quick, decisive motions. In a few minutes the fire began to crackle.

"Not for me," the Delaware said at last. "You whites talk too much anyway." He stood by Whirlwind with his wounded arm resting on the front shoulder of the horse, his other hand gently stroking the neck and fingering the mane. The scalp at his waist played peekaboo as his arm moved. Charley hadn't noticed the corn-colored scalp until they set out together on Montoya's trail. From the color he wondered if it was Billy's.

When the Delaware joined him to follow Montoya's trail Charley was uncertain what was going on. He knew the Indian could have shot him from ambush and taken Whirlwind and gone on his way with no one the wiser. But the Indian had engaged him instead. What was the Delaware thinking? Charley wondered. Finally he decided the Delaware was going to help Charley catch Montoya before reclaiming Whirlwind and escaping over the mountains. Maybe the Indian figured that way everything would be square between them. Charley was unsure. After all, had the Indian killed Billy?

"No, I guess it's not a fix for you," Charley said, pushing himself to his feet. He blew his nose with his fingers, walked over to Whirlwind, and untied his foodbag containing coffeepot and frying pan and tin plate and cup, aware the Indian still watched his every move. With his big knife Charley hacked some ice from the waterfall into the coffeepot and set the coffeepot on the fire. Then he took a pouch of coffee and a slab of bacon from the food bag and the two loaves from inside his coat. Another half inch of snow had fallen and light was failing by the time the coffee boiled and thick slices of bacon sputtered and curled in the sizzling fat. The fragrance of cooking coffee and frying bacon filled the air. All this time none of the men said a word. Montoya had inched back a bit from the bigger fire and sat impassive with his bare foot extended towards the fire, massaging his ankle and staring into the flames. The Indian stood watchful, rooted by his horse.

Charley sawed one of the small Mexican loaves in half with his knife and poured coffee and lifted some bacon onto the plate and presented the cup and plate to Montoya, who looked surprised, then smiled sadly. The Mexican dipped the bread into the coffee and gnawed off a mouthful and chewed appreciatively, still distracted. He slurped the hot coffee with relish, but never raised his eyes. He ate the bacon with his fingers, saving the last of his bread to wipe the greasy plate clean.

Charley studied the Mexican as he ate, not sure what to think about the sad man's part in the bloodshed. The Delaware had told Charley on the trail that he hadn't seen Montoya among the rebels until they were all assembled for the march to Santa Fe, when some of the men had helped Montoya up onto a cart to make a speech in the plaza in Taos. Now Charley wondered why Colonel Price was so hot about Montoya. Was a man who made a speech worse than a man who pulled a trigger or took a scalp?

After Montoya finished eating Charley poured more coffee and invited the Delaware to eat by proffering another plateful of bread and bacon. The Indian at last left his horse to squat by the fire, his musket canted between his legs. He nodded his thanks to Charley as he took the plate and cup.

"You moving on?" Charley asked him.

The Delaware did not answer until he had dipped some bread and chewed and swallowed. "You staying?" he asked in reply.

"Well, I ain't going far with Montoya here, not with that gimpy horse, not tonight. It's a long walk back to Taos."

179

The Delaware looked at him. "Well, at least it's all downhill," he said, and smiled to himself at Charley's rueful expression.

They sat around the fire looking like cowled monks with their blankets over their heads and shoulders, too weary from days of marching and fighting to say much. Charley grew sleepy, and when the Indian offered to take the first turn at tending the fire Charley gratefully stretched out.

That night the snow fell steadily, making white mounds of Montoya and Charley as they slept the sleep of exhaustion. When Charley finally waked in the pre-dawn, his turn at the fire never taken, he was not surprised to find a graying bed of coals and the Delaware and Whirlwind both gone.

During the next two days, separated by the impossible barrier of language, Charley and Montoya exchanged few words. But after they drank their morning coffee that first day the Mexican showed Charley where a sliver of shrapnel had sliced through his boot and buried itself in his heel, Charley deduced what Montoya's dilemma had been on the mountain trail. Unable to dig the metal out, unable to walk without excruciating pain, Montoya had ridden the lame pinto to the point of cruelty in his attempt to escape. But the Mexican obviously felt bad about the smallish horse. Every once in a while he would look at the forlorn animal and say something soft and sad-sounding, as if apologizing.

Charley tried to find the shrapnel in Montoya's heel, first passing his knife over the live coals a few times before beginning to probe. Montoya lay on his stomach, his foot in Charley's lap. But Charley's digging produced such a flow of blood that he couldn't see to work and he gave up when Montoya suddenly fainted. Instead of trying to dig out the shrapnel Charley ended up cutting off the tail of the Mexican's long shirt, packing a cud of tobacco in the wound, and bandaging the foot as best he could. Then he fashioned a crutch and worked for several minutes to cut away the back part of Montoya's boot so he could pull it on over his wounded foot. Later that morning they started down the mountain. Each time Montoya put his foot down Charley saw him wince with pain.

As they slowly made their way back along the snowy track Montoya would sometimes suddenly utter a few words, as if giving voice to a conversation going on in his head. Charley wondered what he was thinking about, whether it was his family, or perhaps what he'd say when he faced the law in Taos.

"You could just shoot me," he said to Charley in Spanish when they had stopped to rest. Montoya's long, sickly face was pale and beaded with sweat. "You're going to hang me anyway." When Charley failed to respond Montoya made a motion of a gun to his head and pulled an imaginary trigger, but Charley just shook his head and made a disapproving sound and after a few minutes motioned the Mexican to his feet.

That afternoon Charley was absorbed in thinking whether he should tie the Mexican's hands that night when he stumbled over a protruding root in the trail and went sprawling, his musket skittering out of his hand and coming to rest not far from Montoya's feet. For a long moment Charley lay stunned. The Mexican watched as Charley gathered himself to rise, then let his head sink to the snow again. He suddenly felt that he had come to the end of his endurance. He could go no farther. For three weeks he'd been living on the edge of life and death and he'd finally reached his end. If Montoya shot him with his own musket...well, that would just be the way it ended. He wouldn't care.

He lay in the snow for several long moments, seeing with unseeing eyes the indifferent mountain scene on the other side of the chasm by the trail.

"Señor?" Montoya leaned on his crutch where he'd stopped, Charley's musket just a few feet away.

At last Charley stirred and slowly picked himself up. He looked Montoya in the eye as he approached to recover his weapon. "*Tsk, tsk,*" Montoya said, his expression sympathetic.

That evening they bedded down in the Delaware's old camp, Montoya's long face flushed with fever. Their only supper was the last of the coffee, but Charley melted snow for hot water to bathe Montoya's foot, now swollen and angry-looking. At the last minute Charley decided to take the Mexican's boots as a precaution, thinking he would sleep more securely knowing that Montoya wouldn't sneak away. But Montoya, fitful and feverish, mumbled throughout the night and kept Charley half awake anyway.

Retribution

The Plaza

Before the rebellion, when winter's midmorning sun began to warm the adobe of the town, a dozen or more old men would drift toward the Taos plaza from different streets and houses, their faces fissured with age, their serapes and blankets faded and worn, their gnarled hands locked on faithful staffs and canes. Generations of custom and usage granted these old men the sunniest walls on the plaza to sit against, where hardly anyone passed without offering a polite nod or a respectful greeting. Little escaped the notice or comment of these elders, and little failed to prompt the re-telling of an old wrinkled story many times told - of wonderful horses and faithful dogs and intelligent pigs and bountiful crops; of fearsome storms, hard times, and desperate men who died alone; of rampaging Utes and Navajos, of out-witted American traders, of the Virgin's miracles, of magnificent cathedrals in the rich cities to the south, of beautiful women and love, of betrayal and bloody revenge. A listening child might stand entranced by their stories until an errand was forgotten, then follow the old men to continue listening as they moved with the sun to a better wall.

The old men would linger on the plaza until the warmth of the sun leaked away in late afternoon, then in ones and twos would pick their deliberate ways home, perhaps never to return again, for old age is fragile. As evening lengthened and the light failed and as the square became deserted, scattered chinks of yellow light from surrounding houses provided the plaza's only signs of life. Even under the light of stars and moon the plaza stayed empty, for in wintertime the center of the town lived with the rhythms of the sun.

But after the battle for the pueblo the plaza belonged both day and night to swaggering American soldiers and government men and loud and boisterous traders and trappers and curious visitors. After the battle for the pueblo, numbed by the carnage, townspeople shunned the plaza and the Americans.

And not just the townspeople. The deaths in the battle for the pueblo and the massacre in the horse meadow numbed the entire valley. Nearly a quarter of the pueblo's population died in the carnage. And untold others from the town and surrounding ranchos. Perhaps 250 were killed in the fighting, Colonel Price figured. The wounded were countless.

The dead became a bloody bond between the town and the

185

pueblo, between Mexican and Indian, which for generations had lived in prickly harmony as they mingled at their respective festivals and celebrations and worked out with wrangling and occasional violence their constant disputes over water and grazing lands and trade. Marriages between the young inhabitants of Taos and the pueblo were grudgingly accepted, though never welcomed. But now more things bound the two cultures together than kept them separate. Now the force of American arms left no doubt that the old order was dead and a new order prevailed. Witness the swift hanging of Charley's prisoner.

The rebels had sued for peace the morning Charley went after Montoya. The white flag he noticed atop the south pueblo was their flag of surrender. Three days later, when Charley brought his prisoner and the gimpy pinto past the pueblo, American sentries stood guard on the rooftops and looked with curiosity at Charley and Montoya. The rebel leader hobbled along on Charley's makeshift crutch, his free hand pressed against his chest in a sign of submission.

In Taos Charley found the townspeople furtive and hangdog. A few of St. Vrain's men on the plaza who recognized Charley's prisoner sent up a ragged cheer. "Shawlee," Baptiste called, pointing to the sad-eyed, gimpy pinto burdened with the men's gear, "where dat big horse? You make bad trade!" Charley grinned at the laughing men and postured a little with Montoya's fancy musket. His cold was much improved and now that he'd gotten Montoya down from the mountain his spirits also lightened. To bring in the rebel leader was a feather in his cap.

Price shook Charley's hand, the colonel's smile broad. "Good work, Otterbee!" he said. At last the Americans had a rebel Mexican general in hand! Now they could present an object lesson to the folly of taking up arms against the government. Colonel Price ordered an immediate military trial of the prisoner.

Scarcely an hour later, the proceedings began. Five officers took their places at the priest's table in the *sala* of *casa Martinez*, now the headquarters of Colonel Price. Spectators who couldn't fit into the room packed the doorways and peered through the louvered windows.

His uniform freshly brushed, his expression pleased, Colonel Price could not hide a satisfied smile as guards brought the prisoner from a back room. On the way down from the sacred mountain a sleeve of Montoya's battle-besmeared green militia coat had somehow ripped on a broken branch and now a long flap of the woolen sleeve hung loose. Montoya looked a picture of defeat and humiliation, of fatigue and pain.

As guards led the prisoner to a chair facing the court, Antonio Martinez whispered an order and a servant disappeared, only to reappear in few moments with a milking stool, which the priest set in place for Montoya's foot. The rebel general sat with his boot and sock off, his badly swollen, discolored foot hanging over the stool's edge. After brief preliminaries concerning the charges, with St. Vrain translating, Price consulted a sheet of paper before him and began the proceedings. The prisoner's answers were brief, almost inaudible. His eyes never left the floor.

"Pablo Montoya, did you not come to Santa Fe last fall and take an oath of allegiance to the American government?" Yes, Montoya answered in Spanish. Price made a checkmark with his pencil, an instrument secured in a holder of filigreed silver. "Did you not sign a document affirming your oath?" Yes. Another checkmark. "Were you coerced into taking that oath of allegiance?" No. Checkmark. "Then, Pablo Montoya, did you not, sometime after, within the last month, put your name to a manifesto, a *pronunciamento*, that called for the overthrow of the American government of New Mexico?" Price seemed pleased he was able to use the Spanish word.

Yes. "Did you know that by putting your name to that manifesto you were committing an act of treason against your government?"

"I did not consider it treason."

"No? You did not think you were violating your oath of allegiance?"

"Some things are greater than mere oaths, important things."

Price regarded him. "Maybe in your scheme of things, señor, but not in a civilized country." The room laughed. Price made two more checkmarks.

"Did you not then lead a rebellion by force of arms against the American government?"

"Yes, but the soldiers elected me to lead them."

"Soldiers! Soldiers elected you! Don't you mean rebels?"

"No, Colonel, soldiers, volunteers, like those who elected

187

you, *sus conquistadoro*. What was I to do? They wanted me to lead them."

When Montoya's answer was translated, Colonel Price darkened. "No, Sir! not like me, not for a minute like me! How dare you compare my election...." He stopped, irritated the Mexican had baited him into an outburst.

Colonel Price studied his paper while he collected himself. Montoya grimaced as he shifted his wounded foot a little. Price resumed, "Did you know that in leading these so-called soldiers against the government, even though you say you were elected, you were committing another act of treason?" Montoya shrugged. "Answer this court!"

"*Si.*" Checkmark.

Price scanned his paper. He rolled the fancy pencil between his fingertips, his lips pursed. "Pablo Montoya, do you know that under the laws of this land, indeed all civilized lands, the penalty for treason is death?" Montoya shrugged again. "You must speak for the record," Price said, his voice showing irritation. He repeated his question and St. Vrain translated again.

Montoya shrugged again. "*Si*," he answered, as if the matter were of no great importance, "I know the penalty."

Colonel Price took a big breath and let it out and exchanged looks with the other officers of the court. The murmur of the spectators rose. Well, there you had it! A brilliant bit of questioning and there you had it. Caught like a fox in the henhouse!

"Pablo Montoya," Colonel Price said, "do you have anything to say before this court renders its judgment on the charges against you?" Montoya gave an almost imperceptible shrug. "In your defense, anything at all?" Price asked. He looked at St. Vrain expectantly, as if St. Vrain should prompt Montoya to say something.

Montoya remained silent, then moved his healthy foot and raised mournful eyes. He drew a long breath. "Señor," he said, his gaze as high as the hastily drawn bill of indictment that lay on the priest's dining table, "I know you will sentence me to die because that is what you must do. Nothing I can say will change that. But I deserve to die by firing squad, señor, because I deserve to die as a soldier, with a soldier's honor. I fought for my country, for my beloved Mexico. I fought with honor and with pride. And that is all I have left now, my honor and my pride. You have taken everything else, you and your army, you and your government, and now you will take your revenge."

He straightened in his chair and looked directly at Colonel Price. "But if I am guilty, señor, remember this: It was you Americans who murdered hundreds of my countrymen trying to surrender at the battle of San Jacinto and you Americans who broke the Treaty of San Jacinto and you Americans who are stealing my country beyond the Rio Bravo and you Americans who steal California from my beloved Mexico!"

St. Vrain glared at Montoya as a handful of spectators who understood the Mexican's speech made a stir. "Well?" Price asked, "what'd he say?"

"You don't want to know," St. Vrain said.

"Damn it, Ceran, this is a military court! What did he say? It's important for the record!"

St. Vrain's tone was petulant. "He says we broke the Treaty of San Jacinto, when Kearny...."

"That's a damned lie!" one of the presiding officers cried as the room erupted. He'd risen to his feet from his place at the judge's table, his face beet-red, his finger accusing. "Remember those murders in Goliad and the massacre at the Alamo! It's you damned Mexicans who came across the Rio Grande in Texas and you damned Mexicans who murdered American prisoners, even women and children! You're all a damned bunch of damned liars and scoundrels!" Shouts and curses directed at Montoya overwhelmed the efforts of Colonel Price to restore order as he banged on the table with the heel of his fist.

After this long, noisy interruption, during which someone flung several musketballs at Montoya, Colonel Price asked the prisoner if he had anything more to say. Montoya shrugged and shook his head. He didn't even look up. A bitter smile played about his mouth.

For a few moments the officers at the table conferred behind their hands. Then Colonel Price announced Montoya had been found guilty of treason and the penalty was death by hanging. The sentence would be carried out immediately.

At his announcement the spectators broke into such a noisy cheer that Colonel Price could only nod his permission for Padre Martinez to approach the prisoner.

Montoya sat woodenly as Martinez knelt beside him, the

priest's face reddened with silent outrage. For several moments he kept his lantern jaw locked to hold his anger in check. Then, white-knuckled, he clutched the huge silver cross he wore around his neck and in the confusion of the makeshift court-room he heard Montoya's confession. As he knelt beside the condemned man with his head close, the priest's other arm em-braced the shoulders of the defeated rebel leader as if protecting him from the excited swirl around them of the self-congratulatory Americans.

Charley was half-finished with his first good meal in days when someone rushed into Asa's Tavern. "Hangin' 'im, Char-ley," the man said. "Better come!" Surprised, Charley looked around to see if anyone took notice of his being singled out. Ex-cept for a couple of strangers who glanced in his direction as they hurried out to catch the excitement, no one paid him at-tention. He remained sitting in front of his food, confused by his sudden sadness. He'd known Montoya faced death, and Mon-toya had known it too. But so soon! What kind of trial was that?

Charley stepped out to stand on the portico of Asa's Tavern, but he couldn't see much. A crowd of perhaps a hundred or more soldiers and St. Vrain's men jostled under a huge cotton-wood tree down by the jail. A few townspeople watched from rooftops. The bayonets of the on-duty soldiers gleamed.

Charley caught a glimpse of Montoya's filthy green coat and his hooded head for only a few seconds before the drums rolled and the condemned man dropped from sight as unseen hands pulled away the big-wheeled Mexican cart the prisoner stood on. After that all Charley saw was Montoya's white hood swinging like a pendulum from a crosstree tied in the branches. The hood swung to and fro in a surprisingly wide arc. A lump grew in Charley's throat and he tasted the bitter stuff of some of his meal. He'd marched Montoya down from the mountain more as keeper than captor. He'd shared his food and coffee with his prisoner and had tended the man's wound. Now he'd just witnessed Montoya's immediate, ignominious death. Charley felt used, cheapened, and betrayed.

Yes, he'd known he was bringing Montoya back to face the law. But was this law, what he saw, this...this...this lynching?

Charley went back to his place in Asa's tavern and sat skewed sideways in his chair staring at the dirt floor for a long time. He wondered if anybody else had figured out what he was starting to figure out, that once you start killing you can never go back to the way it was before. Taos would never be the same. So many dead and gone forever - Simeon Turley, Charles Bent, Stephan Lee, Cornelio Vigil, a dozen more. And how many in the pueblo? Now their families would have to live with the pain of loss and grief and loneliness. And for what?

After a while Charley started wondering whether Serephina would ever feel the same about him for bringing her country-man in to be hanged. Then he started wondering whether he would ever feel the same about her.

Charley's shoulders lifted high as he drew in a long, long breath and let loose a huge sigh. He sat staring at the floor. Everything looked so hardscrabble.

By order of Colonel Price, Montoya's body was left hanging in the noose for twenty-four hours as a lesson to the town.

The way some told the story later, the Esquival brothers sneaked off after Charley told about the tracks he saw beyond the pueblo and how it had looked to him like the Esquivals had met up with Montoya and talked. Hell, the brothers skedaddled before they had to explain themselves and their danged holed hat was nothing but a sneaky trick.

But some said that it was Charley's brother Tom who could read sign like an Indian, not Charley, and that Charley was probably wrong about what he saw. Why, the Esquivals were as good Americans as anybody, and what kind of fool would shoot holes in a perfectly good hat anyway?

The way St. Vrain told the story, the Esquival boys resigned from the mountain man company because they were unhappy at seeing the Pueblo Indians treated so badly - men forced into labor to load and unload supplies, dig graves and latrines, cut wood and carry water. "This isn't why we volunteered," they told St. Vrain. "To see all this," and they gestured towards a half dozen Pueblo men hitched up like mules to pull a wagon-load of firewood for the Army.

The day before Charley brought Montoya in to be hanged St. Vrain had accepted the resignations of the Esquival brothers.

But it wasn't just the Esquivals. Some even resented the

191

way Charley went after Montoya all by himself. They remembered shaking hands on a deal in Asa's Tavern that they would all set out together and run Montoya down. But then that darned Charley had sneaked off and hogged the whole $100 reward himself. Listen, why did he think he could come and go like a danged Indian?

The mood of the mountain man company was sour.

With the rebellion put down, a rebel general hanged, and other rebel leaders like Chavez dead in the fighting, Colonel Price made desultory efforts to piece together the puzzle of the uprising. There had been widespread conspiracy, no doubt about that. But first-hand information was impossible to come by. Only one principal known to be in the van of the rebellion was in custody, the pueblo leader named Tomasito. But Colonel Price was unable bring himself to put the Indian on trial as a military man in a military court. The idea of an Indian being accorded the status of a military officer was unseemly. Indians at war were savage warriors, not military men. In any event, Tomasito refused to speak, which made the matter "mute" as many said in Asa's Tavern. So Colonel Price kept Tomasito imprisoned while awaiting instructions from Washington about what to do with the Indian rebel leader.

According to rumor, one other rebel leader was still at large - "a half-breed," some said - a shadowy figure who was holed up on the other side of the Sange de Cristos mountains. And there were probably others.

Some like St. Vrain suspected Antonio Martinez knew more than he let on and that he'd actually helped prepare the rebels' *pronunciamento*. But Taos remained tight-lipped and protective. Instead, townpeople maintained the trouble-makers were "outsiders" who'd come up "from the south," that they were "not from around here."

St. Vrain snorted his contempt at these explanations. "They were all in on it, every damned one of 'em, in some way or other, but they all know that if anyone talks...." He drew a finger across his throat.

Colonel Price shrugged off St. Vrain's petulant suspicions. Truth was, the colonel was more than ready to quit the dirty little town in this dirty, unfriendly land. The enemy's army destroyed, he was ready to leave the clean-up to civilians. With three or four makeshift jails full of prisoners accused of involvement in the various murders and in the rebellion's widespread looting and arson there was certainly plenty to occupy the civilian courts. Charles Bent's widow and her sisters had already identified Bent's killers, and a few other witnesses also came forward.

But much remained unknown. Who killed Stephen Lee, Elliott Lee's brother? Who killed James Leal, an American who'd come to town just a few days before the rebellion? Who killed Simeon Turley? Who killed Cornelio Vigil and Narcisse Beaubien and Pablo Jaramillo? And what of the two trappers killed up at Rio Colorado? And what of the men at Turley's mill? Jesus! How would they ever sort out Turley's mill? The authorities had a hundred questions, and Taos produced a hundred stories.

Some said Cornelio Vigil was the first to die in the uprising. A longtime Taos notable, uncle to Charles Bent's wife, Vigil had made the mistake of accepting a position in Kearny's government. Locals muttered he was also in cahoots with St. Vrain and other Americans in shady land deals and that he had got just what he deserved. Whatever the case, in the pre-dawn darkness the day of the uprising a hooting mob of two hundred or more torchlit faces assembled outside Cornelio Vigil's house. They banged on Vigil's door and windows until he appeared in hastily donned pants, his nightshirt hanging out in back. Looking frightened, and a little silly in the nightcap he still wore, he stood barefoot just outside his portico door, jostled this way and that by the crowd while his wife hovered nearby wearing a terrified expression. "Come back in!" she cried. "They're going to hurt you!"

"Are you with us?" the mob demanded. "Are you going to get our men out of jail?" Someone snatched off Vigil's nightcap. "Traitor!"

"No!" he cried. "I'm not a traitor! I love my country! I'm one of you!"

"You're a traitor." "You sold out!" "You're helping the Americans whore our country."

"No, I love my country!"

"You're a whore-master! Traitor!"

Vigil didn't have long to live after he challenged the mob. "You fools!" he cried. "Do you think you stand a chance against the Americans with your few muskets and your bows and arrows? Do you think you'll succeed by trying to fight them? You'll die! You'll all die!"

"No, you'll die!" "You'll be the first!" "Traitor!"

Even in a violent land the first blood in a fresh conflict is hard to shed, especially a countryman's blood. But in the pushing and shoving that accompanied this exchange someone suddenly thrust forward to strike a blow with a tomahawk. Blood spurted from Vigil's head. For a moment those in front fell silent as the stunned man staggered backward and put a hand to his wound. Dazed, he uttered his last words. "You fools!" he cried. "You ignorant fools!" and he sank with an awful, prolonged cry of agony beneath a sudden, frenzied onslaught of slashing blades.

The Poinel

News travelled slowly in the vast reaches of New Mexico. On Thursday, January 28, nine days after the first murders in Taos, young Lewis was still enjoying the exotic allure of O-ne-o and his Cheyenne friends when an employee of Bent, St. Vrain & Company dismounted from his exhausted horse in front of John Smith's teepee with shocking news: Governor Bent was murdered! Where was William, the governor's brother? Someone ran to fetch him at his teepee.

The messenger was ravenous, having scarcely stopped on a beeline from the company's grazing camps on the east slope of the Sangre de Cristos, more than 100 miles distant. Wolfing down chunks of buffalo from John Smith's simmering pot, he told of how he and the other company employees in the grazing camps had been attacked just a couple of days before by a horde of Mexicans and Indians. From a Mexican they captured in the ensuing skirmish they learned about the deaths of Charles Bent, Stephen Lee, Cornelio Vigil and young Narcisse and others.

"Narcisse?" Lewis cried. "Narcisse dead?" The idea seemed too large for him to encompass, like the vault of the prairie sky that stretched from horizon to horizon in every direction.

"*Waugh!* True enough!" the rider said. "Damn Mexicans have gone plumb crazy!"

As Lewis conjured up his last image of Narcisse at Bent's Fort when they bid farewell - the young New Mexican's smile wide and friendly, his hand warm and soft - the youth felt an odd sense of detachment overtake him. He saw rather than heard the messenger tell of mayhem and looting and repeat his story of how a horde of Mexicans and Indians had crossed the mountains to swoop down and create havoc among the company's livestock and the Army's grazing camps. Animals not stolen were scattered all over the hills. Soldiers and teamsters of the Army's grazing parties were huddled on the "Picketwire" convinced another horde in the mountains was waiting to swoop down again. And word was out that a 1,000-man army of Mexicans was marching up from the south.

William Bent left for Bent's Fort early next day. He rode in silence, his chin buried in his coat, his manner brooding. A few years earlier Comanches had murdered and scalped his

younger brother almost within sight of a company wagon train.
Now a Taos mob had murdered his brother Charles. Were the
Bent brothers mad to have made this violent land their home?

A dozen yards behind William, young Lewis rode in respectful silence. Inwardly he relieved the older man's funeral gloom
with youthful fantasies of coming battlefield glory and a daring
rescue of St. Vrain's daughter from Indian captivity. So far he'd
been unable to feel anything but sham sorrow for the death of
Narcisse.

Scarcely stopping, the two riders reached the fort by sun-
down, arriving just before another weary messenger hurried in
from Fort Pueblo with John Albert's news of the massacre at
Turley's mill. Turley's mill too? Jesus, was the whole of New
Mexico in revolt? What about the Army in Santa Fe? Was it
also under attack? Speculation ran wild.

The military men at Bent's Fort seemed at a loss. What
should they do? They had no orders! They looked to William
Bent for his opinion. William's expression was stoney. What the
Army did was of no concern to him. It was the damned Army
that had brought on all this trouble anyway! William waved
away their appeal with an impatient gesture and posted extra
lookouts on the bastians to watch for signs of movement on the
hills across the Arkansas. William's stoney expression didn't
fool those who knew him well. The man was deeply wounded
with grief.

The next morning he stood over the snowy grave of the
brother who'd been killed by Comanches, one hand covering his
face. Perhaps he stood in prayer. At the faint crunch of winter-
dry grass he turned. His eyes were teary. Drawn by curiousity,
Lewis had followed and stood a short distance away. "Lewis,
damn you!" William barked. "You think this is all a damned
game?" He looked ready to pounce on the youth and beat him
with his fists. Lewis scuttled back through the gate to the fort.

That afternoon at William's direction Lewis and a voluntary
expedition of two dozen Americans and French-Canadians
crossed the Arkansas into New Mexico. Some of the men were
worried about wives and children in Taos. So far they'd heard
nothing of rape and captivity, but what if...? And what could
they hope to accomplish anyway, a handful of men with a handful of muskets, most of them shuffling along afoot because they
lacked horses?

Well, if called upon by the Army, William instructed, the

men who worked for Bent, St. Vrain, and Co. could help put down the rebellion, but their principal task was to round up company livestock on the "Picketwire." Unless they were asked to help, he emphasized, they should leave the fighting to the Army.

William stayed behind. As soon as he saw the tiny expedition on its way he retired to his room, not to emerge for the rest of the day.

The going was rough for Lewis and the little band of "Bent's Fort volunteers." Winter temperatures plummeted. Their first night out several inches of fresh snow buried them under their blankets. Finding fuel and water on the bleak, winter desert was a chore. But they slogged along.

Four days later, gathered around quick-burning but smokey fires of greasewood, they heard a rumbling in the mountains that rolled on and on. Thunder, they wondered? Thunder, in February? Not likely. Could it be cannonfire? American artillery? Yes! The Americans must have carried the war to the rebels in the Taos valley.

They thought Taos lay about forty miles across the mountains "as the crow flies." In the mountains, the more experienced men agreed, sounds can carry forever. The "Bent's Fort volunteers" took heart.

Next afternoon Lewis and his companions reached the "Picketwire" and the small detachment of soldiers and teamsters still huddled behind a hastily erected barricade of ditchwork and wagons. For the next several days, watchful for the return of the phantom savage horde that had scattered the livestock, Lewis and the Bent's Fort men scoured the surrounding land rounding up horses and mules and oxen and beef cattle. Then they set off to the south to round up livestock grazing along the Poinel River. Those herds too, they learned, had been victimized by rebels.

They were descending the southern slope of the Ratan pass when a rider bound for Bent's fort brought word of the American victory in Taos. The messenger was a Mexican who worked for the Bents. Although he spoke no English, Lewis's party was able to determine that the wives and families of the Taos men were unharmed. They also learned upward of 200 rebels had been killed in the battle for the pueblo and dozens more were imprisoned while awaiting justice. The pueblo church was a smoldering ruin. One prominent rebel, Pablo Montoya, had already been hanged. The Bent's fort volunteers breathed a collective sigh of relief.

On an afternoon shortly after, at his ease on the verges of the Poinel, Lewis looked up from writing in his journal to see two riders approaching from the direction of Taos. White men. Americans. One was a grizzled Bent's fort employee named Bill. The other was a U.S. Dragoon whose haggard face and scruffy weariness could not disguise a sly smile. It was Fitz, of Captain Burgwin's company.

"He what?" the men on the Poinel asked, almost with one voice.

"Shot the son of a bitch!" grizzled Bill said. "Yup, pulled out his pistol and shot him dead, right in the heart."

"Jesus!"

"Yup, right in the jail. Shot ol' Tomasito deader'n hell!"

"Jesus!"

"Yup, and then he got away!" The grizzled man proceeded to sketch the story.

Curious like many of the other American soldiers, Fitz had gone to see the pueblo prisoners in one of the jails, and had suddenly shot Tomasito dead.

Arrested, Fitz was put in a windowless room near the plaza to await trial for murder. Late one night he complained to the sentry about the cold and asked for more firewood. Fashioning the wood into a pile that enabled him to reach the ceiling, he pried away the roofwork, covering his efforts with boisterous Irish song. After he had made a hole large enough, he hoisted himself through, waited on the roof until the sentry was around a corner, then swung to the ground and sneaked off to his company's bivouac.

Rather than turn the escaped prisoner in, his messmates gave him a coat and pistol and food and set him on a trail that crossed the mountains. Grizzled Bill had caught up with Fitz late the next day, leading a saddled horse supplied by sympathetic American civilians.

"Yup, I tell you he's somethin', all right," grizzled Bill said, "but nobody's blamin' 'im."

They watched Fitz return to the firelight, swaggering a bit, probably aware the men around the fire talked about him while he'd gone off to relieve himself. He took his place again, one booted leg stretched towards the fire, a forearm resting on the cocked knee of his other leg. He became aware of the men looking at him, young Lewis with fascination. "So Bill here tells us you shot Tomasito," someone finally said. A couple of men around the fire were familiar with the pueblo chief, a dignified man in his fifties.

Fitz glanced at grizzled Bill, shrugged, and made a face with a downturned mouth, as if the deed were no great matter. He didn't reply, but neither could he contain a smug smile that played around his lips, and when the men kept looking at him, waiting, he suddenly sat up, his outraged words at odds with his now-broad smile, "You're damned right I did! Gave the son of a bitch just what he deserved!"

As Fitz told it, shooting Tomasito was an act of justice. After all, his company of Dragoons had lost seven men in the fierce fight for the pueblo - seven good men - men with wives and children. Three had died when they charged through the hole in the church. And dear, gallant Captain Burgwin died after three days of suffering from his wound. And there were men maimed and wounded so bad some of them were going to die, too. And not just from his company, although Company G had borne the brunt of the fighting. Every American unit suffered casualties, including quite a few killed.

Oh, it was a hot fight, all right, and he gave the pueblo its due for putting up a damned good resistance, but the real fighters were the Indians, not the Mexicans. He told of Dragoons in hand-to-hand battle in the smoke and tumult inside the church, bayonet against tomahawk and knife and spear. Then his expression suddenly deepened and his voice trailed off. He stared into the coals.

"But they were gonna hang Tomasito anyway, weren't they?" someone asked after a long silence, "like they did Montoya?"

"Oh, I don't know," Fitz said, rousing himself to sit more upright. He scratched his stubbled jaw, "Maybe. But I didn't think I'd see him hang before we got sent back to Albuquerque. Who knows how long before theyd have a trial and hang the son of a bitch." A few heads nodded understanding. "But I really didn't plan to shoot him. Honest! I didn't even know who he was until somebody said, then all of a sudden I saw myself pull out my pistol and put the barrel right to his chest and pull the trigger like I was watching someone else's hand and pistol. I saw the pistol go Blam! and the Indian went backwards like he was yanked with a rope." Again the twisted, almost pained smile of Fitz was at odds with his words. Young Lewis chuckled nervously, but when he caught the glances of the others around the fire he quickly fell quiet and looked away.

Fitz surveyed his listeners. The silence was long and awkward.

Finally he said, "Listen, boys, it ain't just that. I ain't that hard. You won't find an Irishmen with a heart that hard."

"So what, then?" someone finally asked.

"Well, this," Fitz began, and from beneath his shirt he pulled the battered silver cross he wore around his neck. What looked like a shriveled human ear shared the leather thong. He fingered the silver talisman as he told the story of his brother's death at the hands of a cruel Mexican captain.

In early summer just five years earlier, his brother Archibald had set out from Austin, Texas with an expedition called the Santa Fe Pioneers. Numbering more than 300 men, with 20-some wagons and a cannon, the Pioneers were bound for New Mexico. Financed in part by government, this semi-official assembly of government representatives and traders and teamsters and curiousity-seekers was supposed to determine if New Mexico might welcome a trading relationship with the newly independent Republic of Texas. Of course the Pioneers were heavily armed; to cross the land of the Comanches otherwise would be folly. They were also organized into military-style companies. Among the wagons in the expedition were two belonging to Archibald and his partner, loaded with trade-goods for the New Mexico market.

But their expedition was jinxed from the start. Confused guides, inept leaders, harassment by hostile Comanches, and a multitude of other difficulties made for a plodding disaster. Six weeks after setting forth the expedition was lost but didn't know it, following a trail that led them ever farther from their goal. Many of their supplies and trade-goods, including Archibald's, had burned up in raging wild prairie fires. What beef on the hoof they hadn't yet consumed had been driven off by Indians or was dying of thirst.

200

Weak and failing, the expedition began to disintegrate. Some of the more discouraged turned back for home. Others died at the hands of hostile Indians. A few simply disappeared into the desert wilderness, perhaps deranged by their ordeal. When at last the rest of the expedition figured out where it was, still miles and miles from New Mexico, several small parties with the best horses pushed ahead to seek help from the nearest civilized habitat. Archibald was in one of those parties.

As soon as Archibald and his companions reached the first New Mexico settlements a captain of the Mexican military arrested and disarmed them. Then the Mexican officer lined up a dozen of his soldiers as a firing squad.

"Jesus! I can't believe this," Archibald cried. "He's going to shoot us!" He wanted to jump the ragtag Mexican soldiers, snatch back their guns, and put up a fight. But just then an elderly gentleman rode up on a fine horse and began to harangue the Mexican officer, telling him he didn't have authority to shoot the prisoners, that only His Excellency, Governor Armijo, could order a death sentence. Archibald and his party ended up in the local jail.

Before long the entire remainder of the Santa Fe Pioneers expedition was in the custody of New Mexico authorities. Many of them saw their arrest as deliverance from a desert hell, but New Mexico saw matters differently. Rumors had circulated for weeks that an expedition from Texas intended to seize Santa Fe and all territory to the Rio Grande and to assume the powers of government on behalf of the Republic of Texas. Priests warned the people of rape and pillage by the invaders. By the time Archibald and his party were captured, New Mexico was primed to treat the Santa Fe Pioneers not as potential trading partners, but as marauding invaders.

Governor Armijo confiscated the expedition's horses and weapons and valuables and began marching groups of the prisoners down to Mexico City to be turned over the national government. Two months later the last group, including Archibald, began the 1,800-mile march.

These were the men who suffered the most, especially at the hands of a captain named Damaso Salazar, the same man who'd wanted to shoot Archibald and his companions out of hand.

Although Captain Salazar was given cattle and grain and beans and money to feed his charges, he withheld the prisoners' rations to line his own pockets. On some days a prisoner's food was an ear of uncooked corn. After their long desert ordeal, the men's clothes and shoes were in tatters. The October nights were cold. Frostbitten toes and bloody feet were common. Other men suffered from fever and dysentery.

Salazar harried the laggards and beat them with the flat of his sword. Other guards smacked the hobbling prisoners with doubled ropes as if they were beasts of burden. When the procession passed the encamped wagon train of an American trader bound for the trade fair in Chihuahua, the prisoners were forbidden to speak to anyone or to receive any kindnesses. That was when Archibald, perhaps realizing this was his last chance of rescue, fell to his knees and insisted that he was unable to walk any farther. Salazar pulled out his pistol and shot him dead with a bullet in the chest. Then he cut off Archibald's left ear and strung it on a thong around his neck. By the time Salazar turned over his prisoners to another military authority in El Paso he wore a necklace of ears as a tally of those who'd failed to survive the march.

"He left my brother's body for the wolves," Fitz said, his eyes glistening with tears in the firelight. "This was the cross my brother wore around his neck. My mother got it from one of the men who made it back home from that God-awful prison down in Mexico." Fitz was crying openly now. Tears streamed down his cheeks. "Listen! That damned Mexican left my brother's body for the wolves! That's why I shot that Indian son of a bitch. He deserved it because they're all the same, the sons of bitches! Salazar, Tomasito, all of 'em. Ain't even human! That's why I shot the son of a bitch!" No one around the fire said anything for a long time.

"Wasn't that something, that story?" Lewis asked. He rode with grizzled Bill as they followed a gushing creek in search of livestock. The pace of their horses was leisurely.

Fitz's tale of the Santa Fe Pioneers had swung the men around the campfire to his side, and he was no longer the cold-blooded murderer of Tomasito. He'd found rightful revenge for his brother's murder.

"Yup, some story all right."

"And the way they helped him get away, the Army, I mean."

"Yup."

"And the Americans too, in Taos, giving him that horse."

"Yup."

"So nobody's coming after him?"

Bill reined in, turned in his saddle, and looked at Lewis as he scratched his grizzled chin. "Guess not."

Lewis scratched the sprinkling of whiskers on his own chin, his expression puzzled. "So they must think it's all right for him to get away," he said. Bill shrugged and turned away and nudged his horse into motion again. "Well, do you believe him, about his brother, I mean?"

"Could be. Lots of hard feelings in this country. Lots of stories."

"Were you in New Mexico then, when they caught those Santa Fe Pioneers?"

"Nope, I up at the fort. But St. Vrain was. Charles Bent too, right in Santa Fe. They both saw 'em bring some of those Pioneer fellas in. Armijo even put Charles Bent in jail because he figured Bent was in on the whole thing, to take over the country. And not just Bent. They figured we was all in on it, American or Texican didn't matter."

"Why? Because we're white?"

Bill turned again to look at Lewis, his brow furrowed into an odd expression. "Could be," he said, and the grizzled man kicked his horse to get some distance from the pestering youth.

The Trials

Along with several companions from the company camp on the Ponil, Lewis rode over to Taos to see the trials. Absent during the bloodshed and during the weeks of grief and lament that followed, Lewis saw only the allure of the greening valley as he made his first visit to a New Mexico town. Birdsong filled the air on that beautiful April day, which was fragrant with the heady perfume of new greenery. Frisky spring colts frolicked. At the scattered ranchos he glimpsed women and girls carrying water and washing clothes and tending babies and revitalizing vegetable gardens, their animated speech musical and seductive to his ear. He heard snatches of good-natured banter from men working on the irrigation ditches. He paused to listen to the repetitive little song a young cowherd played on a homemade flute as he lolled beneath the new yellow-green leafery of a willow.

People Lewis met on the crude road touched their hats or bowed their greetings. Sometimes they smiled. His ride into the Taos valley was a tranquil journey, almost idyllic, an experience that engendered a sense of well-being that wasn't shaken until he saw Army sentries with fixed bayonets guarding the street corners. "*Waugh!*" one of his companions said. "Trouble still?"

But the streets were quiet. By then the bodies had long been gathered and buried, most in mass graves, and the only visible evidence of warfare was found at the pueblo. There the fire-blackened shell of the church was gouged and pocked by cannon and musket fire; its interior lay a mess of fallen roof timbers and heaps of rubble. The air near the ruins was still acrid with the sharp smell of charred wood, but in the horse meadow the aromatic grass grew thick and luxuriant.

As Lewis and his party strolled about with evening drawing on they spotted St. Vrain crossing the plaza. "Why, hello there, boys!" the bearded trader greeted them, shaking hands all around. He wore his familiar buckskin jacket and frilly-front shirt. "And you, young fella...heard you were working for us." He winked at the others as he asked the youth, "Found a home in the West, have you?"

Lewis looked the look. Lean and hard and shaggy, healthier than he'd ever been, brown as his Indian-made "skins," he was ripe with the accretions of sweat and woodsmoke and meat drippings, seasoned by weeks of demanding range work. He smiled proudly as he shook St. Vrain's hand with his own hardened grip.

But in truth a large part of him wished for nothing so much as the gifts of a civilized life, even for just a day or two...a good wash, clean clothes, good food, and a bed that wasn't a permanent home for half-exposed rocks. When St. Vrain insisted Lewis be his houseguest, the youth's dusty face glowed with gratitude.

That night, weary and worn, but bathed, liquored, fed, contented, and sleepy, a youth again in the security of a home, Lewis lay wrapped in a clean blanket on a bolster in St. Vrain's *sala*. Through half-closed eyes he feigned sleep as he watched the women of the house use the big framed mirror to prepare themselves for a late-night *fandango*. It was an evening he would long remember, for it set him to thinking about women in a different way

St. Vrain's wife was attractive, his niece a budding *ingenue*, but his oldest daughter Felicita was a raven-haired beauty. Since first setting eye on Felicita earlier that evening the youth could scarcely keep from staring. Her eyes were large and luminous, her complexion like coffee rich with cream. Her easy smile revealed strong, even teeth. Her quick laugh was lilting. When she boldly offered her hand during introductions he felt an extra moment of pressure before she released her grip.

That night Felicita dressed in a bright red skirt that reached only halfway between her knees and bare ankles. Above she wore a white, scoop-necked, long-sleeved blouse she tucked in several times as she primped for the party, each time turning in Lewis's view so her breasts caught the light from small oil lamps in sconces on either side of the mirror. When she puckered her mouth in the glass to apply lip rouge Lewis thought he saw her eyes flick in his direction. Perhaps they did.

Life in St. Vrain's house was so different from the stifling formality of Cincinnati! The three New Mexican women went about their business as if Lewis was not even there. Pausing in their preparations to take turns drawing on a corn-shuck *cigarrito*, mother and daughter and neice chattered in rapid Spanish as they applied powder and rouge and something around their eyes and consulted one another about this and that as they combed and brushed and brushed and combed and pulled things out and tucked them back in and turned this way and that and drew in their stomachs and straightened their backs and arranged and re-arranged and patted and smoothed.

They put on and took off a wealth of earrings and bracelets and rings and necklaces and brooches before each found just the right combination. Then they dabbed scent on their wrists and behind their ears and turned from Lewis to lift their skirts to anoint themselves somewhere beneath. In short, they initiated this young spy who had grown up in a household of brothers into the intimate secrets of the female *toilette*.

After the three women left, chattering like busy little birds in anticipation of another night of flirtation and dance, Lewis lay awake for some time reflecting on the differences between these Mexican beauties and his Cheyenne friends.

The young Cheyenne women were playful. And if their lives were the daily drudgery of gathering wood and water, of butchering and cooking, of cleaning skins and tending young ones and of putting up and taking down the teepees, they were always ready to interrupt their work for a few moments of laughter and play. Despite a hard life they found ways to enjoy life's simple pleasures. They too were bold and straightforward, and the more colorful their attire the better. They loved to wear anything that jingled or caught the light or the eye. And although they possessed little, they bathed conscientiously and groomed themselves with care. Their manners, while foreign to young Lewis, were easy.

In contrast, the women of St. Vrain's household lived lives of relative plenty and ease. But they seemed concerned only with the niceties of dress and manners. For all of their leisure and wealth, where were their thoughts? Did they read? It hardly looked so. St. Vrain's household library seemed to consist of little more than a well-worn formulary, a tattered gazetteer, and a new-looking copy of Gregg's *Commerce of the Prairies*. Did they think about life, or history, or art? Did they keep journals or write interesting letters?

St. Vrain's women were ever gracious and kind, of course, and always ready to offer a friendly smile or greeting or to order a servant to fetch refreshment or prepare a *cigarrito*. And if one conceded the Popish religion was spiritual, then they were spiritual. Holy icons and *retablos* and rosaries and crosses cluttered every wall, *"Jesu Cristo"* and *"Santa Maria"* peppered every utterance. But their immodesty seemed contrived, and their predilection for tobacco was most certainly not comely. And in the end, what kind of a wife would raven-haired Felicita make if she did not choose to read or write? Indeed, could not read or write! Did she think there was nothing was more important than the next flirtation and the next *fandango*? *Waugh!*

No, Lewis concluded as he dropped off to a satisfied sleep, better he should marry one who explored the riches of the mind as well as the sweet treasures of the person. Someone like his cousin Clio with her wonderful bluebonnet eyes! And her warm, moist kiss. What did it matter that she was a few years older? And what did it matter that he felt unsettled when she withdrew into herself and gazed into some inner world and seemed to see something beyond him, perhaps a knowledge or wisdom she could not, would not share? Or what did it matter that she was his cousin? Not a whit!

The courtroom was long and low ceilinged, dirt-floored and fusty. Two narrow windows by the street door did little to illuminate its permanent gloom. The judges sat at the far end in a cramped cubicle scarcely wide enough for their table. Appointed by General Kearny before he marched off to invade California, one of the judges was American, a long-term resident in New Mexico whose difficulty with Spanish had earned him the reputation of having a tin ear. The presiding judge, a French-Canadian and also a long-term resident, was Charles Beaubien, the father of Narcisse. Beaubian had a good command of Spanish and could carry on a simple conversation in Tiwa, the language of the pueblo.

On the day Lewis attended the trials Beaubien wore the same funeral black frock coat he'd worn since the first day of the proceedings, during which time he had sentenced six rebels to death, each time intoning: "*Muerte, muerte, muerte.*"

In front of the judges, separated from the spectators by a peeled pine barrier as simple as a hitching rail, two small tables served the defense and the prosecution. Except for a chair reserved for witnesses, everyone involved in the proceedings sat on backless benches. Beyond the hitching rail barrier, relatives of the accused shared three or four benches or made do on the dirt floor or stood with the other spectators, while a handful of townspeople enjoyed the luxury of chairs and stools they carried in from home. And then there were the same few aged Mexican women who, Lewis was told, showed up every day to take their places on the floor against the back wall and tell the beads of their rosaries with voiceless, moving lips. Nearer the street door, curious on-lookers - Americans mostly - crowded in and left as their interests moved them.

The courtroom was crammed the day Lewis attended, for it was trial day for Bent's murderers, and if someone left the courtroom another person immediately elbowed in to fill the void. The defendants were four Indians from the pueblo who sat in manacles beyond the pale with hooded eyes.

After the clerk read the charges brought by the grand jury, with St. Vrain translating the information into Spanish for the accused, the defense counsel moved for dismissal. A Missouri soldier pressed into service to represent the Indians, he argued that American jurisprudence had no standing in New Mexico by right of conquest. Carlos Beaubien summarily denied the motion. Defense then moved for a change of venue because the judge was not without prejudice; his own son had been a victim of the uprising. Beaubien hotly rebuked the young man and denied the motion. Then defense moved for a change of venue because there were no Indians on the jury and it was therefore not a jury of peers. Beaubien denied that motion also. Then defense moved the case be dismissed because the accused did not understand the charges brought against them.

"You mean these men don't understand they're being tried for the murder of Charles Bent?"

"No, sir, I mean they don't understand the complexity of our laws. I'm told the Indian way is, one man one death. The defendants don't understand how four men can be guilty of one man's death." Beaubien and his fellow judge conferred, then denied the motion.

Defense asked then to be relieved as counsel because he didn't understand the defendants' language and therefore could not properly represent their interests.

"Do you mean you can't argue their side?" Beaubien asked. "What kind of lawyer are you anyway?" The courtroom laughed at Beaubien's unwitting gibe at the legal profession, even the defense, who remarked in an aside, "Well, who said I was a lawyer?" Beaubien denied that motion also.

The defense counsel hardly seemed upset. He knew the trials were a charade. After seeing six quick convictions earlier in the week he held little hope of better success with Charles Bent's alleged killers. Everyone in town knew deep down that the trials were just a formality.

The maneuvering of the defense blocked, Beaubien ordered the trial of Bent's murderers to proceed.

The district attorney was a 23-year-old Princeton man named Blair whose family had political connections in the East. Shortly before Kearny's invasion young Blair had come to the West for adventure and ended up with an appointment in the new American government. His first witness in the trial was Charles Bent's widow, who sat quietly with her two younger sisters, the three of them clad in black skirts and blouses and draped with lacey, black *rebosas*.

In her late thirties, Charles Bent's widow possessed the aplomb of a woman used to public scrutiny. She made her way to the witness chair with a natural dignity. Attractive but not striking, fulsome, her black, unadorned hair was tinged with gray around the temples. She wore it pulled into a tight bun that smoothed the skin over her cheekbones and around her dark eyes. When sworn as a witness she kissed the Bible with simple reverence. Within hours after the start of the uprising she had lost both her younger brother, her husband, and her uncle. And so far Ignacia Jaramillo had told no one but her sisters that she was three months pregnant.

The young prosecutor approached, nervously cracking his knuckles, a rudeness that caused Ignacia Jaramillo to drop her eyes in momentary embarrassment for the young man. When she looked up again her eyes expressed such disappointment and disapproval that Blair was taken aback. "Ah, ah, *buenos dias, Señora*," he mumbled, a greeting which was not quite the full extent of his Spanish.

As the morning's principal witness, Ignacia Jaramillo painted a word picture of Bent's murder that had the courtroom hanging on her every word. When she paused for St. Vrain's translation, the jurors would turn to him with open-mouthed anticipation. Sometimes young Blair interjected an obvious question to emphasize a point. "Your husband did what?" "He said what?" Several times he turned to the jury with a play-acting furrowed brow, as if puzzled by her description of the patience and forbearance of the murdered governor. Ignacia Jaramillo's voice was matter-of-fact. Her only sign of emotion was the constant worrying of a lacey, black handkerchief. She unconsciously twisted it tight, then untwisted and smoothed it on her knee, then twisted it tight again.

It was early morning but still dark when she and Charles Bent were waked by commotion and a violent pounding at the street door of their house. Bent grumbled and pulled on his pants and boots to investigate. The afternoon before he'd come home weary from the long ride up from Santa Fe, still upset by his confrontation with the pueblo delegation just outside town. But he looked forward to a lazy day or two before making his speech on the plaza and returning to the capital with his family. Now his first comfortable night of sleep in several days was disturbed by the impatient pounding.

Muttering under his breath, Charles Bent shrugged into his coat as he made for the door in the darkness. Ignacia trailed behind, hugging a blanket against the cold. Was someone sick or injured? Or was it trouble at the pueblo? For weeks she and her sisters had heard rumors that men were stirring up the *pueblanos*. She stood in the doorway of their house while Charles stepped onto the portico of the little courtyard. Above the wall enclosing their courtyard they saw the smoky glow of firelight in the street. From the raucous voices and blasphemus speech they knew a large, unruly bunch was gathered outside. Some sounded drunk.

Bent crossed the courtyard to the *portillo* and opened the wicket. From the way he recoiled at what he saw Ignacia could tell he was taken aback. The narrow street seethed with a mob of torch-lit, painted faces brandishing guns and spears and bows and arrow-filled quivers. The mob continued to yowl. Ignaicia shuddered, suddenly frightened for their safety.

When the tumult quieted for a moment at the sight of the opened wicket Charles Bent asked what they wanted. Someone (a Mexican, she thought) said, 'Open this door, *gringo*, we want your head!"

"Those words," Blair interrupted her. "'We want your head?'"

"*Si.*"

The young prosecutor turned to regard the jury of twelve American and French-Canadian men, most of them former mountain men or traders. "We want your head?" he repeated for their benefit.

"*Si.*"

"Go on, please," he said, sweeping the defendants with a look of contempt. They sat stone-faced, staring at the witness. How much they understood of either the testimony or the proceedings was unclear.

Ignacia then said that Bent shook his head as if dismissing the remark as drunken nonsense and told the mob, "This is foolish. Go home and let me go back to sleep. You're disturbing my family."

Ignacia stopped, dropping her eyes. Something in those last words evoked a sudden welling of emotion. She took a long moment to gather herself as she twisted and untwisted her handkerchief. The courtroom remained dead silent. From outside came the sounds of a passer-by whistling a sprightly military marching song. In the back of his mind young Lewis recognized "The Girl I Left Behind Me."

"I'm sorry, señora," Blair said. "Can you go on? I know this is very difficult for you."

Ignaicia dabbed at her eyes with the handkerchief, then gathered herself and went on to describe how Bent crossed back to the portico where she waited, but he had left the wicket door open, a small, head-high window to view visitors. Perhaps, she remembered thinking, he left it open so he would not give offense.

By this time the racket had waked the entire household. Their son Alfredo appeared in the doorway behind Ignacia with their household servant, a young Ute girl. Then Ignacia's younger sisters emerged from the back of the house with Teresina, the Bents' five-year-old daughter. Her sisters had been staying with Maria Jaramillo while their own husbands were out of town. The entire household crowded near the open door, white-faced and wide-eyed with fright. Little Teresina started to bawl at the noise and confusion. That seemed to make Bent angry, because he turned back to the mob and told the men to quiet down. They were scaring his family. He would talk to them in the morning. "You, Tomasito, you should know better," he said, pointing to the pueblo chief, one of the torchlit faces he recognized through the wicket.

Then Alfredo stepped onto the portico with a small-bore musket he'd received for his last birthday. A 12-year-old, he said, "We should fight them, Papa."

"No, son," Bent said. "We won't fight." He took the little gun, leaned it against the wall inside the doorway, then put his hands on Alfredo's shoulders and steered him back inside the house. "I'm the governor and I have to see what the trouble is and work things out."

"He what?" the young prosecutor asked, breaking Ignacia's narration again. She repeated what she'd said, that Bent had wanted to work things out. Blair turned to the jury, shaking his head, his expression studiously incredulous.

"Señor," Ignacia explained, "he has always been a fair man. He always tried to help. He never thought those men would hurt him."

"Yes," Blair said sympathetically, "we all know he was a good man, a very good man." He paused, then asked, "Now, can you go on?"

Her eyes still tear-filled, Ignacia resumed her story.

The mob was angry and would not listen. 'Now!' they cried. "Now! We want to talk now!" and someone poked an *escopeta* through the wicket. Ignacia screamed at the sight of the gun-barrel and as Bent turned back towards the mob the gun let loose a smoky blast.

The scatter of shot wounded Bent in the face and chest. Luckily, the weapon had been poorly loaded and its force was weak. Lucky too that at that moment Ignacia had bent to take Teresina into her arms or she would have been peppered also.

Bent staggered, momentarily stunned. He wiped blood from his face. "What are you doing?" he cried.

"Run!" Ignacia implored. "Run! Get a horse and run!" She couldn't understand why he still wanted to try to talk to the mob, but he kept saying, "No, no, I'm the governor and I won't run away and leave my family." Ignacia retreated into the house and ordered her sisters to run to safety with the children. They fled for the stableyard gate, but when they heard the noise of the mob beyond the stableyard wall they knew they were trapped. They retreated to the house to a room that shared a common wall with a neighbor and began frantically to dig through the back of the big fireplace to reach the other house.

By then men had climbed atop the courtyard wall in front to shoot arrows at Bent, who ducked his head in and out from the safety of his house to cry, "Wait! Wait! We can talk this out!" All this time Ignacia fought in vain to pull him back from the doorway, imploring him to come into the house. "You fool!" she finally yelled. "They're going to kill you!"

Then one of the missiles skewered the top of Bent's scalp so he looked like he wore an arrow on his head. That was when he finally slammed and barred the front door and when the insurgents succeeded in battering down the *portillo*. The mob swarmed into the courtyard.

Meanwhile Ignacia's sisters and the Ute girl, terrified and sobbing, took turns hacking at the heat-weakened adobe in the back of the fireplace with a small axe until that proved impractical, then took turns gouging at the stubborn clay with a big iron cooking spoon. On the other side of the wall, hearing their cries for help and the sounds of their digging, the neighbor woman began to gouge at the adobe from her side. Above them on the roof the women heard the mob trying to dig their way down into the house.

When Ignacia reached the safety of the back room with the wounded Bent, the others had dug a hole in the fireplace big enough to crawl through. Teresina slithered through first, then Alfredo and the sisters. "Go!" Ignacia cried to Bent as they heard their front door begin giving way with a horrible rending of wood. "They won't kill me." Bent dropped to his knees and reached through to hands waiting to pull him to safety. By this time he was woozy from shock and barely able to see for the blood streaming down his face. He screamed when the arrow sticking through his scalp caught the edge of the hole. He backed out of the fireplace and snapped it off, roaring like a lion to mask the pain, his sudden rage giving him extraordinary strength of will. He disappeared through the hole.

Ignacia had gotten part way through the hole when several men rushed into the room. Blocking the fireplace with her body and outspread arms, the Ute girl was felled by the point-blank blast of a musket that sent her sprawling. The murderer could only try to club Ignacia's disappearing foot with the butt of his weapon as those in the neighbor's house yanked her through to safety.

For the moment the enemy was frustrated. Only a fool would have tried to pursue them through the escape hole, but Bent and his family had just a few minutes of respite, for the relentless mob then began attacking the roof and door of the neighbor's house.

Bent seemed to lose his focus. He sat heavily on a straight-backed chair, then after several moments took a little memorandum book from his coat pocket. His movements were so slow and deliberate as to seem almost surreal. He kept wiping blood from his eyes with a sleeve.

213

"What are you doing?" Ignacia cried. "What can you write now?"

Bent looked up at her as if confused by the question. Then, regarding the memorandum book on his knee, he said in a dream-like voice, "I...I can write who's killing me," he said. "Go on and save yourselves. Take the children." Then he seemed to withdraw into himself. He sat glassy-eyed, the little memorandum book opened on his knee, a forgotten pencil in his hand. Ignacia realized their situation was hopeless. They were trapped in the back room of the house and surrounded by the mob. They could retreat no farther.

She was standing beside Bent with her arm around his shoulders, dabbing at the blood on his face with a corner of her nightgown, when she heard the door give way and the scream of their neighbor and saw several men burst into the room. "What do you want?" Bent asked in a strange voice as he roused himself from his torpor. He sat looking at them with uncomprehending eyes, making no effort to rise or resist.

"We want your head, *gringo*," they said, and pushed Ignacia roughly aside. They shot Bent with a musket at point-blank range. The blast knocked him over backwards on his chair. Then they shot him with several arrows. Bleeding profusely, choking, he made a feeble effort to pull an arrow from his throat as one of the intruders took Bent's scalp with three quick slashes of a skinning knife and a ripping sound.

After Bent was dead, other men came in and stripped him of his coat, trousers, and nightshirt and left his bloody, nearly naked corpse on the floor.

For what seemed like hours a succession of brutish men ranged through the two houses, threatening the women and plundering Bent's belongings, scattering papers and smashing whatever they could not carry away. Still clad in their nightgowns, numb with terror, the women and children cowered on the floor near Bent's body. Teresina no longer cried. She sat frozen in the nest of her mother's arms and legs, her thumb in her mouth, her eyes fixed on the corpse of her father. Alfredo also sat wide-eyed with shock. At one point the women tried to cover the corpse with a blanket, but another looter appeared and snatched off the makeshift shroud as plunder. Only at mid-afternoon, almost nine hours after the initial disturbance, did the last of the mob leave the huddled survivors.

Young Blair's question broke the trance-like state of the listeners, "Did you know them, señora, those men?"

"Señor?"

"Did you know them, the men who came into your house and killed your husband, the governor?"

"Yes!" Ignacia Jaramillo cried, half rising, her eyes terrible, her hand shooting forth like an arrow to point an out-stretched finger at the four Indians. "Them! Them! They killed him! They murdered him! God in Heaven, I'll see their horrible faces until the day I die!"

Beaubien tried to gavel the uproarious courtroom to order.

It was Charles Beaubien's appointment in the new American government that cost the life of his son, Narcisse, Lewis's travelling companion on the Santa Fe Trail. Having spent the Christmas holidays visiting with relatives in Santa Fe with the rest of his family, Narcisse returned to Taos with Bent's party the afternoon before the uprising. He travelled with another boy about his age, Ignacia Jaramillo's brother Pablo. The two youths stayed the night together at Beaubien's house.

Soon after daylight they were awakened by the sounds of hubbub in the plaza. Half dressed, they scampered barefoot across the wintry courtyard and opened the *portillo* to see a yowling mob making its way up the street from the direction of Bent's house, the early morning light catching the dull gleam of blades and gunbarrels. Charles Beaubien's stableboy was running in panic ahead of the mob. "Run, señores, run away!" he cried. "They've gone crazy! They're killing everybody!"

"Who?" they shouted back, confused. "Who?"

"Señor Bent! They killed Señor Bent and cut off his head! They killed Señor Vigil. Run!"

The boys looked at one another, dumbfounded. Killed Bent? Bolting the streetdoor, they fled to the stables in the rear.

But the mob had spotted them and poured toward Beaubien's house, where several men used a heavy bench that sat under the portico to batter down the door. In the stableyard the panic-stricken boys struggled to bridle their mounts. They could still get away! But in moments they heard the mob in the courtyard. "We can't!" Narcisse cried, giving up one last vain effort to climb aboard his plunging horse, "We've got to hide!"

They spanked their horses and burrowed like panicky mice under a rickety manger half-buried in old hay and barnyard clutter.

While some of the mob began to loot Beaubien's house and store, others dashed to the stables and made a hurried search for the boys. Their prey had gotten away!

"There! There!" a woman cried from her vantage on a nearby roof. She pointed to the ugly heap of the manger, "They're hiding under there! Kill the little lice!"

One of the rebels laughed an awful laugh as he pulled a squirming victim from hiding. Screaming, scrabbling to get back under the manger, the boys held up their hands to ward off the knives and tomahawks, but the weapons found their flesh again and again and again. Bleeding from dozens of wounds, scalped, the two youths were left to die by a dungheap. Looting Beaubien's store to its bare shelves, the mob then set it afire.

Friday of that first week of the trials was set for hanging day, the last day of life for the six men convicted earlier in the week. So far there had been ten convictions, for Bent's killers were also found guilty the previous afternoon. Some of the jury for Bent's trial were ready to return a verdict of guilty as soon as they heard Ignacia Jaramillo's testimony, but they were forced to sit through corroborating testimony from her sisters and the neighbor woman. When finally they were told to retire to consider their verdict a few cooler heads cautioned that a semblance of deliberation was necessary. They couldn't just walk into the jury room and turn around and walk out again with a verdict of guilty.

For appearances' sake the jurors spent an hour or so listening to a man of the West, a jury alternate named Antoine LaRoux, tell of his adventures as a scout with General Kearny's expedition to California. A few days earlier he'd returned from California to his Taos home and learned for the first time of the rebellion. Now he entertained the jurors with a description of Kearny's big fight at San Pasqual, where eighteen Dragoons had died in a skirmish with a troop of Mexican lancers. Using his own big skinning knife to demonstrate, the former fur trapper showed how a Mexican lance had wounded Kearny in the groin. The men winced. Then LaRoux showed his own wound where an Apache arrow had struck him in the wrist on the journey west. General Kearny's surgeon had probed and pried for almost an hour before getting the arrowhead out. "*Sacre!* that hurt!" he blurted.

The storytelling of the jurors going good, Baptiste Chalifoux then told of seeing St. Vrain wrestle with a wounded pueblo Indian in the fight in the horse meadow. Shamming death, the Indian suddenly sprang up from the snow with an arrow in his hand and tried to stab St. Vrain in the back, but something alerted St. Vrain and he spun around in time to catch the Indian's wrist. Both burly men, they grappled like bull elks, the Indian with his arrow, St. Vrain with his tomahawk. "Like dance," Baptiste laughed, whirling an imaginary partner. "Roun 'n roun! Den dat St. Vrain take Inyun hair. Ha, ha, ha, ha! Ha, ha, ha, ha!"

Charley Autobees shook his head at the French-Canadian's thoughtless laughter. He wanted to vote and be done with the whole ugly business.

After a few more stories, a decent interval having passed, the jury had returned its verdict of guilty for all four men.

Not a single Mexican sat on the juries that first week. Like Beaubien and the other court officials who conducted the trails, almost every juror had some connection to the victims of the uprising. By the end of April, seventeen would be hanged as a result of this first round of trials.

Elliott Lee also sat on a jury, but it was the grand jury, made up mostly of Mexican elders, although its foreman was George Bent, a younger brother of the slain governor and a man who also made his home in Taos. Some said the murder of Charles Bent took a terrible toll on young George, who escaped death during the massacre because he was away on a horsetrading expedition. Some observed young George seemed to grow more gaunt each day.

In lighter moments Elliott Lee came in for some good-natured ribbing about his conversion to the True Faith. The story around town was that after Padre Martinez had rescued Elliott from the mob, he hurriedly baptized the American to help insure his immunity from further violence. "Mite quick, wasn't it, Elliott?" someone winked. "Did you get the full instruction?"

Elliott's smile was sad. His brother Stephen had been twenty years in the True Faith, but he was shot with arrows after he challenged the mob from atop his store, and was killed by an arrow in the heart that saved him from worse suffering. The mob scalped him, cut out his tongue, and supplanted it with his penis.

The mob had also shot James Leal with arrows, but just enough to make him helpless. Then they scalped him and left him to die. A popular officer from the 1st Missouri, Leal had resigned his Army commission to accept the civilian post of Circuit Attorney and had come up with Charles Bent's party the day before the uprising. His tenure in office was brief. With blood streaming from his scalped head and body wounds, he crawled through the streets of Taos for what seemed an interminable time, pleading for help. But no one would approach him. Finally, with the man begging to be put out of his misery, a passing Mexican in a militia uniform shot him in the head. Leal being a stranger in town, no one claimed his body, and townspeople said dogs and pigs had disposed of his remains.

With Stephen Lee dead, the acting sheriff was Metcalfe, St. Vrain's 1st lieutenant in the Santa Fe volunteers. As the trials proceeded he oversaw the building of a gallows on the north outskirts of town, two waist-thick tree trunks sunk into the ground and notched at the top to accommodate a stout crosstree. The gallows stood a short distance beyond one of the makeshift jails, an abandoned rancho holding several dozen prisoners in one large room. Some accused of murder, some of looting or arson, some of treason, all of the prisoners shared jail space with those already condemned to die, who were acceded the sun-drenched floor near the doorway to soak up as much sun and warmth as possible before eternal darkness descended. Beyond the rancho's gateway a howitzer loaded with grapeshot stared point blank at the prison. The prisoners' families - women and young children - brought food and what comfort they could. After saying the regular Mass that Friday Padre Martinez walked out to the prison to offer another service for the prisoners and give the last sacraments to the six condemned men.

While Martinez administered to the prisoners, Metcalfe sat in Asa's Tavern fashioning the six nooses he needed. By this time St. Vrain's men had long been discharged from volunteer service, Captain Burgwin's Dragoons had left for Albuquerque, and Colonel Price had returned to Santa Fe. But the 2nd Missouri was still a major presence in town and martial law still prevailed. To insure the executions were completed without incident, the local commander of the 2nd ordered every American in town - military and civilian - to stand to under arms.

Feeling important at being called to duty, young Lewis presented himself with his musket at Asa's Tavern and helped Metcalfe fashion the nooses. Charley Autobees also joined the dozen or so men from Asa's tavern that later ambled out to attend the hangings. The streets were eerily deserted. Only a few women and children stood silently on rooftops to see what would transpire at the gallows. The men of the town were conspicuously absent.

By now the howitzer had been hoisted onto the rooftop of the prison where it could range the place of execution, but except for an empty Army supply wagon and two mules waiting beneath the gallows, the scene was empty. As the appointed hour of execution approached the 2nd marched out in formation from their bivouac to assemble in a large, inward-facing circle surrounding the gallows area. Then the six condemned were brought forth from the makeshift jail, their arms tied behind, their white, execution hoods rolled up and worn like caps. A hollow square of Army and civilian guards formed around them for the short walk to the gallows.

Along with several others, deeply pleased to be numbered in the company of such men, young Lewis helped form the civilian rank of the hollow square that escorted the condemned to the gallows. He walked with a half dozen mountain men slouching along behind the soldiers, their muskets casual on their shoulders, an eccentric assembly of lank frames and weatherworn skins and faded, patched shirts and battered hats and long knives and tomahawks and powerhorns and mocassins, true originals of the already-mythic American West. So unlike the gussied-up soldiers!

Walking in that rank of mountain men, Lewis couldn't help staring at the condemned men ahead as they took their last barefoot steps on the soil they'd been born to, fought for, and now would die for. Were they counting their last steps on this earth? Perhaps fifty steps to go. Now forty, now thirty! What did they feel? he wondered. Were they aware that their pounding hearts were measuring out their last moments of life? A thousand heartbeats left! Now just nine hundred! Now just eight hundred! How could they not shriek with terror at the sure and certain knowledge of impending death, of eternal perdition?

219

And yet...and yet...*dulce et decorum est*...and Lewis found himself imagining his cousin Clio observing him at his grisly office, her face framed with soft curls of gold, her soft lips pouted in an expression of disappointment and hurt, her eyes sad, as if she saw the impending violation of some wiser thing beyond the ken of him. Oh, Clio! Do not think the less of me for being here at this awful time, for doing *this*!

Metcalfe and the wagon driver helped the condemned men climb into the wagon, then step onto a broad plank at the rear that was laid across the sideboards.

As Lewis watched the scene unfold a confusion of image and sound and smell and emotion crowded his senses, a confusion he would dream about for years and never sort out. As he grew older he recreated the scene in his mind's eye again and again...the wavery circle of soldiers with grounded arms and fixed bayonets and the patient mules with their ears twitching and tails swishing; the Army commander atop his fine white horse and a soft-scented breeze that smelled of green and flapped the loose, dirty-white trouser legs of the condemned. The prisoners, with their hair glossy black in the sun, their swarthy faces masked with terror and sorrow and resignation and hate. Is this why he had come to the West? Yes, he'd wanted adventure. Yes, he wanted to prove himself a man. But this? A part of him felt ashamed and saddened at his part in the grisly drama. But wasn't this manhood? Wasn't this was something he had to do?

The six to be executed crowded shoulder to shoulder on the plank as Metcalfe set their nooses. His adjustments seemed to take forever...shorten here, lengthen there, tighten here, loosen there. All the while the on-lookers stood silently, awed by the power of the moment. Good God! These six living, breathing human beings would be dead in minutes!

As Metcalfe systematically prepared the men, Lewis stood open-mouthed, wondering, how Metcalfe could perform his office. Educated, fun-loving, an easterner come west for better fortune, Metcalfe had become a hangman. Were his hands shaking? Was his heart in his mouth? Had he ever imagined he would be the instrument of such ignominious death?

At last all was ready. Metcalfe took a seat next to the driver on the wagon. Looking sad and tired, he twisted on the seat to face the condemned. He stared at his handiwork as he sat quietly for what seemed like a long time. Then he took a big breath. When he spoke his soft words were almost carried away by the gentle breeze: "Anybody want to say anything? *Hablar?*"

No one spoke. Then a sudden spring gust whipped up a dustdevil and sent it racing across the gallows ground, spooking the mules so the driver had work the reins hard and say "Whoa! Whoa there!" and the condemned men on the plank had to struggle to maintain their balance. Metcalfe, half rising to go to their assistance, suddenly sat down with a dumbfounded look at the absurdity of the situation.

When all was calm again, one of the condemned men shifted his feet and in a strained voice said he deserved to die because he had gone against God's word and had taken another man's life and hoped that he would be forgiven and that his soul would find peace in Heaven. His shoulders shook as he bowed his head and wept. After a few moments another said he prayed his mother and father would forgive him. Others nodded and muttered agreement.

No one else spoke for perhaps a full minute. Then one who had stood silent, his bearing defiant, raised a voice husky with emotion and declared his execution was murder. He could not be guilty of treason for opposing an enemy that had conquered his country by force of arms. He was being murdered by a tyrannical government. "Listen to me," he cried, his husky voice rising. "They're stealing our land. How long have we lived here, our fathers, and our fathers' fathers? Our blood and sweat have watered this land, the blood and sweat of our fathers."

"Listen to me! Do you think we stand on American soil? We have been an independent country for twenty-five years! A quarter of a century! A whole generation has never known the yoke of Spain. Do these *gringos* think we will now bend our necks to the American yoke? No! Never! Never! We will never submit! Never!" He seemed to be appealing to the scattered spectators on the nearest rooftops. It was unclear because of the distance whether they could understand him.

Few of those surrounding the gallows understood this patriot's speech, but they all understood his meaning as Metcalfe stood and performed his penultimate office, pulling down the hoods. As Metcalfe carefully rolled down the man's hood, the defiant Mexican cursed his executioners with his last view of the world: "*Carajo, los americanos!*"

Metcalfe climbed down to the ground and studied his work again. The driver sat twisted on his seat watching Metcalfe, who at last turned to engage the eyes of the Army commander on the white horse. With a barely perceptible nod the commander indicated "Go ahead." Metcalfe regarded the condemned men again and raised a hand as if in halfhearted greeting or farewell. After a moment's hesitation, he let it fall, at the last instant averting his eyes from the gallows.

"HUP! HUP!" the driver cried, snapping the long reins. The mules surged, leaving the condemned men swinging and kicking and colliding with each other, fighting their inevitable suffocation. The ropes creaked and the gallows swayed and the crosstree groaned with the violence of their struggles. Two of the men, swinging so their backs made contact, grabbed hands and held on to one another until they expired, which took several minutes. Here and there a soldier in the ranks moaned or choked a sob, the only other sounds audible above the violent struggles of the dying. Lewis felt his stomach churn and bent over to spit up a vile tasting mess as quietly as he could. "Steady, hos,'" someone said.

The bodies were left hanging for almost an hour, when at last the deed was declared done and the American soldiers marched back to bivouac. Lewis made himself stay to help cut the corpses down so they could be claimed by relatives. When all were freed of their nooses (which Metcalfe carefully coiled up in preparation for the next round of executions), Lewis walked back to the plaza with the last of the civilian volunteers. There they retired to a backroom at Asa's Tavern.

Before long, when Asa's "good stuff" was flowing freely, Lewis made the formal acquaintance of Charley Autobees. He met an ugly man, a crude, unlettered, almost incoherent soul, and the only impression the mountain man made on the young adventurer was the way he guzzled his liquor with the fierce determination of a man who wanted a quick drunk. "Don' know," Charley kept mumbling to no one in particular, shaking his head side to side. "Jus' don' know, sometimes I jus' don' know."

"What don't you know, Charley?" young Lewis asked, ever the curious Boswell.

Bleary-eyed, Charley stared at Lewis as if he were looking at a two-headed calf. "Don' know," he mumbled, waving off the youth. "Jus' don' know." Within the hour Charley had fallen off his chair and passed out on the floor. And young Lewis also proceeded to get quite drunk.

Turley's Mill

The Sunday after the hangings, done with his jury duty, done with drinking, Charley headed home. Riding just ahead of him, also headed back to their farms, LeBlanc and LaRoux chattered away in French, LaRoux telling more stories about his western adventure with General Kearny. Half sick with a hangover, Charley rode in silence, regretful of his excess as only a man with a massive hangover can be regretful. Jesus, what good was getting drunk?

But Charley had a lot on his mind. Things were not good at home with Serephina, and he wasn't sure whether it was because he'd left his family alone and lit out for Santa Fe the night of the attack on Turley's mill or because of all the killing afterwards. Or maybe it was the sniping and quarreling now going on between him and Jose. Charley realized his drinking only made matters worse, and he was beginning to wonder if maybe the problem was just his wife's hard, lonely life, stuck out there in the middle of nowhere. Worse, they didn't even have enough words in common to talk about it. Maybe what they needed was a fresh start at a new place, maybe in Dolores or Rio Colorado. At least she'd be with more of her people. Anything to get his life back to where it was before the uprising. Land be damned! There was more to life than a piece of land.

"Charley," LeBlanc said, turning in his saddle, "Turley no marry, *n'est-ce pas?*"

"What? Turley marry? Nope, don't think so."

"*Qui mal!*" LeBlanc said, shaking his head. "*C'est pauvre femme!*" Charley flushed. So far he'd told no one of Turley's gold pocketwatch. In fact, until that very morning he hadn't known what he would do. For weeks the question had tried his conscience:

-- Go ahead, keep the watch! It's gold! No one will ever know!

-- No, it wouldn't be right, you've got to give it to his widow!

He wasn't sure why, but that morning he'd awakened knowing he would return the watch, and he now felt less guilty as the French-Canadians clucked about the widow's situation. Although Simeon Turley had taken Rosita to his bed and fathered a pocketful of children, he'd never embraced enough of the True Faith to marry her. Some said she might be left with nothing but the children and the charity of Turley's family, most of them strangers back in Missouri.

"Wha'chu tink, Charley?" LeBlanc asked, waiting for Charley to catch up. "She get some ting, *n'est-ce pas*, some *pico* ting?"

Charley shrugged. "Yeah, I s'pose, somethin'," he said. He would let Rosita struggle with the right and wrong of keeping Turley's gold timepiece from his relatives.

He'd come across it at the place where they killed Turley when he spotted a gleam of gold that had somehow escaped notice. Perhaps Turley tried to hide his watch when he realized the approaching riders were bringing death rather than help. And maybe the wolves had helped keep it hidden when they tore at Turley's corpse and churned the debris of the forest floor as they squabbled over their portions. So voracious were their appetites that Jose was able to gather what remained of the miller in a small flour sack. But there the watch lay in the pine-mottled sunlight, a chance gleam of gold. Its chain was broken and mostly missing, its cover was sprung, its hands stopped at 3:17. Was that when Turley had died that afternoon, when his timepiece was stopped by a blow that dented the case and made a starburst of the crystal? Or had the piece run on, slowing as the spring lost strength, at last stopping at 3:17 the next morning, or the following afternoon?

Charley pondered the question as he studied his discovery. He'd been relieved to discover Turley had died some distance from Charley's home and that it was probably Lucero who had betrayed the miller to the rebels. That knowledge had eased Charley's conscience about Serephina and Jose.

Examining Turley's watch, he gave his newfound treasure a shake and held it up to his ear. A brief *tick-tick-tick-tick*, then nothing. Inexperienced with pocketwatches, he wound Turley's timepiece until he heard a strong ticking, then for good measure continued to wind the stem against increasing resistance until suddenly he heard something snap inside, a metallic *tink!* in the forest stillness. Then the stem rotated freely. After a day the watch stopped and further winding was fruitless.

By the time the trail from Taos reached Arroyo Hondo and the cutoff to Turley's mill, LeBlanc and LeRoux had turned off for their own homes. Charley saw smoke rising from the chimney of Turley's house and started down the steep cart track, not knowing what he would say to Rosita. Although the interior of the house was a shambles, the mob had left the structure fairly intact. In contrast, the mill and distillery and the other outbuildings lay in ruins, their roofs fallen in, their walls smoke-blackened. The fire-charred millwheel canted crazily, paralyzed in the rush of icy water through the millrace. Through a yawning gap in the millhouse wall Charley could see where Turley's five-foot millstones had fallen through to the floor below. One of them looked split in two. The air was still faintly pungent with the acrid, sour smell of fire-residue.

Charley saw children playing among the sooty timbers and the slumping rubble of the mill. When they discovered Charley they stood staring until they recognized him, then waved and called "Otabee, Otabee!" and scampered from the rubble to greet him. Rosita emerged from Turley's house.

Charley dismounted from his new mule, a large brown jack bought with the $100 reward and the lame pinto. He tousled each of the children's heads in turn as he led his mule to where Rosita stood. Old for her years, she stood holding her *rebosa* tight around her chin with one hand and waited impassively for whatever news Charley might bring. Her other hand pressed her youngest child's head against her hip. The little boy's eyes looked enormous.

Charley cleared his throat. "Found this," he rasped, reaching into a pocket for Turley's broken watch. He'd wrapped the treasure in his none-too-clean handkerchief. "Thought you might want to keep it."

Rosita's round face was expressionless as she wordlessly held her *rebosa* close with her elbows and made a cup of her hands to accept the offering. Unwrapping the handkerchief with great care, she at first regarded the useless timepiece with puzzlement, then seemed suddenly to become aware of its significance. Her mouth worked wordlessly as she gently stroked the dented cover with a single finger. Her face showed loss and grief and resignation. The curious children crowded close to see what Charley had brought. "*El reloj de Papa!*" one cried, her voice expressing amazement.

"*Si,*" Rosita said sadly. "*Es el reloj de Papa.*"

They said in Taos that Turley's brother back in Missouri wanted everything liquidated and that whatever remained of Turley's goods and property should be sold off and his debts cleaned up. What they might do about making things right with Rosita was still unclear, but under the law neither she nor the children had any legal standing with regard to Turley's estate. His children did not even carry their father's surname. Despite the law, most folks figured the valley would somehow find a way to take care of Rosita for a while at least, and the authorities would let them live in Turley's house and work some of his land along the creek. It was good land. For a while there was much speculation around town about the gold Turley was supposed to have secreted around his place. Besides what gold and specie he'd acquired by trade, rumor had it he was also taking gold out of a secret mine somewhere up Hondo Creek on the big mountain. Others said the rebels got the gold. Still others hinted that maybe Rosita was hoarding it. In any event, no evidence of the hidden treasure ever turned up, at least that anybody admitted to.

Over time much of the other property looted in the rebellion was reclaimed by survivors and heirs. That is, what wasn't drunk up, burned up, eaten up, shot off, or ridden to death. Not only Turley's chattel, but Bent's and Lee's and that which belonged to most of the other victims too. In the end, what was most irretrievably lost was life itself.

By then it was known that the rebels had discovered the bodies of Hatfield and Slim in the grain long after they suffocated in the smoke. They were found lying side by side, faces turned to each other and their eyes closed as if in sleep. Slim's hands were crossed on his breast as if he'd prepared himself to be found a corpse ready for burial. Hatfield still clutched his crotch. No one knew where they came from and no one inquired after them; Slim and Hatfield become just two more of countless men over the years who left homes and families to journey into the vast reaches of the West and simply disappeared.

It was one of Rosita's relatives who discovered the bodies of Brushie and the narrow-faced Englishman. Marshall lay in the rubble of the mill, his charred corpse intertwined with the dogs. The remains of Brushie indicated he'd rested his head on his arms near the escape hole in the foundation, as though unable to make up his mind whether to risk a break for safety, and so decided to sleep on it. With the discovery of Brushie and Marshall, all the men known to be at Turley's establishment on that fateful day were accounted for.

Soon after his victory over the pueblo, in a ceremony replete with military pomp, Price buried the twelve American soldiers who were killed in battle or who had succumbed to their wounds. By then several civilians killed in the massacre had already been buried in the town's cemetery: Charles Bent, Stephen Lee, what was left of James Leal, and the three New Mexicans - Cornelio Vigil, Narcisse Beaubien, and Pablo Jaramillo. Colonel Price also took a few wounded soldiers back to Santa Fe with him. Some would recover, and some died.

Parties sent forth to fetch the dead from Rio Colorado and Turley's mill returned with ten bodies. They were interred in a single grave topped by a large wooden cross near the final restingplace of the American soldiers. No one could identify the tenth body, a charred corpse found in the ruins of Turley's mill, but by then no one much cared whether this was an unknown visitor - American or otherwise - who got caught up in the fighting, or perhaps one of the rebels. All told, 28 men who suffered death during the uprising - Americans and those associated with the American government - were interred in the little Taos cemetery. Where and how the rebel dead were buried is not recorded. Indeed, how many rebels died in the battle for the pueblo is uncertain. Some said it was 250. Some said 300.

227

Fort Mann

Lewis wanted one more adventure before heading home. He wanted an Indian fight. Along with shooting a buffalo and, by some accounts, bedding a copper-skinned maiden or two, banging away in a good Indian fight was said to be the crowning experience for a Western adventurer. And so far Lewis had only shot a buffalo. Actually he'd only finished the beast off, when he was on his journey west with St. Vrain. Wounded by another hunter's ball, the brute was sunk to its knees with a mortal wound. As Lewis approached afoot the beast snorted and glared and threatened so diabolically that both the youth and his horse nearly turned tail and ran.

But an Indian fight! He pictured his cousin Clio's bluebonnet eyes, wide with wonder at the dinner table. "I tellee," he heard himself saying as he affected John Smith's high-pitched, nasal mountain man speech, "fer this chil' there's no boudins what docks off a good inyun fight, yer all-out bitin', gougin', stompin', hair-raisin', hoodeehah kine'! That'll bile yer blood som, hos! *Waugh!*" Perhaps feigning embarrassment, Clio would raise her fan to conceal a smile. His heart would swell at the sight of the amused sparkle in her eyes.

The problem was, Lewis didn't want to kill Indians but only to fight them. Until the city-bred youth shared three months of his life with the Cheyenne near Bent's Fort, Indians to him had been the caricatures of Cincinnati's broadsides and newspapers. Now they were human. Well, not quite white human, but at least Indian human. As for the possibility that he might actually suffer mortal harm, why the thought scarcely crossed his mind. A good Indian fight promised excitement and glory to the youth, not the possibility of hurt or death.

Perhaps, like an adventurer who sets forth alone to scale a snow-capped mountain, Lewis wanted to challenge both his courage and his resolve. Perhaps he even wanted to challenge death, that mysterious, black-caped stranger, that phantasm that had taken away his father long before. *Pish!* What was death to the youth, really? To young Lewis death was an announcement from the pulpit, an anonymous grave on Pawnee Rock, a story told around a campfire. Those fresh Pawnee scalps a Cheyenne raiding party carried into camp in yipping triumph while young Lewis was living with John Smith? Indian dead, of no real significance. Charles Bent? His murder meant nothing to Lewis. Even Narcisse.

Well, actually, news of Narcisse Beaubien's violent end had cracked the youth's shell of bravado a bit, but he still couldn't help picturing the boy's expiration as the light of life leaving the soft brown eyes of a dying buffalo cow. As with all the other deaths in the Taos massacres, the death of Narcisse remained an abstraction...until Lewis participated in the hanging of those half dozen men in Taos. Then something in the youth began to change.

The Sunday after the hangings Lewis found himself walking over to Judge Beaubien's house, not sure why his feet were taking him there. Hat in hand, finding Beaubien at home, he politely paid his condolences. He said he'd thought Narcisse to be a fine young man and had enjoyed their time together on the Santa Fe Trail. Judge Beaubien shook his hand as he thanked Lewis for his kind words, then offered coffee, which the youth declined. Beubien then asked if Lewis would like to see where Narcisse and Pablo had died. Not waiting for a response, an arm around Lewis's shoulders, probably thinking of how his arm would never again be around his own son, Beaubien led Lewis back to the stableyard. "Here," Beaubien said with a gesture. Lewis saw a cleanly raked space and a few chickens scratching at the dirt. Then a surprising thing! As Lewis raised his eyes to the mountains in the distance that Narcisse so loved, the youth experienced an unexpected welling of grief. "Narcisse loved this place," he blurted, his voice catching. "We talked about it on Pawnee Rock."

Beaubien squeezed Lewis's shoulder in appreciation and said he was glad Lewis had been such a good friend to his son, that Narcisse had spoken of him often. And Lewis suddenly burst into tears. Feeling small and dishonest and unworthy, he sobbed on Beaubien's shoulder for the loss of the man's son, for a young life wasted in foolish violence, for his own fatherless life, for his alienation and loneliness, for his silly bravado and supercilious behavior. He sobbed for some time as the grieving father held him close and sobbed along with him.

Yes, in Taos young Lewis had stood so close to dying men that he'd seen and smelled their fear and the final humiliation of their last evacuations. Witnessing a human being's violent death was uglier than anything he could ever imagine, and he was not sure now whether he could ever take a man's life, even an Indian's life, certainly not close up and real and certainly not looking into the man's eyes, even the eyes of a painted savage.

But while he wished he'd been friendlier to Narcisse and more understanding of the pain Narcisse must have felt at the loss of his homeland, and while he wished he hadn't tried to appear so brazen at the hangings in Taos, his shell of adolescent bravado was only cracked, not shattered.

At bottom he was still a callow youth, and he still fantasized about an Indian fight in which he and a few other brave hearts, innocent of provocation, beat off a hundred or more frightful, howling savages, perhaps wounding three or four, but not seriously. For a memento he would recover a battlefield trophy, perhaps a lance with a scalp attached or a blood-stained war-club lost by the vanquished foe, a souvenir his cousin Clio would hesitate to touch, then would tentatively explore with long, tremulous fingers, her face averted, her golden curls quivering at the vicarious thrill.

His opportunity for further adventure actually came rather easily. Quitting New Mexico and his western adventure, Lewis was homeward bound on the Santa Fe Trail when his party stopped for the night at a new, small, unfinished Army fort on the Arkansas River. After supper and stories and a strong drink or two, Lewis had an inspiration: he would enlist in the Army and help defend the little fort.

Actually, his decision was not without a certain prudence. After the previous officer in-charge suddenly called it quits (for such were the incongruities of military life at the time), nasal John Smith was persuaded to assume command of the fort as his patriotic duty. Well, Lewis thought, if anyone knew how to handle himself in an Indian fight it would be John Smith. Indeed, John Smith and his Cheyenne wife and little son Jack were talismatic. What harm could come to Lewis so long as he was under the wing of "Blackfoot" John Smith?

But Lewis didn't really fit with the fort's company. From a privileged Cincinnati family, he'd grown up with books and learning in a society of manners. In contrast, his new military comrades came from the lower walks of life and were a scruffy menagerie of tall and short and fat and lean. Some possessed a kind of primitive cunning, some were as dumb as rocks. Several were useless as an axe with a broken handle. His new companions were alike, however, in having low ambition and scant respect for the law. Nonetheless, rubbing elbows with these unlikely comrades (all twelve of them!) was adventure. And at the very least, Lewis thought, he would experience enough adventure to enrich his storytelling.

If four small log structures surrounded by an unfinished palisade is a fort, then Fort Mann was a fort. But even the men of the garrison saw it as a fort in name only. Situated at "The Crossing," where the southwesterly "dry route" to Santa Fe branched off from the "mountain route," Fort Mann possessed a small cannon with a meager supply of ammunition, a small American flag, and a scant store of provisions. Its primary purpose was to provide reasonably safe surrounds for repairing broken-down freight wagons, which now in their hundreds supplied the Army of the West along the Santa Fe Trail.

Fort Mann was unquestionably a great place for finding a fight with Indians, Pawnees and Comanches especially. Incensed by the growing incursions of whites onto their lands, roving bands of agrieved young braves were harassing wagon trains, running off animals, and scalping and sometimes killing laggard travelers. Just days before Lewis enlisted a band of Comanches had dispatched one of Fort Mann's men within sight of the lookout. Now every man in the fort believed lurking savages would murder them all if given a chance, and false alarms and panicky flights to the safety of the buildings were all too frequent. Truly, what finer place for fighting Indians than this isolated, under-strength outpost in the middle of Indian Territory?

But Lewis fought no Indians. On most days he stood guard or made adobes or fetched wood and water and wondered why he'd enlisted.

He did have an unexpected opportunity to broaden his Indian experience. But not in warfare. When nasal John Smith realized after a few days that commanding a fort was not his avocation after all, he also resigned on the spur of the moment and joined an eastbound wagon train. In the absence of anyone else more qualified, he designated young Lewis as *chargé d'affaires indien*. Lewis was still seventeen years old and all of ten months in the West.

The youth's responsibilities weighed heavy, especially after a touchy band of Arapahos decided to set up their teepees nearby. But Lewis used his rudimentary Cheyenne and sign-language to communicate, not only with the Arapahos but with several other passing bands, and for a couple of weeks he found

himself in the surprising position of offering, not combat, but coffee and tobacco and conversation. So much for fighting Indians.

In later years Lewis made up a private little game he played while waiting at ferry terminals, busy hotels, famous street corners, railroad stations, or any place of great coming and going in a world that numbered far fewer people than today. He would speculate how long he might have to wait before someone happened along that he knew. In a place of familiar intercourse such as the Cincinnati railroad station, he thought twenty minutes might be long enough. Somewhere less traveled he might have to wait two days or a week. At the Taj Majal he imagined he would wait for half a year, and at the Great Wall of China perhaps for a lifetime.

These speculations of place and probability and coincidence were born at Fort Mann where, despite its apparent isolation, it seemed almost anyone might turn up. The fort saw constant traffic of military and civilian travelers. Most camped nearby, because the grazing was still good around Fort Mann, and the protection of the fort's small cannon was reassuring. Thus, on many evenings there were campfire sessions among the travelers that Lewis often joined to socialize and exchange news, and not always as a stranger, for he discovered he'd made a wide acquaintance in his brief western adventure. Scarcely a party happened by that didn't include someone he knew from his days in Independence or at Bent's Fort or in the grazing camps near the Sangre de Cristo mountains or in the Taos valley, or even in Cincinnati. Invariably the older men took Lewis to task for putting himself in harm's way at Fort Mann. St. Vrain was aghast when he discovered Lewis among the fort's company.

"This is foolish!" the bearded trader expostulated. "Don't you realize this is serious business? You could be killed! This whole miserable place could be wiped out! There's Indians out there looking for hair, any hair, including yours!" He begged Lewis to resign immediately and return to the States under the protection of St. Vrain's entourage.

Lewis scuffed his moccasins, unable to look St. Vrain in the eye. For months the older man had watched over him like a father. St. Vrain had performed a hundred courtesies and kindnesses and made Lewis a guest at his home in Taos and had so much as invited the youth to court his daughter. But Lewis had reached a watershed. Although he wasn't yet 18 years old, he nonetheless believed he had more experience with elemental life than most men in Cincinnati twice his age, He'd braved snowstorms and duststorms and hunger and thirst and was a man in every respect (except for his secret virginity). Except for that carnal secret he no longer thought of himself as a youth. And he didn't like being called "young fella" either.

But something else worked at Lewis. Something more elemental. For all his adventures, he felt deep down that he'd somehow fallen short of the real thing. He'd always been on the fringe, held back by his elders. On the trail west he'd traveled like a tourist and been watched over like a greenhorn. Among the Cheyenne he'd lived under the avuncular protection and tutelage of nasal John Smith. By a quirk of fate he had missed the rebellion in the Taos valley and the bloody battles to put down the uprising and therefore any chance to shine in patriotic service. And at the hangings, he now saw, he'd been a brash Johnny-come-lately. Really, by what right had he marched in the company of those mountain men as they escorted the condemned to the gallows, him in his greenhorn buckskins? Oh, sure, he'd helped to "sweat the worth out" in the grazing camps of Bent, St. Vrain, and Co., but that was common labor, not the real stuff of the West.

No, just once before resuming the tedium of student life back in Cincinnati, Lewis wanted to be in the thick of things. He wanted to be a principal. Someone who mattered. He wanted to prove his manhood. And he saw Fort Mann as his last opportunity.

As respectfully as he could, Lewis declined St. Vrain's advice.

But think of my situation! St. Vrain argued. How can I ever explain to your family that you got killed because I left you out here in the middle of nowhere? Don't you realize how hard you're making it for me and everyone who cares about you. Think of your mother and brothers!

Lewis said nothing. He looked away, and a familiar image came to him of his father's face looking away, a shadowy memory of some boyhood moment of disappointment and disconnection.

"And what about your future?" St. Vrain persisted. "Do you really want an arrow in the back when you're running for your life? Have you ever seen a man scalped? It's not pretty! Listen, Lewis, if the hangings in Taos made you sick, think of being run down by a wild Comanche and having your scalp ripped off while you're still running! You think your hide's so thick it can't happen?"

Lost in his own thoughts, only half listening, Lewis was obdurate. "I know," he said a dozen times, "but it's something I gotta do, Mister St. Vrain. It's hard to explain, but it's something I gotta do, please."

At last the older man gave up. "Well," he sighed, "I guess a man's gotta do what a man's gotta do." He clapped a hand on the youth's shoulder. "Anyway, come around tonight for a bit of humpmeat, young fella. You must be tired of eating salt pork and beans." Lewis gave him a smile of relief and appreciation and affection.

As eight or ten men sat around a fire that evening, supper done, their pipes lit, St. Vrain puffing a cigar, the long-time trader announced, "You know, it was just about a year ago when Charles and I ran into some Dragoons right here. Just luck how we met up with them."

"Of course this mighty Fort Mann under the command of young Lewis here wasn't built then," he added with a wink to his listeners. A chuckle ran around the fire.

St. Vrain then told the group how he and Bent had been heading back to Missouri, knowing war with Mexico was imminent, when their party came upon a small encampment of Dragoons. The soldiers were escorting Major George Howard, sent racing west by President Polk to bring news of the war. War with Mexico! The major had first hurried up to Fort Leavenworth to bring Kearny his orders for the invasion and was now heading into New Mexico to warn the Americans there. As secretly as possible, because maybe the New Mexicans were ignorant of the state of war. Major Howard had a secret communication for Charles Bent too, a request from the president to come to Washington as quickly as he could.

Knowing the politics, Charles Bent had suspected (and hoped) President Polk might want him to be governor of America's prospective new territory.

His voice reflective, his expression distant, St. Vrain said, "Who would've thought so many things bad might come of that meeting? Charles dead, so many dead." Except for the snapping of the fire and a distant chorus of wolves, the silence was long before talk around the fire moved on to other things.

On a sunny Sunday morning when a few men from the fort headed down to the river to wash clothes and cavort in the shallows under the pretence of bathing, Lewis went along with his musket as a lookout. He also took his journal. Splashing across the shallow, rain-freshened Arkansas, he wandered downstream a little distance until he came to the remains of a familiar fallen cottonwood, its branches and roots already hacked off for the fort's firewood. He leaned his musket against the windfall, made himself comfortable, and wetted his pencil point with his tongue. "June 13" he wrote. Two days until his 18th birthday.

Keeping a promise to his brothers, he had journalized his experiences since his first days in St. Louis. Now he was glad he'd kept his word. The pages of his quarto-size, leather-bound notebook held hundreds of notes and sketches and ruminations from his months in the West, and several unposted letters to his cousin Clio. Its early pages he now recognized as the work of a greenhorn...lengthy commentary on things that now seemed obvious or irrelevant, eager sketches of objects he could now draw from memory. But even those pages were useful for jogging his recollections, which, he was sorry to discover, time's wingèd chariot was already obscuring, changing, obliterating. Sometimes, lost in his memories, seeing the faces, hearing the voices, he would suddenly be drawn up short. Was *this* when that happened? Who said that, *him* or *him*? Sometimes, driven to search his notes for a name he couldn't recall, he was relieved to find he'd written it down, or chagrined if he had not. Sometimes too he saw his entries as little better than a schoolboy's daybook, a painful record of his learning, complete with flaws and pretensions and judgments that in retrospect made him look young and foolish – especially when he indulged himself with grand speculations and Latinate observations. On this particular morning, however, his thoughts were troubled. He didn't know whether he would actually write anything in his journal, but sometimes just the prospect of writing helped sort out his thoughts, and that is what he certainly needed to do.

What troubled him was the discovery at St. Vrain's fire the night before of two men travelling back to the States: Frank Blair, the youthful prosecutor at the Taos trials, and Fitz, the Dragoon who'd murdered the jailed Indian chief. Prosecutor and escaped murderer travelling together, bantering at the campfire as if the law and murder had no connection.

235

The sun had been sinking into the horizon when Lewis shook St. Vrain's hand goodnight and asked in an undertone if Fitz was under arrest. St. Vrain put a hand on his shoulder and steered him towards the fort. They walked slowly, St. Vrain's arm heavy on his shoulders.

"There's more to this business than the law, Lewis. Some things are beyond the law."

"Beyond the law? What can be beyond the law? If we don't have law, what's left?"

"Sometimes, Lewis, it's better just to let things slide."

"Yeah, but...you mean because of Fitz's brother? The one the Mexican killed? Is that why they're letting Fitz go, because he killed an Indian in revenge?"

"Lewis, Captain Salazar never killed Fitz's brother. That's just a story Fitz made up."

Lewis stopped in mid step, flabbergasted. "What? Salazar didn't kill his brother?"

"No."

"Well, Jesus, why are we letting him go then? He's a murderer! Is it because Tomasito was just an Indian?"

St. Vrain and Lewis had reached the fort. The older man patted the youth's back and indicated a crude bench that leaned against the palisade near the gate. The reddish orange rim of the sun disappeared even as they looked at a western sky piled high with a spectacular palate of billowing reds and yellows and streaks of purple. In the east the sky was already a deep, murky blue, almost black. Appreciating the spectacle, Lewis found a part of himself thinking, Oh, how I love this wide, wide land!

St. Vrain lowered himself to the bench with an audible groan. "God, I'm getting too old for trail life." He fished another cigar from his leather case and lit it with a sputtering match, a method of making fire that was still a novelty in the West. He gave the box of matches to Lewis for his pipe. "You know about the Santa Fe Pioneers?" he asked.

"Sure," Lewis said, getting his pipe going, "Fitz told us his brother was one of them. That's when Salazar killed him."

St. Vrain puffed on his cigar until he had a good coal going.

Their separate shrouds of smoke mingled above the youth and his mentor. "Well, no" St. Vrain said, "that's not true. What really happened is this."

In the late 1830's the newly independent Republic of Texas and Mexico squabbled constantly about their disputed border, and the Santa Fe Pioneers were just more one instance of Mexico imprisoning what they considered to be illegal intruders into their country. Although the forced march of the prisoners down to Mexico City and their subsequent imprisonment were hard ordeals, almost all the Santa Fe Pioneers eventually got back to Texas. Nonetheless, before long Archibald Fitzgerald was back in Mexican captivity again, this time because he was taken prisoner in a raid Mexico made on the city of San Antonio, which both Texas and Mexico claimed as their own. Some time later, when the Mexicans were marching Archibald and about two hundred prisoners towards Mexico City once again, the Texicans (for so they called themselves) decided to make a break for freedom before they were marched any farther from home. Bedded down for the night in a compound at a place called Salado, the Texicans next morning stormed the compound gate while the guards were cooking breakfast. Archibald Fitzgerald was right in front of the hurly burly mob. Completely surprised by the hail of stones and war cries of the charging prisoners, the Mexican guards fired their weapons in the general direction of the mob and fled for their lives.

St. Vrain looked directly at Lewis. "That's when Archibald got shot. At Salado. He was one of those leading the charge and caught a ball in the stomach. Salazar wasn't even there." Archibald was one of four or five Texicans wounded by the fleeing Mexican guards.

Next day, not a hint of Mexican authority evident anywhere, the Texicans started for home. They pulled the wounded on a handcart for a while, but Archibald died that first day and they had to leave him by the road.

"So you see," St. Vrain said, "it wasn't Salazar who left him for the wolves, it was his own men, Texicans. But what could they do?" St. Vrain took several reflective puffs.

"Well, what happened then? Did the rest get away?" Lewis was rapt.

St. Vrain shook his head. He leaned forward, his elbows on

237

his knees, his cigar forgotten. When he resumed speaking he sounded tired.

The escaped prisoners walked north in the direction of Texas for almost fifty miles before stopping. Armed with abandoned and looted weapons, they were a rogue force that the rattled Mexican authorities gave a wide berth. Then the Texicans got into the rough, dry mountains of Chihauhua. "Until you see that country, Lewis," St. Vrain said, "you don't know how bleak a place can be. It's dry, it's hot, it's endless. Like a rocky Hell." After weeks of captivity, some of the men were giving out from weakness and fatigue and hunger. Some were ill. All of them suffered from thirst.

They decided to split up, every man for himself.

Within two weeks those who hadn't died of thirst were back in Mexican captivity. Lost in the mountains, frantic with thirst, half starved, some gave themselves up for the promise of a drink of water. Most surrendered with the relief of knowing that at least they wouldn't die wandering alone in the wilderness. Out of the 200 or so who escaped at Salado, perhaps three or four made it safely back to Texas.

Things looked bad for those who were recaptured. The Texicans had killed five Mexican guards in their breakout, and so far as Mexico was concerned the Texicans were nothing more than bandits anyway. Under Mexican law they could have been shot out of hand. But they were not. Instead they were taken back to Salado to await word of their fate from higher authority.

President Santa Anna finally sent orders up from Mexico City. He would not shoot all of them. Just one in ten.

The Mexicans put a clay pot containing 176 beans in the courtyard, one for each remaining prisoner. Seventeen of the beans were black, the rest white. One at a time the men were compelled to approach the pot and, with eyes averted, reach in for a bean. When one of the unlucky drew a black bean, guards led him over by a wall, and when the last black bean was drawn they gave those 17 unlucky men a half hour to make their peace with God or do whatever needed doing. Then the rest of the prisoners were compelled to look on as a firing squad shot them.

"Shot 'em!" Lewis exclaimed. "All seventeen?"

"Yup, all seventeen."

"God!" the youth breathed.

"Yup, the Black Bean Men. That's what the newspapers called those poor souls. The Black Bean Men. Pretty soon the news was all over the country. And that was just four years ago."

"Jesus!" Lewis said, imagining himself drawing one of the black beans. What would he have done? What could he think to say in a half-hour?

He pictured his cousin reading his last words, her head bowed, her hand covering her face, stricken with grief. Oh, Clio! How I regret....

St. Vrain rubbed his knees preparatory to rising. "So you see, things might not seem right, Fitz and all, but sometimes they sort of balance out." He stood and massaged his lower back. Lewis stood too. "Actually," St. Vrain said, "I doubt Archibald Fitzgerald was even this fella's brother. There's lots of Fitzgeralds and lots of those big silver crosses around."

"How do you know all this, about Archibald Fitzgerald, I mean, about how he got shot in Mexico? Did you know him?"

St. Vrain shook his head. "No, I never did. But you remember that major I was telling about last night, Major Howard, the one we met right here last year, the one President Polk sent out to find Charles Bent? Well, that major was Archibald's business partner and they were both with those Santa Fe Pioneer fellas. Both of 'em were held prisoner by the Mexicans for months." St. Vrain raked his cigar three or four times on one of the palisades. A small rain of burning tobacco drifted to the ground. "The major told us the whole story the night we met up with him here." St. Vrain scrunched the embers with a boot until they were obliterated.

"He was half drunk when we got here and I didn't think much of him. But after that night I could see how he had a lot on his mind. See, even though he had orders from the President himself to go into New Mexico, he was afraid of being found out. What if the Mexicans found out he was one of the Santa Fe Pioneers and one of the fellas who broke out of Saledo? He was afraid if they knew who he was he'd be shot for a spy. And maybe so. For sure there's no love lost between Mexicans and those Texican fellas."

St. Vrain massaged the small of his back with both hands. "And so it goes, round and round." Then to Lewis's surprise St. Vrain gave a brief, humorless laugh. "You didn't see Montoya hanged, did you?" His utterance was a statement. "And anyway you wouldn't have noticed or thought anything about it because you don't know the history, but Montoya really wanted to wear his militia coat when he was hanged, a dirty green coat with a ripped sleeve. Even Price's men wondered why. But Montoya wore a special badge on that coat, see, a badge Governor Armijo gave the men who captured the Santa Fe Pioneers. It was a special insignia, the Mexican eagle, worn right here where his sleeve was ripped." St. Vrain pointed to the upper part of his left arm. "Pablo Montoya somehow got that sleeve sewed up so we could all see that Mexican eagle when we hanged him. He wanted to remind us that Mexico had got the best of us once too. That's what was important to him in the end.

"The thing is, Lewis, after a while things all start to look the same. It's just the same thing over and over. We go round and round and round about all this land out here. We're like Indians stealing horses. Indians out here keep stealing the same horses. First the Cheyenne steal Comanche horses, then the Kiowa steal those horses from the Cheyenne, then the Pawnee steal those same horses from the Kiowa, then the Comanche steal their horses back from the Kiowa. Hell, the same horse might get stolen four or five times." St. Vrain laughed another humorless little laugh.

"But horses aren't the hurt," he continued, his voice sober. "Until nowadays most times an Indian wouldn't harm a man if all he wanted was his horse. But when we kill a man we leave a mighty big hurt, Lewis. I think of Bent's little girl seeing her papa die, and little Alfredo, and Bent's wife, pregnant now. They're going to live with that hurt for a long, long time. And that's just the start of it, Lewis. Think of all the others - all the pueblo kids, all the Mexican kids, Turley's kids, all the women and old folks with nobody left to look after them...they're all going to live with a lot of hurt for a long, long time. And for what, Lewis? For revenge? For getting what we think is ours? For getting more? Because we think we know what's right or what's true?" St. Vrain was silent, lost in thought. "But then it never ends, does it? And for all that I'm guilty as anybody. *Vraiment.*"

After another pensive silence he sighed and extended a hand. "Well, young fella, enough preaching for one night. Early day tomorrow." He shook the youth's hand. "I'd say this is good-bye."

In the deep twilight Lewis could barely make out St. Vrain's sad smile as they shook hands for a long time. The older man clapped Lewis on the shoulder as he turned and walked slowly toward his wagons. When he had gone a little way he called without looking back, "Mind your hair, young fella."

The Delaware figured there would be a lookout for the soldiers who were doing women's work in the river, and he spotted him reclining against a fallen cottonwood in the sun, a musket handy, his head bent over a book, his floppy wool hat pulled low. Moccasins and "skins" burnished by wear suggested a man of the west, but after observing him for several minutes the Indian did not see the man raise his eyes. What kind of lookout was that? Was he reading? Or sleeping?

Across the river, on the flat roof of one of the fort buildings, a sentry leaned on his weapon and watched the men in the river.

The Delaware rolled on his back and lay looking up at the beauty of the cottonwood leaves against a bright blue sky. The soft rushing of the river, the sweet rich grass, the intense colors...how easy it was to find beauty in the world! He spotted a tufted owl asleep in the branches of the willows.

He lay on his back for some time. Despite being just a stone's throw from the armed lookout by the cottonwood he was oddly at ease. How strange, he thought, that of all those in the Delaware nation he was the only one unable to approach the fort across the river as a friend. Delawares were General Kearny's guides and John Fremont's hunters. They were farmers and artisans the whites accepted almost as equals. The Delaware were a "civilized" tribe.

Indeed, En-di-ond could speak the language of the men in the fort with ease and could write it better than most. But he had fought for the Taos pueblo and killed the pueblo's enemies and was supposed to be dead, and if anyone in the fort recognized him they would kill him now for sure. And not just the whites. He knew the Cheyenne and Arapaho and Pawnee would also take his Delaware hair as payback for old tribal hurts.

241

How foolish! he thought. Around and around we go, raiding each other's camps, stealing each other's horses, taking scalps to avenge old hurts...hurts that are quickly made but slow to heal. The One Below must be laughing!

What a fix! he thought, I'm like a lone buffalo on the prairie surrounded by hungry wolves!

The Indian eased up for another look at the man by the fallen willow. He could take the white man's scalp as a trophy to show the Comanche band he was following. The Comanche were no friends to those tribes that would gladly take his Delaware hair, and he hoped to work his way east under their protection. But he needed a gift to present, some demonstration of his respect. A fresh white scalp would be good, a symbol of strength joining strength.

The Delaware saw where he could sneak up to within a dozen yards of the inattentive lookout. A swift rush from behind. No war cry. Just knock off his hat, grab his hair, expose his neck, cut his throat, rip off his scalp. Before anyone in the river got to his weapon he would be gone, maybe before anyone even noticed.

"Hey, Lewis! You awake?" The sentry on the rooftop bellowed like a bull elk. The lookout jerked, obviously startled into wakefulness, and got awkwardly to his feet. He seemed momentarily dazzled by the bright sunlight. He took a few steps to a better point of vantage and doffed his hat to wave it at the sentry on the roof, who waved his own hat back.

The Delaware saw the lookout was a youth. He watched him return to his resting place, hesitate, then come a few steps nearer to urinate, his white member pissing a white stream as he yawned and looked around at the river scene.

So easy, the Delaware thought. An arrow in his throat, a second in his heart, and one less white man.

Done pissing, the youth milked his penis and turned it this way and that in examination before returning it home and relacing his leather pants. Huh! the Delaware thought, mildly amused, what I do!

The youth ambled back to his place, picked up his musket, examined it, tracked an imaginary target across the prairie, and jerked his weapon in imaginary recoil. "POOM!" he said aloud. He leaned his musket against the log again and sat.

As he observed the youth's actions the Indian realized he could not go back to Delaware land if word followed that he had possessed white scalps. Word would spread among the whites: Big Nigger was a renegade! No, he would have to present the Comanche with the corn-colored scalp of the brave youth from Turley's mill too, his revenge trophy for Red Willow's death.

He slid two arrows from his quiver, poked one in the ground, rolled on his side, and fitted the other on his bowstring. He figured to draw the youth's attention with the *chuck-chuck* of a prairie chicken. The youth would stand and grab his musket by its barrel and look towards the source of the sound, wondering if he'd heard right. Then the Delaware would rise to shoot from one knee, an obscure form in the reedy grass, drawing the bowstring as he rose, a swift fluid motion discernible for just an instant before the arrow was on its way to the youth's throat. Then a second arrow in his heart. A silent killing.

When the Delaware got back among his people he would have to lie low. He would have to blend in and be a good Indian and think up a story to explain why he'd been seen on the pueblo church roof shooting at the American soldiers and insulting them in their own language. The elders would stick up for him. They would make up some story for the inquiring authorities. Whites were gullible that way.

The young lookout had picked up his book. The Indian saw him wet a pencil with his tongue and sit with his hand poised to write.

The Delaware imagined his proud approach to the Comanches on Whirlwind, now filling out and getting stronger with the spring grass, the two fair-haired scalps affixed to the muzzle of his musket. He imagined shouts of welcome and praise.

Then he heard a sudden soft sound and looked up to see the tufted owl taking flight. He watched it flap and glide, flap and glide along the fringe of the river trees as it headed downriver, growing smaller and smaller until it was a light-colored speck against the sun-dappled green. Then it disappeared. So effortless, so pure.

The morning had seemed so peaceful, the earth so fresh and pristine from the night's rain, Lewis actually felt that the day was too beautiful to be dangerous. Now, however, waked by the sentry's call, he felt embarrassed by his unsoldier-like lapse and was glad he'd been able to cover up his failing.

He'd fallen asleep while musing about St. Vrain's admonition "to let things slide." For while he esteemed St. Vrain, his instinct told him it was wrong to let a cold-blooded murderer like Fitz go free, even if he had only murdered an Indian in a fit of passion.

But the youth's musings had gone in circles, side-tracked by memories...of his Indian adventures, convivial campfires, the awful hangings, of O-ne-o, of his cousin's surprising farewell kiss almost a year earlier. Of his father.

He wondered, why do I still wonder how Father might react to what I do? He's been dead for years! Why do I still wonder what the look on his face might be? Why do still I hope that he'd be approving and proud? Why, Lewis wondered, is he still so much with me? Will he always be with me this way?

Among his musings the youth had gotten nowhere with the dilemma of the murderous Fitz. Words like "justice" and "legal" and "right" and "wrong" seemed to lose meaning in the tangle of the story. And it wasn't just Fitz. Yes, the rebellion had begun with bloodshed, and that was wrong, but we were wrong too, he thought - we took more land than what was rightfully ours.

And then the trials in Taos! It seemed to Lewis that what happened in Taos had twisted the law in a terrible way. The Americans had rushed in to mete out punishment so swift and certain that no reasoned voice could rein them in. What happened in Taos and was called justice was a perversion of justice. Taos had cloaked revenge as justice. What was missing in Taos, he thought, was...was...restraint!

And yet Fitz was free.

Here was restraint! Here was judicial temperament! Here was a murderous deserter returning home with no more stigma than perhaps a dishonorable discharge for desertion. Fitz was a comrade still, one of "us" on the Santa Fe Trail. Why? Because he was on the side of victory? Because he was white?

All right, the youth thought, so you let Fitz slide, you let the Taos trials slide, you let this slide and that slide and say it all looks the same and goes around and around until it makes you weary to think of it. And then what? Do you always just let things slide? Don't you ever draw the line? Don't you ever say, Enough is enough and this is right and that is wrong. And know that you know the truth?

You must! Lewis thought. There must be a time in our lives when we draw the line...or life would be hopeless! But when? When will we know something is so important that we have to stand up for what we believe? When will I know...

A swift hiss. Lewis looked up from his journal, his pencil still poised, his words still unwritten, uncertain what he might have heard. He looked in the direction of the passing and saw, perhaps thirty yards beyond, just visible in the vibrant green of the luxuriant grass, the bright-colored bands of a quivering arrow. He made a grab for his weapon and crouched, his heart pounding, his darting eyes seeking the source. Then, after a time (it might have been just a few seconds or a lifetime) there came from the distance the whinny of a horse and then a long, wild howl, a howl so despairing and so full of loss and sorrow and hopeless rage that Lewis thought for a confused moment he was hearing the cry of an animal in great pain. And as the nude white bodies of the soldiers scrambled from the river for their weapons they heard the cry again, farther and more muted, a wail of wrenching sadness. Lewis knew then that the wail was human, and the youth stood transfixed, wondering at the depth of such a hurt. And then, with an inchoate insight, he shuddered at what such a hurt must portend.

The End

Afterword

The notice was in the Taos newspaper in the summer of 1991: "Turley Mill ruins, ultimate riverside homesite, historical ruins, serious inquiries only...." Serious inquiries only?

A short walk from the Taos plaza I inquired of a young park worker scraping rust from a cooking grate. A nearby historical marker noted that Simeon Turley and six others from his mill were buried together in the park cemetery. I was unable to find their common grave.

"Ah," the young worker said with a tone of regret, "when I cut the grass I notice depressions in the ground and I know somebody's got to be down there, but there's no markers anymore. So much vandalism all the time, you know."

Small headstones in the cemetery were broken off, the tops disappeared. Some large headstones were fallen facedown, perhaps too heavy to be raised again by enfeebled survivors.

Such bleak repose, I thought, to lie looking up at the chiseled summary of one's life...when born, when dead.

Although I knew Charles Bent's body had been removed to Santa Fe for an honorific burial, I found the grave of his widow, Ignacia Jaramillo, and the showier marker of their traumatized daughter Teresina, who lived for the rest of her long life in this same little town.

Pursuing the story of the massacres, I sought out the ruins of Turley's mill a dozen miles north of Taos. There I found low walls of tumbled foundation stones that confused interpretation. 150 years old. Which heaps of stones were the mill? Which the distillery, the house, the granary? Except for these ruins and a sketchy word-description by Ruxton, the "English spy" who interviewed John Albert at Fort Pueblo, there is no record of what Turley's establishment looked like. And no indication today of the historical significance of these tumbled ruins.

Indeed, the absence of official recognition of the rebellion is puzzling. Plain to see in the topography, the battleground near La Cañada is unmarked. Likewise the battleground near Embudo. And the remains of the fortress church of the Taos pueblo is an unidentified mound of weed-covered soil. Why? Perhaps only New Mexico can explain. Perhaps its reasons are the same as Missouri's, where the site of the Haun's mill massacre is accessible only to the persistent.

A century and a half ago reportage of the rebellion in Taos was heavy with themes of heroic Americans and mean-spirited, untrustworthy Mexicans and Indians. Racism was rampant. History, of course, belongs to those who write it, and there is little acknowledgement of New Mexico's grievances or the carnage Colonel Price and the Americans wrought in suppressing the rebellion. In addition to those Mexicans and Indians killed outright, many more died of wounds and infections. At least eighteen were hanged in Taos for their crimes in the rebellion, including the crime of treason (but the records are incomplete and there may have been more put to death). The effect on the Taos valley of so much death among so few people must have been devastating. Small wonder that most New Mexicans were meek and submissive for long after.

Further news of some of the characters depicted in this story might be of interest. Not surprisingly, we know more about the Americans and French-Canadians than about the Mexicans and Indians.

Major George Howard, born in Washington, D.C., joined the emigration of Americans to the new Republic of Texas in 1836 and just happened to be back in the city of his birth when the U.S. declared war on Mexico. Because of his knowledge of New Mexico as a Santa Fe Pioneer, he was pressed into service to bring news of the war to the western frontier. Completing his mission for President Polk, Howard returned to Texas to serve with the Texas Volunteer Cavalry for the rest of the war. An entrepreneur in Texas for many years after, he supported the Confederacy in the Civil War, and died in Washington, D.C. in 1866.

Ceran St. Vrain died in 1870 at age 68 at his home in Mora, across the Sangre de Cristos from Taos. Some 2,000 people reportedly attended his funeral. By then the U.S. Congress had reduced his original holdings of more than 4 million acres to fewer than 100,000 acres, and squabbling would go on for years over that remnant. He remained a patriarch of the American West, however, and had the satisfaction of dying rich and honored.

Young **Lewis Garrard** cut short his enlistment on his 18th birthday to abandon Fort Mann (near present-day Dodge City, Kansas) and return home with a passing wagon train. Back in Cincinnati he wrote *Wah-to-yah and the Taos Trail*, a narrative of his adventure that he dedicated to St. Vrain. Some call his book a western classic. At the very least it is a remarkable performance for a young writer. Before reaching home Lewis got into the Indian fight he was looking for...a thrilling pursuit by howling Comanches back to the safety of his encircled wagon train. A gun battle continued until the Indians withdrew. It is likely that En-di-ond was among those Comanches. Other than a few thick-hided oxen stung by nearly spent musketballs, however, there were no casualties in Lewis's wagon train, and apparently none among the Indians either. And no battlefield trophies.

It is interesting that Lewis attended law school for a time before ultimately earning a medical degree. He was married at age 33 (not to his cousin!) and thereafter lived a rather ordinary life in Minnesota and in Cincinnati; he raised two daughters, and died at age 58 in 1887.

A year after the rebellion, **[Joseph] Elliott Lee** escaped death once again, this time from an Apache ambush. Although badly wounded in the leg, Elliott crawled to safety in the darkness. After cleaning up the affairs of his brother Stephen in Taos, Elliott returned to St. Louis, where he died about 1858.

Just two years after the rebellion an epidemic of cholera wiped out half the tribe of southern Cheyenne who were wintering near **Bent's Fort**, including William Bent's wife, Owl Woman. With the deaths of his Cheyenne relatives and his brothers (including his brother George, who died a year after he served as foreman of the grand jury in the Taos trials) **William Bent** could not abide the symbol of sorrow that Bent's Fort had become. Stripping the fort of everything of value, he rolled barrels of gunpowder into various rooms, set fires, and rode away. He heard the explosions from miles distant. After decades of neglect the adobe of the abandoned fort melded with the earth.

Today, however, the fort stands as Lewis Garrard first saw it, a reproduction managed by the National Park Service a few miles from La Junta, Colorado. From its bastians on a clear day one can see the Spanish Peaks and Pike's Peak, but because of the air pollution they are not as visible as when young Lewis saw them more than 150 years ago.

Soon after events quieted in Taos, **Charley Autobees** abandoned his ranch on Llama Creek to pursue farming near Rio Colorado, then on some of St. Vrain's land just south of the Arkansas River. His farms were never very successful, however, in part because of continuous Indian trouble. Both Charley and his brother Tom served as scouts for the Army in several Indian campaigns. Charley was among those who led Colonel Chivington to the Cheyenne encampment on Sand Creek, where more than 100 were slaughtered, including two who had befriended young Lewis, **O-ne-o** and **Smiling Moon**. Little **Jack**, John Smith's son by his Cheyenne wife, also died in the Sand Creek massacre. By then a 20-year-old, Jack was executed by soldiers who had orders to kill every male Indian they encountered.

Charley Autobees died at age 70 in 1882, unsuccessful in his efforts to secure a government pension for helping put down the Taos rebellion and for capturing Montoya.

John Albert never returned to the Taos valley. When his wife died soon after the rebellion, John forfeited whatever he owned at his farm near Turley's mill. He abandoned New Mexico and sought a new life in southern Colorado. He would outlive all other Americans with firsthand knowledge of the events at Turley's mill, dying in 1899 at age 93, a chain-smoker to the end.

After his jury duty in the Taos trials, **[William] LeBlanc** returned to his little farm near Turley's mill where he remained for many years as the friend and helper of Rosita Turley and the seven children she bore for Simeon Turley. LeBlanc died in 1872 after more than 50 years' residence in the West.

En-di-ond became mythic, perhaps because of his white man's name of Big Nigger, perhaps because he taunted the Americans in their own language in the battle for the pueblo. On Delaware tribal rolls and in most writing he is known only as "Big Nigger" (or sometimes as "Big Negro"). Those who described the battle for the pueblo to young Lewis told him the Delaware's body was found in the ruins of the church "riddled by thirty balls." **En-di-ond** actually escaped from the battlescene, only to be caught up in controversy a few months later when he was accused of being among a band of Comanches that murdered an American fur trader returning to the States, the same Comanches who attacked the homebound wagon train Lewis joined. It was an Indian agent's report of this incident that provides Big Nigger's Delaware name months after the rebellion, En-di-ond. "He-who-was-seen" might be a subtle joke perpetrated by the Delawares to confuse the Indian agent. In any case, nothing came of the charges against En-di-ond, and he later moved to Oklahoma in still another resettlement of his tribe. He married a Delaware woman named Qua-qua-chuch, became a councilor in the Wolf clan, fathered several children (including a son named Nicholas), and died sometime after 1867.

Baptiste Chalifoux served as a memorable juror in the Taos trials. Once the jury retired from public view he stood ready to vote guilty with no further discussion. In time Baptiste moved from Embudo to take up farming near Charley Autobees on the Arkansas. Like so many French-Canadians engaged in the early beaver trade, Baptiste came to know vast reaches of the Rockies, but other than his wealth of knowledge he accumulated little more than a large family. He died in 1860.

Although **Francisco LaFôret** figures in this story only by reference, the French-Canadian's reputation suffered in the aftermath of the rebellion when rumor held that he was involved in killing Mark Head and William Harwood in Rio Colorado as they passed through on their way to Taos. Some said the murder of the two men was simple banditry. When LaFôret was found with their furs, he denied any involvement in the killings and maintained the pelts were owed him for past debts.

This tumultuous period of New Mexico history is rich with such stories.

Colonel Sterling Price returned to politics and was elected governor of Missouri in 1852. Eight years later as a Confederate general he found himself fighting men in Missouri who had been his comrades-in-arms in the Mexican War. He died in 1867 of cholera.

[Archibald] Metcalfe, son-in-law to Asa Estes, proprietor of Asa's Tavern, had little to do with Taos after the hangings. For a while he traded with the Kiowas near Fort Mann, then attempted to build a bridge over the North Platte near Fort Laramie to cash in on the growing traffic on the Oregon Trail. There he apparently died of cholera about 1849.

While Fitz's murder of the pueblo chief **Tomasito Romero** is a familiar story in the lore of the uprising, the deserter Dragoon is never identified in contemporary accounts other than as **Fitzgerald**, and he disappears from Western history after Lewis records his appearance at Fort Mann. Who was he?

Although hundreds of Fitzgeralds served in the American military in the 19th century, there's little doubt the man in question is Entry #58, on page 80 of Microfilm #21 of the official enlistment rolls of the U.S. military. John Fitzgerald, born in Cook County, Illinois, enlisted in Company G (Captain Burgwin's company) of Kearny's 1st Dragoons on August 6, 1844. He is described as 27 years old, 5 feet 9 inches tall, with blue eyes, dark hair, and fair complexion.

In the normal course of events Fitzgerald would have completed his term of service in 1849. However, this record notes his service expired on March 18, 1847 with a dishonorable discharge at Albuquerque, Company G's headquarters. This was about six weeks after the battle for the pueblo. He apparently deserted. Why he was never pursued by military authorities for killing a prisoner in custody is a mystery. In the end it's safe to say that John Fitzgerald of Cook County, Illinois literally "got away with murder." And if indeed he was Archibald Fitzgerald's brother, his revenge was misdirected.

Father Antonio Martinez remained controversial until his death twenty years after the rebellion. A man distrusted by many Americans, he was venerated by most Taoseños. A complicated man in a complex time, he is portrayed for posterity in Willa Cather's *Death Comes to the Archbishop*. Her portrait is not flattering.

Six months after the murder of Charles Bent, **Ignacia Jaramillo** gave birth to a daughter (Rumalda). Some say this daughter was born later and that she was St. Vrain's issue, perhaps because Rumalda was not party to a settlement of Bent's portion of a huge landgrant years later. But as Rumalda existed only *in vivo* at the time of Bent's death she was not legally an heir. In any event, Ignacia Jaramillo never remarried, and Ceran St. Vrain and the legendary Kit Carson, her brother-in-law, became guardians of her children. Ignacia died in 1883 at age 68. Her son **Alfredo** was murdered in Taos in 1865 (oddly, his murderer is described as a "Mexican," as if the appelation was enlightening information). Ignacia's daughter **Teresina** died in 1920.

A year after he was hanged in Taos for high treason, cursing his executioners with "*Carajo, los americanos!*" **Polo Salazar** was found by the U.S. Secretary of War to have been wrongfully convicted and put to death, an opinion upheld two years later by the United States Supreme Court.

Although the battle for the pueblo broke the rebellion in the Taos valley, strife did not end in New Mexico. Writing to his superiors after putting down the rebellion, Colonel Price reported: "Rumors of insurrection are rife, and it is reported that a large force is approaching from the direction of Chihuahua. I am unable to determine whether these rumors are true or false, but it is certain that the New Mexicans entertain deadly hatred against the Americans, and that they will cut off small parties of the latter whenever they think they can escape detection." The New Mexicans Colonel Price refers to were mostly roving bands of Mexicans and Indians on the east slopes of the Sangre de Cristos, some of them veterans of the battles at La Cañada, Embudo, and the Taos pueblo. For those patriots the rebellion continued.

Such conflict continued in New Mexico long after Price wrote, even after New Mexico assumed official territorial status in 1851. Many more whites would die in isolated assaults by resentful (and revengeful) New Mexicans. Increasingly, however, attacks in the southwest became a matter of Indians fighting for their survival as the undercurrents of Manifest Destiny wore away the foundations of Indian culture. In that great expanse known as Indian Territory increased traffic along the Santa Fe and Oregon trails brought on by the California gold rush, the Pike's Peak gold rush, and the Civil War disrupted the buffalo migrations and the life-rhythms of thousands of Indians. These escalating intrusions into the Indian way of life would result in years of enmity and massacre, on both sides.

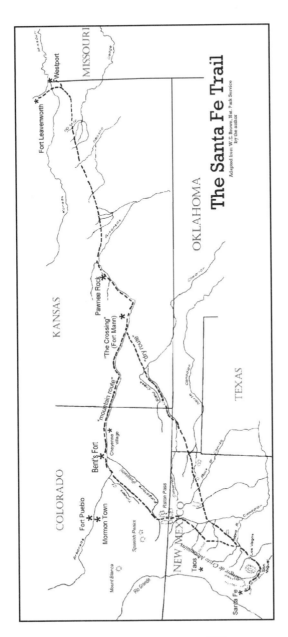

The Santa Fe Trail

Adapted from W. E. Brown, Nat. Park Service
by the author

The Santa Fe Trail was a commercial route stretching across an area mapmakers sometimes labeled Indian Territory and sometimes the Great American Desert. The distance from Westport (near Independence, Missouri) to Santa Fe was roughly 775 miles. Mexico maintained a customs house in San Miguel at the southernmost loop of the Santa Fe Trail because many traders headed from there to Mexico by way of El Paso. This "dry route" became the most popular route to Santa Fe because it avoided the torturous mountains of Raton Pass, notorious for wrecking the heavy freight wagons.

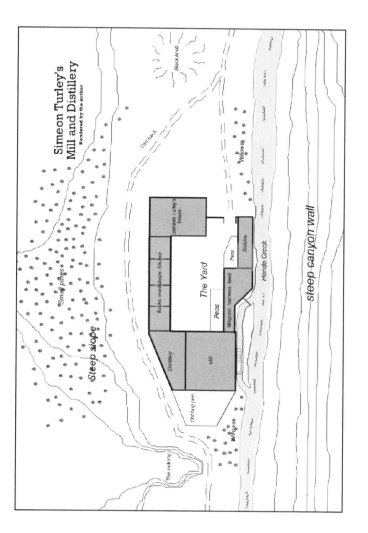

Simeon Turley's
Mill and Distillery
Rendered by the author

Although no historical views of Turley's Mill have been discovered, the ruins were still visible in Arroyo Hondo in 1991. The schematic shown here is based on the author's visits to those ruins and on descriptions and incidental references in various writings from the period.

John Albert's Flight to Safety

Approx. 10 miles

Arkansas River

Wet Mountains

Mormon Town

Greenhorn

Sangre de Cristo Pass [Veta Pass]

Mount Blanca

Spanish Peaks

Rio Grande River

Sange de Cristo Mountains

COLORADO

NEW MEXICO

Rio Colorado

Charley's Ranch

Rio Grande River

Turley's Mill

Sange de Cristo Mountains

Taos Pueblo

Taos

From Turley's Mill, John Albert followed a mountain track to the settlement at Rio Colorado (today's Questa), then aimed for Mount Blanca to reach Sangre de Cristo Creek. Crossing today's Veta Pass brought him within sight of the Arkansas River, the boundary between Mexico and the U.S. before the war of 1846-48. Once safe, he never returned to his family and home in New Mexico.

256

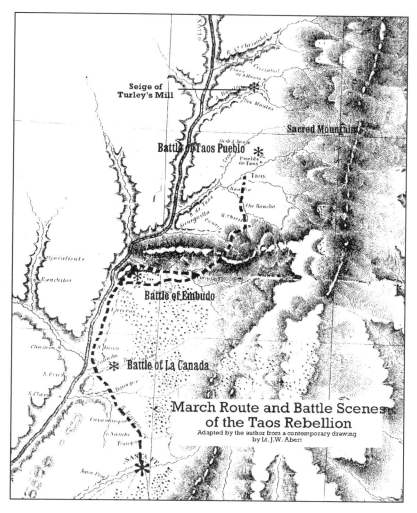

March Route and Battle Scenes
of the Taos Rebellion
Adapted by the author from a contemporary drawing
by Lt. J.W. Abert

When word of rebellion reached Santa Fe, Col. Sterling Price set out for Taos to put down the uprising. At La Cañada he met a large rebel force. Routing them after a pitched battle, he met them again at Embudo and routed them once more. The final battle took place at the Taos pueblo. Showing important locations in *The Taos Massacres,* this map is adapted from a much larger map of the area by Lt. J.W. Abert, a military cartographer who also diagrammed the battle scenes.

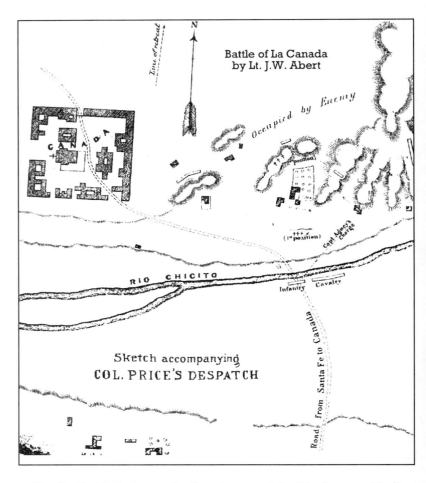

The first battle between the Americans and the Mexicans and Indians took place near La Cañada, where the rebel force held positions on the north side of the Rio Chicito in several ranchos. Lacking artillery and effective arms, they were soon driven from their positions by withering cannon fire. This diagram by Lt. J.W. Abert and the two battle diagrams following were printed after the war as U.S. Senate documents. For readability the author has made slight modifications to the originals.

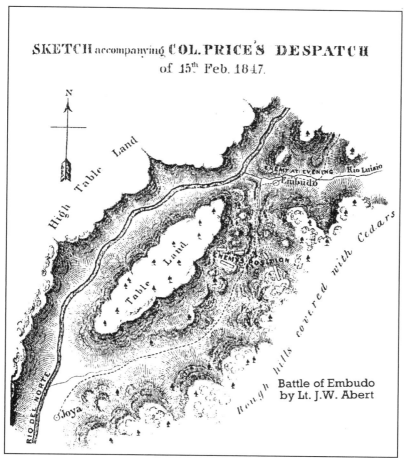

SKETCH accompanying COL. PRICE'S DESPATCH
of 15ᵗʰ Feb. 1847.

Battle of Embudo
by Lt. J.W. Abert

In a steep-sided draw near Embudo the rebel force made a second stand against the advancing Americans. Here the "royal road" to Taos choked to a track scarcely wide enough for three men abreast. After a hot fight during which they were flanked on both sides by intense musket fire, the rebels scattered northward. Underestimating the strength of the Embudo rebels, Col. Price had divided his force before the battle and sent his supply wagons along a friendlier route to reach the mountain pass leading to Taos. Today Highway 68 splits the Embudo battle scene, which remains unmarked. The Rio Grande was known as the Rio del Norte.

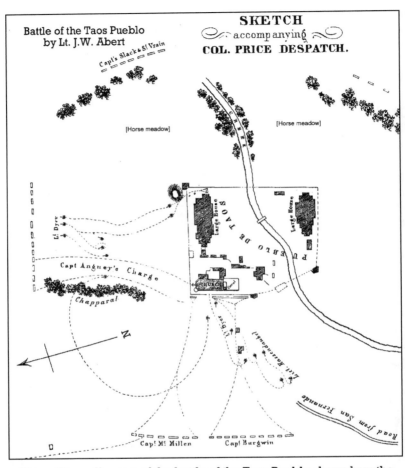

This military diagram of the battle of the Taos Pueblo shows how the Americans focused their fire on the pueblo's huge adobe church, which offered the rebels the "high ground." The battle began after mid-day on February 3, 1847 and lasted through the following evening. By then the Americans had gained control of the church and the north pueblo. Driven from those two strongholds, many rebels fled for the mountains through the horse meadow, only to be massacred by a mounted force of volunteers. At daybreak of the third day the rebels hoisted a flag of surrender atop the south pueblo. The "Road from San Fernando" came from Taos, whose official name was San Fernando de Taos.

260

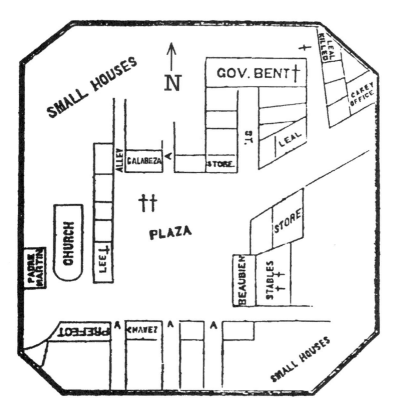

This contemporary view of central Taos and the locations of the murders appeared in the *St. Louis Reveille* in February 1847, a representation confirmed by a "gentleman familiar with the town." Although Charles Bent, Stephen Lee, and James Leal were the first American victims of the uprising, the rebels also took the lives of Cornelio Vigil, Narcisse Beaubien, and Pablo Jaramillo because of their affiliation with the Americans. Charles Town, an American warned of the rampage by his Mexican father-in-law, escaped to the safety of Santa Fe, and Stephen Lee's brother Elliot was saved from certain death by Padre Antonio Martinez, whose house and church are labeled above. Several other American residents escaped possible death in the uprising because they were away on horse-trading ventures and other business.

Chronology of Events
Pre-1845

Following years of conflict between the distant government of Mexico and the thousands of American and European settlers moving into sparsely populated areas that today comprise much of Texas, supremacy in the region is settled in 1836 at the battle of San Jacinto. In that battle a volunteer army under the command of Sam Houston defeats a Mexican army under the command of Antonio López de Santa Anna. Santa Anna is held captive until he signs a treaty conceding the disputed territories to the nascent Republic of Texas. Conflict continues however, because Mexico rejects the legitimacy of the treaty. Under pressure from American settlers in Texas, the United States is drawn into the dispute.

1845

Unable to secure Mexico's recognition of the Mexico-Texas boundary by treaty, out-going President John Tyler forces a resolution through the Congress offering annexation to Texas, and thus setting up a conflict with Mexico to greet in-coming President James Polk, a political rival. Having run on a platform of expansionism, however, Polk does not seek to reverse Tyler's policy.

March •Polk is inaugurated as President. •Mexico recalls its ambassador to the United States. •America recalls its ambassador to Mexico.

May •Zachery Taylor is ordered to hold his Army of the Southwest in readiness. •J.D. Sloat, commanding the U.S. flotilla in the Pacific, is ordered to seize ports along the California coast in case of war.

July •Texas accepts annexation into the United States.

November •Elements of the American Army of the Southwest take up positions just north of the Rio Grande, which the United States intends to establish as its boundary with Mexico.

1846

April •American and Mexican cavalry skirmish on disputed territory near the Rio Grande. Reports of these skirmishes and the loss of American life is pretext for Polk's declaration of war.

May •President Polk declares war on Mexico on May 11, an act ratified by the Congress two days later. • The Secretary of War dispatches Major George Howard with orders 1) for Missouri's governor to raise two volunteer regiments for service in the West 2) for Stephen Kearny at Fort Leavenworth to occupy New Mexico as far as the Rio Grande with his 1st Dragoons 3) to find Charles Bent and send him back to Washington, and 4) to warn Americans on the Santa Fe Trail and in New Mexico that they should be prepared for the coming conflict.

June •Kearny learns by a new communication that President Polk's object is now to take California as well as New Mexico. •Charles Bent and Ceran St. Vrain meet up with Major George Howard at The Crossing and learn that President Polk has summoned Bent to Washington.

August •Kearny's Army of the West occupies Santa Fe without bloodshed on the 18th.

September •Kearny (now General Kearny) appoints Charles Bent as governor of New Mexico on the 22nd, then sets out with 300 men to invest California. •Lewis Garrard leaves Westport with St. Vrain's wagon train.

October •Sterling Price arrives in Santa Fe with his 2nd Missouri Mounted Volunteers and assumes military command of New Mexico from Alexander Doniphan (1st Missouri Mounted Volunteers), who marches south to Mexico.

December •The American government in Santa Fe learns of a conspiracy to rid New Mexico of every American and American sympathizer.

1847

Thursday, January 14 •Governor Bent, Stephen Lee, Cornelio Vigil, Narcisse Beaubien, and James Leal depart Santa Fe for Taos.

Monday, January 18 •Governor Bent and his party are met near Taos by a party from the Taos Pueblo demanding the release of jailed Indians.

Tuesday, January 19 •In the very early morning a mob murders Cornelio Vigil, Charles Bent, Stephen Lee, James Leal, Narcisse Beaubien, and Pablo Jaramillo. •Charles Town is warned by his father-in-law and flees for Santa Fe. •Town meets Charley and Tom Autobees on Picuris mountain with news of the uprising. •Charley hurries north to warn the men at Turley's mill, then goes to his ranch, where he finds En-di-ond. •In mid-afternoon an organized force attacks and besieges Turley's mill in Arroyo Hondo. •Charley and En-di-ond return to Turley's mill, then Charley heads for Santa Fe.

Wednesday, January 20 •Town reaches Santa Fe with news of the uprising. •Rebels attack the grazing camps of the U.S. Army and Bent, St. Vrain & Co on the east side of the Sangre de Cristos. •En-di-ond's wife Red Willows is killed at Turley's mill. •At nightfall John Albert, William LeBlanc, and Simeon Turley escape the siege of Turley's mill.

Thursday, January 21 •Charley Autobees reaches Santa Fe with an Indian prisoner and confirms the news of the uprising with a captured document. •Simeon Turley is murdered on the trail to Rio Colorado. •John Albert passes by the camp of Mark Head and William Harwood on the west slope of the Sangre de Cristos mountains.

Friday, January 22 •John Albert crosses the Sangre de Cristos pass.

Saturday, January 23 •Price marches from Santa Fe as far as Pojoque with elements of his Missouri 2nd and a "mountain man" company of volunteers under the command of Ceran St. Vrain. •John Albert is carried to the Greenhorn trading post by Blackhawk.

Sunday, January 24 •Price and the "mountain man" company defeat the rebel army in the battle of La Cañada. •Mark Head and William Harwood are murdered on the outskirts of Rio Colorado.

Monday/Tuesday •Price regroups at La Cañada. A number of horses from one of the Army grazing camps are delivered to Price. •John Albert reaches Mormon Town after dark.•Rebels raid Army and Bent, St. Vrain & Company grazing camps on the "Picketwire."

Wednesday, January 27 •A rider leaves Mormon Town to bring word of the rebellion to Bent's Fort. •Price marches from La Cañada to Lucero.

Thursday, January 28 •At the Cheynne encampment on the Arkansas, a company rider brings William Bent news of Charles Bent's murder and of the attacks on the company's grazing camps. •Captain Burgwin and Company G of the 1st Dragoons join Colonel Price at Lucero.

Friday, January 29 •William Bent and Lewis Garrard depart the Cheyenne encampment and reach Bent's Fort. •Bent's Fort learns of the rebellion by way of the rider from Mormon Town. •Elements of Price's force under Burgwin rout the rebels in the battle of Embudo.

Saturday, January 30 •Lewis Garrard leaves Bent's Fort with a small party to round up livestock scattered in the attacks on the grazing camps. •Burgwin marches to Trampas to await the arrival of Price and the supply wagons.

Sunday, January 31 •Price reaches Trampas and joins up with Burgwin. The unified command continues as far as Chamisal.

Monday, February 1 •Price crosses the summit of Picuris mountain and starts down the other side, but spends the night on the mountain.

Tuesday, February 2 •Price marches as far as Rio Chiquito and spends the night.

Wednesday, February 3 •Price reaches Taos and attacks the Taos pueblo in early afternoon. •From their camp on the east slope of the Sangre de Cristo range, Garrard and his party hear the cannon fire of Price's attack.

Thursday, February 4 •The battle of the pueblo continues, culminating in the massacre in the horse meadow.

Friday, February 5 •Charley Autobees sets out to track down Pablo Montoya and encounters En-di-ond. •The Taos pueblo surrenders, giving up Tomasito Romero, one of the rebellion's principals.

Sunday, February 7 •Charley Autobees reaches Taos with Montoya. After a quick military trial Montoya is hanged. •Burgwin dies of his wound.

Monday, February 8 •Private John Fitzgerald shoots Tomasito Romero dead.

Sunday, February 14 •An employee of Bent, St. Vrain & Company on his way to Bent's Fort informs Lewis Garrard and his party that Colonel Price has put down the rebellion.

Monday, February 15 •Returned to Santa Fe, Price completes his report of the rebellion and of his military actions.

Saturday, April 3 •Lewis Garrard enters Taos.

Monday, April 5 •A grand jury is convened in Taos.

Tuesday, April 6 •The grand jury indicts Jose Manuel Garcia for murder. A jury finds Garcia guilty.

Wednesday, April 7 •Garcia is sentenced to die by hanging on April 9. •A jury finds Pedro Lucero, Manuel Romero, Juan Ramon Trujillo, and Isidor Romero guilty of murder. The four are sentenced to die by hanging on April 9. •A jury finds Polo Salizar guilty of high treason.

Thursday, April 8 •Polo Salizar is sentenced to die by hanging on April 9. •A jury finds Francisco Naranjo, Jose Gabriel Romero, Juan Domingo Martins, Juan Antonio Lucero, and El Cuerroe guilty of murder.

Friday, April 9 •Court agrees to postponement until April 10 of the trial for four more indicted for murder. The trial of one indicted for high treason is also postponed. •The first six men found guilty are hanged.

Saturday, April 10 •The court sentences the five convicted on April 8 to be hanged on Friday, April 30. •A jury finds Manuel Miera, Manuel Sandoval, Rafael Tafoya, and Juan Pacheco guilty of murder.

Monday, April 12 •A man identified only as Asencio is tried for murder and found not guilty. •Franciso Revali is tried for high treason and found not guilty.

Tuesday, April 13 •Juan Antonio Avila is tried for murder and found guilty. He is sentenced to be hanged on May 7.

April 14-24 •Additional trials are held for theft, larceny, horse stealing, mule stealing, and receiving stolen goods. •Lewis Garrard and his party return to ranching work on the east slope of the Sangre de Cristos mountains.

May •Lewis Garrard leaves New Mexico by way of Bent's Fort and arrives at Fort Mann, where he signs on as a volunteer and later assumes command of the small outpost. From a passing wagon train he learns that William Bent had granted Dick Green and his wife Charlotte their freedom.

June •A wagon train that includes Ceran St. Vrain, Frank Blair, and Private John Fitzgerald camps at Fort Mann. St. Vrain tries to persuade Lewis Garrard to leave his post and join his party; Lewis demurs. Within a few days Lewis Garrard is relieved of his command by a military officer and joins a wagon train bound for the States. En route he and his party fight off a party of Comanche raiders.

THE STORY OF GOV. BENT'S MASSACRE AS TOLD BY HIS DAUGHTER, TERESINA BENT SCHEURICH, WHO WAS A WITNESS[1]

[Grammar, spelling, and punctuation not corrected]

He was killed in January 19, 1847 about six in the morning. We were in bed when the Mescicans and Indians came to the house breaking the doors and some of them were on the top of the house tearing the roofs, so we got up and father step to the porch asking them what they wanted and they answered him, we want your head gringo, we do not want for any of you gringos to govern us, as we have come to kill you. Father told them what wrong have I done to you, when you come to me for help I always helped you and your familys. I have cure you people and never charged you anything. Yes, you did but you have to died now so that no American is going to govern us, then they commenced to shoot with the arrows and guns, while he was talking to them. Mother went to him and said why don't you jump on one of those horses that you have in the corral and go somewhere. Father told her would not do for a Governor to run away and leave his family in danger, if they want to kill me, they can kill me here with my family. Mrs. Carson and Mrs. Boggs, and an Indian slave dug a hole to the next house; so between the four women they took him where they had dig out the wall. So he comence to put all of us children first then Mrs. Carson, Mrs. Boggs. He wanted my mother to go next, but she told him, you go first, as I do not think they want to kill me but you, so she had him go first, but when he was going to go through the arrows that he had in his head hurt him so he pull them out, and crushed them against the wall so he went through the hole to the next house. Then mother was going and an Indian had found where they went, he was going to shoot Mama, but the slave woman stood in front of mother and the

---

[1] Reprinted by permission of Governor Bent House and Museum, 117A Bent Street, Taos, NM. Copies of the typescript made from the original written by Teresina Bent Scheurich (1841 - 1920) are offered for sale by the museum.

269

poor Indian was killed. Then he struck mother on the back with the butt of the gun. Father went with all of us to a little room, and he sat and took his memorando book, suppose he wanted to write something, but by that time the whole crowd of Mesicans and Indians got to the room where we were so they commence to shoot at him and scalp him and strip him of his clothes and when they killed him, some of the crowd wanted to kill all the family but some of the Mescicans said, no, women folks and children we must not kill, but we will not help them in anything. So they left us about three o'clock. A man by the name of Manuel Gregorio Martin came to see us, and ask mother what are you going to do about the burial of the Governor and she said I have nobody to see about it. I have no clothes for him nor nothing, so this man told her that he had a pair of trousers and a vest, so he went to his house and brought the clothes and then he went to see if he would find somebody to make the coffin, so next day, he had the coffin and buried him. So we stayed in the Lashones house for three days till Mrs. Catalina Lovato de Valdez sent for us. Before we went a man by the name of Juan Bautista Vigil, one of the best to do gentlemen, use to come to the house of Lashones about three o'clock In the morning and brought us provision and clothes as we did not have anything, as they stole everything from our house and all of us were with our night gowns. We stayed at the house of Mrs, Valdez till the Americans came that was 15 days after Father was killed and the American soldiers got here the 3rd of February 1847 and they went to fight the Mescicans and the Indians the 4th of February, they killed about 250 there in the Pueblo, had 6 Mesicans hanging here in the middle of the Plaza and if I am not mistaken, 16 Indians were hung too somewhere near Mr, Phillips Studio. At the same time that father was killed they killed here in town Shirif Luis Estaven Lee, Cornelio Vigil, Mother's Uncle, Provote Judge, Lawyer Leal, Pablo Jaramillo, Mother's brother and Narcizo Beaubien. In Arroyo Hondo they killed Turley the owner of the Distelary and seven men more that were working there.

This is my recollections, as a child of 5 years.

Further Reading

Chavez, Fray Angelico *But Time and Chance: The Story of Padre Martinez of Taos, 1793-1867* Sundstone Press, 1981

Down the Santa Fe Trail and into Mexico: The Diary of Susan Shelby Magoffin, 1846-1847 Stella M. Drumm, ed. University of Nebraska Press, 1982

Garrard, Lewis M. *Wah-to-yah and the Taos Trail* University of Oklahoma Press, 1987

Lavender, David *Bent's Fort* University of Nebraska Press, 1972

LeCompte, Janet *Pueblo, Hardscrabble, Greenhorn: Society on the High Plains, 1832-1856* University of Oklahoma Press, 1978

Loomis, Noel M. *The Texan-Santa Fé Pioneers* University of Oklahoma Press, 1958

Ruxton of the Rockies: Autobiographical Writings by the author of Adventures in Mexico and the Rocky Mountains and Life in the Far West LeRoy R. Hafen, ed. University of Oklahoma Press, 1982

Twitchell, Ralph Emerson *The Conquest of Santa Fe, 1846* The Tate Gallery, 1967

Weber, David J.

   The Mexican Frontier, 1821-1946: The American Southwest Under Mexico University of New Mexico Press, 1982

   The Taos Trappers: The Fur Trade in the Far Southwest, 1540-1846 University of Oklahoma Press, 1971

Would you like someone else to enjoy
The Taos Massacres?
Order copies signed by the author

Yes, I want _____ signed copies of *The Taos Massacres*.

I am including $15.^{00} per book, plus $3.^{00} shipping and handling for one book, and $1.^{00} for each additional book. (Wisconsin residents add 75¢ per book sales tax)

(Canadian orders must include payment in U.S. funds, with 7% GST added)

Payment must accompany order.

Allow two weeks for delivery.

My check or money order for $_____ is enclosed.

Send to:

Name _____

Address _____

_____

City _____

State & ZIP _____

Make your check or money order payable to

Puzzlebox Press

Send to:
**Puzzlebox Press
PO Box 765
Elkhorn, WI 53121**
Thank you!

www.puzzleboxpress.com